CUT AND RUN

BY

ALARIC BOND

Fireship Press
www.FireshipPress.com

Print ISBN: 978-1-61179-169-3
e.Book ISBN: 978-1-61179-170-9

BISAC Subject Headings:
  FIC014000   FICTION / Historical
  FIC032000   FICTION / War & Military
  FIC047000   FICTION / Sea Stories

Address all correspondence to:
Fireship Press, LLC
P.O. Box 68412
Tucson, AZ 85737

Or visit our website at:
www.FireshipPress.com

1.1

DEDICATION

To David and Jean

Acknowledgements

Writing can be a lonely business, and those odd enough to indulge in historical fiction have an additional disadvantage; not only do they shut themselves off in another room, but a completely different time.

I have been lucky, and kept relatively sane, by the company of a group of people who have encouraged and supported me throughout *Cut and Run*, and other books. In no particular order they include Rick, Roy, Tom, Lesley, Mike, Mary, Susan, Malcolm, Linda, Ron and Dee. Some are tall ship sailers, others historians, still more readers or just plain nice folk. All have been ready with help and advice, and many I consider amongst my greatest friends and yet I have not met, or even spoken with any of them. The internet has many failings but this is one of its nicer aspects, and I am glad to be able to acknowledge and thank them now.

CUT AND RUN

To cut the cable for an escape. Also, to move off quickly; to quit occupation; to be gone. [1]

---

[1] From: *THE SAILOR'S WORD: A Complete Dictionary of Nautical Terms from the Napoleonic and Victorian Navies.* by Admiral W. H. Smyth, Edited by Vice-Admiral Sir Edward Belcher. *Fireship Press,* 2007.

CHAPTER ONE

It was raining outside the church. The couple paused for barely a moment, before hurrying down the damp stone steps and on to the street. Kate clutched at her dress with one hand, raising it out of the winter slime. The other, holding a seasonal posy, was firmly threaded through the arm of her new husband. They laughed as they hastened down the street, while from behind came the sound of their guests scurrying after them in the sudden shower, and laughing as well.

"Ship an' Turtle," Robert Manning shouted, pointing across the road at the dimly lit tavern slightly ahead. A crack of thunder heralded a further increase in the rain as they paused to wait for the crossing sweeper to carry out his work.

"Struth, Robert, I've never known such weather," Tom King said, when he and the others had caught up with them. "It is worse than Biscay in the depths of winter!"

Manning turned to grin at him. "Perchance I shall be knowing that myself in a week or so."

"Ready gents, ladies." The crossing sweeper stood respectfully aside as the party crowded across the road. He wore a waxed canvas sheet tied tightly about his head, and his eyes were half closed, but one hand shot out instantly to catch the coin that Adam Fraiser threw to him. He slipped it neatly into his pocket, knowing the value without any need to look.

I

Inside, the tavern steamed with the smell of beer and wet clothing. Kate and her two friends brushed down the damp folds of their dresses while the men shook London rain from their dark blue uniforms. The water settled into raised puddles on the waxed wooden floor. It had been a bright, clear day when they arrived at the church and, despite being the middle of January, no one had thought to bring coats.

"Party in the name of Manning," King told the young serving girl who was sent to greet them. A larger wedding breakfast would probably have warranted the landlord's appearance and attention, but this was a small affair, and they were shown through to a gloomy, bare room at the back of the building. Manning looked about, clearly disappointed, although his smile was quick to return when he caught Kate's eye.

"Could we have some light, miss?" Fraiser asked the girl. But at that moment the landlord entered, looking slightly harassed, and carrying a taper and a bundle of long yellow candles. "You will have to forgive me," he said, glancing around at the guests. "We sprung a leak over the pantry, and I had to attend to it."

The room and atmosphere grew lighter as the landlord bustled about between the pewter candelabras mounted on the wall. The girl found a white cotton cloth for the table, and the party began to seat themselves, self-consciously jostling for places. Soon, the first of the wedding breakfast was being laid out, and the landlord re-appeared with four dark green bottles.

"Wine, sir?" he asked cautiously. "It was requested." Manning opened his mouth to protest, but Michael Caulfield was there before him.

"My treat, Robert; I trust you will not object?"

The first cork was pulled with a spectacular popping sound that was quickly followed by a ripple of expectant laughter. Manning shook his head. The wedding, and their accommodation for the previous month or so, had been paid for by the last of Kate's father's money. He, of course, could not be present, the staff in the asylum who kept him safe were adamant on that point. Consequently, little had been spent on anything that was not essential. Manning could not guess how much the wine, which was almost certainly smuggled, would have cost—but he did know that as an unemployed naval lieutenant, Caulfield was hardly in a position to afford such a gesture.

"I am grateful to you, Michael," he said, but on feeling Kate's gentle nudge, he corrected himself, "We both are."

Caulfield grinned and nodded while the landlord quickly opened a second bottle, and soon all around were standing and toasting them. Manning raised his glass and touched Kate's with a gentle clink. They were both smiling now, radiantly, and quite without reserve.

"It is a shame that Sir Richard could not be here," Kate said, effectively breaking the moment for her new husband. "He did say in his letter he might, 'though I know there are many matters to concern him since giving up the ship."

"Plans to stand for Parliament, or so I gather," Fraiser said, his tone completely flat. "A pity. We had a good crew in *Pandora*."

Kate Manning's gaze swept about the naval officers at the table; all solid reliable men who had proved themselves in action, and yet it seemed they were no longer needed.

Clara, one of Kate's friends from her days as a midwife, spoke up suddenly. "I do not see why you cannot be reemployed. Surely, a boat will take only so long to mend?" Jane, Kate's other colleague, snorted into her glass as the room became strangely silent.

"Can you not wait for it to be fixed?" Clara added lamely.

"Sadly, madam, that is not in our control," Fraiser murmured. "Had the captain chosen to stay with the ship, we might well have been recalled. As it is, a new man is to take his place, and he will doubtless have his favourites."

"And what if Sir Richard had taken another command?" Kate enquired.

Caulfield considered this for a moment, "Why then, he may have requested our presence. Instead, we have to bide our time and hope for a position elsewhere."

"Aye, well, I for one shall not be waiting," Doust said, sipping his wine reflectively. "The sea is for young men. I require something a mite less demanding for my old age."

"Come, let us eat!" Manning said suddenly, conscious that the conversation was in danger of becoming maudlin. Indeed, the food was being ignored by all, though not a bad spread, considering the time of year. Plates of cold roast, bread, a raised pie, and potted meats were passed about, and soon the company settled into a quiet reverence as they began.

"But I gather you have secured yourself a berth, Robert?" Caulfield asked Manning as he cleared his plate for the first time and helped himself to more.

"Aye, joining the Company Bahadur, is that so?" Fraiser regarded him genially.

"Yes, the Honourable East India Company. I have signed for an Eastern trip—we are both going," Manning added hurriedly.

"Both?" Doust started. "Only just got her wed, yet you are takin' the wee lassie to India?"

"Oh, it was my decision," Kate said firmly, and King suppressed a grin How could it have been anything else? "We shall be gone by the end of the month," she continued. "India, then on to China for a spell. It might be two years they reckons, but we should be the better for it when we return."

"Aye, and that's a fact," Doust nodded. "Providing you take care of yourselves."

"In what capacity will you...?" Fraiser stumbled. He was about to enquire if she would be employed, or was simply travelling as a wife. A fair question, but somewhat artless when asked of a woman such as Kate.

"I shall be working my passage," she said quickly. "It seems the time I spent in *Pandora* has served me well."

"You were commended for it, so I believe," Caulfield agreed. "Set a bad mess right, and with little trouble. Not many could have achieved as much."

"That's as maybe, though the Navy would still not consider appointing a woman as a purser." There was a harshness in her voice that was not lost on the officers.

"But John Company had other ideas?" Doust asked hopefully.

"Not exactly," Kate replied. "Even in that quarter I met with opposition. A woman might be capable of the work, it seems, but it would be totally wrong to recognise the fact."

"So officially you will be merely accompanying Mr Manning?" Fraiser asked.

"Yes, whilst in truth acting as an aid to the purser. A sort of Jack Dusty, I suppose, 'though it be a different position in a trader."

"Aye, and you will have the Company's accounts to keep," Caulfield spoke again. "That will be no easy task, I'll be bound."

"Easy or not, I look forward to the prospect."

4

"Indeed." Caulfield switched his attention to Manning. "And what of you, Robert? Still the sawbones?"

"I will be assisting the surgeon, as before," Manning replied. "There should be plenty of time for study. When I return, I hope to stand for my own ticket."

"And no finer man can I think of for the position." Doust drained his glass and accepted more from Caulfield.

"What ship?"

"*Pevensey Castle*," Manning told Fraiser. "An eight hundred tonner. She has completed one India trip already. Just come down from Blackwall and is lading at Gravesend. Captain's a first timer, though."

"Ah, a Guinea Pig!" Caulfield laughed.

Manning looked at him quizzically.

"They calls those who have yet to make the run to India, Guinea Pigs," the lieutenant explained. "But I am glad to know the ship is a professional, even if you cannot say the same for her captain."

"Oh, I gather him to be reasonably experienced; he certainly behaves that way. A former Navy man, or so I am told."

"As often is the case," Caulfield shook his head sadly. "An' more's the pity. Country's in the worst plight I can remember, and there are so many of us on half pay." He caught Fraiser's eye and felt a little guilty. As a senior warrant officer the Scotsman would receive nothing at all until he secured a position in another ship.

Again there was a brief silence while the party took this in, before Manning continued, "Well, there are places in *Pevensey Castle*, of that I am certain." Fraiser and Caulfield looked up quickly. "I've tried to interest Tom here, but he seems set for a life in white britches."

"And I cannot blame him for that," Caulfield said a little sadly. "The East India Company has many merits, but try as it might, it can never match the Navy."

King was about to speak, but Manning was already asking of Fraiser.

"What of you, Adam?" The surgeons' mate asked. "Surely a trading vessel would fit with your thoughts?"

"Aye, it is something to be considered, but I have to agree, and would prefer to stay with the Navy. Your average merchant officer is of a separate mould, though not inferior in any way," Fraiser added quickly. "Still, the two contrast more than most allow. On the whole, they have different temperaments, and values: maybe you will see what I mean when you have served awhile."

"But Kate says you are against fighting," Clara struck up again. She had already drunk two glasses of wine and was finding the taste very much to her liking. "Surely you would be happier on a merchant boat?"

Fraiser smiled. "Sadly lassie there is no guarantee of the peaceful life in a trading ship," he said, emphasising the last word only slightly. "And as for my Christian faith, well, let us just say that there is more good to be done amongst the sinners than the saints."

A wave of gentle laughter passed about the table.

"So that is the way of things," Kate said suddenly. "We are off to see a new world, and this must be the last time we will all meet for two years or more. It is a sad thought."

King wriggled in his seat. "Well, actually, there is one you might be seeing rather more of." He had the attention of the whole table while he reached into his waistcoat and pulled out a letter. "Word came today, but I thought it better to save it until now." Slowly, and in silence, the paper was unfolded. "I shall not bore you with the details, but I have notice from a certain captain accepting my application to be appointed as an officer under his command."

"Employment!" Caulfield and Fraiser spoke almost as one, while they gazed at the note with a mixture of pleasure and envy.

"Why that is excellent news, Tom," Kate beamed. "What ship is she?"

"Aye," Manning was grinning as well. "And where bound?"

"She is the *Pevensey Castle*," King told them. "And bound for India."

* * *

Pevensey Castle was a queer-looking craft to anyone more used to looking at His Majesty's ships. Similar in size to a frigate, her hull appeared unnecessarily long, with a bluff bow and lines that would give far too much leeway when sailing close to the wind. They'd be lucky to see five knots from her, even in the hardi-

6

est of breezes. Moreover, she would be cranky, rolling like a drunkard and turning all the fat passengers green. She was low in the water, presumably well laden, although there was plenty amiss with her rig that required attending to before she sailed. A shout from one of the lightermen brought Johnston back to the real world.

"Won't take us more'n an hour to load this lot," the man told him. "Then, you can be up and on your ways."

It was the arrangement they had agreed upon—Johnston would help with the small cargo in return for a free passage to his new ship. He nodded, stuffed his ditty bag next to his sea chest, and moved towards the pile of barrels, crates, and sacks that lay waiting to be loaded. Some were tagged, presumably ordered by individual officers or passengers, but the majority were shipboard stores.

"We will send nets down for the bread," a voice from above informed them while the lighter bumped gently against the hull. "Barrels can be parbuckled." Johnston looked round. The other lighterman was standing next to the parbuckle rails on the side of the hull. Two falls came down, and they began to attend to the first cask, looping the line about so that it could be dragged up the side and into the ship. The net began to descend from the fore and main yardarms, and soon Johnston and the first lighterman began to fill it. An hour was a generous estimation. Well within that time, he had swung his own chest into the last net, bid farewell to the crew of the lighter and clambered aboard the vessel.

"Thought you was a touch well dressed," the boatswain's mate told him when he announced himself. "Marked for being aboard, are you?"

Johnston nodded. "Signed at Leadenhall Street the day afore yesterday." He looked at the petty officer more carefully, and it was not an impressive sight. The man was short, but well built, with a mop of unruly brown hair that fell in front of his face. His jacket was tatty and decidedly unkempt, with a slight rip to the sleeve that had been allowed to run and fray. The trousers were no better, being heavily stained at the knees, and the varnished stiff hat, usually a proud mark of rank, was dented and shabby.

"Well, you took yer time getting here," the boatswain's mate snorted, wiping his nose with the back of his hand.

"Said my pay wouldn't start until I comes aboard," Johnston said defensively.

"Oh yes," the man's face softened slightly. "But there be a wealth of work on, and no one to do it, so we needs all the 'elp we can get."

"Short of 'ands, are you?"

"Aye, loaded us up, then most buggered off. More's a commin', an' we 'ope to pick up further at the Downs an' probably the Channel. But, it ain't just the lack of Jacks that has put us out." His voice softened, and he darted a quick look about before continuing, "We got new officers, an' they're the biggest bunch of nigits it has ever been my misfortune to sail with."

Johnston pulled a face. "So we're in the suds?"

"Up to our necks." The shorter man eyed Johnston knowingly. "You a King's man, are you?"

Johnston stiffened slightly. "I served, a while back."

"Well, we'll keep you safe in the barkey," he said, understanding much. "Can't stop 'em if the Andrew comes lookin', but no one will tattle, not while you're in the Company's service, you can be sure of that." He held out a tar-caked hand. "Name's Ward, captain of the maintop in *Sovereign*, afore I sees the error of me ways."

Johnston took the iron grip while the man continued, "An' I don't want you thinkin' I'm usually in such sad trim; like I says, plenty of hard work for us all afore we sail, and not the time for the dolly. Better go and make your mark, then I'll finds you some entertainment. An' ditch that shore goin' rig if you want to keep it tidy."

* * *

King turned and gave his hand to Clara who stood awkwardly at the carriage doorway, her long dress all but hiding the small wooden step. The coachman tied up the reins, and reached back for the first of the luggage.

"So which one is it?" the girl asked, when she was safely deposited on the ground. King looked about the crowded anchorage. There was a mass of shipping in various states of readiness, some with topmasts up and clearly set for the off, while others might just as likely have been in ordinary.

He shook his head, "We'll know soon enough."

"Ain't you just a little bit interested?" the girl asked, as Manning clambered down after them.

"He'd be keen enough were she a warship," he said, giving his hand up to Kate. "But then he'd have been aboard afore now, not leaving it to the last second."

"It's a means to an end," King said simply. "Employment for a couple of years, and hopefully a decent return."

"Set you up, will it?" Clara asked hopefully.

"Hardly that, but I have a need for funds, and this appears to be the best way of providing them."

Kate was with them now, and looking about expectantly while Manning began to take the luggage down from the driver. "Better get a porter, Robert," she said.

Manning shook his head. "Not for this little lot." He turned and passed the first of King's possessions to his friend, then reached back for the single sea chest he was sharing with his wife. King walked towards the quay where a line of wherries sat waiting for trade. Clara stepped close alongside him, and awkwardly pushed her hand under his arm.

"You really will be gone a full two years?" she asked.

"Two years is probably the most," King said, strangely eager to please her. "More'n like it'll be a year an' a half, maybe even less."

Silently she took the information in.

"How much for four an' luggage?" he asked when they reached the nearest boat.

"Sixpence for the hire, penny a person, and sixpence for the dunnage," the grizzled seaman answered. "It's the standard charge; any boat you like, to any ship in the pool."

King looked about. All were manned and of roughly the same size, so he chose the one owned by the speaker. Robert arrived, and gratefully swung the chest down to the wherryman, while Clara stepped uncertainly into the small craft. In no time, they were out on the murky waters of the Thames. There was hardly a breath of wind, so it was likely to be a slow passage.

"What ship?" the stroke oar asked, once they were underway.

"*Pevensey Castle.*"

"I knows her; India bound, so they says."

King nodded. He didn't need reminding. Feeling a faint pressure on his arm, he noticed that Clara had taken possession of him yet again. She smiled and looked up into his eyes. She had a pert nose and a pleasant face, and King supposed that she was really very pretty, although he only registered the fact as one of many that did not concern him. Kate beamed at them both from the seat opposite, while King's attention drifted to the shipping about them. They were passing a Navy frigate, a sixth rate similar to his last ship, just in the process of setting up topmasts and probably to be gone with the next tide. She was likely to spend the rest of winter scraping an enemy lee shore on some relentless blockade duty, but it might well be something better; an independent mission, possibly even a cruise. In that case, there would be prize money for all, and a lieutenant's share was not inconsiderable. The ship was sharp as a razor. Even the ironwork gleamed, and her lines promised speed and a weather helm. He sighed, turned back and caught Clara's expression as she looked intently at him.

"That your boat then?"

He tried not to wince, "No, I'm afraid it is not."

She leant closer. "I'll be missing you," she told him quietly, pressing her body gently against his. He wriggled uncomfortably on the thwart.

"Thank you, I..." It was difficult to express his emotions, especially under the scrutiny of two women, but he did not want the girl to be under any illusions.

"You will write?" she persisted.

"If you wish," he said. "But also to another."

"Another?" Her voice was suddenly loud; a screech almost, and one that attracted the attention of all in the boat as well as some further away.

"I have told you," King said softly. "There is a young lady; we have an understanding."

"She's Dutch!" Clara all but spat, before pulling away and continuing just as loudly. "An' she ain't hereabouts!"

For the first time in many months, King was rather pleased about the last point. Kate was still watching them both, a sly look on her face.

"No, but I intend to send for her, when I return." His words were spoken especially clearly, as if talking to a child. "I have said this before; you must understand."

Whether she did or not, Clara's hand was swiftly removed from under his arm, and the journey continued in an awkward silence.

They neared an Indiaman, and soon King could make out the name on her counter. He looked across at Manning. "That's her," he said.

Clara came out of her sulk to look. "Pretty," she said, although neither of the men agreed. The ship was painted well enough, a fresh job, probably the result of her time at Blackwall, and there was nothing exactly wrong with the vessel itself. Fresh dark marks below the scuppers told a different tale, however, and there was a free end of line swinging uselessly from the taffrail, while a length of mouldy canvas hung down from the lip of an empty gunport. A grubby wooden landing stage was rigged at the starboard entry port. The wherry drew closer, but there was no shout from a lookout. King and Manning exchanged glances as the boat rubbed against the stage, before coming to a gentle halt. Standing, King reached into his pocket and passed the fare to the stroke oar.

"You'll be taking this young lady back," he told him. Clara did not look up, or even acknowledge his leaving and he stepped quickly out of the boat.

"Comin' aboard, sir?" A head appeared at the entry port; an ordinary seaman, although the greeting was friendly enough.

"Indeed. Have this luggage swung up, will you?" The man knuckled his forehead before disappearing. Manning and Kate joined him on the stage; he looked back at Clara, and received a cold smile. There seemed little else to do, so he turned and made his way up to the entry port.

On deck, the ship was clearly in a state of turmoil. That was to be expected, and really, nothing was terribly out of place. But to a seasoned officer, the general impression was not favourable. The main grating to the hold was left open, even though no work was being carried out, and it was clear that several weeks had gone by since any of the decks last received the attention of a holystone. The only men present were working at the falls, bringing the luggage from the wherry, and they were hardly setting any records.

"We have to get used to a different routine," Manning said philosophically when he joined him. "It's bound to be different; merchants just don't have the man power, so they cannot be so spick."

King nodded, although he had heard different. Of course, the East India Company mainly used leased vessels, but they were supposedly built and maintained to a very high standard. The Company even ran their own naval service, the Bombay Marine, equipped with proper warships that had proved able to match most of their size and many much larger opponents. He simply could not believe that this was a typical example of an East Indiaman.

"Captain's probably ashore," Manning said, following his thoughts. "An' also the first luff, or chief mate, as I suppose we shall have to start calling him."

The party at the falls were finished now, and the luggage lay heaped on the deck. One of the men approached, and King noticed he was wearing the uniform of a boatswain's mate.

"Are there officers aboard?" King asked, as the man saluted.

"Only yourselves, sir. Captain's been a day or so back, an' Mr Willis, the chief mate, he was here yes'aday. The others 'ave not been down yet; you're the first."

"I see," King said, coldly. "And you are?"

"Ward, sir."

"You are poorly turned out, Ward."

The man nodded. "I am sir, an' the sorrier for it, but there's a measure to do, and no one else to do it. The other boatswain's mate 'as a party sortin' in the 'old, an' I was trying to make some sense of the bosun's stores. We finished lading last week, then most of the crew took their tickets; there's less than twenty men aboard, sir. Another joined us today, but we was promised a whole lot more."

"Where is the bosun?"

"We ain't got one, sir, not no more. Mr Hodges left several days back, 'long with t' carpenter an' sailmaker."

"Indeed? Something of a massed exodus."

Ward's eyes fell. "Bit of a disagreement with the cap'n. They were all good men, sir, but used to doing things their own way."

King sighed and looked about. The wherry was heading back to the quay, and Clara could be seen sitting in the stern. She had turned around and was desperately waving in a hopeless and quite pathetic manner. Instinct told him to hail the boat; he had made a mistake, a big one, and the sooner things were sorted the better. He looked to Manning.

"This don't augur well, Bob. What say we leave out of this?"

Manning snorted, "I'm inclined to agree."

"And how do you intend to live?" Kate asked sharply. There

was a cold look on her face. She might have shared their concern, but was clearly considering the practicalities. "Father's money is spent, now it is our turn to maintain him."

Manning nodded silently, but she was not finished.

"We have already accepted pay for the first two months of our service. Do we give that back? A berth aboard this ship might not be the best, but it will take time to find better. Really, we have little option."

"The surgeon, is he aboard?" Manning was addressing the boatswain's mate.

"Aye sir, but he'll be asleep b'now."

"Asleep?" That seemed like the last straw. It was nine in the morning. He glanced back at King, carefully avoiding Kate's stare. "I fear you might be right, Tom."

"Been up all night with Clegg, one of the hands what 'as the fever," Ward continued. "It finally broke just afore breakfast, and he said he could be left for a while."

"I see." That was better. "When do you expect the captain to return?" King again.

"This eve'nin, sir. An' we should be getting more 'ands afore long. Rumour 'as it a detail's a'coming from the *Boreham*, what docked last week. The old girl's to be condemned, so we'll probably get 'er standing officers, and a few of the crew. Me'be enough to make up the numbers."

"Right, well I feel we should make the best of a bad job." King clapped his hands together and looked about. "We'll strike our luggage below. Then, I want to see all the petty officers. I'll need a full report on fabric, rig, and stores, both held and expected. We have the rest of today; what say we start to make some measure of order?"

Ward's grin owed much to relief. "That suits me fine, sir," he said, knuckling his forehead.

King turned to Manning and Kate. "There's clearly a deal to be done, and I'm not saying I'm happy with the situation, but we may as well make what we can of it."

"I think you're right," Kate said. "I can't see it getting any worse."

"Aye, an' if it does," Manning agreed, "we can always jump ship."

* * *

By four that afternoon there had been a mild transformation. Despite his appearance, Ward had a good understanding of what was needed, and actually seemed keen to sort matters out. As for the remaining men, the arrival of a proper officer and the promise of order provided them with the impetus they so clearly wanted.

King walked out of the carpenter's workshop where two mates were freeing the blocks in a jumble of tophamper, and looked along the lower deck. He was tired. Several weeks had passed since he was last on board a ship, and this one, with her novel architecture and ramshackle state, seemed destined to wear him out. There had been so much to attend to; not everything was exactly in his domain, but all needed to be done. Word had come from one of the shore boats that the captain was due back aboard at any time, and King wanted to deliver a better prospect than the one presented to him that morning. He moved on, continuing his tour of inspection. In steerage, the cattle stalls were empty, as they must have been for a month or more. But, the lack of ventilation meant that there was still a distinct smell of the farmyard about the place. As a mate, King guessed he was berthing with the senior officers and better class of passengers at the stern of the ship. Steerage was for the juniors, and he was glad not to be joining them. A figure working in the near darkness caught his attention. King could hear the splash of water and the sound of brushing.

"All well there?" he asked, walking forward. The man was on his knees, scrubbing out the stalls with water and what smelled like vinegar. He turned back and looked up at King.

"Aye, sir. Just giving a bit of a scrape out; ain't been clean in ages. No good putting fresh beasts in a dirty stall." The seaman stood up awkwardly and grinned. King noticed the long pigtail that marked him as a man of several years' service. His gaze fell to the deck and even in the dim light he could see that a workmanlike job was being done.

"Very good," he said, and went to pass on, when he noticed the man regarding him strangely. "Was there something?"

"No, sir." The man looked away quickly and, slinking back to the deck, began to scrub again.

King paused, uncertain. "What is your name?"

The brush stopped for no more than a second. "Johnston, sir." His voice was low, almost muffled, but there was something about that pigtail that stuck in King's mind.

"Have we served together in the past?"

"Don't believe so, sir." The scrubbing continued, possibly a littler harder than before.

Johnston. It wasn't a name he remembered. There were noises from above. Something was happening on the upper deck that may well require his attention. But, the man did seem oddly familiar and he opened his mouth to say more when another voice came through the upper grating, "Mr King, are you below, sir?"

"What is it, Ward?"

"Looks like captain and chief mate are a comin' aboard, sir."

King snorted. There was still a deal to do but at least he had a better ship to show them. "Very good, Johnston," he said, and moved on.

* * *

The gloomy winter afternoon was just starting to give way to dusk when King joined Ward on the starboard gangboard. The boatswain's mate pointed out to where a wherry was approaching, crowded with officers. King looked around; there were no sideboys on board, no marine guard; he would have to greet his new captain without any Navy ceremony.

"Boat ahoy!" Ward's hail rang out across the water just as Manning came up from the depths, followed by an inquisitive Kate.

"*Pevensey Castle!*"

The reply confirmed Ward's suspicions, King tried to make out the dark figure dressed in a boat cloak who sat in the sternsheets. The captain of any ship held the ultimate power: he could make or break a commission. A bad report from this shadowy man would seriously influence his future in the merchant service. They waited in silence while the boat drew nearer, and finally came to a halt next to the staging.

"Right then, line up and pay some respect." Ward was forming six ordinary seamen up into a welcoming party and, as the captain's hat appeared above the entry port, the squeal of a bosun's pipe shattered the silence of the dark afternoon. Manning and Kate drew forward in anticipation, but King stayed right where he was. The man was in full view now, and glared down the line, appearing to find fault in all that he saw. His gaze swept round to the officers, softening slightly and pausing to take in the young woman appreciatively. Then, it rested on King, and a hint of evil humour appeared. He smirked, and nodded his head very slightly.

"Mr King, what a joy it is to see you once more."

King's mouth was dry; a store of seemingly forgotten memories flooded into his mind, bringing back the very atmosphere of the officers' quarters in *Vigilant*. It had all happened several years ago, but the recollections were fresh and not in the least pleasant. And here was the cause, the man himself, standing in front of him, and wearing the uniform of an East India Company captain. *His* captain, *his* superior officer, and for the whole of the commission.

"Rogers!" he said. The word came out involuntarily, but he was alert enough to bite back those that were keen to follow.

"Indeed it is, Mr King," the man said coldly. "And I am not insensible to the fact that the pleasure appears to be entirely mine."

CHAPTER TWO

King pulled himself together and attempted to wipe the expression of horror and disgust from his face.

"I'm sorry, sir. I just didn't expect..." His voice trailed away.

"Apparently so, and yet you applied for a position in my ship, and I was good enough to accept you."

Still, King's mind refused to function. Yes, it was a Captain Rogers he had written to, and the signature had been clear enough on the letter of acceptance. Yet never in his most troubled nightmares had King connected a senior naval officer in a respected merchant service with the incompetent buffoon standing in front of him now. Rogers was second lieutenant in *Vigilant*, where his bullying ways caused no end of friction, both in the wardroom, and throughout the ship. The man had proved to be impossible to work with, and yet here he was, not only in front of King, but apparently his commanding officer.

Captain Rogers turned to the two men who now joined him on the gangboard. "Mr King here was an officer in *Vigilant*; I have told you of my time with her, I believe?"

"Indeed," the first spoke. He was probably mid-twenties, short, with greasy black hair and sallow skin that was pockmarked with old chickenpox scars. "A gallant action, sir."

"Willis, my chief officer," Rogers gave an offhand nod to the man who stepped forward to shake King's hand. "Mr King has joined us as midshipman," the captain continued.

King's jaw dropped. "Sir, I have passed my board; I was made lieutenant in my last ship."

Rogers showed little surprise or emotion. "Indeed? Then, I wish you joy of your commission, but you will be rated as midshipman aboard *Pevensey Castle*."

"That was not the agreement, sir." The last word was added hurriedly, and there was a noticeable stiffening from the two at Rogers's side as King continued. "I was at East India House, I have been sworn in, as...as an officer of the Company."

"I do not doubt it." The captain studied him for a while, as if wishing to remember the moment for always. "And the agreement, sir," he continued with emphasis, "was for you to join as an officer of this ship; that is what you committed to, that is what I accepted. No mention was made of actual rank, however."

King knew that his face was glowing red, but Rogers left him no room to speak.

"If your work meets my exacting standards you might act as sixth mate, but midshipman is your station, and be glad of it. You will find it a slightly different role to that of the Navy; but then many things are, aboard an Indiaman." He glanced at the two officers and received knowing, worldly looks in return. "Besides, I could not appoint you as mate, with so little knowledge of the service." King wondered how much experience Rogers claimed. "It would be wrong, and totally contrary to Company rules."

"How so?" It was Kate's voice. She had been watching with interest and now stared hard at Rogers who looked appraisingly back at her.

"Beg pardon, madam; I do not believe we have been introduced."

"Katharine Manning," King began, but she continued for him.

"I am to assist the purser."

"Then, as your captain, you will address me as sir!" Rogers's roar was powerful, although the only reaction it elicited from Kate was to bring a slight reddening to her cheeks.

"I said, I was appointed, sir," she spoke clearly. "But I fear it is not to be. From this brief exposure, I can say that I should rather serve as a lily white in hell than stay a moment longer in a ship where you have command."

"Is that so?" he looked from one to the other. "Well, ain't that a fine welcome to a captain?"

King's eyes fell momentarily.

"Fine indeed; I comes aboard to greet my new officers, and this is the respect I am given. You see here?" he indicated Kate and King. "One has not been aboard more than a watch, and he's demanding promotion, an' the other swears she won't serve with me, though we have never before met, and I have yet to even read myself in!"

The two officers nodded sycophantically while considering the utterly deplorable creatures before them.

"Let me tell you this, Mr Midshipman King." Rogers's words were close clipped and carefully chosen. "A mate is a respected and senior position. You are unable to serve in anything other than an acting capacity aboard a Company ship until you have accrued sufficient sea time. That is not time with the Navy, it is with this service, learning our ways and the proper procedures aboard an Indiaman. And that ain't my ruling; you may take it up with those at East India House if you have any dispute." He gave a brief nod towards the men next to him. "Mr Willis here has made three India trips, and Mr Seagrove two." It was a point well made, and King felt suitably humbled. Then, Rogers's eyes fell to Kate.

"And madam; be in no doubt that you may leave this ship whenever you choose." She raised her head slightly as he continued, "but to undertake a responsibility only to decline when a ship is about to sail is not the act of an honourable person. I will see to it that anyone who has dealings with merchant shipping is well aware, before they deem it right to employ you in the future. I will also require your two months' advance payment returned this instant. The same will apply to you, Mr King, 'though in your case I shall have no hesitation in speaking with Earl Spencer. He is a personal friend of my father."

King swallowed. He had forgotten about Rogers's family connections.

"I am sure he will wish to learn of any officer who is not inclined to abide by his word, be they humble midshipmen or lofty lieutenants. And, as First Lord of the Admiralty, he is in an excellent position to see that they are suitably remembered, should they be foolish enough to apply for employment in the future."

The silence lasted all of thirty-seconds, before Rogers's gaze finally switched to Manning. "And you, sir; we have met before, I recall; remind me of your name and position, assuming, of course, that you intend to take one up?"

Willis and Seagrove simpered as Manning searched for words. "Robert Manning, sir," he said, finally. "I called on you some weeks ago. You posted me as assistant to the surgeon. I have since satisfied the Company's medical board who agreed to the appointment."

"Very good, Mr Manning." Rogers indicated Kate. "And this is your wife, your sister, or perhaps your mother?"

"M-my wife, sir. We are just married."

"Indeed." A lewd smirk was not very far away, but Rogers continued, "Well, I trust you will learn to keep your rib under better restraint in future."

Kate flushed, but said nothing.

"And so, Mr Manning, are you to honour your commitments, or do you also threaten to desert?"

"I will stay, sir," Manning said quietly; he was aware of having no other option.

"And I am glad of it. Welcome aboard; I hope your time is pleasant. Now, if you will excuse me I have important matters to discuss with my senior officers." Rogers walked smartly towards the quarterdeck with Willis and Seagrove who paused only to deliver further contemptuous looks, before hurrying away. Ward touched his hat and dismissed the seamen, all of whom were witnesses to what had been said, leaving Kate, Manning and King alone by the entry port.

"Well," said the woman. "That might have fared better."

"Do you think he means what he says?" Manning asked. "About his influence? Could he really break us—and even if he could, would he?"

"Oh yes," King was positive. "I'm afraid I know Mr Rogers of old. And believe me, he would like nothing better."

* * *

"Aha!" Ward said, finding Johnston settling for the night. "Secured yourself the best berth, then?" The forecastle accommodation was intended for senior hands and petty officers but with so few aboard and little order, Johnston felt justified in slinging his hammock there.

"You don't mind?"

"Na." Ward slumped down at a nearby mess table. "Finer perch than in steerage; better still when the galley stove's properly alight. And we got the heads close at hand." He reached for the chunk of dark yellow cheese that was left over from supper and cut a generous slice with his knife. "Takin' on fresh hands tomorrow; upwards of fifty, so you can expect it to be a bit more tight. But, you may as well stay there for now, if you've a mind."

"Fifty? That's a lot to magic up in one go. Are they Lascars?"

Ward shook his head. "No, most'll be British, come down from the old *Boreham* so I believes. Young Seagrove told us not ten minutes ago. An' they got a load more officers; should make a difference—might even get this barkey back into order. Mind, we made a good start today." He bit into his cheese and chewed meditatively. "That new bloke, King; he's a live one, right enough. Thought he were a mate, the way 'e was behavin', but now it seems he's naught but a middie. Still, a few more like 'im, and this could turn into a decent berth again."

"I knows him," Johnston said quietly.

"Do you now?" Ward looked across with interest. "Good as he seems, is he?"

"As an officer yes, there'd be few to beat him; but my worry is just how keen. We was in a previous ship, see. An' I didn't stay to see me wages."

The boatswain's mate took in the information without comment.

"So, do you think I got to worry?" Johnston said, after a while. Ward turned round on the bench and faced him.

"Well, maybe you 'ave, an' maybe you 'aven't; I couldn't rightly say, but you won't be the first to run from 'is Majesty, that's for sure. An' those that do usually wind up here, or hereabouts."

"But if he peaches on me..."

"If he does you'll be handed back; but he'd be a fool, and he don't come over that way. It were a different ship, an' a different navy," his eyes twinkled in the half-light, "an' I'll bet a different name."

Johnston nodded, "I was known as Simpson."

"Chances are he won't remember or, if he does, won't say nowt. Can't be certain, mind, but that's one of the 'azzards of runnin'."

Johnston lay back in his hammock and sighed. Of course, he didn't have to take the risk at all. He could go now, this very minute. A simple trip to the heads would hardly attract suspicion; he could be over the side and half way to the shore by the time anyone missed him. And even then, it was doubtful they would do anything about it. He had no real possessions, no ties, and this particular ship didn't seem destined to have a happy cruise.

Yes, it was probably the best option, and he half raised himself up in his hammock when Ward began to speak again.

"But I do know this; if anyone jacks you in, it'd 'ardly show kindly on them."

"No?"

"No." Ward was positive. "There are only so many proper seamen in England, and they got to go somewhere. If every King's man who runs to the Company were given back, there'd be hardly any to serve our ships."

It was a point that Johnston had not considered.

"Better stay, that is if you'd a mind to go," Ward continued. "I reckons your man is not such a fool as all that. Besides, if you're that worried about being sprung, you'll start giving me the jitters an' all."

* * *

Rogers's berth was a good deal better. Set below the poop deck, in an area known as the roundhouse, it was smaller than a captain's quarters in a similar-sized warship, but palatial compared with the other accommodation. There were magnificent stern windows that gave excellent light and ventilation, and room enough for his desk, three chairs and a rather comfortable couch; all that in addition to his bed space which was in a separate room. The entire roundhouse was divided in two by a deal-wood partition that ran down the middle. One half was entirely his; the other was separated into cabins for the better class of passenger. But, most of their rooms were little more than hen houses; nothing like as grand as the space he occupied. And he had his own private washing facilities and head. He closed the door to the cuddy dining room and strode into his domain. It was his right, of course; as captain, he should have the very best. Some masters chose to rent out their cabins to wealthy passengers and berth more modestly, but he had decided to retain this small indulgence as a necessary return for the responsibility and status of his rank.

The door opened, and Luck, his steward, slipped in carrying a small tray.

"Brandy, sir?" the man asked in barely a whisper.

"Set it down," Rogers replied, indicating the desk next to the stern lights. The man left as quietly as he had come, and Rogers lowered himself comfortably in front of the decanter. Despite the wine taken at dinner, the spirit warmed him, and he sat back content.

Since his sudden departure from the Navy, something that his father, who knew little of the facts, was still working hard to understand and justify, Rogers had spent a mildly indulgent life. There was the odd bit of business in the city, of course, and he had taken responsibility for the family's investments and trusts—items that he immediately placed with more competent minds that did the work well enough and passed the credit back to him. Even so, it had not taken long for his father to insist that he took up a true career; something that might actually earn a return on the money already invested. He had thought to have found such a calling with the Royal Navy, but that later proved to be a dead end. He moved on from the unpleasant incident in *Vigilant* with barely a further thought. The years spent in His Majesty's service had taught him much, however, and a position with the East India Company—the *Honourable* East India Company, was really the obvious step. In addition, he could earn a decent pile. Some captains brought back wealth beyond measure, and there was the added advantage that progress within the service was more easily achieved. In fact, like the ship, most of the crew, his personal cargo, and even his future promotion could actually be bought.

His father sorted everything, of course, but then that was always one of his greatest qualities. He knew people. More than that, he knew the right people, and how to handle them, so that he got his way, without anyone apparently suffering. It was quite a talent. The old man had certainly excelled when it came to meeting with the court of directors at East India House. They might have appeared a severe lot but, given time and the right attention, soon proved as willing to take assurances of Rogers's competence, as they were the various gifts, arrangements, and opportunities that were sent their way. It was just a father looking after his son, but he did it admirably well.

And he would see a return—there was no doubt of that: Rogers had all the material necessary. The ship was sound enough. She had just completed one India trip to shake down, then gone through a full refit. He was quietly confident that his knowledge of the sea coupled, even more importantly, with his knowledge of human nature, would be sufficient for everything else. He had two good men to support him in Willis and Seagrove; not the finest of officers maybe, but they did what they were told and could be relied upon to back him to their last breath. Furthermore, their complete lack of social status might also come in handy if a scapegoat were needed. If he had learned nothing from his father about getting his own way, manipulating the junior officers to his will, and generally seeing that matters were done—not actually by him, but to his requirements—then his life to date had been totally wasted.

Pevensey Castle was carrying an official payload of lead, tin, ironware, and woollen cloth that would be sold upon reaching Bombay. A little over fifty tons was Rogers's personal property, as would be the profit. A further allowance of thirty-eight tons' cargo space was also his for the return trip, where the real money was to be made. With earnings measured in hundreds of percent, it would be strange if he were not comfortably set up by the time they next anchored in the Thames. The idea pleased him, especially when he could acquire his fortune by sitting in these pleasant surroundings, and with the reassurance that he was in ultimate control of all he surveyed.

In front of him now was the passenger list. That was another potential source of, if not income, then certainly influence. Listed were the names of people with whom he would be spending several months in close proximity. They would be relying on him and his ship for most of their needs, and he had every intention of claiming future favours in return for his services. He glanced down the page; some were joining tomorrow, others at Deal, and a few more when they reached Spithead. The majority were small traders, factors, minor Company officials, cadets, and writers - the kind who cared not how they travelled, or were doing so at someone else's expense. These were unlikely to be of much use, but then there was also one in a very different station: Charles Drayton esquire, a man of influence, someone truly worth cultivating. A secret and quite unofficial ring known as The Marine Interest held virtual control over all ships offered for hire to the East India Company. Drayton was either a member or at least enjoyed close connections, and anyone who had risen to such a position was likely to be influential in other areas as well. Yes, there were definite possibilities there.

His eyes flowed over the list for the second time. Several female names caught his eye, but most appeared to be travelling with their husbands or, in one case, an adult son. Still, the former might provide a little entertainment. Rogers wasn't above cuckolding the odd insignificant spouse; in fact, he usually found it added spice to a relationship. And even if all were loyal, they were bound to have ladies' maids. Again, he was open minded enough to share himself with women of any level. Besides, there was one, he noted, who appeared to be quite alone; probably being sent to India to secure a husband. That could mean she was as ugly as sin, but even then she might not be discounted, if the time showed signs of moving slowly.

He was pouring himself a second generous measure of the brandy when his servant put his head round the door.

"Officer to see you, sir. Name of Paterson; says he is the new second mate."

Rogers snorted to himself; does he indeed? Well, there was no harm in pulling him down a notch or two. He had long ago learned that, however competent or experienced a man might be, it was always worthwhile putting him in his place, and showing who was really in command.

"Show him in, Luck," he said, before downing his drink in one and standing to meet the newcomer.

* * *

King walked through the door to the steerage mess and threw his ditty bag into the corner of the small, airless room. At the long canvas-covered table, Kate and Manning looked up from the remains of their meal.

"Have you eaten, Tom?" she asked.

He nodded and gave an ironic smile. "I took a bite just before the captain came aboard; haven't felt much like food since."

Manning grunted. "Rather puts you off, don't it?"

"The pity is, it were all starting to go so well," Kate said, as King slumped down at the table. "I'll admit that Mr Myles, the purser, isn't God's gift to accountancy, but at least he has things reasonably in order and some degree of planning for what is to come."

"Likewise with the surgeon." Manning thrust his plate aside and turned his attention to the teapot in the middle of the table. "A trained man, and he seems willing to pass on what he knows. Better medical supply than I've ever seen in a King's ship, and a first-rate reference library to boot. He's got Blane, Lind, and the latest Trotter; a fellow could get educated, were he so inclined."

King collected a cup and passed it across to be filled. "Aye, well up until the arrival of our dear captain, I weren't faring too badly. Ship's in a state, of course, there can be no doubting that, but it's also to be expected with her just out of Blackwall. She needs to work up proper, and there's little chance of that with a skeleton crew aboard." He paused and sipped at his tea, considering. "Mind, what we have are sharp enough, once you get them going. And all are volunteers; far better than the sweepings from the press I'm used to. Together we achieved more in a day than I'd have thought possible, an' I think that in the main the people are happier for it."

Kate had finished eating now and collected Manning's plate beneath hers, neatly stacking the cutlery on top of both. "What really nettles me is the fact that Rogers was quite right." Both men nodded as she continued, "Tyrant and bully he may be, but it weren't the best way to greet a new captain," she looked across at King. "You should have made certain of your rank and entitlement before accepting the post, and I..." She paused for a moment, "I probably should have been a little less forthcoming."

There was a silence as Kate's admission was digested. It was one that, for her, was almost bordering on a revelation. "Perhaps you were a little hasty," Manning conceded, studiously avoiding King's eyes.

"So we will have to make the best of it," she said, standing and taking the plates away. "Purser says they'll be a fresh intake in the morning, both officers and men; it's up to us to make this ship work."

"I doubt that we'll get much help from Willis or Seagrove," Manning said gloomily. "Seems to me they've got their mind set solely on pandering to the captain."

"That's as may be; we'll have to see. But, if we don't try to meet them at least halfway, this cruise is going to be a nightmare for all."

A sound from outside, followed by the opening of the door, made them all look round. A man stood hesitantly in the passageway. Slim, and below average height, his short dark curly hair was cut in the modern manner, and he was dressed in the Company's uniform, with a canvas parcel tucked under one arm.

"Room for one more?" he asked, smiling pleasantly. "I don't take up much space."

"Come in and be welcome!" Both men stood, and King extended a hand. "Thomas King, midshipman; this is Robert Manning, surgeon's mate, and Katharine Manning assistant to the purser."

"Pleasure to meet you gentlemen, madam. John Paterson, at your service; third mate, or so it appears. I had hoped for better, but it seems the captain has already appointed." His look was good natured and genuine. "Sorry not to be here the sooner, there were illuminations in London and not a carriage to be found."

"Third mate?" King asked cautiously. "Are you in the correct berth?"

"Ah, King by name, and do I detect a King's man by nature?"

"I have served in the Royal Navy," King confirmed, guardedly.

"Sure, I gathered as much, and that you aren't used to the ways of the Company." Paterson smiled again, although this time there was something slightly superior in the expression.

"Allow me to explain; the steerage mess is treated very much as a wardroom for junior offices, do you see? Third mate is customarily the president. We don't go for fancy cabins; even those that do are likely to sell them on to the wealthier passengers." Paterson's look grew wistful as he added, "Forty guineas or more, they pay for an outward berth, or so I'm told."

"Tis a tidy sum," Manning commented. King said nothing. He had not asked for an explanation and was a little taken aback by the new man who clearly enjoyed the sound of his own voice.

"Aye, but not for the likes of me, it seems," Paterson continued. "Not for a few more trips at least. Chief and second mates will be in cabins; likewise, the captain. They will eat and drink in the cuddy with the better class of passenger, while we have to put up with each other. You won't mind, I trust?"

"I am sure it will be a pleasure." King said, although his tone was quite flat.

"We might also have to share with a few of what they term the lower class of traveller, 'though I have usually found them to be the better company." Paterson looked about the place. "Belikes it could be crowded by the time we leave Pompey."

"Won't you take some food?" Manning asked.

"No, I ate on the way, thank'e, but if that's coffee, or something like, I could be tempted." He placed his canvas package against the bulkhead and took a seat at the head of the table.

"Tea, perhaps a little cool, and I fear we have no milk," Kate told him, picking up the earthenware pot. "Shall I warm it, or make afresh?"

"It will be welcome enough as it is, thank you ma'am." Paterson nodded, as Kate filled one of the squat china cups, and the two men were seated again. "So, what is the score aboard *Pevensey Castle*?" he asked, after taking a sip.

King moved uncomfortably. "You have met the captain?"

Paterson nodded seriously. "A brief interview, but informative." His voice became deliberately neutral. "I gather he had dined rather well."

"It was always his habit in the past," King replied.

"You have served with him afore, then?"

"In a different ship and a different navy."

"Ah, so our Captain Rogers is another King's man," Paterson chuckled knowingly. "And did he distinguish himself in the service of His Majesty?"

It was King's turn to smile now. "He did, but not in the manner that you intend."

Paterson nodded. "It is often the case that we take King George's bad bargains; present company excepted, though, I am certain," he added hurriedly. "And I should say that Mr Rogers must not be judged too harshly on that account. Many's the man who has made his name and fortune from the Indiamen who never could have progressed in a warship."

King's coat was hanging on the bulkhead and, without speaking, Kate reached for it and began to spread the cloth over her lap. "Well, we shall have to see," she said firmly. "It has not been the best of starts, but it is in our minds to improve matters as soon as the situation presents."

"I was appointed by Leadenhall Street and given to understand it was to be an improvement." Paterson was sipping at his cold tea

28

again. "Second mate at the very least. But from what I have now discovered, the captain has already installed Mr Willis and Mr Seagrove; they are friends from a previous commission, perhaps?"

"It is possible." Manning thought for a moment. "Although when he interviewed me Mr Rogers claimed this to be his first command."

"Then, it is unlikely, and he is probably as blind to their worth as we are."

"You did not take to them?" King asked.

Paterson stiffened slightly. "Forgive me, I have spoken too soon. Sadly, I have the habit for saying too much when it is not required. It's a fault I do try to correct." He grinned at King who found himself liking the man a little better. "Still, I understand he has conjured up a crew; no mean feat in these times."

"His family have excellent connections," King said dryly.

"Then maybe they found him our premier and second." Kate was also one inclined to speak out of turn, although in her case no attempt was made to control the tendency. "And perchance they are not quite so stupid as they appear." She produced a small pair of silver scissors and started to unpick the facings to the lapels on King's uniform.

"That is something we will doubtless find out by and by." Paterson was watching Kate with apparent interest. "Tell me, what are you doing to that coat?"

Kate raised her eyes. "A simple misunderstanding, nothing more."

"I had thought to be shipping as a mate, not a midshipman," King said glumly.

"Ah, another who has found his expectations lowered." Paterson pulled a wry face. "A pity. Still, the distinction is not so very great in the merchant service."

"So I have been advised."

"No, in truth, it makes little difference," the man persisted. "Allow me to explain; if it will not bore you; of course."

King shook his head. "No, please, go ahead."

"Pay for a mid is the same as that of a fifth mate, an' you will still be called to stand watch. Berthing arrangements are also identical, the only way you will be light is in the matter of indulgence."

The three looked at Paterson blankly.

"It is the term we use for private cargo; mates warrant a large allowance of hold space for their own personal trading. Of course, funds are needed to back the goods, but if that is in your mind, I rarely use my full *quota* and will gladly share."

"How many trips have you made?" Kate asked.

"To India, this will be my fourth, but I travelled on to Canton on two occasions, and have also seen New South Wales twice."

"A busy life."

"Indeed." Paterson looked keenly at King. "And one I'd not swap. I understand your loyalty to His Majesty, but John Company has its advantages; guaranteed travel, and most times you know exactly where you're heading, as well as an idea of when you shall return."

"And singularly little blockading duty, I gather?"

Paterson returned King's smile. "We are rarely asked," he agreed.

The door opened again, and this time an older man with prominent sideburns stood on the threshold. Manning rose from his chair at once.

"Come in, sir. Come in do." He turned to the other occupants. "May I introduce Mr Keats, our surgeon?"

There was a brief exchanging of names and handshakes, and soon Keats was relaxing comfortably at the table and accepting a cup of cold tea from Kate.

"Your first trip aboard *Pevensey Castle*?" Paterson asked him as Tomlinson, the steward, entered and began to collect up the remains of their meal.

The surgeon shook his head. "No, I came back from Bombay with Captain Fuller; fine officer, handled the ship well, with always the time for his passengers. The new man - Rogers, isn't it? He'll have his work cut out to match him."

No one said a word, although Keats seemed oblivious to any awkwardness.

"Actually, it was you both I wished to see," he continued, singling out Manning and Kate. "I was thinking of your position, as a newly married couple." They looked at him dubiously. "I am one who likes his fellow's company, yet chance that each of you wish only for the society of the other."

There was another strained silence; even the steward paused in his work, while Kate began to take extreme interest in her sewing. Manning simply blushed.

"So, what say you take my cabin?" Keats asked. "'Tis large enough for two; two who don't mind a little intimacy." His tone was light and pleasant, and there was no hint of mockery when Manning met his eyes. "I'd be more than happy to berth in here, if Mr Paterson permits?" Manning flushed a little deeper, although Kate appeared not to have heard.

"Well, I'd think that a capital idea," Paterson all but shouted, looking at the two for confirmation, while Tomlinson bustled from the room to hide his smirk. Manning nodded silently, but Kate was still totally immersed in her work. "Right then," the mate continued with decision. He stood suddenly, and King was taken by the fact that he could do so without stooping. "But the evening is wearing out and rules state that cabin candles must be doused by ten, don't you know? Besides, if the rumour be true, we shall have more joining in the morning and a wealth to do, no doubt." He looked about the company, now strangely silent. "If no one has any objection, I suggest we calls it a day."

King and Keats were quick to rise, although the remaining couple took a little longer. Both had their possessions to gather, of course, but the impression that there was no rush, and they were actually reluctant to leave, was unmistakable. Keats was momentarily concerned that he had committed some incredible gaff, but they bid goodnight to all calmly enough. However, when Manning held the door open for Kate to leave, the surgeon noticed that they avoided each other's eyes and, when the frail door finally closed, it was to a silence from both sides.

The men in the steerage mess looked to one another. Something was amiss, although none could say what. King cleared his throat to speak when the couple apparently experienced a change of heart. The sound of whispering could be plainly heard, followed by a sudden laugh; then the noise of footsteps that quickly faded as they positively rushed along the passageway and on towards the surgeon's quarters.

CHAPTER THREE

The rumour was spot on. Soon after dawn, when King and Paterson were checking the contents of the signal locker on the ship's tiny poop deck, a pair of longboats and a cutter were spotted making for them in the early morning mist. The first two boats were slightly more than half-full; not enough to make up a complete crew, but a welcome addition, nevertheless. From their vantage position at the stern, the officers watched while the boats approached the landing stage and men began to clamber aboard.

"You, boy!" Paterson turned to a youngster who was brushing out one of the empty poultry coops. "The new intake is coming aboard; pass the word to the captain, then nip down and alert the cook that there's liable to be a few more for breakfast."

The lad was off in an instant and shortly afterwards Willis, the chief officer, appeared to meet the new draft. They assembled in the waist, forming up in ragged lines and facing the break of the quarterdeck. King watched them intently. Their tattoos, gait and attire marked them out as experienced seamen, and he could detect no unduly sullen looks, even though they may well have just stepped off a homeward-bound ship and were probably in need of food.

"Seems like a good start," he said quietly.

"A good start indeed," Paterson agreed.

Then there was a further commotion. The cutter had drawn

up, and soon a collection of petty and junior officers was climbing through the entry port and joining those in the waist. They were known to the seamen who allowed themselves to be arranged into what must have been their previous watches, then stood waiting, a little more formally now. Rogers timed his arrival perfectly, appearing on the quarterdeck just as their attention was about to drift from the new surroundings. King and Paterson watched him from behind as joined by Willis and now Seagrove, he strode forward to the break of the quarterdeck and commanded the assembly's complete attention.

King had to hand it to him. Rogers certainly looked the part; impeccably turned out in full dress uniform, with an embellished sword at his hip, and all the majesty, pomp and swagger of a true commander. The men were also impressed. There was a hushed silence while their new captain read a short statement that nominated him as the overall authority in the ship, the one who controlled her movements and, ultimately, their lives. The fresh intake was dismissed almost immediately, and for a moment stood in small groups, uncertain as to their proper station. Then, following a word from Willis, the petty officers began to shout, and the seamen were herded forward. A party was detailed to man the falls, bringing what personal possessions they might have up from the longboats, while the others were dismissed.

"Mr King, Mr Paterson!" Rogers had not deemed it necessary to turn around, and his call took both men by surprise. "You will attend me, if you please."

King glanced quickly at Paterson who followed him forward and down the short ladder to the quarterdeck. The feeling that Rogers was aware of their presence, indeed had been watching intently, even though his back was turned, was impossible to ignore. Seagrove and Willis chose not to notice them, however, although Rogers touched his hat in return to their salutes with due formality.

"The new men will have to be fed," he said looking directly at King. "See to it, and do not take too long; we have much ahead, and are to be moving to the Downs with Tuesday's morning tide."

"Very good, sir." King was equally formal, although his active mind raced. It gave them barely two days. "Is there a watch list?"

Rogers was momentarily taken aback. "Not at present. Watch lists and quarter bills are something Mr Paterson can attend to."

King could not help but glance across as the third mate

touched his hat. The work would take most of a day in itself and was usually the responsibility of the chief officer.

"There will be a further man joining us later this morning, and the first of our guests by nightfall," Rogers was continuing. "Cows, sheep and poultry are expected at any time, as is the last of the water. I also understand that some passengers embarking at Spithead are sending their personal servants in advance to prepare for their arrival. You will take especial care of them and see that the men do not fraternise with any females."

"Yes, sir." The two men spoke in unison and saluted again. They were about to turn away, but Rogers, it seemed, had not finished.

"Another thing."

They waited.

"From now on Mr King will take charge of the junior officers' berthing arrangements."

The subject came as a surprise, although the young man tried hard not to show it.

"I understand that these have been a little lax until now. Let me make it plain. The only married accommodation aboard this ship is for passengers."

Again, the feeling that the captain had been watching them returned. "Mr Manning will resume his berth in steerage, whereas Mrs Manning can share the female servants' quarters." Rogers paused, glowering at them both, although King who knew him of old, could detect more than a taint of pleasure in his tone. "I expect no further reports of any association between them while they are aboard. You will arrange that, and be certain that I am not disappointed."

* * *

By noon, the ship was in turmoil. Surrounded by an eclectic collection of small craft, with more standing off ready to come alongside, she swarmed with men. Some manned the tackles at the fore and main yardarms, straining to lift in the consumable stores necessary to sustain both crew and passengers on the voyage. Others ran light goods in from a whip at the mizzen yardarm, or loaded smaller casks up the parbuckle rails set next to the entry ports. The decks were dark with spillage, while straw, hay and general filth from the many live animals lay all about, making companionways and ladders lethal obstacles that could only be negotiated with the greatest of care.

Further parties were working below, in the cramped, airless darkness of the hold. Beneath their feet, the ballast shingle, slippery green with bilge slime, was maddeningly unstable, as the heavy casks were patiently coaxed into position. More men were stooping low to dodge the treacherous beams that threatened to knock any remaining sense from their heads, while they carried sacks of flour and hard tack into the bread room, or casks of oil, vinegar, and pickled cabbage to the stewards' pantry. And all would have been in chaos were it not for Paterson, King, Myles the purser, and Nichols, the latter being the new fourth mate who had arrived not three hours ago, yet was already proving his worth.

He was standing at the main hatchway now when King joined him, while yet another leaguer, one of the giant casks of London water, was swung over their heads and those of the straining men who manoeuvred it. Like all the mates in *Pevensey Castle*, Nichols was relatively young; not more than thirty, King guessed, and his stout frame, short, slightly greying hair and a manner that was as dry as desert sand, gave him an air of competence and authority rarely found in so young a man.

"Four more to come," King informed him.

Myles, the purser, made a small mark in his rough book. "Then there're some cattle for Mr Paterson, and another lighter full of water awaiting us."

Nichols nodded. "That should give us our full measure, and I am hoping all remaining will go in the ground tier, which will allow plenty of room for beef on top."

"T'would be good if so." Being both heavy and regularly consumed, the stowage of water dramatically affected a ship's trim. Casks must be stored in a sensible manner, allowing them to be tapped evenly; the same applied to preserved meat, and other heavy provisions. Loading a ship might be backbreaking work, but rearranging stores whilst at sea was even more so, and should Nichols rush his job now, it would be necessary for *Pevensey Castle* to retain an even keel.

All of which hardly explained the absence of Rogers and the other two senior mates. Since making their brief appearance that morning, little had been seen of them, apart from one occasion when Willis was tempted out of the captain's quarters to sign for the spirit issue. King looked about; Paterson, at the fore, was supervising the lifting of several veal calves from a lighter to the pens set below in forward steerage. There had already been two milking cows, which would be swiftly converted into beef when they ran dry, and a breeding bull—the latter being sent to India as cargo. Along with the ducks, geese, and hens lodged on the poop deck, the sheep, shortly to take their place in the ship's longboat, and a pet goat; apparently the property of a passenger, *Pevensey Castle* was fast acquiring all the qualities of an ark.

"Fair amount of livestock," King commented.

"They'll hardly be noticed," Nichols assured him. "Last voyage in the *Clarence* we carried a whole pack of fox hounds; didn't stop barkin' till we reached the Hooghly."

"There's a boat setting for us, Mr King." Ward touched his hat. "Reckons it's the first of the passengers arriving."

King glanced around at the mess. It wasn't the best introduction to the ship, but there was little that could be done about that.

"Very good. Give her a hail and pass the word to the captain if so."

The boatswain's mate nodded and saluted once more. "Shall I swab off the decks a little?"

King was unsure, but fortunately Nichols looked up and shook his head. "A dry brush, nothing more. They'll get used to the pleasures of shipboard life soon enough."

Ward grinned and moved on.

"What is the score with the passengers?" King asked, while yet another cask swung by. "How much sway do they have in the ship?"

Nichols made a mark on his paper and shrugged. "Depends a great deal on the captain. He is in overall charge, and they have to do his bidding in any situation," he gave an ironic grin, "no matter how much they might be paying for their passage.

"If we runs into trouble the menfolk will have action stations and be expected to fight like the rest of us. Should we spring a leak, they'll take their places at the pumps. Other than that, there'll probably be a few steerage class in our mess—junior army officers or the like—but they tend to keep to themselves, specially for the first week or so. Oh, and we're not supposed to mix with the ladies," he added, nodding to the working party in the hold, and pointing to the spot where he wanted the next leaguer stowed.

"That sort of thing is much frowned upon in Company circles. Some captains forbid officers or crew to talk with any woman above ten and below sixty—seventy if they've not seen females for a spell."

The empty lifting tackle shot up and out over the side, ready for another load.

"Don't that seem a might harsh?"

"No, ask me it makes perfect sense." Nichols's manner was quite matter of fact as if he were discussing yet another problem with stowage. "Romance can be a hazardous business in any occupation, but aboard ship the stakes really do stack up."

King noticed that the new mate now bore a distant look as he continued. "Fill a ship with nubile souls and leave them a while to fester, anything can happen. I seen too many arguments over brandy that turned into all-out fights. Duels have been fought, marriages broken, and children conceived, an' all that while still in sight of Spithead."

A call from below told them that the next cask was waiting. King nodded to the party at the falls, and the line grew taut again, just as a hail went out to the approaching boat.

"Yes, they can be an odd lot." Nichols watched while the load was swung up and pulled inboard. "An' it sounds like we're just about to meet our first. Let's hope they're free of kinchins."

"Kinchins?" King had never considered that children would be allowed on board.

"Aye, there's nothing worse in any weather." Nichols turned his attention to the next cask. "They make more noise than hounds," he continued. "And smell every bit as bad."

* * *

There was little to worry about. The first passengers were all fully grown and quite subdued. Two ladies' maids and a valet, sent in advance to prepare quarters for their employers, a cadet from the East India Company's own land forces, and a couple of clerks, or writers, who were to take up positions in one of their many factories. They were clearly lower-class travellers, and Rogers didn't deem them worthy of an appearance, so it was down to the working parties to receive them, and King, as the junior officer, to escort the new arrivals below and introduce the wonders of shipboard life. The cadet, barely more than fifteen, was clearly a little seasick after what must have been a choppy passage out. He was allocated a small partitioned-off cubicle in the great cabin and seemed more than happy to take straight to his cot. The ladies' maids were directed to one of the sternward cabins in steerage, and the writers and valet had been given a similar four-berth hutch almost opposite. Soon, King was returning to the waist, where the last of the water was waiting. As he clambered on to the upper deck, a seaman almost cannoned into him. He grinned instinctively when the man apologised and stood to one side, turning his head away as he passed. King caught sight of a long red pigtail; clearly an old hand, but there was something else about that hair, something that triggered an earlier memory. He stopped and looked more closely at the seaman who, noticing the attention, drew further back, and even lowered himself slightly under the inspection.

"Simpson, is that you?" King asked finally. There was no response, and it was only then that King recalled just why the man had stayed in his mind. "We served together, in *Vigilant*," he continued, a little more cautiously. "You were in Flint's mess; I was your divisional mid."

Slowly the man's eyes rose to meet his.

"Aye, an' I were a runner, Mr King."

"That's right, you were," King agreed. "And missed out on a deal of prize money, if the truth be known."

The man grinned sheepishly. "So I hears, but there was that bit of badness with the master at arms."

"Aye, you split his lip." It was all coming back to King now. "An' awaiting court martial, so I recall."

"I was indeed." Even in the dull light of the upper deck, King thought he could detect a flash of defiance in the man's eyes while he continued. "'E riled me, so he did, an' I hit out. Didn't mean 'im no harm, mind; it ain't happened afore; an' it ain't happened since."

"I'm glad to hear it, Simpson."

"I don't use that name no more, Mr King."

That came as no surprise to King. He studied the man for a moment. Distinctive tattoos, and that brilliant red hair; it was a wonder he had not been picked up long before this.

"You didn't think to lose the queue?" he asked, temporising

while his mind ran through the available options. Simpson must still be wanted by the authorities; not just as a deserter, but one who had also struck a superior officer—struck and drawn blood. The man was clearly destined for the noose, and King should waste no time in having him detained and reported.

The man sighed. "Couldn't bare to cut it, sir," he said quietly. "Nor have it dyed; reckons it would be like flicking off me nose."

"Where have you been?" King persisted. "It must be three years or so."

"About that. I lay low for a time, took some work on a farm inland. Then got restless for the seas. I done one trip in an Indiaman an' liked it well enough, though I were near pressed three times. But, I all'ays got away with it." His eyes fell again. "Until now, that is."

King was still looking at the seaman intently. He had known Critchley, *Vigilant's* master at arms, to be a bit of a bully, and wondered whether he would have reacted in a similar way in Simpson's position. He thought not. King was no coward, but Critchley had been a big man and a born fighter. Simpson was considerably smaller and had shown a fair amount of pluck in standing up to him. And in addition he was a good seaman. Despite the recent intake, *Pevensey Castle* was still desperately undermanned. Of course, Critchley was killed in action a short while later, and when it came to it, King was no longer acting as a commissioned officer. A shout from Nichols at the main hatch brought him back to the present—clearly his attendance was required elsewhere.

"So, remind me what are you called now, Simpson?" he asked, rather artlessly.

"Johnston, sir."

"Johnston." King nodded, as if trying the name out for size. "Well, carry on then," he said, nodded briefly, then hurried on to see to the last of the water casks.

* * *

"Lawks, it' ain't got no lights, nor no windas!" Kate looked up from her seat as the two girls entered the little cabin. They were wrong. A tallow candle burned grubbily in a shielded sconce on the table where she rested her ledger, but the impression was quite understandable. The girls, noticing her for the first time, jumped in unison. Kate looked up and smiled.

"I'm sorry, did I startle you?"

"Startle? I'd say!" The voice was loud, with an edge that made it almost painful to hear. "Fair set me loose below. What you doin' 'ere, anyways?"

Kate stood up and offered her hand. "I'm Katharine Manning, assistant to the purser."

The first girl, whose light blonde hair looked almost green in the poor light, regarded Kate's hand with caution. "Are you indeed? Still don't answer my question."

"No, it don't answer her question," echoed the other girl who was darker, shorter, and running slightly to fat.

"Well, if you are Mrs Drayton's ladies, I'd say we will all be berthing here together."

"Berfin'?" The taller one screeched. "It don't sound decent!"

"It don't," her friend agreed. "Not decent at all."

"That is how they tend to speak aboard a ship," Kate said quietly. "We have to share this space, along with another who is due aboard later."

"I'm not sure that I like the sound of that!" Somehow, Kate was not surprised. "'Tain't enough room for more'n two, I'd chance. There's three of us, an' another coming, you says?"

"I believe so."

The girl pouted. "Na, that can't be right; I'll have to take it up with Mrs Drayton."

"Mrs Drayton will sort it out," the shorter girl assured her.

"I'm sure she will," Kate said. "When does Mrs Drayton embark?" The first girl looked at her strangely, and Kate corrected herself. "When do you expect her to join the ship?"

"She's going to Portsmouth, but 'er husband's comin' later today. That's Mr Drayton," she added, with special emphasis on the title.

Kate nodded seriously. "I see, well what say we make the best of things until Mr or Mrs Drayton arrive? Now, I've told you my name; and you are?"

"This is Susan an' I'm Emily," the dark girl informed her. "Only I'm usually known as Emma."

"Stubble it, girl!" Susan glared at her friend. "You don't want to get too familiar with the 'elp." She looked back at Kate. "Maybe we should make it Miss Woodhouse and Miss Chapstick? I think that would be fitting."

"As you wish." Kate's expression became neutral as the girls inspected the room. It clearly came nowhere near their expectations, and she could do little but sympathise. The place was even darker, and certainly much smaller, than the steerage mess, from which it was separated by several other similarly tiny compartments. Being nearer the stern, the smell of the bilges was also far more noticeable, and almost overpowered that from the animals further forward. How it might be after a few weeks on the ocean she didn't like to predict. And yes, it certainly would be cramped; four shortened cots lay folded against the stretched painted canvas that constituted a bulkhead. She supposed it might be possible to hang them all at the same time, but it would take every inch of available space.

"Well, I'd say it were a pretty queer deal," Susan finally said to Emma. Kate was not included. "We got a mass of stuff to store; there won't be room for the half of it."

"There's personal hold space for every passenger. Anything you do not require whilst on board can be stowed there," Kate informed them. "For that which you do, a space next to the bosun's stores has been set aside."

Susan looked at her doubtfully. "They got to unload it first," she said.

"Then tell the mate in charge."

"Mate?" the girls exclaimed in together, both raising their hand to their mouths and pretending to stifle a giggle.

"A mate is a senior officer," Kate said a little coldly. "One or more will be looking after the party unloading your stores. Speak to them and they will arrange to send what you wish to the appropriate place. The same for your mistress's belongings; you'll find them very obliging."

"Obliging? I'll wager." Emma gave a crude snort, but Susan raised herself above the remark to address Kate.

"What did you say your job was?"

"I am assistant to the purser; he is the officer who allocates provisions and supplies."

"I see, well we are ladies' maids, and don't deal with heavy luggage and the like." Her eyes narrowed slightly. "Besides, we are also paying passengers. It would seem to be a task more suitable for someone such as yourself—a Company servant." She took one more disparaging look about the small cabin before heading for the door with a slight flounce. "Attend to it, will you, Katharine?"

* * *

News of the final passenger scheduled to board at Gravesend came as the afternoon was ending, and it was clear that Rogers would make the effort to greet him. In fact, he came on deck a good half an hour before the man was due. The loading had only just been completed, and the main gratings were still to be secured when the captain appeared, followed at a respectful distance by Willis and Seagrove.

"Hold up, we have company," Paterson spoke, although his lips barely moved when the trio made their appearance on the quarterdeck.

"Mr Paterson, Mr Nichols, your attention please."

King drew back while the two mates approached the captain and saluted.

"The ship is dirty, gentlemen," Rogers informed them. "Extremely dirty; I would have her shining like a new pin, Mr Drayton is an honoured guest, and expected within the hour. He is not to be disappointed and neither am I."

"Very good, sir." Paterson touched his hat respectfully. The hands were tired after the day's activities. Only a scratch dinner had been taken and, as little had been seen or heard from any of the senior officers, it was in his mind to send them to an early supper. For a moment, he even considered asking if they could eat first, but instantly rejected the idea. Rogers wore a relaxed, mildly stupid look on his face, an expression that was shared with the other two officers. Clearly they had been drinking, and Paterson already knew enough about his captain to kerb his inclination to presume or question.

King turned to Ward who summoned a group of afterguard. "Brooms and buckets," he said, catching the man's eyes. "Let's get her put to rights, then we can all eat."

The men responded readily enough, instinctively respecting officers who were every bit as tired as they were and just as hungry. Soon, all was being washed clean of grime, and holystones, the large tablets of granite used to burnish the decks, began to scrape the strakes a shade or two lighter. Throughout the process Rogers, Willis, and Seagrove stood waiting, only deigning to move when their particular area of deck needed attention. By the time evening was descending upon them, the ship lay wet but clean, and a wherry could finally be seen heading in their direction,

"Boat ahoy!" The call rang out just as the last of the water was hurriedly flogged and swabbed away. Rogers stepped towards the entry port, preening himself slightly. His two followers kept close by, although Seagrove stumbled slightly as he moved from the quarterdeck to the gangboard. Willis caught him, and they both staggered, giggling like schoolchildren while they struggled to remain upright. King glanced at Paterson, and received a stone-cold, dispassionate stare in return. Then, the boat hooked on.

Mr Drayton was a man of middle years, greying hair and a strong Roman nose, he was well built, although the immaculate cut of his coat disguised what might have been a slight pot belly. He wore a pleasant, but reserved expression as he walked on to *Pevensey Castle*'s deck and raised his hat in formal salute to the quarterdeck. Rogers stepped forward.

"A pleasure to meet you again, Mr Drayton." The two shook hands. "I hope your trip will be a pleasant one."

"I have been dining ashore," Drayton told him. "And watching your ship while she loaded. A very efficient business, Captain Rogers; very efficient indeed. She appeared to take twice as much as *Admiral Hayes* and *Coventry*, yet I note that all is stowed away, and you are in fine fettle; most impressive. Perhaps you might care to introduce me to your officers?"

Rogers nodded obsequiously, "A pleasure, sir. Mr David Willis, my premier, and Christopher Seagrove, second mate."

The pair stepped forward, immaculate in full dress uniforms, although their grins still owed much to the afternoon brandy. Drayton shook hands with due solemnity.

"And this is Mr Paterson and Mr Nichols, third and fourth mates, and Mr Midshipman King who is acting sixth."

Drayton acknowledged the three, appearing to take no notice of their dress, which was far less formal than the senior officers.

"You do not have a fifth?" he asked, turning back to Rogers.

"He will be joining us at Deal," the captain assured him. "And

Mr Midshipman King is relatively experienced, sir. For a Guinea Pig, that is." He beamed ingratiatingly at the newcomer, giving him the full benefit of his yellowing teeth.

"I see." Drayton considered King once more. "So you have yet to see the East, young man?"

"Yes, sir," King answered.

"I assume you are from the Navy, Mr, er..."

"King, sir. Yes, sir."

Drayton nodded. "Then Mr King, you have much in common with our captain." he switched his attention back to Rogers, whose expression was a little more uncertain now. "That must make for a close bond, eh, Mr Rogers?"

The captain began to mumble something incoherent, but Drayton rode over him in a way that delighted the junior officers when they recalled it later.

"You appear to have a very efficient ship, gentlemen. I congratulate you, and look forward to my time aboard." He smiled again, although his manner remained brisk and efficient. "Now, if you will excuse me? We are to sail tomorrow, is that not right, captain?"

"Yes, sir." Rogers bobbed slightly as he turned to follow Drayton who was moving towards the quarterdeck. "Just to the Downs and in convoy with a Navy frigate. We hope to leave on the morning tide."

"Then I am sure you all have many preparations to make," he said, striding for the stern accommodation as if he already knew every inch of *Pevensey Castle*. "And I, for one, wish to see my quarters."

* * *

"Coo lummy!" Susan exclaimed as she went to enter her berth. "Where's all this stuff come from?"

She remained blocking the doorway, while Emma strained to see past her. The room, which was little more than five feet by seven, was almost entirely filled with luggage. Everything from hatboxes, valises, and trunks to an ornate, but empty birdcage and what looked like a small guitar in a case. All were stacked, neatly but purposely, over the entire floor space. The room could certainly not be entered, and it would be difficult to remove any individual item without cluttering up the passageway outside. Susan looked back to her friend in horror.

"It's all our things *and* Mrs Drayton's," she said. "Silly bitch has put everythin' in 'ere."

"Silly bitch had no idea where else to place them," Kate informed both women who jumped to see her standing so close behind.

"Well, it ain't gonna do you no good," Susan reared up slightly. "You ain't got nowhere to sleep, not neither!"

"I am used to living in a ship," she said. "There are plenty of places I can lay my head."

"Well, wait till Mrs Drayton hears about this!" Susan countered quickly.

"Yeah, then you'll be in trouble!" Emma assured her.

"Oh I do not doubt that there could be a great deal of unpleasantness," Kate said evenly, "as soon as Mrs Drayton finds out that you have spent the afternoon playing cards with two clerks in their cabin when you should have been attending to her possessions. In fact, I'm quite certain she won't be pleased at all."

"You not tellin' no one," Susan informed her, raising one finger. "I'll see that you don't!"

"Whether I do, or whether I do not, is yet to be seen," Kate moved passed them. "Now, you will excuse me, ladies; I have much to attend to."

Chapter Four

Nichols had ordered the boarding stage removed, and singled up to the bower anchor just after six bells in the morning watch. Topgallant masts had been sent up, along with the topgallant and royal yards, which were squared. The hands were back from an early breakfast, and now, with the tide set nicely and what appeared to be the pilot boat approaching, it finally began to feel as if they would actually be leaving. His glance swept about the ordered deck, looking for anything that might detain them further. Nichols had served aboard merchant ships for all his time at sea, with the last four trips being in Indiamen. It was the life he enjoyed, certainly markedly better than any experienced on land, and he was keen to be leaving.

The boat passed by their counter and came up on the starboard side just as the lookout hailed, and Nichols started slightly when he realised it was not the expected pilot. He looked towards the starboard entry port, worried in case, even at the last moment, something might have appeared that must detain them. All passengers due to board at London had done so. Possibly this was just the confidential signal instructions and order of sailing from Leadenhall Street, although it was customary for Company communications to come *via* the pilot who was their own employee. Without the landing stage, and with no man rope rigged, anyone trying to board would have a hard time of it. He glanced down into the boat and received his second surprise of the morning. A woman, long fair hair flying in the breeze, and dark skirt just visible under the oilskin wrapped about her, was sitting in the stern surrounded by an assortment of luggage. Nichols was not pleased.

"You there, rig a man rope, and prepare to take a visitor." The seaman knuckled his forehead, and grabbed the length of line set ready. Soon they were prepared, and Nichols watched as the woman stood uncertainly in the tipping craft, bracing herself for the climb.

It would be one of those hard-faced females, he told himself. Out to preach the Gospel, or whatever other rubbish they had ingested. Probably travelling defiantly alone, trusting their safety to God and all who were unfortunate enough to accompany her. He took a turn across the deck while his mind continued on a familiar track. She would be gripped with a passion to convert the heathens and happy to start with every man on board. Well, she was not expected and would not be welcomed; he would see to that.

The woman had reached the man rope and now held it gingerly in one delicate hand She looked up and, for the first time, Nichols saw her face. It was pale, almost childlike, and so concerned with boarding the ship without falling into the sea that he was able to look, to stare almost, without fear of being noticed. The boat was tipping slightly, and the rise and fall made mounting the entry steps difficult. For a moment, he considered rigging a whip and bringing her aboard in a boatswain's chair, but her other hand went out and took a firm hold of the ship; then she launched herself, not expertly, but with enough force, on to the steps.

"Eyes in the boat, there!" His shout was involuntary but loud enough to cause the boat's crew to look hurriedly away while their passenger clambered up *Pevensey Castle*'s side in a mass of billowing fabric.

"Pass the word to the captain," he spoke to Drummond, a midshipman barely in his teens. "My compliments, and we appear to have taken on an extra passenger."

Nichols doubted that he would get much reaction from Rogers at this hour, but it was right that he should be advised. The woman was almost aboard now, and he walked down towards the gangboard to meet her.

"Captain Rogers?" she asked, as she reached the deck and began to remove the oilskin.

She wore a white lacy blouse, totally unsuitable for shipboard life of course, although Nichols noted that, with the dark blue cotton jacket, grey skirt, and fair hair that was surely the longest he had ever seen, she looked remarkably presentable.

"Ah, Nichols, madam." His customary awkwardness when dealing with those of the feminine gender came to the surface. "I am the fourth mate."

"Well, good morning to you, Mr Nichols." She was struggling to retain some of her hair which was flying about her head like an unruly horse's tail. "Forgive me, my comb was loosened in the journey over."

Nichols was unsure if polite conversation demanded any reply and shifted his weight uncomfortably from foot to foot.

"You will oblige me, madam..." he began. How to put it? Who was she? What was she doing here? Whatever he asked would sound rude, but then as much could be said of a person who plants themselves unannounced on the deck of a ship when she is about to sail.

"I should explain." The hair was under better control now, and being roughly plaited while she spoke. "I was erroneously scheduled to join you at Deal, or so I believe. There was some confusion at East India House; my original application was for London. I sent word to Leadenhall Street when the boarding pass came through for the Downs. They agreed to the change, and said you were to be advised."

"We have heard nothing, I fear," he said. "Indeed, it is more customary to join at Deal, as the passage about North Foreland is not known for comfort."

"I see. Well, it is no matter," she smiled. "I am sure you would not have me depart now, only to join with you again later?"

No, of course that would be ridiculous, although Nichols was uncertain exactly what he should do and, for the first time since joining *Pevensey Castle,* he actually wished that Rogers was on deck.

"My name is Elizabeth Hanshaw," she said, detecting his discomfort. "I assume you have note of me, and accommodation will have been reserved, from Deal at least?"

"Doubtless, madam, doubtless." Nichols blustered, and he knew his face was glowing. It would take little effort to find the passenger list and discover where she was to be put, although again his natural gracelessness had asserted itself, making him appear a fool in her eyes as well as his own. He swallowed. "I will check forthwith and...and arrange for your baggage to be brought aboard." He turned and sought out Drummond who seemed especially eager to assist the young woman. She was reaching into a small bag when he looked back.

"If you would be so kind?" Miss Hanshaw was holding a silver coin to him and, in a morning full of surprises, it rated highly.

"Madam that will not be necessary," he stumbled, looking for the right words while his frustration turned to anger. What did she think he was, a hired hand; a street entertainer who must be tipped to perform? He knew that his face was properly red now, and the woman, however beautiful he might find her, had clearly noticed and was smiling. "As a passenger in this ship you are entitled to certain services and..."

He stopped suddenly. There was a slight and annoyingly attractive twinkle in her eye.

"It is for the boatman," she said.

* * *

Seagrove had been up once, presumably to check that all was in order, but was now below again. Paterson stood next to King on the quarterdeck while Nichols who had appeared unusually keen to leave the deck, ate a hurried meal in the mess. The two young officers had spent most of the evening and some of the night drawing up a workable watch list and quarter bill. With fewer than eighty men on board, a ludicrously small number in King's eyes, care was needed to ensure there were enough experienced hands at every station, whatever the need. Paterson assured him that fewer were required in a merchant. *Pevensey Castle* might be an armed ship, but her twenty-eight, eighteen-pounder cannon were lighter pieces than the Navy type, and only needed a small crew to serve them. Besides, eight of the weapons were currently lying disassembled in the hold. They might be rigged at Portsmouth, when the last of the passengers were due to board or, more probably, conveniently forgotten. Officially, Rogers was liable for a fine of forty pounds per great gun not mounted, but it was unlikely that any check would be made, and if such an instance should occur, the cannon could be ready and in place within a day or so. The convoy they were to join at Portsmouth would be large; twelve John Company vessels at the last count, and maybe more if troops were also to be shipped. It was a size that deserved a powerful escort force, at least until they were clear of the Moroccan coast, and possibly as far as St Helena, so the loss or gain of eight guns seemed immaterial.

Willis now made an appearance, touching his hat in reply to the two officers, but saying nothing. King thought he looked a little under the weather, but then his slightly pale complexion might have been caused from a lack of exposure to the elements. An approaching boat was hailed, and soon the pilot, a stout, ruddy man well into his forties, was making steady progress up the side and on to the quarterdeck.

"Captain Rogers?" he asked.

"The captain is below," Willis said, his voice void of expression. "I am the first officer and will be supervising our departure."

"As you will," the pilot replied. He had taken so many of the Company's ships along to Deal that he could do it almost without his charts, and certainly didn't need some puffed-up blue coat breathing down his neck. "Just got to wait for the Navy signal, then we's off."

"Very good." Willis glanced at the glass. "Retain the watch at eight bells and pipe topmen aloft," he said. Paterson nodded. A frigate could now be seen coming from the west. Presumably this was their escort as far as the Downs. The other two Indiamen were making ready to go. *Coventry* had even manned her yards, so it could only be a question of minutes.

"Ah, and I have a package for you," the pilot said, just as eight bells rang and the new watch began to assemble. He brought out a canvas-covered envelope, heavily sealed and tarred, and passed it to Willis. This would contain confidential signals for the convoy, as well as any last-minute instructions and doubtless notice of the arrival of Miss Hanshaw, the woman Nichols had taken on board. The chief mate scrawled a receipt and handed it to the pilot, while all waited for the signal.

"There it is!" King shouted suddenly. The frigate was almost level with the *Admiral Hayes*, when a string of bunting broke out from her foremast.

"Make sail!" Willis's voice cracked slightly, but soon the cacophony of whistles and shouts left no one in any doubt as to the task in hand. Within moments, the yards were covered with topmen, eager to be back in their natural environment, while the afterguard formed up ready at the braces, and what few that were left began to haul the hemp anchor cable in with the capstan. King watched intently. The breeze was light and coming from the west; it should be an easy run down the Thames, although he had no idea as to the amount of sail *Pevensey Castle* would need.

"We'll take her along Gravesend Reach, then head north, join the Sea Reach, weatherin' Blythe Sands," the pilot told Willis. The other officers took the information in, but made no comment; the man should know his business well enough.

The slow but regular clank from the capstan all but stopped as the call, "Up an' down!" came from the bow.

"Topsails!" It was Willis's voice, and again it hardly carried, but the men knew what they were about, and the ship soon began to gather way as her last contact with solid ground was painfully brought up from the riverbed.

"East nor-east." The pilot glanced at his chart quickly while the ship began to drift into a slow turn. King looked up river. *Coventry* was also underway, and *Admiral Hayes* began setting topgallants as the frigate passed her to larboard.

"T'gallants, lively now!"

"*Shearwater*," Paterson said to King, glancing across at the fifth rate. "Good ship, met with her on the way back last trip, and she saw us safe, despite a couple of Frenchmen with other ideas."

They watched while the canvas filled.

"Mind, we went aboard to thank 'em, back in England," Paterson continued reflectively. "Found the captain an' most of the officers Tynesiders; decent enough people but such strong Geordie accents that we couldn't make out half of what was said."

"Braces there!" King bellowed.

The frigate cut through the water with all the panache of her class. *Pevensey Castle* was moving steadily, now that the extra sails were starting to draw, but her bluff bow seemed to stub the water head on. King had the impression of driving a nail upside down, and it was perfectly clear that she would never set any records. At that moment Drayton, dressed in a very superior greatcoat but without a hat, made his way on to the quarterdeck.

"Good morning, gentlemen," he said in reply to their greetings. "I trust I will not be in your way?"

"No sir." Willis's complexion had grown slightly darker. Clearly, the fresh morning air was doing him some good. "You will be very welcome."

"Mr Rogers is not abroad?" Drayton asked.

"He has matters to attend to in his cabin." Willis appeared slightly awkward. "Shall I send for him, sir?"

"Thank you, no. It would be better that he were not disturbed." Drayton's voice was low and quite without emotion. "I am sensible to the heavy responsibilities a man such as he must carry." He treated the group of officers to a genial look. "Sure, he will be busy enough later, let him take his rest while he may"

* * *

The convoy made steady progress, but by four bells in the afternoon watch, was only just passing the anchored shipping at the Nore. King looked out at the well-remembered scene. Less than a year ago, and in the very same channel that they now navigated, his previous ship, *Pandora* had been forced out to sea in the dead of night. The threat that caused their sudden departure had not come from any foreign force: *Pandora* was actually running from British seamen. Led by Richard Parker, himself a former junior officer, they had disgraced themselves by daring to defy the Admiralty and hold their own countrymen to ransom. King recalled the night well. The lack of wind meant the frigate had to be towed as far as the estuary, and he had been a lieutenant in charge of one of the boats. It was a bad time for the ship, the service, and the country in general. All appeared lost, and imminent invasion seemed certain. Much had happened since, of course; but now, as they passed the dockyards at Sheerness, King questioned whether his own position had actually improved.

At that moment Paterson who was not on duty for some time, appeared on the quarterdeck, and walked across to join him. King had only known Paterson for a matter of days. At first, he had been put off by his somewhat direct approach, although their common purpose in getting *Pevensey Castle* ready for sea, as well as the conflict between them and Rogers, had started to forge a friendship.

"Slow work, Tom," Paterson said. His voice was loud, and Willis who had the conn, stood with the pilot barely twelve feet away. "By this rate, it will be ten hours or more before we make the Downs."

"There might be a better wind presently."

"Aye, and rain, if I'm not mistaken. T'will mean rounding

North Foreland in darkness, then we have to negotiate the Good-wins; not my favourite sport on a winter's night."

"How long do we stay at the Downs?"

"As little time as possible," Paterson replied. "A day or so to take on passengers, then off for Pompey just as soon as the wind sets fair. We may be lucky and gone within a day or so, 'though I've known ships trapped at Deal for almost a month."

"Do we collect more at Portsmouth?"

"Aye, an' the rest of the convoy. Reckon a few more escorts as well; can't be too many for my liking."

King had served in warships detailed to protect convoys and did not remember overly enjoying the work, although now he was starting to see the other side of the coin. *Pevensey Castle* might be the size of a heavy frigate, but there all similarity ended. Her armament was modest, her crew would have been considered insufficient for a warship half her size, and the last few hours had already shown that she possessed many of the sailing qualities of a house brick. The idea of her putting up a reasonable defence against a determined force was frankly laughable, and he shared Paterson's wish for a strong escort force. The wind was growing more fitful by the minute and was slowly veering.

"So, ten hours to the Downs?" he asked.

"At least that. We have to round North Foreland first, and I reckons that'll take us six."

King glanced at *Shearwater*, valiantly holding herself in check while she waited for the clumsy merchants to catch up. Paterson was right. It was slow work indeed.

* * *

In fact, it was all of eight hours later, and Paterson had the deck when the pilot finally ordered them round the tip of the north Kent coast. In the absolute black of night little could be discerned apart from a single guiding light off to starboard, a visual anchor for them all to centre upon.

"Eighteen lamps a burning there," Paterson told King who had brought him a mug of hot tea. "An' bless the Lord for each an' every one of 'em."

The wind grew steadily and was blowing from the northwest as they settled on to the new course, and soon *Pevensey Castle* began to wallow in the slow chop. The pilot took a bearing on the light and looked forward to the frigate, several cables ahead. Rogers appeared, his second visit of the evening, although this time he was more suitably dressed in a heavy watch coat and tarpaulin hat. Seagrove was with him, and they beckoned Paterson and King to join them as they approached the pilot.

"Navy's cutting it close, usual," the older man was saying. "I'd prefer to give them sands to starboard a wider berth."

"The Goodwins?" Willis asked brightly. The pilot stared at him in mild contempt.

"That's the Goodwins," he pointed over the larboard bow. "We's headin' for the Gull Stream what runs between them."

"The Gulf Stream? Surely not?" Seagrove gave a slight laugh that was stilled by a stony stare from the pilot.

"Gull—like in the bird," the disdain was evident. "It'll take us into the Downs an', hopefully, a safe anchorage."

Rogers looked up at the weathervane. "Should we be concerned?"

The pilot shook his head. "Na, cap'n; not at present, though I'm not taking her any closer. Ask me, the Navy's more afraid of the French than runnin' aground, or they wouldn't be holding such a tight course. But, the Frogs can come and go, whereas the sands is always with us."

The man was probably right, but still King felt a measure of sympathy for their escort. It was a thankless task, shepherding three rolling merchants through difficult waters, and on a night when all of them would have been far happier abed. However, it was not unheard of for privateers, or even small enemy national vessels, to take such an opportunity to snap up a fat prize. *Shearwater* must keep an eye out for just such a threat, as well as watching the weather, the tide, and the treacherous shoals through which they were heading.

King looked across at the pilot's chart. A small mark showed their present position, and it was clear that it was going to be a delicate business, threading through the channel to their final destination. Paterson also peered over his shoulder, although the others seemed content for the pilot to continue managing the ship without their assistance. King was about to comment when, quite abruptly, the third mate turned and rushed for the lee rail, dropping his mug with a clatter as he went. They watched in surprise while he leant deep over the side.

"Something he ate?" Willis said, in a voice void of concern.

"It appears that Mr Paterson is unwell," Seagrove was quick to join in. "Belike he is not so experienced with the sea as he might have us think."

King stirred uneasily. There was little shame in seasickness; a condition famous for being no respecter of rank or station. It could spring up without notice, setting its evil claws into the least suspecting and most seasoned of men, and was relatively common during the first few days of any commission.

Rogers snorted. "Takes our first blow to settle the wheat from the chaff," he added disparagingly.

King turned his back on them and approached his friend. He had experienced the condition just once in his life, but could remember only too well the feeling of absolute despair and desolation. "T'will be better bye an' bye," he said, placing his hand awkwardly on Paterson's shoulder. "Is there anything I might do for you?"

The mate turned to him, his face looking ghastly in the low light.

"Kill me," he commanded softly.

"Perhaps I could arrange a relief?" King temporised.

"No, I can finish the watch, Tom." Paterson gave a faint smile. "And, in truth, will be right and normal again in a year or so."

King followed his gaze across to where Rogers and his two senior mates were grinning openly. "Would that you could suppose the same about our dear officers," he said.

* * *

Below, the situation was not pleasant. In her small cabin Kate sat at the table, picking at a bowl of cold greasy lobscouse, while the two girls were swaying gently in their cots. As an idler, one who need not stand a night-time watch, Kate was allowed several hours to herself and could have taken to her own bed, had she so pleased. However, the room really was too small for more than two cots to be rigged at once, and she preferred to squeeze herself into the corner and eat her meal. She might slip out to the sickbay in a moment or two. Clegg, the seaman with the fever, was mended now and back in his quarters. There were berths a plenty there, and relative privacy. She had no wish to stay in this little room with her two companions, especially when they both appeared to be dying.

One moaned as the ship gave a particularly severe lift, before falling into the trough with a surge that even took Kate momentarily aback.

"When will it end?"

She looked up to see Susan's face peering over the side of her cot.

"We shall be at Deal before long," Kate told her. "Then, we will anchor, and the motion should be less." Her tone was deliberately matter of fact; she saw little purpose in sympathising with either girl. This was not due to any animosity she might have felt. Her father had been a lifelong victim of seasickness, and Kate who never suffered, had learned that empathy or attempted understanding on her part would usually be taken the wrong way. A stiff word was all he usually needed; then at least he might leave her alone.

"Can't we go ashore?" Emma whispered.

Kate snorted. "Land is the last place we should wish for at the moment."

"Well, ain't there a cure?" Susan spoke again, her voice a little stronger.

"Oh yes, there are a number."

Both heads appeared now, and Kate felt herself very much the centre of attention.

"Proper ones?" Susan asked doubtfully.

"Some say," she was assured.

"Well, what are they?" Emma demanded.

"Food, but you have to know exactly what to eat." There was a pause, then the groans began again as Kate continued. "Uncooked salt fish is supposed to be efficacious, though I prefer mine in a cream sauce with maybe a fresh raw egg. And there are those who recommend a rich turtle soup, 'though I have never tried it myself."

"You're an evil bitch, you know that, don't you?"

Kate looked up sweetly. "Or I have heard a long ride on a bay mare works wonders," she said simply, and continued with her meal.

* * *

Despite an initial increase in both wind and the motion of the seas, Paterson remained on deck while *Pevensey Castle* headed uncertainly down the Gull Stream. He still felt giddy and nauseous; still longed for the moment when the universe stopped moving about him, and still hated all and everyone who were so annoyingly healthy in his distorted world, but the effects were slowly dissipating and he was able to make a passable impression of an officer of the watch.

Of course, the pilot had charge of the ship. Paterson's only duties were to implement his orders, and see to any emergency that might occur. Rogers seemed strangely happy to leave him, taking Willis and Seagrove below with sarcastic advice against the overfeeding of fish. Paterson was not totally without support, however; Nichols, due to relieve him at eight bells, had come on deck early. In company with King who was also apparently at a loose end, he was taking much of the responsibility, leaving Paterson to his misery. An hour ago, they ordered the topgallants taken in, and all thought it likely to follow with a reef in the topsails, although this had proven unnecessary. The pilot who had been standing on the quarterdeck for more than twelve hours without any sign of fatigue, had just taken another bearing, and was talking to them now, while the third mate watched from the shelter of the weather bulwark.

"South Foreland Light!" King turned and yelled at him, pointing ahead. Paterson dutifully peered out to sea. Sure enough, even through the dizzy haze of his nausea, the dim gleam of a lighthouse could just be made out. Paterson stepped forward. The deck heaved and swayed when he moved, but the motion was certainly less; either that or he was starting to become accustomed to it.

"Keep that dead ahead an' we'll come through to the anchorage," the pilot was telling the other two as he approached. The elderly man seemed pleased. Paterson assumed that this was just a normal day's work for him, and wondered how anyone could repeat such a dreadful passage on a regular basis. He took a firm grip on the reassuringly solid binnacle. The other three ships were still in sight. *Shearwater*, almost dead ahead, had seemingly decided that the merchants were no longer in need of her protection and was simply heading straight for safety. *Admiral Hayes* and

Coventry were a little way behind. Paterson thought *Coventry* might be drifting slightly too far towards the Brake Sands, but he was in no position to judge and had enough to do on his watch to bother about other shipping.

"I see lights!" It was King. Paterson peered forward again, but could make out nothing further through the heavy rain.

"That'll be the first of the moored shipping," the pilot replied, almost smugly. "You're to anchor off the western bank; it won't be long now."

A rocket went up from *Shearwater*, followed by a series of lights at her mainmast. After a pause of no more than a minute, a deep blue glow shone out from the shore, was shielded for several seconds and then appeared again. Paterson held tight to the side of the binnacle while a fresh wave of sickness began to gather. They had announced their arrival, and the pilot was right; it would not be long now.

CHAPTER FIVE

The dining room cuddy was really quite impressive with the candles alight. Rogers allowed his gaze to sweep about the room, and gave a self-satisfied smile to the assembled guests. The silverware was only plate, of course; one does not waste the best for sea travel. But, his servant had made it shine bright enough, and the white muslin tablecloth contrasted well with the darkness of the beams. It was customary for the captain, senior officers and important passengers to have the main meal of the day at four bells in the afternoon watch—two o'clock—although Rogers had called this first introductory dinner during the evening to allow the new arrivals to acclimatise to the ship. Besides, he always preferred to eat later, when the aftereffects of any drink he might have taken would be numbed by sleep.

And this really was the most splendid of evenings. The food, having in the main been taken aboard that morning, was just as good as any on land, and it had been worth broaching that case of claret which was intended for his arrival in India. Drayton certainly seemed to appreciate it, along with the port that was now making its tortuous journey round the table. Tradition was that the base of the decanter must not leave the surface of the table, on fine of the purchase of the next bottle. Rogers watched the progress with interest. His port was of the highest quality and could never have been considered cheap.

"Five guineas that robber wanted, for to take us out here," an elderly army officer was broadcasting to the table in general. "I told him to take a powder, but it seems they are thick in their trade, and have the monopoly."

"Landlord knew how to charge at the George," the fair haired son of a factor confirmed. "If *Pevensey Castle* hadn't made it by the end of the week, I'd have been following a 'whereas'."

The army officer looked at him strangely. "Whatever do you mean by that?"

The younger man grinned. "Following a whereas? Don't you read *The Gazette*? Whenever there is a notice starting 'Whereas', you know some poor Joe is about to be announced bankrupt." The company gave a good-natured laugh, although the officer appeared mildly cross. Rogers continued to watch the decanter, now very much on the home straight as far as he was concerned.

"You were to tell us of your time in *Vigilant*, captain," Drayton prompted him, setting his own glass down and selecting an apple from the bowl.

"Ah yes." Rogers leant forward and beamed generously. It was the ideal occasion; his senior officers and most of the better class of passengers were present, including that darling little yellow mot who had come aboard at Gravesend. She was actually only a steerage-class traveller and had no right to be at his table at all, but on first seeing her he made certain she would be invited. She was sitting there now, at his right hand, and just waiting to be impressed. He paused until the full attention of the table was his, then he began to speak.

He made it good, very good. First, the events that led up to the action; his ship protecting the gallant merchants, the dividing of the convoy, and finally one heroically small two-decker charging in to beat off all those nasty Frenchmen. The captain was killed early in the fray. Dyson, the first lieutenant, was not a fighting man and proved rather short of the mark. Therefore, it had fallen on Rogers, as second lieutenant, to take charge. *Vigilant* suffered severely, of course, and many of the crew were dead or wounded, but with Rogers in command, they caused enough damage to the enemy squadron to make their eventual destruction inevitable. *Vigilant* finally limped back with a returning convoy to the thanks of a nation. Of course, it was unfortunate that full recognition was not given to him, he looked about deprecatingly, but he was still officially only second in command and Lieutenant Dyson had written the report.

The company were quite fascinated by his performance, with only the occasional whistle or sigh from Seagrove or Willis, both of whom had heard the story at least once before, to break the respectful silence. As he finished Rogers wondered if he might have exaggerated his part slightly too much; but, on reflection, and after receiving the decanter for the second time, he told himself he had pitched it about right.

Drayton's apple lay on his plate untouched. "It seems the merchant navy has much to be grateful for," he said, collecting his glass and twirling it in his hand meditatively. "And the East India Company must have been especially pleased when you applied to become a commander in their service."

"I was equally delighted," Rogers hurried to assure him. "To be honest I expected promotion following my actions. When none was forthcoming, I decided my true destiny lay elsewhere, and was very pleased to accept their offer."

Drayton nodded. "I was returning from China at that time, but was soon made aware of your joining the Company, of course."

He caught the man's eye, and for a moment nothing was said. Then, Drayton turned away, and began a neat dissection of his apple. For the first time, a doubt began to form in Rogers's mind. Might he have gone too far? There had been no direct approach as such; no tempting proposal from Leadenhall Street following valiant, yet unrewarded service. His formal application to become a ship's master was made in the usual manner, and even initially rejected. Several times, in fact. The lengths that his father eventually went to in securing his command were considerable, and might well be common knowledge in the higher circles of the Company. Drayton was known to have both status and influence; it was one of the reasons Rogers was pleased to have him on board, but just how far did it reach? And rather than do him good, could it possibly be dangerous?

The uncertainties began to multiply in the rather fuddled regions of Rogers's mind until the sober parts temporarily, regained control. He reached out and downed the rest of his port in one swallow. This would not do. It would not do at all. As soon as he allowed another person to exercise power over him, he would be lost. He closed his eyes while the drink made its way past his throat. Whatever Drayton might or might not know, Rogers was the captain of this ship, and while he remained so, there was nothing the man could do to harm him.

"Well, I think we must all be very glad to have you in command, Captain Rogers." The voice came from further down the table. It belonged to a rather harsh northern woman travelling with her husband, a small man who traded in tea and had a hair lip. Rogers's delay in asking the ladies to retire was due partly to the lack of suitable quarters to receive them; although, in truth, he was quite content for them to stay, as it gave him greater chance to impress. In fact, this particular woman's husband was not present, still suffering from the aftereffects of seasickness apparently. Rogers might have no current intention of exploiting her, but who could tell what the future might bring? What was their name, Cralltree? Coltree? Crabtree; that was it.

He lowered his head and muttered a brief, "Thank you, ma'am." Miss Hanshaw's reaction was far more important to him at present. He glanced to his right and was delighted to see an expression of stunned surprise on her face. He gave her one of his more caring looks.

"Did you enjoy your meal, Miss Hanshaw?"

The girl seemed to jump slightly as she was addressed. "Why yes, captain; thank you, it was quite delightful."

"You have a cabin in steerage, have you not?" He was every bit the dutiful, concerned commander.

She raised one eyebrow delightfully. "Indeed, sir, what of it?"

Rogers's expression deepened. Talk had begun about the table, and he lowered his voice so as not to be overheard. "Can get a little noisy down there, and crowded; of course, what with the animals..."

The girl was looking at him doubtfully now. "My quarters suit me admirably, captain, I do assure you."

"There is, I believe, a spare position in the roundhouse," he persisted in little more than a whisper. "On this deck and with excellent stern windows. You will have light and air and be able to take meals at this table. It really would be far more comfortable."

"If better accommodation is available, captain, I would know of it." Mrs Crabtree's ears were clearly as powerful as her voice. He leant back and surveyed the woman.

"Sadly, madam, the quarters are designated for one only, and I should be the last to separate a wife from her husband."

The woman gave out a giggle that was horribly skittish. "Oh, I might have no objection, sir," she said, amidst slightly awkward laughter from those around her. Rogers bowed his head again, making a mental note to treat Mrs Crabtree very carefully in future. She would be saved for extreme emergencies only.

He turned back to the contrast that was Miss Hanshaw. Her blonde hair was dressed in the most elegant manner, and he almost had to physically restrain his hand from reaching out to touch it.

"Let me make enquires, my dear," he continued. "I will speak with the officer responsible for cabin allocation and see if a change cannot be made."

"It is kind of you, sir."

The decanter was with him again, and he helped himself to a generous measure. "Oh no, it will be my pleasure," he said.

* * *

The following morning, their second at anchor at the Downs, was lit with the sort of bright, clean, and vaguely warming winter sunshine that was especially welcome. King had the quarterdeck to himself; the hands having carried out the twice-weekly holystoning earlier. The carpenter with two of his mates was working on a minor repair to the forward hatchway, while painters were on a stage at the larboard bow attending to a scrape. Odours of marine glue and paint mixed oddly with cooking smells from the galley chimney, and both almost overrode the farmyard stench which was quickly taking over most of the ship. The wind was predicted to change soon, and the prospect of sailing on tomorrow morning's tide seemed more than likely. The new fifth mate was due to join them at Pompey, and Paterson had again intimated that further hands could also be expected. With a fresh officer and more men, it was possible that this trip might not end up as poorly as he had expected. In fact, King was feeling quite optimistic.

The mail boat had called on them the previous day, and by some great stroke of fortune, there was a letter for him from Juliana. It was less than three weeks old and might well be the last he received before seeing India. He thought of her now, while he looked out over the forest of masts that spread out about him. There was a mass of shipping, and most were waiting for the fair wind to take them south, although few would be travelling so far as *Pevensey Castle*. In a matter of weeks he should be several hundred miles away, although in truth, the war, and Juliana's home on the coast of enemy Holland, were as effective a barrier between them as any distance. He had seen her regularly for less than a month and in circumstances that were hardly ideal, but they had come to an understanding almost straight away. King did not believe in fate, but as a born seaman, he trusted his instincts and was determined to send for her as soon as it was feasible. She might have problems getting out of the country, of course, and for him to keep a Dutch wife in an England currently at war with most of Europe would not be accepted by many. But they could go elsewhere. He had left the Navy in the hope of eventually sharing his life with Juliana, and moving to a different land need not be too much of a hardship. There was always America; they had a fledgling navy, and he knew of several who had already made the change and taken to it readily.

Manning came on deck and sauntered over.

"Taking the air, Tom?"

King smiled readily. "It is a pleasant morning. Have you spoken with Kate?"

Manning rolled his eyes. "We managed a word or two in passing. She cares little for her travelling companions, I fear."

"Captain asked me for another change in accommodation this morning," King said, his voice matter of fact, but slightly softer. "Lady berthing alone in steerage is to be moved to the roundhouse."

"Is that so?"

King nodded confidentially and continued in little more than a whisper. "We're taking on more passengers at Spithead, but I think we may still have the space if Kate prefers to berth alone."

"She would welcome an exchange," Manning mused, his voice equally low.

"Well, say nothing for now, I should hate to give false hope. It is almost the size of a double berth, but..."

The surgeon's mate raised his hand. "Fear not, Tom. I will keep my distance."

"The captain seems to know much of what occurs below."

Manning pulled a wry face. "Indeed he does."

* * *

It was certainly far more spacious than her cubicle in steerage, although even her new cabin, presumably one of the finer in the ship, could never be considered luxurious. Elizabeth walked to the small portion of stern light that was allowed her and peered out. She could see Deal, hazy in the winter sunshine and slightly distorted, thanks to the thick crown glass. A low smudge of coal fire smoke seemed to hang over the small town, one that was rumoured to exist wholly to service the constant supply of shipping anchored in the Downs. The captain had offered to take her ashore in one of the ship's boats, intimating, not too subtly, that they might share a meal at the George or one of the other hostelries that evening. He had been politely, but determinedly, declined. Doubtless she was misjudging his intentions, but Elizabeth felt little inclination for Mr Rogers's company and had no intention of spending further time in England. Her ticket, bought at a cost of most of her late father's money, would take her to a new world, and she could not wait to leave the old one behind.

She turned back from the windows and looked about the cabin again. There was only a bed and a chair, both presumably left by the previous occupant. Even that was a distinct improvement, as her previous berth had been extremely bare. Of course, she knew that passengers were expected to provide their own furniture, but had decided before the trip that her sea chest, a wash stand, and a travelling cot would be sufficient for her purposes. She could do very well without more, and indeed had done so; but a chair, especially one with such a comfortable back, was most welcome. She settled herself into it and then reached for the knitting that always accompanied her. Within minutes, her mind was wandering many miles away, and the knock that came at the cabin door startled her back to the real world. She rose and opened it, to find a young woman about her own age, with dark hair tied back in an efficient bun.

"Miss Hanshaw? I'm Katharine Manning, assistant to the purser."

"Miss Manning, won't you come in?"

Kate entered, and together they stood, rather awkwardly, in the middle of the small room.

"I am to see you regarding victualling. You have paid your fare, and food and drink are, in the main, provided, but some passengers require a little more to supplement; maybe wine, or further fresh milk?"

The woman smiled. "Yes, I was told when I purchased my ticket and read it again in the regulations on coming aboard. Tell me, Miss Manning, what is the usual practice?"

"That appears to be rather vague; some require nothing, others a herd of cows and a small distillery." Kate's manner was slightly guarded when dealing with any of the passengers, but she found herself warming to Miss Hanshaw. "And it is Mrs Manning; my husband is the surgeon's mate."

"Oh, how wonderful for you!" Elizabeth beamed.

"Forgive me?"

She shrugged, raising her hands slightly. "To be travelling the world, and with your husband; I cannot think of anything nicer."

"Yes," Kate found herself smiling in return. "Yes it is; we were only recently married."

"Then my congratulations. Won't you sit down? Take the chair, I will sit on the bed."

"No, thank you, I really cannot stay long." She glanced about the small cabin. "Is the rest of your furniture arriving at Portsmouth?"

Elizabeth laughed. "No, what you see is what I have; I'm travelling to India to join my brother; he is a missionary in Calcutta and speaks highly of the country. I'm afraid there is little left over for extras, so I doubt if I will be prevailing on your offer regarding extra provisions."

"But this is a roundhouse cabin?"

"Yes, the captain provided for me."

"Did he?" Kate's expression faded slightly, and she gave the woman a careful stare. "You are old friends, perhaps?"

"No, I only met him properly at dinner yesterday. My berth was in the steerage. Is that the right word?"

"And he moved you in here?"

"Yes." She felt her face go slightly red. "It was very kind of him."

"It was." Kate continued to look at the girl who began to recognise vague warning signals.

"Mrs Manning, this won't cost me more money, will it?"

The smile returned suddenly, as Kate came to a decision. "No, my dear, it certainly will not; and the captain is quite within his rights, of course." She raised her hand and, after considering, placed it gently on Elizabeth's. "I'm sure he only has your welfare in mind, but please do be careful."

* * *

Rogers could hear very little. Even a bulkhead made of thin deal muffled most of the sound, but the room was brightly lit, and the two women were right in the middle, so he could see perfectly. That confounded female from the purser's officer was to one side, while Elizabeth stood almost facing her and was clearly worried. Twice her eyes flickered towards him; for a moment he even thought he could be observed, but that was unlikely. He had checked the crack when her cabin had been empty. It merged in beautifully with the grain of the light wood and could barely be seen. But, they were talking about him that was almost certain, and should Mrs Manning have anything to do with it, he knew the conversation would not be complimentary.

He gently eased himself away from his spy-hole, choosing a time when both had their attention elsewhere. Elizabeth, as he now thought of her, even though she had not given permission for him to call her so, Elizabeth was gift from heaven. If that cat even thought of spoiling things for him he would find a way to make her pay; of that he was quite determined.

* * *

The wind held fair, and they sailed with the following morning's tide. By noon, they were off Dover, and, as the first dogwatch began and the afternoon light started to fade, the dim coast of Dungeness could just be made out on their starboard bow. The merchants were travelling in line, with *Pevensey Castle* leading and *Shearwater* keeping station well off their larboard beam, her lookouts hopefully intent on spotting any enemy raiders from the nearby French coast. And it was just as the new watch was being called, and the old was going below for supper, when a flurry of bunting broke out on the frigate.

"What of it, Drummond?" Willis demanded. He was officer of the watch and, for once, had not allocated the duty elsewhere. The signal midshipman leafed through his book.

"Enemy sail in sight." His voice quivered slightly, worried in case he had made some terrible mistake. "Maintain present course."

"Send for the captain," Willis snapped, while all about him began to grow tense.

Rogers appeared as if by magic, his coat unbuttoned and his stock awry. Clearly he had been asleep, although there was no sign of drowsiness as he stared out to larboard. *Shearwater* could be seen faithfully plodding along in her usual station, but nothing more. He raised his eyes to the masthead.

"What do you see there?"

"Nothing to note, sir. Horizon beyond *Shearwater* is clear."

"Midshipman!"

Drummond touched his hat automatically. "Not you, damn it," Rogers cursed. "I want an officer at that masthead now, and not one in signals. Mr King!"

King stood nearby taking the air after eating his meal. Following convention, he was not wearing a hat so as to signify being off duty. He turned to Rogers awkwardly, trying to remember how a salute should be given in such a situation.

"Get to the top; tell me what you see."

He grabbed the deck glass handed to him by Drummond and made for the weather shrouds without a word. Soon, he was skimming up the ratlines just as the masthead lookout made a further report.

"Deck there, sails to larboard, bearing..." he paused. "Bearing nor-nor east. Looks like two, maybe three small ships, in close company. An' there's another further to the east. She's a good deal nearer, and seems to be making straight for us."

That must be the sighting which alerted *Shearwater*. Being that much closer she would have seen them first, and by now might even know their exact course and type.

"Clear for action, captain?" Willis asked.

Rogers glared at him for a second, then turned away and began to pace the deck. This was a nice problem; to clear for action meant a great deal of effort and discomfort to the passengers. Cabins would be knocked down, furniture dismantled and moved to the hold and the guns cleared away. It would be a major disruption to the ship, and all for probably little gain. If the sighting proved to be an enemy force, and if *Shearwater* were unable to avoid, deter, or blow them out of the water, there might be little *Pevensey Cas-*

tle could do with her tin-pot guns and scaled-down broadside. Should they be boarded, which was the likely method in these cases, success or defeat was almost certain to be decided by hand-to-hand fighting, having clear decks would make very little difference either way.

Yet, not to do so might be judged foolhardy, and could scarcely inspire confidence in him as a commander. Those same passengers who were appearing now, to gossip and speculate in childlike ignorance on the possibility of being taken by raiders, might not look so kindly on a captain unprepared to do all he could to protect them. He peered back at the horizon, still empty apart from *Shearwater*.

"Summon the watch below and send them to quarters," he said, coming to a decision. It would do the hands no harm to have their meal curtailed. "Douse the galley fire and issue small arms. Clear away guns three to eight." The cannon were in the waist, where no cabins could be disturbed. Rigging them would make some sort of impression, as well as giving a limited amount of firepower for the least possible disruption.

"Seven an' eight are quakers, sir," Willis reminded him cautiously, and Rogers let out an oath. It was true; the two guns beneath the break of the quarterdeck were just wooden half barrels, lodged to make the ship appear to be fully armed, while the real pieces were stowed in the hold for want of space.

"Then run out the quarterdeck batteries as well," he spat.

"Deck there!" King's voice rang out. "I have them in sight."

"What do you make?"

"They're sailing fast, and look to be privateers." The last part was very much a guess, although they were behaving exactly like privateers with a rich prize in their sights.

"Colours?"

"Not that I can see, sir; but there are definitely just the two to the north. They're bearing down on the rear of the line, while the third seems bent on cutting us off. Wait, one is signalling." Flags had broken out on the southernmost vessel, and everyone waited while King trained his glass upon her. There was an answering hoist from one of the other ships. "Looks to be a recognition signal, sir," he said.

So, the three ships were from two separate forces, and had either met by chance or design, although it was clear they were after the same prey, and any question that they might not be sailing un-der a letter of marque could now be discounted. *Pevensey Castle*'s departure from Deal may well have been witnessed, but the infor-mation could not have been conveyed in time without semaphore. No, it was far more likely that the French raiders were already at sea, staying out in the middle of the Channel and biding their time. When the wind favoured ships leaving the Downs, they would simply move closer inshore and see what was blowing their way. Rogers grunted to himself and took another turn about the deck. It was all happening so clinically. Really, the Navy was to be blamed. How many had been lost in just these circumstances? Yet, they allow one solitary frigate to protect three juicy Indiamen. His own ship might be taken from him by the end of the day; a splendid end to matters. He turned back and glanced across to the grey Kent coastline—and it was all being done within sight of British soil.

CHAPTER SIX

The news radiated about the ship, and reached the other off-duty officers. Paterson and Nichols hurried up the quarterdeck ladder, followed by Seagrove who was still buttoning his waistcoat.

"Mr Seagrove!" The second mate jumped slightly at the sound of his name. Rogers strode towards him and pointed back down to the waist, where several groups of passengers now gathered.

"Organise the gentlemen into parties to repel boarders," he said. At that moment, Kate came up the main companionway. "And get that purser woman to take the females below." Seagrove touched his hat and turned back towards the main deck.

The women were soon shepherded away, and Rogers examined the male passengers while the second mate gathered them. Several were officers in the Company's army and could be expected to handle themselves adequately enough. The rest, the civilians, were mostly clerical types, but fit enough in the main. In fact, it mattered little that some were decidedly elderly. They might not fight terribly well, but the very act of being killed should at least slow the enemy down. At that moment the gunner and four seamen emerged from the forecastle with two small arms chests and began to solemnly hand out cutlasses, pikes, and firearms. Some of the civilians took them, with varying degrees of amusement and expertise. Seagrove was dancing about and rabbiting like an idiot, although no one seemed to be taking much notice of him. Rogers's glance swept the deck for a replacement. Osborne, the master at arms, caught his attention; a powerfully built brute with square shoulders and a bullet head, he looked up from the waist and met the captain's eye with total competence.

"Mr Osborne, Mr Seagrove has some recruits for you, station them where you will."

The man gave a knowing look and touched his hat as the men were surrendered to him.

"Form up on the gangboards, if you please, gents," he growled, roughly organising the chattering passengers into a line and all but pushing them into place. "Plenty of time to play with your toys when the enemy comes a callin'."

* * *

"John, you will cover for me for a moment?"

Paterson looked at the fourth mate, surprised. "Of course, will you be long?"

"Five minutes, no more," Nichols assured him. He had a worried look on his face, and Paterson suspected he needed to relieve himself in some way.

"Take your time, I'll see that the fightin' doesn't start without you."

Nichols nodded briefly before turning away. The captain seemed to be engrossed by the vision of the oncoming privateer, and he was able to slip behind his back and on towards the round-house entrance, under the poop.

He walked through the empty dining room cuddy. There were two cabins to one side, but both lay open, and the rooms were clearly empty. Nichols was not entirely sure where she berthed. Indeed, she might already be safe in steerage, but there were still a couple more to check, and he had come so far. A short narrow passage led to the cabins immediately next to the captain's quarters. He knocked at the first door and cursed under his breath when a male voice answered. It was Drayton.

Nichols drew back when the door opened. "Forgive me for disturbing you, sir." He looked past the valet to Drayton who stood in the centre of the room adjusting his stock. "Privateers have been spotted, and we are likely to be in action."

Drayton nodded and came forward to meet him. "We wondered at the commotion; it was good of you to inform me. I assume the captain sent you?"

"Yes, sir," Nichols replied a little doubtfully. "I am to clear the roundhouse," he continued, deciding that two lies were no worse than one.

"Then, I shall not detain you; we will leave immediately."

Nichols waited until they were gone before knocking, a little more gently, on the door at the very end of the passage. Elizabeth Hanshaw answered and seemed surprised, but not displeased, to see him. He repeated his earlier warning, and she nodded seriously. "Is there danger?"

"I fear so, ma'am." Again Nichols felt strangely stupid in her presence. "But naturally we will do all we can to see you come to no harm. Perhaps if you made your way below?"

"Of course," she smiled, and it was a pleasant expression. "Thank you for coming to tell me."

Their eyes met. "I could conduct you if you wish?"

"No, that will not be necessary. But thank you again." She paused. "I...I do not know your name."

It was his turn to smile, but he knew that his version was far less appealing. "Nichols, ma'am; fourth officer."

"Yes, yes; I am aware, Mr Nichols. I meant your Christian name," she laughed. "I assume you have one?"

Now, he knew he was blushing. "Aye, ma'am; 'tis George."

"George, like the king?" she asked, delighted.

"Aye, ma'am, just like the king, though not many call me by it."

"Then indeed it is exactly the same, I am certain few address him as such!" Her look was still every bit as bewitching. "But you would not mind if I do?"

He shook his head almost sadly. "No, ma'am; I would not mind at all."

* * *

The enemy was in plain view from the deck now, and clearly the vessels were moving quickly. Rogers looked up to the masthead. "What do you see there?"

A pause, then King's voice, slow and considered. "They look

quite light, sir. Flush decked and twin masts. The easterly one's course appears to be to the southwest; I'd say they were trying to cut us off."

Rogers grunted; typical privateer craft, and typical privateer tactics. *Shearwater* was doing the right thing in staying on station to windward but, with three attacking, the likelihood was strong that at least one would make it past her and to the rich prizes beyond.

"The two are changing course," King called again. "Seem to be splitting up, one heading further south, t'other more to the east."

With the wind in the northeast, they were in the perfect position to divide, making *Shearwater*'s job that much more difficult and the possibility of at least one of the Indiamen being raided more certain.

"*Shearwater* is making sail," Willis this time. All the officers looked to see the frigate raise royals above her topgallants. The canvas was soon full, and the ship began to cut deeper into the water as she surged forward. *Pevensey Castle,* the leading merchant, was soon overtaken, while several cables behind, the other two Indiamen also began to ply on extra canvas in an effort to close up.

"She's tacking!" Paterson's voice cracked slightly. Sure enough, the frigate was turning swiftly into the wind, her sails momentarily slack as she nosed her way about. The privateers were plainly heading in a fanlike formation for the merchants. Then, *Shearwater* was fully on the starboard tack beating back, as near to the wind as she could make.

"They'll be in range of the frigate at any time," Paterson muttered. Certainly, the southernmost enemy, the one most likely to take *Pevensey Castle,* was nearing the escort's arc of fire. Presumably the Frenchman was risking one broadside, and at the speed she was travelling there must only be time for one, against the chance of getting to grips with their ship. A line of smoke engulfed the British frigate, followed by a murmur of approval from the passengers. But, the shots must have been poorly laid for by the time the dull report of the broadside reached them, the privateer was still flying in their direction, apparently unharmed and closing fast.

The British frigate was turning to larboard, and her intention was clearly to fire broadsides at the other two ships, then wear and come back with the wind on her quarter. They were good tactics and should account for one or both of the privateers, leaving her poised to bear down fast and have a second try at the remaining ship, but it also meant that this last craft would be allowed to continue heading for *Pevensey Castle*. Rogers began to fume. They could fire their puny broadside, rig boarding netting, use spars to fend them off, and do whatever they could to repel the boarders, but the privateer would be crammed full of men and, once alongside, there would be little point in resisting further. He glanced at his watch and then at the oncoming privateer which was closing on them with a bone in its teeth. Less than half an hour, he reckoned, certainly no longer, and they would be taken.

* * *

The women were huddled together in the hold. Kate had removed the gratings and arranged for ladders to be lowered. After a token amount of persuasion, all had descended. Now, they sat on crates and casks, their long dresses held clear of the damp shingle in the dim light of three lanterns. Kate had also collected a small spirit stove along with crockery from the third mate's mess, and a kettle which was almost boiling.

"Susan, Emma, lay these out and distribute them, will you?" She pointed at the pile of white china cups that sat next to the trays. The girls stared at her, but did nothing.

"Did you hear what I said?" The water was boiling now. She began to spoon a generous measure of tea into the pot.

"We ain't your servants," Susan said, a sullen expression on her face.

"No, you are employed by Mrs Drayton," Kate replied in measured tones. "With luck, she should be joining us at Portsmouth, and I'm sure she will be overjoyed to hear how helpful you have been to her fellow passengers."

Kate turned back to the pot, but watched out of the corner of her eye as the girls rose and began to assemble the tea things. Her gaze continued round to the other women, mostly passengers, and mostly chattering excitedly at the novel surroundings and the fact they might shortly be in action. Kate could not tell how they might react if it actually came to fighting, but was reasonably certain that the present high spirits would not last. She noticed Miss Hanshaw, sitting quietly next to a tier of beef casks and knitting. Their eyes met, and both smiled.

"Will you take tea?" Kate asked as she approached. She caught her eye and held the pot up. "I'm sure it's within your victualling allowance."

The girl laughed. "In that case, it shall be very welcome."

Kate began to fill her cup. "I'm afraid there is no milk."

"Really?" Elizabeth looked surprised and then considered for a moment. "That is a shame. Do you perhaps have a bucket?"

Kate eyed her quizzically. "A jug, might that do?"

She returned to the stove and held up a large pewter jug.

"Capital!" The girl put down her cup and knitting, sprang to her feet, collected the jug and made for one of the ladders. "Some of the cows above are Company property, I assume?"

"Why, yes." Kate looked mildly puzzled. "And I suppose I should know which, but fear I do not."

"It is no matter," Elizabeth said, hitching her dress up with the hand that held the jug, and starting up the ladder. "We only need a pint or so; I'm certain it will not be missed."

* * *

Rogers looked about his ship in mild desperation. The male passengers were standing along the larboard gangboard, fingering their weapons with rather more respect. Seamen were stationed at those larboard guns that had been cleared and ready. It took six men to serve each, so he was left with fewer than thirty actually sailing the ship. To starboard, the sands off Dungeness effectively blocked any chance of escape in that direction, and to turn and attempt to find shelter behind *Shearwater* would only present themselves to the privateers and make matters far worse. He had yet to take his ship through the eye of the wind, but even the poorest of seamen knew that a lubberly barge like *Pevensey Castle* would wallow hopelessly, taking forever to see the opposite tack. He glanced up. They were carrying topsails and topgallants, along with the forecourse and staysails; there was little more he could do in this wind—ominous creaks were coming from aloft as it was.

Shearwater was firing again now, this time at the centre of the three ships. A small cheer went up as the enemy vessel was neatly straddled by the shots, wiping her masts down as if they were nothing more than matchsticks and leaving her helpless.

"One down," Nichols murmured to Paterson. They watched while the frigate, now heading almost directly away from them, made for the northernmost craft. The next Frenchman would be in range in minutes, but by the time *Shearwater* had dealt with it and turned about, *Pevensey Castle* would be fighting off the nearest of the privateers.

"Mr Paterson, Mr Nichols, you will assist Mr Seagrove in the waist." Rogers had already decided that a fight was inevitable and wanted his third and fourth mates well out of the way, should he choose to surrender. He turned to the men at the nearest gun. "How are you set?"

"Round shot, sir."

Ideally he should order the weapons drawn and reloaded with grape, but the time to think of that had long passed. To attempt to do so now, with inexperienced men, would probably see the guns empty as the enemy came alongside.

"Very well; each of you will hold your fire until you are ordered." He looked up at the approaching privateer. She was well armed, with seven guns a side; they might be six or even nine pounders, and almost certainly more accurate and with a greater range than his own blown-out eighteens. *Pevensey Castle's* guns threw a heavier ball, but the barrels were short and the bores generous; point-blank range against a large enemy was about their limit. The Indiaman would probably be feeling the force of the privateer's weapons at any moment, and he was far more confident of their effectiveness.

Then while he watched, the enemy turned a couple of points to starboard, and the immediate threat was postponed. The French were clearly intending to close as fast as possible, then round their stern. Like everything else that was playing out before him, the tactics were eminently sensible, although that hardly lessened his frustration. He felt his hands begin to shake and thrust them behind him, as he sought to adopt a determined attitude. If he allowed the enemy to attack from behind, *Pevensey Castle* could be raked, round shot running the length of the ship, smashing everything in their path. He bit his lower lip. There would be carnage. It must not happen, especially as he, standing on the quarterdeck with only the frail timbers of the poop to protect him, would be a likely casualty.

"A desperate situation, captain."

Drayton's voice combined with the suppressed tension made

Rogers physically jump. Where had he come from? Presumably the man was in his cabin in the roundhouse and had not been alerted until now.

"It was good of you to see that I was advised of the danger," Drayton said.

Rogers looked at him cautiously, but made no comment. Thoughts of the roundhouse brought an obvious association, however. Elizabeth might still be in her cabin. He really should see that she was safe as well. For a moment, he considered despatching one of the midshipmen, then changed his mind. The girl could look after herself; she was only really steerage class, after all.

"Are we in danger, sir?"

"I fear so, Mr Drayton." His tone was forced but strangely, even in such a situation, Rogers found it easy to speak lightly. "T'would be a shame to lose the ship so early into the voyage, and while still in home waters."

"You think that likely, Captain?"

"It is indeed possible," he continued, almost casually, as if there were nothing odd about indulging in light conversation while his ship was about to be attacked and boarded. Rogers thought for a moment. Was this the bravery that other men displayed in battle? He supposed so, and had certainly met with those who behaved in just the same way. He remembered even despising them a little for it. Rogers had been in action on several occasions, and each time fear, something he considered quite healthy, had made itself known. This was his first time as a captain, and he found himself performing like those stalwarts he always vaguely scorned. But did they also have to clamp their hands behind their back to prevent such a shaking? Rogers told himself that they did not, even though a curious inkling said that they might.

"She is coming up on our stern." This was Willis who ought to know better than state the obvious. But, the enemy was certainly creeping closer, and should be able to fire on them from a different angle very shortly. The question was, would they do so? Damaging *Pevensey Castle* might make her easier to raid and ransack, whereas holding back, and taking her by boarding was the better option if she were intended as a prize.

"*Shearwater* is signalling!" Drummond was watching the frigate, now a good distance to the north. Sure enough, bunting had broken out, and she appeared to be about to wear, even though that meant leaving the remaining merchants to the other privateer.

"What does she say?" Rogers barked at the midshipman.

"Nothing in the Company code, sir." The lad was clearly worried and went through the book several times. "Think it might be a Navy signal."

It was, and soon the reason became obvious.

"Deck there, ships in sight." King's bellow from the masthead made them all look up, then across to the empty horizon. "Two maybe three, heading from the north, an' I think I can make out a commissioning pennant."

Rogers drew breath while he considered the approaching privateer again. She was now comfortably in range, although still making no preparations to fire. If the sighting turned out to be British warships, and if they really were heading directly south, they must surely deal with the northernmost Frenchman, as well as cutting off any chance for the nearest to escape. Should the enemy attempt to board and take *Pevensey Castle* she would be recaptured almost immediately. However, the main advantage lay in the fact that *Shearwater* had been able to wear earlier. Even now, she was coming round and would soon be hurtling down on them and the last privateer.

"Sighting is two frigates," King was reporting more confidently now. "British colours, and coming up fast."

Rogers glanced up at the horizon. The topmasts were in sight from the deck. His gaze dropped back to the privateer, and he thought there might be movement about the deck. Yes, hands were taking up the braces; she was going to turn and run for her coast while there was still the chance. He felt the relief flow down his body, and it was all he could do to stop himself from laughing aloud. However, this was not the way to behave. The conniving part of his brain was very much awake, and he sensed there was an opportunity to turn the situation to his advantage.

"Larboard battery, are you ready?"

The gun captains turned to look at him, surprised at the question. "Aye sir," one replied, and the rest hesitantly raised their right arms.

"Quartermaster, take us to larboard. As close to the wind as you can make!"

"Braces there!" Willis was alert enough and took up the call while the ship began to ease over. He had been right, the privateer was turning and would soon be heading away on the starboard tack, much faster than the stately old East Indiaman on the larboard. But, the raider's guns would not be able to bear, whereas *Pevensey Castle* should have at least a chance for a single broadside.

"Hold it now, on my word!" It was not the best way of signalling a broadside. Paterson or Nichols in the waist were probably better placed, and it was hardly a captain's responsibility. But, Rogers was not expecting to hit the ship. It was more a dramatic gesture, one that he knew would impress the men, the passengers, and hopefully Drayton, still standing behind him and doubtless watching all that went on.

Pevensey Castle was slowing as she came closer to the wind; the time was very near.

"Hold it, steady..." He wished he were wearing his sword, so that he might raise it in a spectacular fashion. The gun crews were desperately levering their pieces to bear on the enemy. Rogers held his hand up high, bringing it down with a flourish.

"Fire!"

It was not the snap discharge of a crack warship. The sound rolled out in an erratic staccato, but the sudden noise and flash of bright flame that stood out against the smoke and late afternoon gloom made a dramatic impression, as Rogers knew that it must. All rushed forward to see the fall of the shots; some were very wide, another ridiculously short. Two might have found their mark, but no damage was evident on the privateer.

"A hit, sir!" Willis's face was ecstatic. "I'm certain of it!"

That was all Rogers needed to hear. The story was now in place and could, in time, be embroidered upon. He chuckled inwardly to himself. At that moment they might have been fighting off a flood of desperate privateers, but instead he had apparently seen them off. Carefully handled, this should do his reputation no harm at all. His standing with the East India Company would be greatly improved, and all on board must acknowledge him for his true worth. Legends had grown from smaller beginnings than this. With care and a little elaboration, he could go on to build his reputation as a true fighting captain.

CHAPTER SEVEN

They arrived at Portsmouth the following afternoon, the late January sun picking out the famous seafront in spectacular fashion. Their luck held, the wind was still fair and in the north, contrary to what usually prevailed in the Channel, and as they crept up to anchor off the Mother Bank, Captain Rogers was clearly in a buoyant mood.

"Passengers expected, Mr Nichols," he said, smacking his hands together while he bustled about the quarterdeck. "Have the decks holystoned and pipe clay the man ropes."

"Very good, sir."

"With luck, we can keep this wind and be off by nightfall."

Nichols glanced at the assembled shipping; it would indeed be a lightning stop if so.

"Oh, and the fifth mate should be arriving." Rogers took one more look about the deck, before starting for his quarters. "Send him to me when he does."

Nichols touched his hat and passed the instructions to Drummond, before returning to check the ship's bearings. The current was negligible. There seemed no risk of the anchors slipping, but procedure was there to be followed, and Nichols was a methodical man. *Admiral Hayes* and *Coventry* were close by; just beyond them the rest of the convoy lay, apparently ready for the off. There were fifteen ships in all and most the same size or larger than

Pevensey Castle. Something of the captain's optimism was probably wearing off on him. All had topmasts set up, all appeared ready to sail, and it did seem a crime to waste such a useful wind.

A party of seamen came on to the quarterdeck with a sack of sand and several holystones. Nichols stepped to one side as they began to work. Memories of the previous afternoon's adventure were still fresh in his mind although strangely it was not the actual contact with the enemy that haunted him. He had seen the woman on several occasions since she boarded at London; in an eight hundred-ton ship that was inevitable, he supposed. Still, each meeting had stuck in his mind as he usually managed to embarrass himself in some minor way. The rule about not mixing with passengers was strict Company policy, but it was also one he readily approved of.

When a midshipman, on his first voyage, he had fallen desperately in love with the youngest daughter of a senior East India Company factor. He realised now, with the benefit of hindsight and experience, that she had led him on, enjoying his frustration as much as he had their few clandestine meetings, and was determined never to allow himself to become so embroiled again.

He was almost thirty now, his hair was prematurely greying, and he knew that with each passing year he became less attractive to the opposite sex. It was a change he welcomed, as it made his life of celibacy that much easier. Only occasionally, as with the recent meeting with Miss Hanshaw, did he wonder, wistfully, just what a normal married life would be like.

Marriage, ha! It was a measure of his true state of mind that he need only meet a presentable woman to start to think about weddings. Stupidly, he realised he was still holding the azimuth compass and hurriedly replaced it in the binnacle locker. He might pretend to accept growing old and grey. He could fool himself that he was in no need of feminine contact and greet the prospect of a chaste life with all the relish of a true enthusiast. But deep down inside, he knew himself to be longing for that comfort which can only come from the close company of a woman.

The last time someone had truly attracted him was two years and ten months ago. After that misfortune, he really thought he might be able to settle down to a bachelor existence. Sadly, Miss Hanshaw had come to spoil things—sadly for her as much as him. However, hard he might try, it was inevitable that he would continue to annoy the girl and embarrass himself with each subsequent meeting. By the time they finally saw India, she would be so desperate to free herself from his attentions that escape at the first opportunity would be her only desire. It had happened before, on several occasions, and he accepted with grim resignation that it was about to happen again.

* * *

The frigates, whose appearance had been the true cause of *Pevensey Castle*'s reprieve, had followed them to Spithead and were now dropping anchor close by. King had come on duty a few minutes before and noted how they took in sail and secured with smooth efficiency. Then the nearest began to attend to her long-boat, which was cleared away and swung out from tackle at the fore and main yards.

"It appears the Navy are to pay us a visit." Willis was on deck and watched with him as the boat, now manned with a crew as well as six armed marines made for them.

"But surely, they cannot be coming for us?" King asked.

"Would be strange, if so," Willis snorted. "But then His Majesty never misses a chance to collect a few more hands."

King always found that the forced upper class whine in the first mate's voice made everything he said sound mildly disdainful.

"But we are desperately undermanned," he persisted, feeling vaguely incensed that his previous colleagues should even think of taking men from their ship. He himself had been involved in many such raiding parties in the past, but always from homebound merchants. The Navy was allowed to press men then, even if their prey might be sighting England for the first time in many years. "Surely there are rules against taking men from outward-bound ships?"

"Rules there may be, but they make little difference to the Andrew," Willis replied, curling his lip slightly. "They can write their own, and would leave us with the captain and the ship's cat if they needed the people bad enough."

Sure enough, the longboat was soon alongside and a young midshipman clambered through the entry port. He was not more than fifteen, although he carried himself more like an admiral. Four sailors, broad bodied men with arms like hams and expressions of pleased anticipation, followed the lad on to the newly whitened quarterdeck. They were clearly looking forward to their morning's work. The detachment of marines, crisp and lethal in red, white, and silver, formed up smartly behind them.

"Name's Gordon, from *Phoebe*," the lad said to King. "Captain Barlow sent me to wait upon your captain. You are to provide us with some men, I believe."

King had not held his lieutenant's commission for long, but still it rankled that a warrant officer should presume to speak with him on equal terms.

"You have no jurisdiction here, sir," Willis replied. "We are outward-bound, and as such may retain our people."

The boy met the mate's stare with equanimity. "It is a private arrangement," he said. "Between our captains. A matter of honour, or so I understand."

Watching, King felt he could guess the story. Rogers had probably got himself in debt to this Navy captain, and chosen to see himself clear with members of his crew. A despicable trick, but one he could well imagine of the man.

"Mr Midshipman Gordon." The devil himself was on deck now, he must have been roused by the hailing of the boat. "I am the captain of this ship, and you will address yourself to me."

Gordon rolled his eyes at King and then turned away.

"Captain Barlow's compliments, sir. I have been sent to collect four experienced hands, if you please," he said.

Rogers nodded. "I will assemble the people, and you may select, although I cannot vouch for any individual's qualifications; that was not in the understanding."

At a word from Willis, the sound of a pipe broke the still morning air and soon both watches formed up in the waist. The men stood waiting knowing what was to come and that there was little that could be done about it. They might have the law on their side, but that hardly mattered against a group of Navy roughs with marines to back them up. King and Willis followed the lad down to the waist, while Rogers stayed watching from the quarterdeck.

"Cap'n said topmen only, and not to be fobbed off with no landsmen," the boy informed them.

Willis regarded him with scorn. "I fear we have been at sea but a few days, Mr Gordon. The men have yet to prove themselves. You may take four hands, as I believe you intend, but pray do not expect us to aid in your selection."

The boy looked along the rows of tanned faces. All appeared to be experienced, in fact there was very little to choose between them. Eventually he selected four, pretty much at random. The men stepped forward muttering slightly as the others mocked them gently from behind. King noticed with a start that one had long red hair tied back in a queue.

Johnston's eyes met his for a moment, but no words were spoken, even though the man was probably about to face a minimum of two years in the frigate. The chances were that no one would recognise him immediately, but once in the Navy he was likely to stay there, and for all the time he served, he would be under constant threat of the noose.

"Give your names to the purser, then assemble your immediate possessions." King spoke quietly wondering if, even now, there might be something he could do to save Johnston. From his position at the break of the quarterdeck, Rogers watched in silence. The captain had also served with the man, and it was possible he recognised him as well. But, even if that were the case, little could be done to avoid Johnston's departure. The chosen men went below; appearing again almost immediately with their ditty bags. Myles, the purser, began to mark against names in a large brown ledger.

"Some will have chests." Willis turned to the midshipman. "You have room for them in your longboat?"

"Indeed, sir." The lad was about to say more, when one of the men caught his attention. "Hey, there! What goes with that fellow?"

Johnston was mounting the gangboard ladder and looked back. The midshipman approached him.

"What have you there?" The midshipman tugged at a small canvas and leather device that Johnston carried over one arm.

"It's me spare truss, mister," he said, holding the thing up. "I'm allowed one for washin' and one for wearin'." Johnston lowered the belt of his trousers slightly to show a similar implement in place.

"I'll have none with the bursten belly," the midshipman scoffed. "Send him back, I will choose another!"

"You have already selected, Mr Gordon," Rogers informed him curtly. "Now take your men and leave."

"Don't want no man with a rupture," the lad repeated.

"Take him or leave him, but you get no more choices." Rogers's tone was one of complete unconcern. "This is a Company ship, lad; not a penny bazaar."

The midshipman hesitated, wondering if a seaman who was clearly no good for most purposes would be welcomed. Five men were already on light duties, and one was to be discharged ashore that very day. To take another, only to have him similarly dealt with, might reflect badly on him and his judgement.

"I'll just have the three, then," he said, his tone somewhat grumpy.

"Very good; do give my compliments to your captain." Rogers turned away as three of his men trudged reluctantly up to the entry port and into the waiting longboat.

The rest were also dispersing, some to duties, others to return below, and Johnston was one of the latter. He swung his truss and ditty bag jauntily over his shoulder as he passed King. Again their eyes met, although this time the seaman closed one very slightly, and his face bore a look of quiet triumph.

* * *

Another boat drew alongside at the beginning of the afternoon watch. In it was the last of the passengers, along with an older man. He was dressed in a mate's uniform of a very superior cut, although the buttons on his sleeve proclaimed him as merely a fifth officer. Paterson who had the deck, greeted the newcomer on the gangboard just as Rogers was fussing over Mr Drayton's wife who had also arrived and was amid a vast collection of luggage.

"Anthony Langlois," the man informed him.

"Langlois?" Paterson regarded him carefully before adding, "A French name?" with his customary lack of tact.

"I am a Guernsey man, sir," Langlois replied smoothly. "And am to join you as fifth mate."

Paterson blushed slightly, extended his hand and introduced himself. "Forgive me, I spoke rashly. There is such talk of foreign agents and spies at present."

"It is to be understood," the man regarded him with an easy expression, "though I doubt that even a Frenchman would announce himself quite so boldly."

Paterson grinned in return. Langlois had a pleasant way about him that was both welcome and reassuring. The arrival of any new officer was always a worrying time. So much depended on him and his abilities. He might be an excellent seaman, or an outright lub-

88

ber. In either case, they must work together, and a friendly demeanour was a definite bonus. Langlois not only carried himself well, but he also possessed an inner confidence that spoke volumes of his qualities, both as an officer and a seaman.

"I should introduce you to the captain," they reached the quarterdeck, and both turned to look as Mrs Drayton was holding up a small pug dog for Rogers's admiration. "But now might not be the time."

"I have enjoyed the benefit of Mrs Drayton's company for five days or more." Langlois's voice was smooth and low, although his twinkling eyes spoke loud enough. "And could not contemplate depriving anyone from such an experience."

Paterson grinned again and considered the newcomer further. He was older than the other senior officers, and yet he had not progressed in rank: curious. At that moment, Rogers noticed them and gratefully seized upon Paterson as a distraction.

"And this is my third officer, John Paterson."

The mate stepped forward, raised his hat and took the woman's hand.

"Delighted to meet you, ma'am," Paterson gushed. "I hope you will enjoy your time aboard the *Pevensey Castle*."

"You will have to meet Bella, Mr Paterson," Mrs Drayton informed him, proffering the pug.

Paterson was not sure quite how to greet a dog. He extemporised by holding out his hand and attempting to pat the animal's forehead. This was taken in quite the wrong manner, and he snatched his arm away as the beast erupted into a paroxysm of snapping and barking. Rogers chuckled with uncharacteristic good humour, while Mrs Drayton cooed like a young mother and began explaining how much Bella liked a game. Paterson stepped back and looked sidelong at Langlois. The man's face was respectful and attentive; he might have just witnessed a senior captain being introduced to an admiral. One thing was certain; whatever had checked the new mate's promotion, it was not a lack of diplomacy.

* * *

King looked up from his journal. Someone had entered the steerage mess, and instinct told him it was not one of the usual inhabitants. He was behind him now, collecting up the teapot and cups from their earlier meal, so it must surely be a steward. The new mate, Langlois, had impressed them all by being unusually tidy, but this would be taking things too far. He was about to return to his work when the man coughed ostentatiously, clearly wanting his attention. King sighed at the interruption, the last in a long line that had stretched from first light. Placing his book down, he swung round in his seat and then gasped in surprise.

"Michael! Michael Crowley!"

The man grinned self-consciously. "Good afternoon, Mr King."

"What a grand surprise," King rose from his chair. "How did you get aboard?"

"Well, I volunteered, so I did." Crowley shook the offered hand. "Heard from some old Pandora's that you had gone for the Indiamen. I figured you might be needin' a hand, an' brought m'self along."

King who always considered himself to be virtually friendless, was taken aback at hearing the man was here because of him. They first met when Crowley had been aboard a French prize. An Irishman by birth, he had spent his life travelling the world and was all but stateless. When given the chance, he readily accepted the Navy as his home and signed on for service in *Pandora* as a gunroom steward. Together they had seen fleet actions and mutinies, and when they finally said goodbye, King promised to send for him if he took another ship.

"I hadn't expected you to want for John Company," he said, slightly embarrassed at the memory. "Surely you are a Navy man now?"

"Ah, I might have said the same for you."

King laughed briefly. "Alas, there are few postings for a lieutenant at present. I considered the Impressment Service, but it were not for me." He regarded Crowley carefully; a trained hand, one who would be welcomed aboard any warship. He could have chosen his berth with ease and yet had opted for *Pevensey Castle*.

"Would you be needing a steward?" Crowley asked.

King cleared his throat. Surprise at meeting an old friend coupled with the knowledge that he had been especially sought out, had quite shaken him. "Whether we do or do not, you're in." He laughed again as a thought occurred. "Never did trust that Tomlinson fellow: too many stories finding their way back to the captain for my liking. Perhaps we can discover another station for him, an' move you in his place?" There was an awkward pause before King, unsure of what to do, yet wishing to convey his feelings, reached out and touched the man gently on his shoulder. "And if you even think of changin' your mind, I'll have you confined until we sail."

* * *

Rogers's prediction was wrong. It was not until the following morning that they finally set sail. Amidst a flurry of unnecessary signals from the commodore, the group of ships made a decidedly stately progress as they crowded round the north coast of the Isle of Wight. The wind, which had backed slightly, was in the north-west and gave them every assistance, although some still strayed dangerously close to each other, and on more than one occasion, shouting was heard between quarterdecks. Nevertheless, before long they rounded Bembridge Point and a more regimented order of sailing was established, with two columns of vessels roughly three cables apart, and the frigates snapping about amongst them like dogs herding sheep. By four bells in the afternoon watch, they were in the Channel proper, although the commodore seemed strangely reluctant to increase sail and take full advantage of the obliging wind.

As the first dogwatch was set, this was becoming frustrating. King who had just come on duty, looked about at the other ships in the convoy. None were making more than three knots, and yet there was easily another two in this breeze. He was aware that In-diamen had a habit of snugging down at nightfall, but darkness was still several hours away.

"Once more, slow work, Tom," Paterson said, joining him.

"We seem destined to remain in home waters," King agreed. "If they continue at this rate, most will be dead from old age afore any raise India."

"Well, this time there may be a reason," Paterson nodded authoritatively. "Just wait and see."

There was, and it became obvious less than half an hour later, when the sails of a merchant convoy were spotted. It was a home-bound fleet of Indiamen, beating up towards them from the southwest.

"Commodore's signalling" Paterson shouted. "Drummond, look alive there!"

The midshipman was already focusing on the leading ship in their fleet. "General, to the convoy," he said. "Heave to."

Paterson ordered the braces round, and the ship began to wallow in the gentle chop. Alerted by the change of motion, Rogers appeared from the roundhouse and strutted up to the binnacle.

"Trouble, Mr Paterson?" he asked.

"I think we might have met with a homebound convoy, sir."

Rogers nodded knowingly and examined the new arrivals. "Pretty much on time, and just as well, else we might have been scraping round the south of Wight for an eternity. Clear away the longboat and both cutters."

King watched, mystified, while Paterson simply touched his hat. Without the power of the wind, both convoys were starting to break up and ships soon began to drift in the swell. Only the outward-bound escorts retained any degree of order. Taking advantage of the opportunity to drill, they cruised back and forth, tacking and wearing like automatons.

"A spell in the tropics does not favour a vessel." Patterson commented.

King looked at the home-coming Indiamen. All appeared weathered, with mended sails and paintwork that, even at this distance, appeared bleached and patchy. Their escorts, two line-of-battle ships and a frigate, looked in far better order, although they would have only joined the convoy at thirty-seven degrees south.

"Come from India?" he asked.

"Me'be China for some," Paterson considered. "Stuffed full with all the wonders of the East, yet there is only one commodity that interests us."

The truth was starting to dawn now. The longboat had been cleared of sheep and swung out, soon it was joined by both cutters. Rogers pulled out a slip of paper from his pocket and looked about. King felt his eyes on him.

"Mr King, you and Mr Langlois are for the *Salisbury,* take both cutters. I need at least forty, but more if they can be spared. Lascars if you must, but Englishmen are preferred. Mr Nichols will take the longboat to *Harlequin,*" he indicated the ships concerned with a wave of his hand. "Now away with you."

"Lascars is all you'll get," Paterson told him when Rogers was out of earshot.

"Are we to press them?" King asked.

"Hardly," the third mate snorted. "They'll be only too pleased to come with you. Given the choice of a quick trip back home and carrying on to England, I'd say you'll be hard pushed to keep the numbers down."

"But they've not even reached home waters."

"Why should they want to? If they did, if they landed in England, they'd only be laid off. Then, they gets another choice—starve to death or freeze. Few Company ships will take them back. There are laws against employing too many Lascars—laws that we're about to flout, 'though no one will report us for it."

King looked across to where boats from other ships were already bearing down on the homebound convoy. It seemed a strange system, but then no stranger than taking a man from a farm and forcing him to serve at sea. If what Paterson said was so, they might well be doing the Lascars a favour, and no one could pretend *Pevensey Castle* did not need the extra men.

His cutter was the last to leave, and as he settled himself into the sternsheets, he noticed Johnston seated as stroke oar and without any sign of a truss.

"We're making for the black-hulled number over there," King said, pointing at a ship about half a mile from them. "Might as well rig the canvas."

The crew quickly erected the twin masts, and soon the small boat was skimming through the seas behind the other cutter. The late winter sun was welcome, and King began to enjoy both the trip and the brief time away from *Pevensey Castle*. He found himself beaming at Johnston. The seaman also appeared to appreciate the change and grinned in return.

Close up, the *Salisbury* looked in even worse order. Her black paintwork, although touched up in places, was badly blistered and peeling, revealing dark, damp wood beneath, and a small stream of water from the scuppers told that the pumps were currently being manned. King's cutter stood off her starboard beam, waiting while Langlois's boat was loaded. The cargo was human, a line of apparently emaciated bodies that slowly descended and settled themselves in the boat. All were slightly built, dark tanned and wore a variety of headgear ranging from light skull caps to full turbans. Some carried small bags, some short rolls of cloth, but there were no birdcages, no monkeys, no musical instruments, or exotic fruit; none of the usual baggage so beloved by British seamen. And, neither was there any banter. They continued in silence until the boat, finally filled, pushed off and passed them, with Langlois sitting, equally impassive, in the sternsheets. King noticed that not one of the new intake looked back at their old ship or forward to the new. Their expressions, if the word had any meaning at all, were totally neutral. They appeared to expect nothing and were willing to accept all, without a hint of curiosity, complaint, or even understanding. What was happening to them might just as well have been affecting someone else, and on the other side of the world. The other side of the world where they came from, where they would shortly be returning to and where their minds apparently still lay.

Then, it was their boat's turn. The cutter bumped once against the side of the merchant ship and was secured. King stood up gingerly, expecting to board, but before he could do so a line of men began clambering down and into his boat. A head appeared through an empty gunport just above him.

"This lot will make thirty-eight." A sheet of paper was thrust down. "Details are there for your pusser; all fit, all healthy, and all about as much use as a bald man's brush."

King looked about, slightly embarrassed. The man, a fourth mate, identified by the buttons on his sleeve, laughed readily.

"You ain't had much to do with our foreign friends, 'ave you?" he asked. "Some can't speak the language, an' those that can don't care much what we says. Long as they 'ave their food, a place to caulk, an' a chance to pray, they'll do you no 'arm, but don't expect much more."

"They're trained, though?"

"Oh yes," the officer assured him. "Most 'ave done several trips, an' can 'and, reef, an' steer with the best of them. Feel the cold somethin' awful, mind. An' wind blows 'em away easy as sneezin'. Lost two in Biscay just the other night, an' three to the fever since Helena."

"Fever?"

He grinned. "Na, not real fever; we'd call it a cold or a chill; drop of burnt rum and a dab of butter would 'ave sorted an Hinglishman out, but not these little fellows." He looked at the last as they settled themselves in the boat. "Na, as seamen they're more 'elp than hindrance, but not my choice for shipmates. I wish you joy of 'em."

The Lascars were all aboard now, and King ordered the cutter off. Johnston caught his eye as he leant into his stroke.

94

"Ain't as bad as he says," the seaman muttered. "I known a few good uns in my last passage, and most can handle theirsel's on deck sound enough. Though 'e's right about the sickness. Get 'em near fever, or action come to that, an' they're sure to let you down."

King looked at him questioningly. "How so?"

"It's the one thing everyone agrees about Lascars," Johnston told him. "They're always the first to die."

* * *

The convoy, now considerably better manned, was back on the wind by the time the sun began to lower in the sky, and with dusk they had left the homebound ships far behind. A group of fresh passengers who had gathered at the rails to take their last look at England stayed to be heartily sick over the side when the regular chop of the Channel asserted itself. And as the first call went out for supper, there were noticeably few takers. Paterson, now seasoned to the motion, had already eaten and sat in the steerage mess, working through yet another draft of the watch bill with King, while Kate stole a few clandestine moments talking quietly with Manning over the light of a shielded pusser's dip. Langlois, the new fifth mate, sat at a table on the opposite side of the small room and appeared to be sketching on a white tablet of paper. King leant back from his work and rubbed his eyes.

"We've all passengers aboard now," he said, turning to the couple in the corner of the mess. "An' I can certainly fix it so that cabin I mentioned is free."

Kate looked up, and Manning grinned. "Is that right, Tom?"

King nodded. "Reckon so."

Paterson glanced round. "Mind, it would only be for the one. If the captain gets to hear of you sharin' there'll be the devil to pay, an' no pitch hot enough."

"Still, t'would be a marked improvement," Kate sighed.

"We're not too filled with passengers, then?" Langlois asked.

"No." King consulted another list. "Several that had been marked down were actually taken in the *Surrey* or the *Glen Eden,* and that detachment of troops never did materialise."

Manning looked up. "Strange, surely?"

King shrugged. "Not for us to know the goings on in higher circles. Maybe Mr Rogers has caused some upset."

"Maybe he has," Langlois agreed. "Or perhaps other captains offered better terms."

"Quite possible," King nodded. "But we are certainly left with a deal of space; I'd say it must be twenty or so light at the very least."

"Those are homeward numbers," Paterson grunted. King looked at him, and he explained, "Always get more going out than coming back; it's usually two-thirds or so. At this rate, we'll be returning to England empty."

"Do that many stay?"

Paterson shook his head. "That many die," he said bluntly.

"But then this is the captain's first trip," Manning added. "Surely he has not had time to properly make his mark?"

"Even this far into the voyage his reputation will be established," Paterson continued. "He might claim the breeding, but ain't got the prestige; doesn't know how to handle the better class of passenger."

"And I suppose word soon gets around," Manning agreed. "Surgeon said he heard all manner of stories when he were ashore at Pompey."

"But we've hardly been clear of Gravesend more an' a week." King was still not convinced. "And we only called at Deal before Portsmouth; how can rumours spread so wild?"

"Bad word knows no bounds," Paterson replied enigmatically. "And it seems to me that our dear captain's repute started some while ago."

"I should chance that a man in his position has to be more than just a seaman," Kate mused. "There is also a need for diplomacy, and Mr Rogers seems somewhat remiss in that quarter."

"Aye, his position is far more complex than it might appear." Paterson sat back in his chair. "The seamanship he can leave to us, but he must manage the passengers, in the same way he does the crew. Respect is every bit as important in a merchant as a warship—probably more so. When folk are paying a good deal and risking their very lives, they don't want some puffed-up drunkard in command telling tales of derring-do."

Langlois regarded him over his sketchpad. "And that is how you consider our captain?"

The third mate pulled a wry face. "There I go again; speakin' out of turn: it's a fault with me I am aware, and I apologise for it," he said, a little abashed. "But, in truth it is hard to respect such a man."

"I fear John is right," King added. "The voyage is hardly started, and Mr Rogers has already worked up quite a feeling."

"Mr Keats said you was a-staying at the George." Manning looked at Langlois. "Along with Mrs Drayton; did you hear anything?"

"Not that I can recall." Langlois began to take more of an interest in his work.

"You were with Mrs Drayton's party, though?" Paterson asked.

"On the same floor," the new man agreed vaguely.

Paterson looked round from the watch list. "Drayton's pretty high up with the Company, ain't he?"

"So I believe."

"Odd then that he chose to sail with us, don't you think?"

"In the extreme." Langlois looked up and met his eyes. "But then I have learnt not to anticipate the workings of the Company."

"You seem quite experienced," Paterson persisted. He had turned in his seat and was speaking to Langlois directly. "And yet you are only rated fifth; can I ask, is there a reason?"

The man laughed and placed his pad down on the table. "Call it a lack of dedication, I suppose, but my aim has never been promotion." He regarded Paterson genially and then, sensing that more was called for from him, addressed the room in general. "'Tis one life that we are given and one only; that of an officer in an Indiaman suits me fine. I get the opportunity to travel, a fair wage, and a chance to practice my art." He indicated the sketchpad on the table in front of him. "I do not ask for more."

"Can I see?" Manning made to collect the pad.

"You may indeed," Langlois nodded, sitting back. "And can keep it, should you so wish."

Manning lifted the pad and gave an involuntary gasp at the image. It was Kate, sitting in the corner of the mess, just as she was now, and with that look of beauty and purpose that he found so attractive.

"It is very good," he said, eyeing Langlois somewhat suspiciously.

The new man stretched and yawned. "Alas my work is hardly equal to the subject," he smiled at Kate. "But do keep it, if it pleases you."

Manning nodded and carefully removed the paper from the tablet. The drawing was certainly of a high standard; in no more than a collection of lines the man had captured her mystery exactly. It was an act that, as her husband, Manning felt mildly disconcerting.

Kate reached across and took the paper from him. She pulled a face and gave a short snort. "Don't look nothin' like me," she said, holding it up for all to see. King and Paterson laughed more from embarrassment than anything. It was plain to them that the sketch was indeed good, and no one could ignore the air of tension which was suddenly present in the mess. Manning took the drawing back and looked at it once more. Kate was wrong, it was her to a tee and almost indecent in its perception. He looked across at his wife noticing that her face was now a shade darker, and made a mental note to treat Langlois with a deal of caution from now on.

* * *

"Not in 'ere, Abdul," Ward told him. "This is for senior 'ands and warrant officers only." The Lascar paused, uncertain. "Down in steerage," the boatswain's mate continued. "That's where you lot berth."

"It is the deck below." Johnston sounded out each syllable separately while he pointed downwards with his finger.

"Would you want me to show you?" Crowley, the steerage mess steward, asked him, not unkindly.

"Thank you, no." The newcomer placed his small canvas bag down and looked about. "This will suit me very well, thank you, gentlemen."

Ward raise himself up in his hammock. "You don't understand, matey. It's for senior 'ands; Hing-glish-men." He sounded the word out and raised his eyebrows. "*Comprehende?*"

The man's deep brown eyes were made darker by the poor light. "I am an officer," he said quietly.

Johnston looked across at Ward and Crowley, then back at the man. Certainly, he was better dressed than most of those who had recently embarked, but there was little about his small skull cap and loose-fitting clothes that spoke of rank or station. "You're a Lascar," he said bluntly. "A native."

"I am a serang," the man replied with dignity. "I take charge of my countrymen, and anyone else below. For that duty I was originally treated as a bosun by my masters, and I have learnt such skills to make the entitlement fair."

Johnston gave out one loud laugh and clapped his hands together, as he grinned across at Ward, who looked distinctly disconcerted.

"Belike he has us there!" the Irishman said, smiling also.

The boatswain's mate scratched at his chin. "Bosun, you say? No rapper?"

"On my word," the Lascar replied seriously. "No rapper."

Ward threw himself out of the hammock and straightened up. "You'll have to excuse us, we weren't aware." He stepped across and extended a hand. "Name's Ward, bosun's mate. This 'ere's Johnston. 'E's rated able, but there ain't a finer Jack aboard, and Crowley which is Irish, but not completely useless for all that."

The boatswain shook hands with the men. "I am pleased to meet with you. I am Khan," he said. "Though you can call me Abdul if it pleases you."

The men looked at him dubiously. "He didn't mean no disrespect," Crowley began.

"And none was taken," Khan nodded. "Abdul is also my name; I was most impressed by your perception."

Johnston laughed again and pointed to a bench, "Get yourself sat, Abdul," he told him, although Ward continued to view the stranger cautiously.

"Thank you, but I must see that my men are provided for. I may leave my bag here?"

"Of course," Ward told him. "An' if you got a chest, we'll strike that below, or 'ave it in the mess; there's plenty of space."

"Thank you; this is all I own," he smiled briefly. "We natives do not have the need for many possessions."

* * *

It had been another difficult evening with the captain. Even now, as she changed into her nightdress and brushed out her long fair hair, she could still smell his breath and the very odour from his oily body. The cabin was fine; she liked the fresh air and the fact she did not have to bend double to stand. However, when all roundhouse passengers shared the same dining table in the cuddy, and her place was inevitably laid so convenient to the captain's right, and increasingly nomadic, hand, Elizabeth wondered if she might not be better returning to her allotted berth in steerage. And if she must listen to that tale again, the one about how he had fought off the ravaging pirates virtually single-handed, she knew she was going to scream. The actual event had only happened a day or so ago, and already she could repeat the story word for word. They had taken on the final passengers, but even that had not changed things. Some were clearly prosperous, and she expected her constant rebuffs to Rogers's advances to have weakened her position in some way. But, the newcomers were found cabins elsewhere, while she, with her standard ticket and minimal furniture, was allowed to enjoy all the benefits of roundhouse accommodation, together with the captain's apparently undivided attention.

Elizabeth briefly considered a spell of knitting, but the bed was far too welcoming, and she climbed in, wriggling herself comfortable and wondering vaguely if continuous rebuttals and the occasional slap were not a worthy price to pay for this nightly luxury. It was a proper bed, not a cot, not a bunk, but one as might be found in any well-to-do house. It had cotton sheets that tucked under a real mattress, feather pillows and several woollen blankets to place on top. And it was hers.

But, she could still sense him, which was the strange part of it. Even now, even in her most intimate moments, he always seemed to be there. She closed her mind to the problem and blew out the candle. It must be close to ten o'clock. After that unpleasant experience on the first night, she wanted to give no further reason for him to come and tap on her door. He claimed to be checking that Company rules about lights in cabins were being obeyed, but it had taken almost half an hour, and finally one determined push from her, to be rid of the beast.

A movement from the room next door made her turn her head. Clearly the captain was less concerned about enforcing the ten o'clock lamp curfew on himself. She could see several small points of light through the thin deal partitioning, but there was one crack large enough to illuminate her own room slightly. As she considered it, the hole went suddenly dark. She watched, fascinated, as it reappeared, followed by the sound of footsteps close by. Slowly she pushed the covers back and climbed out of bed. Standing on the cold deck in her bare feet, she stepped over her knitting bag and crept closer to the bulkhead. It was really quite a large opening, about half an inch across, although she had not noticed its existence in daylight. Intrigued, she pressed her eye to it and gave a sharp intake of breath.

There was the captain's cabin, well lit and on show for her; and there was the captain, slumped in front of his desk, drinking from an overlarge balloon of brandy. He had taken off his jacket and looked far more slovenly in an unbuttoned waistcoat and britches. As she watched the man gave out a belch, lent to one side, and scratched his behind. The sight, along with the realisation that her cabin must be equally exposed, caused Elizabeth to shift her weight slightly, making the deck beneath her creak.

She held her breath as Rogers turned, and it was all she could do to contain a small instinctive shriek when he rose up from his chair and began to walk towards the spyhole. Thinking he had spotted her, she drew back and stood to one side. The light from the hole was still visible, but she, hopefully, was not. He could be heard as he drew close, and even the smell of his breath was apparent. The room dimmed slightly; his face must be barely inches from hers, with only a thin wood partition separating them. A thin wood partition, with him looking through, seeing into her private world. No doubt he had looked before, probably several times, over the last few days. A wave of revulsion all but overcame her. She felt both uncommonly angry and physically sick when she fully realised the outrageousness of his crime and reaching for the knitting needle, so conveniently placed in her bag, her hand was shaking quite violently.

CHAPTER EIGHT

The scream alerted everyone, from the officers on the quarterdeck to the watch below, just two hours into their caulk. Even the lookout, cold and lonely at his perch on the snugged-down ship, even he was aware of the commotion, and none of the passengers in the great cabin or further away in steerage could have remained asleep, while the noise spread easily throughout the wooden vessel. Drayton, abed in his roundhouse cabin, emerged, blinking and pulling on a silk dressing gown. He was followed by his wife, hair in papers and face pasted, who carried a bemused Bella for general encouragement and interest. Elizabeth's cabin door remained shut, although it was her name that was called when Rogers staggered out into the cuddy, a hand clapped firmly over his right eye.

"Bastard Hanshaw woman!" he yelled as he crashed into the dining table and slumped forward. "The blower! The bitch! The whore!"

Drayton regarded the captain with apparent curiosity as he leant over the table and continued to moan.

"I'll see her thrown off this ship, and—and flogged at the grating."

Luck, the captain's servant, appeared dressed in a nightshirt. "Are you hurt, sir?"

"Hurt?" Rogers reared up, his hand still covering half his face, although there was a slight trickle of blood seeping from underneath. "That drab has put my damned eye out!"

"Is she in your cabin?" Drayton asked peering, none too subtly, through the opened doorway.

"No, she blasted well is not," Rogers roared. "And neither will she ever be; accursed witch that she is. I'll see her off my ship!"

Drayton regarded him seriously. "So you have already said. But I fail to see how Miss Hanshaw did you any damage when she does not appear to have been in the same room."

Rogers appeared to think for a moment. "Damn it man, I need a surgeon, Get me to sickbay. Luck!"

The servant collected his master, holding him awkwardly under the shoulder. "Very good, sir. We'll take you to see Mr Keats; I'm sure he will effect a cure."

Drummond entered the cuddy and looked about. He was midshipman of the watch and had been sent to see what all the noise was about. The captain, clearly wounded, was being helped towards the door by Luck. Mr Drayton, presumably the instigator of the injury, appeared bemused, while his wife, the only other occupant of the room, seemed more interested in consoling her dog.

The lad looked from one to the other. "What's going on here then?" he asked, without any hope of an answer.

* * *

A light tap came at the door. Elizabeth jumped and looked up. Her face was strained, and she had clearly been crying.

"Who is it?" she all but whispered.

"Nichols, ma'am; fourth officer." He paused and, feeling slightly foolish, added, "George."

It appeared to be one fluid movement: Elizabeth sprung from her chair, opened the door, reached up and hugged him. The mate tried to pull away, but the grip was too firm and her words, though hardly distinguishable, spilled out like too many cats in a barrel.

"Steady, steady." He found himself rocking her gently as a child, and as a child she told him everything, her sentences long, breathless and unbound. Nichols looked across to the partition. There was no obvious hole, although the room was lit only by the opened door to the cuddy. Her knitting bag lay on the deck. The room darkened slightly as Drayton entered.

"Is the young lady all right?"

Nichols regarded him over Elizabeth's still sobbing shoulder. "She needs to get away from here," he said. "She has had a dreadful fright."

"The captain is injured." Drayton regarded them both quizzically. "He would seem to blame it on her."

"The captain is a pig," Nichols replied, his voice surprisingly controlled and unemotional. "If there were any justice he would hang."

Drayton considered this for a moment. "My wife is outside and will look after the girl."

"Thank you, sir, but I think she will be better away from the roundhouse. I shall take her down to steerage; I'm sure accommodation can be found for her there."

"Very well, you might seek out my wife's maids, I'm sure they will assist."

Nichols went to go, but the girl held him firm, and he had to gently coax her into moving.

"I'm not certain what has been going on here," Drayton's voice was slow and considered, "but some form of enquiry will be needed; the captain is clearly hurt. We should signal the commodore at first light."

Nichols paused and looked back. "I'm sure the chief officer can take charge, sir."

"Maybe so, maybe so." Drayton nodded. "But Mr Rogers has the ultimate power in this ship. I think the young lady should be transferred to a different vessel, if only for her own safety."

That made sense, and Nichols was silently glad that one with Drayton's intelligence and authority was present.

"You will look after her until first light?"

Nichols nodded. "Yes, sir. I will," he said and ever so gently he began to ease Elizabeth through the door.

* * *

"If you will try and keep a little still, sir." Keats peered at the man's face, pale and sweaty in the dubious light from the lantern. Rogers twisted slightly and winced when the surgeon gently eased back the lid of his eye with his thumb. "Swab, if you please, Mr Manning." Manning passed a small piece of tow, and the surgeon wiped away some fluid. He then collected the lamp and slowly moved it across Rogers's line of sight.

"It is impossible to say until morning," Keats replaced the lantern and sat back, wiping his hands on some more cotton waste. "But my guess is badly bruised, no more. The initial impact appears to have been away from the eye; there is a cut to the skin below the *medial canthus*, but no sign of puncture to the orb itself. Though badly bloodshot, it appears not to have been penetrated."

Freed from the surgeon's examination, Rogers's hand returned to his eye. "Hurts like hell, doctor. You'll have to give me something for the pain."

"Yes, my mate will mix you a draught. Other than that, I will prescribe a cold application at the beginning of every watch; we will undertake that if you wish. Antiphlogistic treatment might be necessary, that will be decided upon later. In the meantime, you must rest. I'll prepare a protective bandage for when you are on deck, but the dressing can be removed below, as long as you are not exposed to bright lights." The surgeon began to make notes in his pocket book. "Tell me again, this was caused by a pen quill, you say?"

"That is correct." It was the only story he could concoct during the journey to sickbay. "I was writing at my desk."

The surgeon considered him. "The incision was made with some force; perhaps you sneezed?"

"Of course!" Rogers's voice rose as if in triumph. "I sneezed, whilst writing, and the next I knew there was this terrible pain."

"At the time you appeared to blame Miss Hanshaw." It was Drayton's voice, and Rogers opened his good eye in surprise. How long had he been standing there?

"Did I?" Rogers appeared confused. "Me'be it were the shock?"

"You seemed reasonably certain. Her name was definitely mentioned—several times."

The captain's face cleared as a fresh idea occurred. "I was writing to my cousin, my cousin Elizabeth, that might have been it."

Drayton said nothing.

"Have you taken any alcohol?" The surgeon knew the answer, but felt it right to ask the question.

"A little wine with my meal, doctor, no more."

"Very well, we will give you a small draught of laudanum. It should help you to sleep, and may even reduce the swelling."

"Will this affect Mr Rogers's ability to command?" Drayton spoke softly, although all were well aware of the importance of his question.

"There should be no commands given while under the medication's influence," the surgeon said.

"Hold fast there," Rogers's voice rose up. "I am the captain. It is for me to decide if I am fit and able."

"That is not so." Drayton's voice remained quiet, although he spoke with authority. "Mr Keats also has a duty to the ship, her passengers and crew. If he feels you unsafe to take charge, it is right that he say so. And, as a member of the Company, I will back him."

Rogers pressed his hand to his eye and moaned slightly.

"I am certain your officers can see the rest of the night out, and so there seems no call for you to take charge for the next few hours at least. Mr Keats will examine you in the morning, and a more detailed diagnosis can be made."

The surgeon nodded, although Rogers made no sign of hearing.

"You will advise me of your prognosis, Mr Keats?" Drayton asked.

"Indeed sir. A light dressing for now and the laudanum should make the captain comfortable. I will attend him at first light and hopefully begin to administer a remedy."

"Very well." Drayton looked at the captain for a moment as he lay on the bunk, hand held to his face and groaning slightly. "Then I shall wish you all a good night."

* * *

"It was in steerage," Elizabeth told him. "To the left; the larboard side, that's correct, isn't it?" She was still resting against him as they walked down the companionway.

"Spoken like a true salt," Nichols reassured her.

"Here!" She pointed at a closed door.

It was past ten o'clock, and only one shielded lamp lit the corridor. Nichols tapped hesitantly, and a female voice answered.

"Nichols, ma'am, fourth officer."

After a brief flurry from inside, Kate opened the door, a gown pulled about her nightdress.

"Miss Hanshaw has had a nasty shock," Nichols informed her. "She will need her cabin."

"Of course." Kate stood to one side and allowed them in.

"You may light a candle," Nichols said, as he seated the girl on Kate's sea chest. "I will not stay, but guard the flame and keep it burning all the night if you so wish."

A yellow glow soon lit the tiny room. Kate replaced the tinder striker and turned to them.

"I will leave also, there is another berth," she said.

"No, please!" Elizabeth's hand went out to the other woman in supplication. "You may stay, there is room for two, surely?"

Nichols looked about. "I will have another cot brought. And arrange for your things from the roundhouse cabin."

Elizabeth reluctantly released his hand. "You have been very kind."

Freed from her contact, Nichols felt his old stumbling stupidity return. "I regret the need, ma'am," he said, lying only very slightly, "but trust you will enjoy a better night now."

"Thank you, George."

He smiled awkwardly, before turning and ducking out of the small door.

Kate looked at Elizabeth. "It would seem to have been an eventful time," she said.

"I've known nights more restful. Is there news of the captain?"

"The captain?" Kate's eyebrows rose. "He was shouting rather loudly earlier - was that anything to do with you?"

"I fear it might be."

A tap at the door, and Crowley appeared with a cot.

"Sling it to the other side, Michael," Kate said. "There should be room."

There was, and soon the two women were alone again.

"All may be told in the morning, should you so wish. But now I think sleep is called for."

"Sleep seems a very long way off at present." Elizabeth sighed.

Kate nodded, "So I would suspect, but no talk of the captain, eh? In my experience nothing good has ever come from that quarter—though you can surely tell me more about George, if you wish."

* * *

Drayton's next visit was back to Elizabeth's roundhouse cabin, but finding it empty, he called on the captain's quarters instead. The room was very much as it had been left. He looked about, noticing Rogers's writing desk, empty apart from a decanter of brandy and a half-filled glass. He glanced round when Luck, the servant, entered.

"The captain is returning; you may make preparations to receive him. I assume he will be retiring forthwith."

"Very good, sir."

"And he is not to be disturbed during the night. See to it; sit up outside his door if need be." A thought occurred to him. "Tell me, has anything been moved since Mr Rogers was taken from here?"

"No sir, I have been waiting for news."

Drayton nodded and glanced about. All appeared to be in place, although there was no sign of a quill or any letter in preparation. His gaze swept around as he went to leave, and it was then that he noticed something amiss. Luck had gone, and Drayton stepped quietly as he moved across and collected the small wooden knitting needle from the deck. Examining it for a moment, he touched the point experimentally with his finger. Many seamen indulged in all types of handicrafts, from lace making to scrimshaw, but Rogers did not strike him as one who might knit. He looked about the cabin again, searching for inspiration, and was about to replace the needle where he found it when something else caught his attention. It was the hole in the bulkhead. He moved across and examined it, then cautiously proffered his eye and peeped through. There was little to be seen as the girl's cabin was in darkness, but Drayton thought he had discovered enough. Slipping the needle back through the hole, he strode briskly out of the captain's quarters and returned to his own.

* * *

By the following day, the mood in the ship was considerably lighter. Paterson, transcribing the traverse board on to the deck log at the calling of the first dogwatch, decided that *Pevensey Castle* was now properly on her way. Nearly all the passengers were free from the constraints of seasickness; in fact several had already appeared to take in the fresh winter air that carried the faintest hint of spring and a promise of southern latitudes to sweeten it. Aloft, hands were skylarking and an unofficial game of crown and anchor was being played in the lee of the forecastle, something that Paterson and Langlois, the relieving officer, were quite prepared to tolerate for as long as it remained controlled.

Eight bells rang and the new men mustered. The quarter-master and helmsmen were replaced, and Paterson was about to go below when he noticed that an unusual number of Lascars were gathering in the waist. Some were clutching small cloths or rugs, and under the direction of the serang, they began to make for the forecastle. The men playing crown and anchor stopped to watch as Lascars from the old watch joined and grouped themselves in a tight pack on the deck. The serang pointed over the stern, and his men fell to the deck, prostrating themselves in a series of deep bows. Paterson and Langlois, standing on the quarterdeck, stirred uneasily at the sight of a group of men apparently paying obeisance in their direction.

"*'Asr*" Langlois said, finally. "Afternoon prayers."

"You seem to have picked up the lingo," Paterson grunted. The new man was certainly full of surprises.

"Their faith has interested me for a while." Langlois studied the log and made a small mark at the end. "Found a translation of the *Qur'an* last time I were in Bombay. I have it below now; you may see it if you wish. Made as much sense to me as any Bible."

"Each to his own, I suspect," Paterson mused, while the praying continued.

"Well, I can't pretend I am a follower of this, or any other religion." Langlois replaced the log in the binnacle, removed the pegs from the traverse board and wiped it clear, then dusted the chalk from his fingers with an elegant handkerchief. "But then I would not stand in the way of those who are."

"You don't believe in God?" Paterson asked, amazed.

Langlois gave a short laugh. "Oh I would be happy to," he said, "should He ever choose to believe in me."

The two officers relaxed as the Lascars completed their venerations and dispersed. The men playing crown and anchor returned to their game. Paterson realised that they had stopped throughout the period of prayer. "Well, if that's all they need to keep them content, I have no problem," he said.

The third mate was about to leave the deck when Langlois stopped him. "Any news of the captain?"

"Not a peep." He lowered his voice so that the midshipman, quartermaster and other nearby hands were forced to strain quite hard to hear. "Word is he's laid up an' the surgeon won't sign him back for duties until he's off the laudanum."

"Has Willis been on deck?"

Paterson nodded. "Noon sights, an' he showed his face at six bells; took a look about then left me to it."

Langlois glanced across to the other ships in the convoy, all maintaining reasonable order, with the nearest escort, *Shearwater,* keeping watch to windward. The light was starting to fade, and before long they would be reducing sail for the night. "Can't pretend I miss him," he said.

* * *

Nichols was with Elizabeth in her cabin. He had been so since giving up the forenoon watch and seemed likely to remain until he was expected on deck again at the call of the second dog, in less than two hours' time. His very presence was flouting Company regulations, although neither of them appeared to care. They had shared several cups of tea, some biscuit and cheese and a conversation that had grown more intense with every bell. Now, with Kate due back at any moment, they were seated on her sea chest, their heads close together, and hands unashamedly entwined.

"But a school teacher; is that really you?" Even after knowing her for so short a period Nichols felt instinctively that it was not. "Spending each day with someone else's children? I can't think of anything worse."

"I can certainly think of plenty better," she said, smiling into his eyes.

"So why?"

She sighed. "Because there is little else a woman can do in this world, and I find eating rather essential."

"You hated being a governess."

"I hated being a governess working for that man Chesterton. You only had to see the way he treated his valet, and it were clear what he intended for me."

Nichols stirred uneasily at the thought. "It will not be easy," he said, trying to steer the conversation away. "The East India Company have total control over the country, and do not sanction missionary work of any type."

"Yes, my brother has said there have been problems; but his heart is set on a native school. It is needed, and must certainly make his work easier."

"And that is your ambition? To travel several thousands of miles on the open seas, to do a job that you will probably be unsuited for, and live in a country where you are not welcome?"

"Whether it is, or is not, my path is set."

"I do not believe that is ever the case, Elizabeth," he said, surprising himself. "You must always be in charge of your own life, and are certainly entitled to change your mind, should you so wish. To do otherwise is to be a slave."

"I wish that it were so easy."

"It could be. You can alter your course now, this very minute."

"And step into the sea?" she asked. "Thank you, George, but I should consider that rather a waste of life."

"Is ignoring your own dreams, in an attempt to fulfil your brother's, any less of one?"

There was a silence as both considered this. It was hard to explain that one of the main attractions of remaining in *Pevensey Castle* was sitting right beside her. The pause lasted slightly too long and something of their intimacy diminished, although neither tried to remove their hand from the other's.

"What would you really like?" he asked, finally. She shrugged.

"Strange as it may seem, I have been enjoying my time aboard ship. There is little that I miss on land."

"But you could go back." His words were measured, and he felt his throat begin to tighten as he spoke. "We are to call at Madeira, it would be little difficulty to arrange a transfer to a home-bound ship."

With his hand gently enclosing hers, she could find no credible answer. "I will continue to India," she said finally. "Even after all that has been, I find the travelling really rather pleasant."

"The travelling only takes a matter of months; you must expect to be in India for many years."

"What will you be doing?"

"Me?"

"Yes, you and this ship."

"After India?" he thought for a moment. "Why there will be some delay while we unload and resupply. Many will go ashore for a while, and some of the crew are bound to be exchanged. But I should think *Pevensey Castle* would be sailing within the month. On to China, probably a similar wait then and, once the grand chop has been granted, back to England."

"Grand chop?" she laughed. "It appears they will be feeding you at least."

"It is the procedure necessary for foreign ships to leave China," he explained.

"So you will be home within a year?"

"If I can call it home," he laughed. "No, a little longer, maybe next summer."

"Tis a pity I could not stay with the ship."

His eyes widened slightly, although he was quick enough to follow her thoughts. "I should like nothing better." He gave her hand the gentlest of squeezes. "But I fear that one aboard might raise objections."

She looked away, her thoughts elsewhere, and he found himself staring at her face. Mention of the captain had taken the child from her expression; she suddenly seemed more mature, even worldly. And she did not seem to notice, or mind, his attention.

Nichols had never been allowed to consider a woman so closely before. He had known many to be beautiful, but a chance to study that beauty in detail had always escaped him. Her mouth was perfectly formed with lips far less red when examined closely. The desire to kiss them was very hard to resist, although he felt instinctively that in doing so he was merely postponing the pleasure.

"But maybe another ship?" she turned back to him. "There must be jobs for women aboard?"

"Precious few, I fear," he said. It was on the tip of his tongue to say that many women who wished to travel married officers, but either sense, or stupidity, stopped him.

"Still, I am sure there is something I could do," she pondered. At that moment, a hesitant tap at the door brought them back to the real world. Both quickly dropped the other's hand and assumed as independent an attitude as was possible when sharing the same sea chest. Kate entered, wearing the warrant officer's jacket she favoured when working with the purser. She gave a knowing look to the couple as the ship's bell began to strike.

"Why, that's it!" Elizabeth laughed and turned to Nichols, squeezing him with sudden affection. "Kate here has all the joy of travel, and she is with her husband. I think I know the very thing!"

* * *

It was more than six days later, after *Pevensey Castle* had rounded Ushant, left the Channel and was truly in the North Atlantic, when Rogers was next seen. Striding out on to the quarterdeck he took King, the officer of the watch, quite by surprise, so much so that he was greeted with a less than formal gasp of astonishment, rather than the salute a captain was entitled to expect. Rogers glowered at him. Half of his face was covered in bandage, and what was not appeared pale and loose. It was as if he had suddenly grown too small for his skin, although the fire in his remaining eye still shone out, bright and defiant.

King hurriedly corrected his mistake and removed his hat. "Good morning, sir," he muttered, his voice slightly higher than usual. "I trust your wound is recovering well."

"My wound, and its present condition, is not of your concern, Mr King." The captain sniffed loudly, before reaching for the traverse board and glaring at it.

"We're heading..."

"I can see our heading, and will thank you to keep any further observations to yourself." He looked up suspiciously and stared at the convoy.

King withdrew to the leeward side of the quarterdeck. *Pevensey Castle* was the sternmost ship, as she had been for the past three days, but nothing else had changed since the captain was last abroad. There was little unusual in Rogers's behaviour, he told himself. The vast majority of ship captains, be they merchant or Royal, would behave in a similar manner, first call in the morning. And many might suspect their officers of all manner of misdemeanours; sometimes with good reason.

But then, the last week or so without Rogers had been extremely pleasant, and a great deal that was not officially ordered had taken place without the captain's knowledge. There were the exercises with the great guns, as well as sail drill from the Lascar boatswain, who had proved to be an exceptional seaman. And progress was made in other areas. The passengers were settling down to the rigours of shipboard life and starting to form their own social groups. Now that Rogers's extended lunches no longer monopolised the dining room cuddy, a whist school could meet there every afternoon. Some of the finer details about the captain were also starting to grow hazy, and many were actually looking forward to the rest of the voyage. But, now his presence was back, the old regimen looked likely to return.

It could have been intuition, or he might have even heard the captain leave his cabin, but Drayton made an appearance on the quarterdeck shortly afterwards. King withdrew even further as the two men fell into deep conversation. They spoke quietly, but with passion, for several minutes. At one point, Rogers broke away and took a stride or two about, but King noticed he soon returned to Drayton, waiting patiently by the weather bulwark.

Seven bells rang, the new watch was to be set in less than half an hour, and the ship would come alive, but still they talked, although it was clear that Rogers was now doing most of the listening. Then, with a swift turn on his heel, the captain walked away and made for his quarters under the poop. Drayton remained and took a pace forward to the binnacle. He stood there for a moment, hands clenched behind his back and greatcoat flapping as he rode with the ship's motion through the swell. Looking at him, King reminded himself that this was merely a passenger and that Mr Rogers, who apparently had just been dismissed from his own quarterdeck, was the captain.

CHAPTER NINE

They made good progress for a convoy of merchant ships. Clearly, the commodore was not in favour of slow passages, and the wind, blowing from the east, was aiding him by growing stronger with every passing day. The glass had also been dropping, although none of the experienced sailors needed any mechanical aids, they understood only too well that a storm was in the offing. Khan, the Lascar boatswain, had noted several deficiencies in their rig that he wanted to rectify before the bad weather arrived. Ward and Johnston were part of the team assisting him, and as they finally wound a fresh larboard mizzen topmast shroud tight, all shared in a brief moment of triumph.

"That'll hold," Ward informed them, pulling back on the line with grim satisfaction. It was on the lee side and remained relatively slack, but all knew it would tighten to iron hard once they changed tack. "Jus' 'ave to reeve in the ratlines, an' there's one more we can rely on."

"The others are not as bad." Khan spoke with quiet authority, while Ward gave a thumbs up to the party below at the chains. "All can now wait until we reach harbour, although I wish to attend to the serving in several areas, and there are still the foretopmast braces."

"Aye, they gets a measure of use," Johnston agreed. "Want that we look to them next?"

Khan sniffed the wind and looked about. "I think we can leave those as well," he said finally. "The bad weather is getting closer, and we should prepare for work in different quarters."

"It'll be a bit of a blow, that's for sure," Ward nodded. "The cap'n might be asking for preventer stays."

The Lascar's eyes rolled slightly. "If he does, you can be certain we will have little notice."

"I'll rouse out the lines and have them ready." Ward glanced across to Johnston. "Better make a start on the ratlines, we may not get the chance later."

A sudden gust of wind blew a high-pitched whine through the taut stays. All three tightened their hold while the ship gave a lurch to leeward and plunged down into the depth of a wave.

"Reckon that's a taste of things to come." Johnston grinned, recovering himself. "It's going to be a proper thumper an' no mistake." The ship was surging forward now, and the spars about them creaked alarmingly; it could only be a matter of minutes before the officer of the watch called for a reduction in sail. The men watched in silent fascination while the storm bore down on them.

"We're going to be in for a night of it, sure enough," Ward muttered, when the first drops of rain began. Dusk was coming early; the horizon had already grown dark and indistinct, and the slatches on the windward waves were large and almost upon them. *Pevensey Castle* gave another surge, one that broke the pattern which was already becoming established, and this time they were all caught unawares. Johnston, in the act of transferring himself to the shrouds, felt his feet slip away, until he was hanging by his hands from a ratline. Ward noticed his friend's predicament and reached out for him, only to find himself stumbling in the process. He fell against Khan, knocking the man free of his own hold. The two clung to each other for mutual support and were in danger of falling from the crosstrees when Johnston, who had now regained his footing, swung himself in and grabbed at them both. The top twisted and heaved as the trio hurriedly secured themselves, before giving way to mutual laughter. Johnston, now steadied, reached again for the shrouds.

"Take us for a party of landsmen," Ward snorted, wiping his eyes with one tarred hand.

"I seen a bunch of Newgate offerings act less lubberly." Johnston was back on the shrouds now, and about to descend.

"Better remain for the present," Khan said. "If the t'gallants are not taken in immediately they will blow out."

"Aye, if you got to go, take a backstay," Ward agreed. The call from deck was surely only seconds away. "Head down the shrouds now an' you'll be stampeded in the rush. Most of 'em will be Lascars, so they won't knock you off; but you could be tickled to death."

* * *

"Take in t'gallants!" Paterson roared. The captain's standing orders stated clearly that no change of sail should be undertaken without his or the first mate's consent, but then Paterson had already sent two messages without response and now regarded the situation as dangerous. The quartermaster, tired of wrestling with the wheel, bellowed at the sheltering topmen. Soon the tight weather shrouds were dark with clambering bodies, fighting to keep a grip of the naked ratlines. Ward, who had followed Johnston down, watched as the sails were taken in.

"Begin with the lee clew!" he shouted. If the weather sheet were started first the sail would belly off to leeward, being of a lighter cloth than that used for topsails or courses. However, the mizzen topgallant was already heavy with moisture and could be controlled and brought in relatively easily.

The movement on deck, though not as extreme as that at the crosstrees, was no more predictable. *Pevensey Castle* bucked and twisted in the growing swell, her ponderous bow and kettle bottom giving the action little grace. Like a cow trying to dance, she lurched and shuddered in the heaving sea, while her heavy hull, freed from the steadying pressure of the upper sails, began to roll sickeningly.

Shearwater was stationed to windward, and making far better of the weather. She had also taken in topgallants, although her reduction was less critical than the one Paterson called for. The frigate's hull was sleek and flowing; she might even have carried more canvas rather than less. Right now, she could as easily be flying past at an incredible speed, instead of being chained to this crowd of lubberly, overweight tubs who were in very real danger of losing spars.

Willis finally appeared on the quarterdeck, followed a moment later by his servant carrying neatly folded oilskins and a sou'wester. The chief mate acknowledged Paterson with no more than a single glance before looking up to the sails and across to the convoy. The rain was easing off slightly and now came in hard individual drops. Powered by the wind, they stung any exposed flesh. Paterson pulled his watchcoat about him, while Willis clambered clumsily into his oilskins.

"Reckon it will be worse before better," Paterson chanced. Willis merely grunted in reply. He stared up at the sails once more, while leaning forward slightly and gauging the ship's motion.

"Reef topsails," he said suddenly. Paterson looked at him. The ship's motion had already eased considerably.

"Take in a single reef, Mr Willis?" he asked.

"No, fully reef her," the senior mate replied. "And look sharp!"

The boatswain's pipes whistled as the topmen clambered up to the topsail yards. The seamen, now thoroughly wet, leant over the swaying yard, and pulled up the heavy sails, breaking nails and skinning fingers as they did. The lack of pressure from aloft made the ship roll further, and her speed dropped considerably

"Signal from flag." Drummond was the midshipman of the watch and pressed his eye to the deck glass as a string of bunting broke out from the leading ship. "Make all sail commensurate with the weather."

It was clear that the commodore intended to run the storm out; a bold move when commanding a convoy of Indiamen. Paterson cursed softly to himself, it meant another trip up for the topmen. They were under topsails with forecourse, jib and staysails also set, so there was nothing else for it but to shake out those reefs. He looked to Willis, but the senior mate gave no sign of having heard the midshipman, or countermanding his last order. Drummond spoke again—a further signal from the flag, this time for a change of course.

"Steer three points to starboard," Paterson yelled. "Braces there!" The wind moved across their quarter as they turned, until it was blowing almost directly over the taffrail.

"Take in stays an' jib," Willis added, when the canvas fell flat. *Pevensey Castle* was before the wind now and falling behind very slightly. Already the head of the convoy was all but obscured in the gathering storm.

"Chance is we shall keep running till night fall, then heave to and head south again." Paterson spoke conversationally and with little hope of an answer. He was not disappointed: again Willis affected not to hear. Paterson raised his eyes to heaven; clearly the first mate was in no need of advice, even if it had been a fair assumption.

But when the second dogwatch was called, and the convoy was clearly slipping away, there had still been no signal. Willis had gone below some time ago, and Langlois, the current officer of the watch, began to grow worried. The convoy could still be seen under the faintest of running lights, but darkness was closing fast about them. *Pevensey Castle* was decidedly last and even *Shearwater*, the sternmost escort, was gathering speed and now could only be dimly perceived off their larboard beam.

"Afraid of losing the rest." Nichols, who had stayed on after standing the first dog, pointed at the frigate. "She'll be passing us in a trice. Belike we should shake out those reefs."

"Signal from *Shearwater*." Taylor, the curly haired midshipman of the watch, peered through the gloom as a series of lights appeared on the frigate. He was relatively inexperienced in signals, and had yet to master the complex system of lights used for night time communications. There was a distinct pause while he flipped through the book, conscious of the eyes of his superiors upon him.

"Take your time, lad," Nichols told him, with only a trace of irony.

The boy picked up the book from where it had fallen, then miraculously found the correct place almost at once.

"Our number, sir. Keep better station," the lad reported, trying to keep any hint of disapproval from his voice.

"Very good, Mr Taylor," Langlois replied, equally formally. "Thank you."

* * *

"I think we should call the captain once more," Langlois said, some while later. The sky had darkened completely, and there was now no other ship in sight. "The rest have reached ahead of us. If we miss the signal to change course we shall be lost."

"Signal will be by lights," Nichols reminded him. "And bound to be repeated by *Shearwater* and the other escorts."

"But the commodore's ship is way off. For all we knows the signal's been made, the head's turning and we're left ploughing on regardless." Langlois ducked while a rogue wave broke over them. "We could summon Willis again at least," he said, brushing the water from his watchcoat as if it were fine woollen broadcloth.

Nichols nodded and despatched Taylor, who had taken to sheltering by the bulwark.

The first mate appeared shortly afterwards, this time already wearing his oilskins. The ship lurched as he gained the quarterdeck, although that hardly explained the stumble that almost sent him sliding into the lee scuppers. Langlois stepped forward and extended a hand, which was roughly brushed away as the man staggered to his feet.

"Leave me!" he shouted with unnecessary force, while he made his way uncertainly to the binnacle.

"We are concerned about losing the convoy," Nichols explained. "*Shearwater*'s already censured us for falling behind, and we've slipped further since. The last time we called the captain was some time back, but he has yet to appear."

Willis shook his head determinedly, then his eyes opened wide and he took a firmer hold on the binnacle. "Has there been any instruction from the commodore?" he asked, thickly.

"No signal yet, though one could have been made, and not seen."

Willis stared at them both with a belligerent expression. "If you've missed it, I'll see you in the fo'c'sle!" he said.

Langlois looked about. The sea was rising around them, huge Atlantic rollers all but engulfed the ship on either side; the storm was certainly growing to its peak. Willis collected the speaking trumpet from the binnacle and leaned back.

"Masthead! What do you see of the convoy?"

The pause lasted far too long, and for a moment Langlois wondered if Willis had even been heard. Then a faint but hoarse voice replied. "No sign. Last sighting was fine on the larboard bow."

"We appear to have lost them," Langlois said. "I agree with Mr Nichols; the captain must take charge."

Willis placed a hand to his forehead. "The captain is not well," he mumbled. "We were dining together and his wound troubles him greatly."

"Then it's up to you," Nichols said bluntly. "The commodore must surely have ordered us south by now. We should turn; then at least may heave to and gain some respite. To carry on as we are only takes us deeper into the Atlantic."

Willis glared about the deck as if wishing to find something to blame. He snatched up the traverse board; the wooden pegs that indicated heading and speed, were set firm, but any comments that might have been chalked on the slate had been made illegible by the flying spray. "You're certain there was no signal?"

"We saw none, but you can judge the conditions for yourself," Langlois said, marvelling at the man's stupidity. The creaking in the yards told how, even fully reefed, the remaining sails were straining. If they did not heave to, they would have to continue under bare poles. "Reefing the topsails early put us behind; the signal might well have been made, and missed."

"In which case you will answer for it, Mr Langlois," Willis all but spat the words out. Then he sighed and lowered his head for a moment. "Take her to larboard, damn it, and bring her to. Back mizzen," the order came out slowly and without emphasis. The other officers had to struggle to hear.

"Mizzen, sir?" Nichols felt obliged to ask. The mizzen crossjack yard would be liable to foul the main, making the ship more likely to fall off. The first mate looked up and glowered at him.

"Very well, damn you. Back main!"

Nichols touched the brim of his sou'wester and gave the order, and the ship began to turn as the braces were heaved round. The wind was coming over their larboard quarter now, and the waves struck her hull at a slight angle, although in a world that was filled with turmoil, the pressure on the sails kept them relatively steady. Both Nichols and Langlois drew a sigh of relief, the headlong rush into the Atlantic had ended, and they would remain comparatively stationary while the storm raged about them.

"Double the lookout." Willis, who appeared anything but eased, was still standing, clutching to the binnacle cabinet as if it, rather than him, was liable to fly away. "I want to know as soon as we spot the convoy." He paused, as if momentarily unwell, "And if we fail to have sight at dawn, you can both expect to finish the trip in different accommodation."

The first mate turned and made an uncertain passage back to the roundhouse cuddy. Langlois and Nichols exchanged glances as Midshipman Taylor was despatched to the masthead.

"It'll be a spell afore we knows," the fourth mate said, while the youngster started up the larboard shrouds. "Eight hours of darkness at the very minimum, and not much relief after if this lot keeps up."

Langlois nodded, and shook the spray from the front of his watchcoat. "Then we shall just have to pray that it does not," he said.

* * *

But the morning brought no comfort, and very little light. *Pevensey Castle* was still riding tremendous waves, while the wind blew strong and hard, pressing her hull over, making the yards creak and causing the lines to scream like a thousand ill-tuned fiddles. Paterson had the morning watch and found himself joined by Nichols, Langlois and King when eight bells was about to be rung.

"Black as Hades's knocker," Nichols grumbled as the four officers stood on the drenched deck. The new masthead lookouts had already reported no sightings, and it was clear that the bad weather would remain for a good while longer.

Langlois looked at the traverse board and shook his head. "It will be down to dead reckoning; no chance of a sight now, nor probably at noon." By mutual agreement, the group moved to the dubious shelter of the weather bulwark where some form of conversation would be easier.

Paterson was the first to speak. "We've been lying to for so long I'm not sure what Seagrove will make of it." The others nodded. Having been at the mercy of currents for more than twelve hours, the ship might have been swept a hundred miles or ten; even the exact direction was hard to calculate. Responsibility for navigation fell to the second officer, although it would take as much intuition as skill to place them within a fifty-mile radius.

"Captain's not going to be pleased about this," King added, glumly.

"Captain has to take responsibility," Nichols replied. "Right now it should be him and the other two up here getting their faces washed."

"He must know we're not under convoy." Langlois was conscious that it was during his watch that they had lost sight of the other ships.

"Willis will have to speak for that," Paterson said quickly. "It was his decision to shorten sail when we did."

"We won't be the only ones." Nichols brushed some of the surface water from his oilskins and adjusted his cotton scarf. "I'd be surprised if there is more 'an five of them together b'now. Escorts are going to have a lively time rounding them all up."

"But the rest may well have changed course," Paterson reminded him. "They could be miles away and heading Lord knows where."

"We'll certainly be lucky to find them once this clears,"

"So what are we to do?" King asked. "Continue alone?"

"Escorts were to leave the convoy at thirty-seven degrees," Langlois replied. "But I should not care to travel independently, even after that."

"Well, we shall have to; that or make a run for a neutral port." Nichols mused. "Or even over to Gibraltar if needs be."

Patterson shook his head. "Too close to the North African coast for my liking." He was due to go off watch and felt desperately tired. "Fat Indiaman sailing unprotected; pirates would be queuing up to meet us, that's if a privateer or national ship don't take us first."

At that moment, the cuddy door opened and Rogers himself appeared on the quarterdeck. He was dressed in thick oilskins, with a sou'wester pulled tightly over his head and covering his ears. His face was quite exposed, however, and appeared pale and sickly. He stared about the deck, finally spotting the group cowering by the bulwark. As he glared at them, it was obvious that his white bandage had been replaced by a neat black patch.

"Talking of pirates..." Nichols said, as the officers rose to meet him.

* * *

The conditions below grew worse as the storm continued. Each deck was thoroughly soaked, with water seeping in through every conceivable crack; even the solid oak frames seemed to ooze the stuff. The ship vibrated with a constant clatter from the chain pumps, a monotonous noise that irritated beyond measure and mingled oddly with the distinctly agricultural sound and smell of frightened animals. *Pevensey Castle*'s erratic motion had caused accidents amongst passengers and crew alike, and much of the better furniture, the fine pieces ordered by wealthy travellers to indulge and impress, now lay in splinters.

Kate had commandeered the lower steerage mess, where most of the women now assembled. It was not a pretty place; several were severely seasick, and a couple seemed close to madness, although the rest did what they could to retain some degree of dignity. The old social status had started to dissolve from the start, and former ranks and positions now mattered very little. One of the passengers, Mrs Crabtree, the wife of a tea trader, seemed particularly adept at comforting the nervous. In this, she was aided by a robust, tireless *bonhomie* as well as small sips from a bottle of brandy. And Susan, one of Mrs Drayton's maids, had earlier avoided the plunge into hysteria by starting to sing. She was doing so now, with a loud and infectious voice that attracted many others. The small stuffy room heaved and rolled while a chorus of mixed voices ripped through a varied selection of popular songs in a tuneless and often repetitive bellow.

Kate soon abandoned all attempts at making tea, but passed out cups of water or milk as required, and a card school was in progress towards the stern. The only man amongst them had been accepted by mutual consent. Jack, a teenage cadet, had shunned the masculine society of the great cabin and now joined three women, two servants and the wife of a brigadier who were watching with rapt attention as Elizabeth attempted to teach them the intricacies of crochet, the recent craze that was just starting to spread throughout Europe.

The officers who were not on duty took what rest they could in the roundhouse cuddy. Now cleared of the great table, the room was laid out like a dormitory with hammocks hung permanently from the deckhead, quite the best way of sleeping during a storm.

Below, the great cabin had no such luxury, but most of the male passengers gathered there. The majority of the tiny sectioned-off cubicles were equipped with domestic beds. Though secured firmly enough to the deck, it was impossible to lie on them, as the furniture seemed intent on flinging any that tried against the opposite bulkhead. The hard straw mattresses also absorbed moisture as readily as dried-out sponges and were already starting to smell abominably. Instead, the men assembled in the dining lobby, some attempting to sit on the fixed lockers, while most gave up the fight and squatted or lay in groups on the deck. Here there was no singing, although the constant murmur of conversation reassured all, and for others consolation lay in a different direction. Card games were played for impossibly high stakes, and the thick canvas sheeting that covered the deck ran wet with a mixture of sea and bilge water which was oddly coloured with spilled port wine and spirits.

Some of the married couples stayed together. Squashed in their screened-off cabins, they sat hand-in-hand, or in even closer intimacy, while their wooden world rocked itself seemingly to destruction about them. For many it was their first experience of travel at sea, and for most, a true storm. Any dreams of prosperity or contentment that might have brought them to this place were being hurriedly reassessed.

In the forecastle, the senior hands were faring best of all. Though cold, tired, wet and, for the most part, thoroughly sick of working on deck, they were managing life as near normal as was possible. Johnston and Khan were even eating a scratch meal. The galley fire had long been extinguished, but cheese and biscuit were still available and this early into the voyage, both were of a reasonable quality. Johnston was tucking heartily into his, cutting chunks of cheese with his clasp knife. Khan was eating more sedately, dipping the hard dusty biscuit into a small measure of oil, which he found more acceptable than the heavily salted butter.

"Don't eat much do you?" Johnston asked, as he topped his half-filled mouth up to capacity.

"It is sufficient for the son of Adam to have just a few mouthfuls to give him the strength he needs."

"Few mouthfuls won't carry you far in a storm like this." Johnston leaned forward and prodded the boatswain's lithe frame. "You need some meat on you—an' some inside, that's if you're going to live through this little lot."

Khan's expression was quite serene while he watched his friend stuff the last of the biscuit into his mouth and crunch noisily. "If I fill my stomach at all," he said softly, "It is one-third for food, one-third for drink and one-third for air."

Johnston considered this for a moment, his mouth still half full and slightly open. "Drink I can understand," he said eventually. "Though I knows you don't take no strong stuff. But air?" he shook his head dismissively, took a pull from his tankard and swallowed noisily. "A fellow your size, he don't need no air."

* * *

It continued for a further two days and three nights. Throughout that time conditions grew steadily worse and the working men more tired, until many were close to choosing an early death as a suitable alternative to living. Then, when dawn was due to break on the third morning, Paterson was amazed to note a proper lightening in the sky. The wind that had been howling through the lines for so long as to make the sound almost unnoticeable finally began to relent, and was replaced by a strange, uncertain calm.

Langlois and King, who came on deck at the beginning of the forenoon watch, looked about as if in wonder. The waves still rolled the hull, and there was rain off to leeward, but in the distance a faint horizon could be made out, and far off to the east, there was even a patch of clear sky.

"With luck we might be able to take a noon sight," Langlois said, approaching Paterson.

The third mate nodded and pulled his wet scarf from his watchcoat. "Aye, though I'd give a fair sum to know how far we've drifted."

King looked up at the weathervane. The wind was blowing more fitfully now, and all knew it might change in the next few hours.

"Captain been up?" The question was asked with every new watch, and Paterson grinned as he replied. "No, nor Willis or Seagrove, though I fancy one will show their faces during your trick."

In fact, it was less than an hour later when all three made their appearances. The fine weather had come, with even a measure of sunshine. All wore uniform jackets without watchcoat or oilskins, and Rogers's eye, though still bloodshot, was proudly uncovered. Langlois, at his position by the binnacle, saluted smartly and was ignored by all as the three glanced up at the sails and sniffed the air.

"Bring her back to the wind, if you please, Mr Langlois," Rogers said, acknowledging him at last. "Steer south and keep the lookouts doubled."

Langlois gave the command, the boatswain's call sounded, and soon the ship was actually making forward progress. The course made sense. However far they may have strayed from the convoy, a southerly heading would bring them closer to their eventual objective, and there was a strong chance of meeting with the other ships.

"Shake out those reefs and set stays and jib," the captain ordered. The topmen raced aloft, and *Pevensey Castle* began to heel slightly as the fresh canvas caught the wind. Soon they were ploughing ahead, with her rounded bow stubbing the heavy waves. It was good to know they were actually moving with a purpose again. Even the spray that was now being thrown back over the forecastle, the reverse of that experienced for the last few days, made a refreshing change. Langlois found his expression relaxing for the first time as the captain studied the traverse board and read the deck log.

"Not quite sure what's making you so happy, Mr Langlois," Rogers growled suspiciously. "I should have thought that missing a signal and losing us the convoy would be preying on your mind somewhat."

The fifth mate noticed how Willis's attention suddenly seemed to drift. "I have nothing to concern myself with, sir," he said quietly.

"Nothing?" Rogers seemed surprised. "A court of enquiry does not disturb you? Nor the prospect of forgoing your rank? Really, you astonish me."

"I am a fifth mate, sir." Langlois spoke slowly. "There is little to be lost in such a position. And the circumstances leading up to the missing of the convoy do not unsettle me in any measure. A court of enquiry would certainly put matters straight, and I will gladly attend any such investigation, should you wish to summon one."

Rogers snorted and went to turn away. "We shall see," he said, calling the other two officers with a casual backwards wave of his thumb. "But do not make yourself too secure, Mr Langlois. The events of the last few days will not look well in my report, and if there is a penalty to be paid for what has occurred, I shall be certain to see it is you who pays it."

CHAPTER TEN

"There we have it, gentlemen; I'm afraid that, due to the incompetence of my junior officers, we have temporarily lost the convoy." Rogers's glance took in the entire assembly. There were few expressions of surprise or concern; most were well aware of the situation, although he clearly had the attention of every man in the cuddy as he finished speaking.

For a moment there was silence, then Drayton spoke. "So, captain; what do you propose?"

Rogers guessed there would be trouble from that quarter. He gave a confident smile. "Obviously we are doing all we can to regain an escort, and our present position, being some distance from the nearest land, should mean we will be safe from any unwanted enemy attention." *Unwanted enemy attention*, he liked that phrase. It was the kind a true fighting captain used—one who would not be greatly disturbed if an enemy did choose to bother him. "If there are any further questions, Mr Willis or myself will gladly answer them." He repeated his reassuring look and was pleased to note that several smiled in return. Relieved, he made as if to stand when a crusty old officer from one of the Company's military divisions cleared his throat.

"May I ask, sir, exactly when do you expect to regain contact with our escorts?"

It was a damned fool question, and Rogers was about to tell

him so when Willis, sitting at the foot of the table, interrupted.

"That is not easy to predict, colonel." As usual, the first mate's voice held just the right measure of plum, and all eyes turned to him as he continued. "The storm lasted for three full days after the convoy was missed. Naturally we have a good idea where they can be found, but an accurate estimation of our meeting cannot be made."

"Well, how the devil did you come to lose them in the first place?" Rogers was pleased that the officer's question was directed at Willis. He glanced quickly at Drayton, who appeared to be watching the proceedings with no more than the expected interest.

The senior mate spread his hands wide. "A sad mixture of inexperience and foolishness," he said. "I was not on deck at the time; the officer of the watch was concerned that the storm might worsen, and ordered a rather drastic reduction in sail without gaining permission. That might have been bad enough, but it appears that a signal for a change of course was also missed."

"Appears?" the old boy was apparently astonished. "Why were there no senior men on deck?"

"Sadly we cannot be on watch at every hour, sir." Willis said stiffly.

"In my experience that is very much the case." The colonel looked about at the others for support and received murmurs of agreement. "Indeed for any of the superior officers to be on deck at all is an uncommon enough occasion; during the recent storm it I'd wager it was rare indeed."

Drayton stirred in his seat, clearly intending to speak, and Rogers's heart fell. The man was starting to be a nuisance, poking his over-long nose into matters that did not concern him. It was bad enough when he interfered over that damned Hanshaw business, threatening to send in a report to the Company, as if those numbskulls in Leadenhall Street cared a fig what happened between a captain and his passenger. Rogers felt his bad eye begin to throb as Drayton gained the floor.

"If I may interject here, gentlemen, I think you are being a trifle harsh on the captain." Rogers considered him with suspicion while he continued. "It is not an uncommon matter for a ship to lose a convoy, especially considering the storm we have just endured. Indeed, I would be surprised if more than a few ships are still in contact with any of the escorts. What Mr Rogers proposes is standard procedure; the likelihood is strong that we will meet with other vessels, and be able to continue in company to our next stop, when the full convoy will re-form."

His words were spoken with calm assurance, and Rogers felt his concern lessen as he noted the reaction from the other passengers.

"And if not, if we should have to continue independently," Drayton's tone was lifting now, "then I think we can all be assured that Mr Rogers has proven his ability to defend us. One privateer has already felt the weight of our shot, and I am sure there is plenty more in store if it be needed, ain't that right, captain?"

The atmosphere was lightening considerably; even the crusty old officer could be seen to relax. "Indeed, sir," Rogers was quick to reply. "Powder and shot a plenty, and men more than willing to fight. I cannot offer more!"

That was the way to finish such a gathering. The passengers were actually joking with each other when they stood to leave. Rogers looked his appreciation at Drayton.

"I thank you for your support, sir," he said softly, as the last were quitting the cuddy. "It was not the easiest of meetings."

Drayton rose stiffly and brushed some fluff from his jacket. "No captain, I should say not. But it needed to be held, and it would have been of little use if the passengers departed with anything other than confident hearts." There were only the two of them in the room now, and he turned and regarded the captain for several seconds before continuing. "But I will say this to you, Captain Rogers; your performance, and that of your senior officers, has been a disgrace to date. I urge you to make every effort to regain the convoy and see us safely to our destination. Otherwise, you can discard any thoughts you might have entertained of continuing your career with the East India Company. Do I make myself clear?"

* * *

The second of Langlois's sketches was more detailed. It showed Kate from the side, at a slightly acute angle, her long hair mildly adrift and with an expression set in deep concentration, although the beauty of her face was in no way diminished.

"When did he do this?" Manning asked, as he examined the drawing more closely.

"I have no idea," Kate replied. She was sorting clothes and not particularly interested in pictures. "Maybe when I was working in the pantry?"

"You've been with him in the pantry?" Manning said the words and felt instantly foolish. "I mean, it must have taken some time."

"The pantry, or maybe the mess, I really don't know." She finished folding the shirt and regarded him sternly. "He came by the afternoon following the storm," she said. "And stayed no more than a moment. Just long enough to check on supplies of lamp oil, if I remember rightly."

"But this is more detailed," he said, looking again at the many intricate lines that captured her so perfectly.

"Yes, he is a fine artist; but I did not sit for him, if that's what you mean. I don't have the time, and if I did, would not waste it so."

Manning felt more uncomfortable. What Kate said was absolutely right and made perfect sense, but he still could not reconcile the thought that another man should have taken such a careful study of her. She was his wife, after all.

"He is drawing all the while, Robert. Have you not seen?"

"Only the ones of you," he said stubbornly.

"Well, there are many others. Members of the crew; there was one of an elderly passenger—I believe she gave him a considerable sum, though cannot be sure. And a rather good likeness of Mr Seagrove, though it might be better if he did not see it."

"And they are all of people?" Manning asked.

"Yes, now you come to mention it, but then I chance that is his speciality. Some paint bowls of fruit, after all."

He looked again at the picture. So detailed, so beautifully portrayed, so right. "He must have a memory for faces," he said, almost meditatively.

"I think he probably has." She looked again over his shoulder. "It would have taken quite a time." Suddenly tender, she placed a hand upon his arm. "Robert, there is nothing between Mr Langlois and me," she said softly. "I married you and it is you I wish to stay with. If you think otherwise...well, I find it rather annoying. Especially as we are so close to our wedding."

He smiled and put down the paper. "I have never been one so very confident in these matters." Reaching back, he placed one hand over hers. "Never been confident at all, if it comes to it. But when I have something so precious, so..."

She rested a finger gently across his mouth. "Let that be an end of it." Her voice carried that mock firmness that he found so attractive. "Besides, I might hazard a guess that some of his other subjects interest Mr Langlois far more than I do."

* * *

They sailed on for two days in light sunshine and steady winds, conditions that were as welcome after the storm as water in the desert. For more than two hundred miles a stable pace was kept. At no time was either sail or land sighted, and by noon on the third day they were reckoned to be forty-three degrees south. Longitude was less easy to estimate and varied considerably with each working, but it was generally considered that *Pevensey Castle* lay approximately a hundred miles from the coast of northern Spain. With the need to meet up with the convoy paramount, lookouts remained doubled throughout, and when the long-awaited call finally came, they were ready for it.

"Over on the larboard beam," the masthead answered King's question instantly. "Comin' up fast an' sailing large with a quartering wind!"

King nodded to Taylor, the junior midshipman, who made for the roundhouse and the captain's cabin. It was five bells in the afternoon watch, and most of the officers had just finished dining. Paterson, on deck and taking the air, sauntered across to join the acting mate.

"Maybe the first of many, or just another straggler, but at least we seem to have found company," he said.

"Assuming she is British," King reminded him.

"Ah yes." Paterson was relaxed after his meal and grinned rather sheepishly. "That was, perhaps, a premature presumption."

The captain had yet to dine and came on deck with an angry countenance that made both officers stiffen.

"Where away?" he snapped.

"To the east, off the larboard beam." King indicated where the unseen ship should soon be appearing to those on deck. Rogers snorted and glared about him.

"Take that down immediately," he said, indicating the Company flag currently flying from the main. "Hoist the commissioning pennant and rouse out a Navy ensign."

King gave the orders. They were sensible precautions to take. An Indiaman sailing alone was a rare enough sight, to disguise her as a British man-of-war was a simple matter and might fool a long-range inspection. Should the approaching ship be a privateer, or even a small national vessel, it might well be discouraged by what was apparently a powerful British frigate.

"What do you see there?" Rogers bellowed impatiently, as the long pennant was set and streamed out in the wind.

"Ship rigged; and t'gallants showing," Clegg, one of the masthead lookouts replied. "Course seems to be to the sou-west."

Paterson and King exchanged glances. A southwesterly course would intercept them; it was the typical behaviour of a warship intent on closing in the least possible time.

The passengers, who usually dined at three, were starting to assemble for their major meal of the day. There were already several small groups on the main deck, and the officers knew that the quarterdeck was soon to be alive with the more affluent, drinking their sherries and asking the most stupid of questions. Rogers took a pace or two, cursing under his breath.

"I have her courses now," Clegg's voice again. "Not such a deep roach, but still I'd say she were a warship. Small though; me'be a sloop."

King's mind began to race. A British ship of that size was unlikely to be alone in this part of the Atlantic unless escorting a convoy, and her course seemed to rule that out. Really, it was far more likely that they had met with another privateer.

These small, private, men-of-war had been acting independently for the past few years. The risks were high, and manpower hard to come by, although rewards for an enterprising captain or owner were vast—certainly worth the investment of obtaining and fitting out a vessel. Sizes ranged from barely more than open boats to three masted ships that might easily take on a frigate, and the fact that this one was apparently operating alone suggested something larger than the luggers they had seen off in the Channel. A sudden shout interrupted his thoughts.

"Damn it man, I have the business of the ship to attend to!" King looked up to see that Luck, Rogers's servant, was on deck, presumably to call his master to dinner. He retreated, along with two passengers and an Indian servant who was clutching a small gong to his chest. Clearly King's thoughts were shared, and the captain was equally concerned.

"Summon all hands," Rogers said, almost to himself. "Have that ensign bent and ready, and clear away the guns."

"Every one, sir?" King asked.

"Every damn one, Mr King!"

The screams of pipes and rumble of bare feet on deck interrupted some of the passengers, who were just making their stately progress to dine. Others, still in their cabins, were surprised by parties of seamen who burst through the fragile doors of their quarters and began to clear away the trussed-up cannon that had been keeping them silent company since they arrived. Many of these heavy guns had been incorporated into the living arrangements, and were doing service as makeshift clothes driers and wardrobes, or simply draped with cloth to hide their murderous purpose. With few words and no apologies, the men brushed all personal items aside and made the weapons ready for action. Round shot was brought up from the hold and laid out in the garlands that were being used as shelves and contained books and assorted small possessions. Cots, beds and other domestic furniture were roughly pushed to one side to give the weapons, and those who served them, room to work. The guns stowed in the hold were all but beyond reach. It might take several hours to haul up the barrels and mount them on carriages, although *Pevensey Castle* would still be able to offer a reasonable broadside, in terms of weight as well as number.

"Mr King!" Back on the quarterdeck, the young man jumped when his name was called, and he turned as the captain continued, "We'll have the royals on her, if you please, and hoist the Navy ensign."

King collected the speaking trumpet from its becket and bellowed the order. Soon the upper sails, dark rimmed across the heads from lack of use, were set and filling, and *Pevensey Castle* took on an extra measure of speed. It would not be enough to evade capture, however; already a brief smudge of masts and sails could be seen from the quarterdeck, to be gazed at and commented upon by the off-duty officers who were now starting to appear on deck. But the additional sails would buy them time; if they could string this out to darkness and another storm, or even a minor squall descended, it was possible they might escape completely.

"Take her to starboard," The captain spoke again. "Heading... Oh, confound it, man; as far away as we can reach!"

"Steer southwest," Paterson interrupted.

The helmsman turned the wheel, and the braces were brought round. Now that was taking things too far, King thought, when *Pevensey Castle* was settled on the same course as her pursuer. If the sighting was a privateer, there was no chance that their lubberly old tub would out-sail her, and any thoughts Rogers might have of disguising them as a warship were now lost. No British frigate would run at the first sight of a strange sail; the enemy must smoke them straight away.

"She's hull up now," Clegg reported. "I see gunports, an' she's going a fair pace."

"Colours?" King asked.

"Not yet," Clegg replied, his bellow being heard and attended to by all on board. "Weathered sails, though her lines are certainly French."

There were several small groups of both passengers and crew, and his report brought forth numerous discussions. Discoloured canvas meant very little; an active privateer could be expected to be showing worn sailcloth and, for a multitude of reasons, French lines were not uncommon in the British Navy.

"Problems, captain?" Drayton had appeared on deck wearing his ubiquitous greatcoat. King watched with interest as Rogers gave a brief report on the circumstances, his tone containing an odd mixture of respect and arrogance.

The man nodded, apparently understanding. "I notice the guns have been made ready; you will be clearing for action, I suppose?"

"In good time, sir, in good time." Rogers appeared to be physically irritated by the civilian's presence. "But first I intend to outrun."

Drayton looked across at the oncoming ship. Her upper sails were clearly visible from the deck now, and the idea that *Pevensey Castle* could increase her lead in any way was clearly laughable. Rogers sensed this and turned upon the man.

"Sir, you will do me a great service by allowing me to fight my ship." The officers on the quarterdeck cringed slightly, although Drayton seemed to take the outburst in good heart.

"Of course, captain, of course." His genial look encompassed the entire deck. "I will leave you gentlemen to what you do best."

Rogers glared about, seemingly keen to find another target. "Mr Seagrove, assemble the male passengers and equip them with small arms. Mr Robbins, attend to the arms chests, if you please." He paused, long enough for it to seem that he had not been prompted, then added curtly. "Clear for action."

* * *

The women were already heading for the hold, but began to hurry as parties of men started to tear down bulkheads and remove furniture about them. Kate and Elizabeth, who had taken an early meal together, reached the open hatch to find the ladders already in use.

"Give us some light, milady," a dark-tanned seaman spoke, not unkindly, to the first of the bustling line.

"We wish to seek shelter in the hold, Matthews," Kate told him.

"That's as may be, ma'am," the man knuckled his forehead briefly. "But we need to strike all we can below first. Let us carry on, an' we'll see you safe." He stepped back while a large sofa was manoeuvred past him and down one of the ladders. "Safe and comfortable," he added, winking broadly.

The women withdrew and the men continued with their work.

"Most have not dined," Elizabeth said. "Will you arrange for tea?"

Kate shook her head. "I fear that might not be possible, although I will try and send some cold victuals down."

"You will not be joining us?" The other girl seemed surprised.

"I'm sure you can look after the ladies," Kate replied, while further personal possessions were shunted past, with some all but thrown down the open hatch. "This appears to be a major action, and my place is in the sickbay."

"Can I assist?" Elizabeth asked.

"No, you will be better placed below. Share out what food I can find and try and keep everyone talking. Let no man down with you and, if we are taken, do all you can to keep the women together."

Elizabeth reached for her hand. "Do be careful," she said.

"And you, Elizabeth." Kate nodded and left her.

* * *

The bell rang once, it was four thirty, and light was starting to fade. King had been standing on the quarterdeck for over four hours and should have been hungry, although the sight that was on their larboard quarter was enough to quell even the strongest of appetites. The privateer, now in plain view, lay just out of gunshot range, her full sails tight, French national flag flying proudly, and a fine mist of spray breaking from her bow as she broached the Atlantic rollers. King looked away and back to his ship. About him, men stood ready at the larboard battery, and topmen were poised by the shrouds, although there seemed little they could do that had not already been tried. The ensign ruse had failed, as he predicted, although Rogers was not without other ideas. Additional sail was set, only to be taken in again when it was clear the hull would move no faster and they were in danger of losing masts and yards. At one point the captain even decided to wear to the northeast; it had taken the combined efforts of all the officers to dissuade him. A sudden change of direction might have put their adversary off for a while, but there was little that *Pevensey Castle* could achieve that would be both slick and surprising. The privateer, a tidy vessel, well rigged and lithe, was bound to be handier in stays. Now they waited, as the darkness slowly gathered about them, and the enemy grew steadily closer.

"She's intending to yaw," Willis muttered.

Sure enough, the ship was starting to turn; within minutes, she would be presenting her entire larboard battery to the merchant.

"It will cost her." Paterson was watching intently. The action was certainly increasing *Pevensey Castle*'s slight lead, but any gain would be easily offset by a well-aimed broadside.

A puff of smoke came from her side to be instantly dispersed by the steady wind. "She's opened fire!" Seagrove's shout came out in a higher pitch than he intended and he instantly turned his attention to the fastenings of his coat. The sound of a single gun rolled across the water, but there was no sign of any shot, and the other broadside guns remained silent. Langlois was studying the enemy through the deck glass, while Rogers paced backwards and forwards in a stride that was becoming increasingly erratic.

"She's turning back to her original course," Willis said, fingering the hilt of his sheathed sword nervously.

King looked about the crowded deck. It seemed ridiculous that they were simply standing and gaping while the enemy crept closer. Something could be done, something must, else they might just as well surrender immediately. Eventually it became too much, and he approached his captain.

"If we turned to larboard I could muster a broadside, sir," he said, already preparing himself for the rebuke. "Chance we might be able to strike a yard or two. It might buy us time."

Rogers glowered round at the enemy ship that he truly hated. No gun could be brought to bear on her on their present course, yet to do as King suggested would all but finish the chase.

"They are brim full of men, damn it!" the captain spat back. "Even a point will give them sea room; she'd be alongside before you can say knife."

"I don't see many aboard." It was Langlois's voice, slow and measured. He was still examining the privateer closely. "I'd say they were undermanned, sir."

Rogers strode across and roughly snatched the telescope from his hand, while Paterson and Nichols inspected the ship through their own personal glasses.

"Undermanned?" Rogers gave a short dismissive laugh. "Why, I can see enough to take this ship and several others after." He thrust the glass roughly back at the fifth mate.

"We could load round on grape." King felt unable to keep quiet. "That might gain us time, and cut the numbers down."

"You will be silent!" Rogers bellowed, then added more softly, "If anyone else has the temerity to offer advice, I shall dismiss them from the quarterdeck. Do I make myself clear?"

* * *

Manning and Keats had removed a canvas bulkhead and extended the sickbay to incorporate an area of adjoining deck, although the space was still less than twelve foot square, far smaller than the section of orlop reserved for dealing with the wounded in *Pandora*.

"Can I assist, Mr Keats?" Kate asked, as she entered.

The surgeon regarded her doubtfully. "I think not, ma'am; the work will be hard and not in the least pleasant."

"Kate served in the cockpit at Camperdown," Manning said simply.

Keats visibly relaxed. "Then you will indeed be welcome; we have no loblolly boys in this ship."

"And little space," she said, looking about the meagre area.

"I fancy we will not need more," the surgeon continued. "I do not expect a great number of casualties," he smiled grimly. "This will hardly be a fleet action."

* * *

The privateer had yawed again, and another shot came from her. This one struck them, hitting their taffrail and sending up a cloud of small splinters. The debris caught the wind and fluttered down about the men on the poop and quarterdeck like so many snowflakes. Nichols glanced across at Langlois, who grinned winningly back as he brushed the dust from his jacket. Rogers had withdrawn slightly and now stood at the lee side of the quarterdeck, with the bulk of the mizzenmast between him and any French guns.

King moved to the break of the quarterdeck and looked down to the waist where most of the male passengers and some of the afterguard were sheltering under the lee of the gangboards. All were armed, although he wondered how many of those carrying edged weapons were able to use them. The Company blunderbusses, evil-looking beasts with short stocks and gaping barrels, might be a better bet. Even the more reticent of civilians would be likely to have handled a firearm in the past. King knew from experience how much easier it was to squeeze a trigger and watch men fall from a distance, than moving in closer, exposing your own body to injury, and attempt to physically butcher another human.

The privateer did not alter course and a further shot was fired, although this one passed by and fell harmlessly into the sea. The enemy were being left behind, but he fancied he could see movement on their deck. He moved back and collected a glass. Yes, hands were going to the braces. A group clustered about the two cannon that had been fired, but it appeared that the other broadside guns were left unattended. He glanced across at Rogers, still fidgeting nervously by the fife rails. It was useless arguing with the man, his mind was made up and yet, properly handled, King was sure *Pevensey Castle* could put up more of a fight.

* * *

The hold was dark, even with four lanterns burning and Elizabeth found it difficult walking amongst the seated women. Kate had sent down some cold duff that was to have been their dessert, and she was distributing this, along with drafts of lemonade from a large pewter jug. All had been in high spirits at first, the earlier brush with enemy ships having instilled confidence and even bravado in some. But as soon as they received their first hit, the mood changed rapidly. Now they sat, most in stunned silence, although somewhere far away Elizabeth thought she could hear the sounds of gentle sobbing.

"Ain't you got nothin' stronger?" It was Susan, one of Mrs Drayton's maids; her mistress was at the other end of the group.

"Only lemonade," Elizabeth said, offering the jug.

The girl held out her cup to be filled, just as another shot struck. Two women shrieked and the sound of crying was now very apparent. The shock caused the jug to jolt, and liquid spilled over Susan's hand. Elizabeth apologised, but the girl shrugged. "Worse things have 'appened," she said.

* * *

The privateer was pierced for fourteen guns, all of which were bound to be far lighter than *Pevensey Castle*'s main armament. Granted, the enemy's weapons were probably more modern, better served and rigged to allow a greater arc of fire. And any boarding party the French might summon would also be made up of bloodthirsty thugs who were certain to have no interest in mercy. Still, King felt restless as he watched—watched and did nothing. Of them all, he was probably the only true fighting man; certainly no one else had seen action on so many occasions. He alone knew that, carefully planned, they could put up some form of resistance. To do nothing was tantamount to suicide.

The broadside idea was not so far off the mark, he thought, and provisions should be made in case they were boarded. Even now, the men in the waist could be receiving instruction; maybe being formed into individual groups, each under the command of an officer. He felt his fingers physically twitch as yet another shot came past overhead, this time punching a neat hole in the mizzen topsail. The privateer was on their larboard quarter and coming in fast, her guns trained as far forward as they could bear. *Pevensey Castle*'s cannon had antiquated tackle and would not be in range for several minutes. By then the French would be up with them. Alongside or, if King had been in command of the enemy ship, across their stern, with a raking broadside to knock out any remaining fight.

Yes, they were going to be taken, sure as eggs were eggs, yet all Rogers felt able to do was stretch out the inevitable to the last possible moment, while sheltering himself in the lee of a mast. King glanced about for some support. There was Paterson, Nichols, Langlois; men he knew well, men he trusted; yet they were of merchant stock and seemed quite content to stand by and let the enemy take control.

"She's turning!" Seagrove called out, his voice little more than a screech this time as he pointed at the enemy. Sure enough, her yards were being hauled round while the neat bow was pointing straight for them. She held her course for several minutes, eating up sea room as she did, then continued on until the wind came hard over her beam, and she started to creep past *Pevensey Castle*'s stern.

"She'll be taking us from starboard," King spoke, fighting instinct overcoming any reticence he might have felt. His words were picked up and brought on a number of changes; the gun crews hurriedly abandoned the larboard cannon, and crossed to starboard and the men in the waist dutifully formed up and began to mount the starboard gangboard. Rogers glanced nervously back at the enemy, then moved very slightly so that the mizzen still stayed between him and any danger.

The privateer cut across them at a fair rate. Peering through the gloom, King noted that the same men who had left the braces were now running out the guns. With the wind heeling her masts over, these naturally pointed at *Pevensey Castle*'s hull rather than her tophamper. From his vantage point on the quarterdeck, he was starting to lose sight of her behind the poop when the first of a series of flashes pierced the darkening evening. "Here it comes!" he shouted, and a round shot hit them low in the stern. Another smashed through the thin bulwark of the poop, apparently destroying a poultry coop. A man's scream came from below, followed by another shouting hysterically; sounds which mingled oddly with the honking and clucking from assorted poultry that flapped about the poop and quarterdeck in attempted flight. The bulwark next to the larboard mizzen chains crumbled, several shrouds grew slack, and Seagrove staggered, horribly wounded, and fell to the deck.

"Bosun!" Paterson shouted. Willis went to help the second mate, but turned away suddenly to be violently sick. Khan appeared with Ward and Johnston, the latter carrying a length of line. King moved to the opposite side to see the enemy pass them. Her guns were still run out, the crews presumably being used once more at the braces as she turned. Soon she would be coming up on their starboard counter.

"The guns are empty," he shouted at the captain. "They haven't reloaded—they don't have the crew!" Rogers stared at him stupidly, and even Paterson and Nichols seemed stunned. Only Langlois gathered the full meaning of King's words.

"We must turn to starboard," he said. "Give her a broadside."

Rogers took a step forward, and for one glorious moment King thought he might act. Then *Pevensey Castle* began to fall off the wind.

"Rudder's gone!" the quartermaster shouted as he turned the wheel to correct, only to find it spinning uselessly in his hands. The ship started to wallow and sails began to flap. A sudden creaking noise made itself known from the main yard, and slowly the spar separated by the maintop and the main topsail billowed out as *Pevensey Castle* lost speed.

"There's still a chance; starboard battery ready!" King shouted, moving up the quarterdeck and naturally assuming command of the great guns. Langlois was with him and seemed to be of the same mind. "Take the lower battery," King shouted, pointing towards the waist. "Fire on my word; we'll give them a bellyful!" Despite King being the junior officer, Langlois readily accepted his authority and was off, throwing himself down the ladder and calling for the gun captains to attend. King looked back towards the Frenchman. Now was the time to turn and present their full broadside, but with the wheel gone and the ship's way all but spent, there was little he could do. He bent down and peered along the barrel of the nearest gun. It was trained round as far as possible, but the enemy remained just outside the firing arc.

"Leave it, Mr King." Rogers's voice caught him unaware, and

he spun round in annoyance to see the captain standing right behind him. "Leave it, damn you," he repeated and then looked down to where Langlois was standing, his hand raised, signalling the battery ready. Rogers shook his head and Langlois's arm was slowly lowered, a look of mild confusion on the mate's face.

The captain moved back to where his officers were grouped by the binnacle. "Gentlemen, I am grateful for your support, but fear there is little now that can be done, and I, for one, do not wish to annoy our captors with needless violence." He paused in a manner that might have been contrived, had King not noticed the pallor of his face, and the fact that his hands were visibly shaking. "Mr Willis; the colours, if you please."

CHAPTER ELEVEN

They were taken.

The idea did not sit easily with King, as the privateer scraped alongside, and men he had been fighting moments before began to clamber aboard. Soon they were all over the ship, jubilant in victory, cheerfully shouting to one another while the male passengers were roughly disarmed, and gunners pushed away from their weapons. King supposed they were orderly enough, and even relatively well behaved; certainly British seamen would not have acted any better in the circumstances. But he knew instinctively that the act of invading their decks was just the start of many such minor pains of defeat that were to come. And the final insult was now very evident—there were so damn few of them.

The first to mount the quarterdeck appeared to be the privateer's captain; well dressed, with a long-tailed, olive green coat that looked vaguely military, white britches and a silk cravat. He was accompanied by two seamen armed with heavy, businesslike pistols. One also held a large lantern that shone brightly in the gloom of evening, lighting up the scene and making the French officer's black boots gleam. The captain regarded Rogers for a moment, then extended his hand, which was warily accepted.

"Forgive me for detaining you, gentlemen." His smile included the officers grouped on the quarterdeck. "I did not expect to meet with such a fine vessel. My name is André Passon, my own ship is the *Espérance,* and you will understand that I carry the *lettre de course*." The English was perfect, even if his strong French accent made some of the words sound strange.

Drayton, who had managed to separate himself from the other passengers, now appeared at the break of the quarterdeck and strode over to where they stood. A worried French officer, who looked no more than a boy, rushed behind him. Rogers's head was bowed slightly, but he said nothing as Drayton approached and addressed the captain.

"Richard Drayton, *je suis le propriétaire de ce navire.*"

"Ah, the owner of the ship!" The Frenchman exclaimed. "It is indeed a pleasure to meet with you." He shook Drayton's hand, as if he were welcoming an honoured guest.

Rogers looked up sharply and scowled. "I think you will find my father owns this ship," he said, glaring round at Drayton. "And I will thank you all to speak English."

The captain nodded slightly. "I regret, gentlemen, the original owner, or 'husband' I believe you say—that is of no consequence now. And yes, we will continue in English *certainement*."

Another Frenchman approached, not quite as well dressed as his captain, and resting a drawn sword over his shoulder.

"Ah, Marcel; there is no need for that." Passon brushed the naked blade away with the back of his hand. "And perhaps these gentlemen could be relieved of their *encombrements*?"

The boy officer turned and took Paterson's hanger, while the mate housed his own weapon and reached out, neatly removing Rogers's heavily decorated sword. For a moment, he stared in pleased surprise at the embellished hilt and blued, engraved blade, then stepped forward and grabbed greedily at the scabbard. Rogers drew back. The mate gave a short laugh and twisted the belt free.

"One is of little use without the other," the French captain said soothingly. "A fine piece like this will raise good money in France."

Rogers's curse only made the mate chuckle further as he examined his plunder.

"Please, do not concern yourself," the French captain said. "If you choose to cooperate with us, I shall be very happy to return the weapon." His eyes flashed. "Otherwise, I might have occasion to use it."

"What do you want with this ship?" Drayton asked.

"We shall be sailing her to France," the captain said simply. "You will be well treated and should be able to return to your own country in very little time. I regret that I must detain your vessel, and all she carries, however. We will be heading for Bayonne, our homeport, where it will be sold, along with the cargo. My own ship has been at sea for several months. In that time we have been most fortunate, and met with others such as you. *En conséquence* we must now also go home. Many of my men have been forced to take those we have already captured, so we are in need of men as well as stores."

King let out a brief sigh. "We thought you were undermanned."

The Frenchman turned to him. "Whether we are or are not, your captain did well to surrender without firing on us. Had he done so I fear we should not be having this pleasant conversation."

The French mate and boy officer collected the other's swords, while two seamen dragged Seagrove's body to the rail and unceremoniously tossed it over. There was a brief splash, but little more, and no comment from either side.

Drayton gave a start. "This ship is carrying passengers," he said, his voice suddenly urgent. "Ladies amongst them, I demand that they be treated with respect."

The captain's expression hardened. "We are not the Barbarians, sir, your women are as safe with us as they would have been under your care. All passengers will be transferred to my ship to ensure this; your senior officers are also invited to accompany them. As it has previously been our practice to send all prisoners back to France with their ship, there will be plenty of space."

"And the others," Rogers asked. "What of my people?"

"I regret that some of your men and all the junior officers will be needed aboard this vessel. There are repairs to be made and she has to be sailed; as I have already indicated, we are short of hands. But they are expected to behave themselves properly," the man smiled archly. "I am sure you gentlemen will be able to persuade them to cause no trouble."

"You seem to have everything well arranged," Drayton said, with just a hint of appreciation.

"It is our business," Passon agreed. "I do not say that I like it, but war, and the English insistence on blockade, has made such a thing necessary. Now, we will delay no longer, as there is much to do. We all have a busy night ahead of us."

* * *

The first Kate and Manning knew of their capture was when the young French officer forced his way into the sickbay. The man on the operating table bore a splinter wound that ran straight across his chest. Keats had removed most of the debris, and Manning was now wiping down the torso while Kate began to thread a large, bent needle with horse hair.

The boy spoke rapidly in French although the meaning was clear by his very presence. Keats looked up in the act of taking the needle from Kate and addressed him.

"We are busy, you must leave. *Sortez!*"

The lad held a loaded pistol in his hand, and as he waved it in the air, he seemed to notice the bloody body on the table for the first time. He stopped, mouth half open, and gradually lowered the weapon, staring transfixed as the surgeon continued to work. Without a word, Keats deftly brought the jagged wound together and closed it with each successive stitch. The patient was still traumatised by the initial injury and gave a deep and constant moan of pain, but no words were spoken. Then, as Manning wiped a piece of cotton waste over the scar, the surgeon lifted the patient forward, and Kate began to wrap a bandage about the chest. Keats glanced across at the Frenchman.

" We have work to do," he said. *"Nous avons du travail à faire!"* He indicated the second man, waiting patiently on the deck, one hand clasped firmly about a wound to his upper arm.

The boy nodded, looked once more at the body and left.

* * *

In the hold, the lanterns were still alight, but the shadows they cast were starting to disconcert Elizabeth. The ghostly forms seemed to have a life of their own, moving between the tiers of casks and barrels with every flicker of the grubby flames. She had tried to close her eyes to rest, but the feeling of vulnerability was far too great. She longed for a chance for conversation, maybe even a return to the singing that kept them reasonably sane the last time they sought refuge; anything would be better than this dreadful waiting. However, all agreed that, with the privateers so dangerously close, it might be unwise to advertise their presence. Therefore the women sat, for the most part still and reasonably quiet, while shipboard noises and the strange, unexplained sounds of battle filtered down to them.

"If the raiders get on board, what will they do to us?" The sudden whisper almost made her jump—she peered into the darkness and decided that it came from one of Mrs Drayton's maids; the chubby one, Elizabeth didn't know her name. In the half-light, her face appeared drawn and pale, and she sat slightly hunched on her seat, clutching a small bag to her stomach as if it were both precious and dependant upon her.

"Do?" Elizabeth asked, with a perkiness that might have fooled some. "They will do nothing, not if they want to stay healthy, that is."

The girl eyes her cautiously. "But they are pirates, you hear stories..."

"They are most certainly not pirates," Elizabeth stated clearly. "And you can forget all that rubbish the chapbooks might tell you." She noticed that others were leaning closer to hear her words, so she chose them carefully, speaking in a distinct but low voice.

"These will be privateers; they are regulated, and have to keep to very strict rules."

"Will we be held as prisoners?" The voice came from further back, but Elizabeth could not spot the speaker.

"They may well detain us for a short while, but it will not be to their interest that we remain longer."

"I could pay them," a well-dressed woman spoke up. "My husband is carrying a goodly sum. Perhaps if we offered money?"

Elizabeth swallowed. "Madam, I fear that anything you might have will be taken." The silence only lasted a few seconds, and then all began speaking at once. The noise grew into a mild hysteria, with several voices rising above the rest, and there were multiple outbursts of crying.

"Ladies, ladies, please!" Elizabeth tried to whisper through the din, but was unsuccessful. Several were speaking loudly now, and from further forward a small dog began to bark. Then the sound of a man's cry came from above and instantly brought a shocked silence to the cramped space.

"Below there!" The call was repeated; it was an English voice and one that Elizabeth recognised. There had been no gunfire for a while now. Was it possible that they had been victorious, and chased the Frenchman off? She stood and hurriedly made her way over the legs of the seated women until she stood under the open hatchway.

"Elizabeth, are you there?"

"George!" She looked up and could see him standing by the coaming, although he seemed to be looking back along the lower deck.

"Stay where you are," he said, holding his hand out to her. "The French have taken us, they are coming aboard."

Her heart fell. "What shall we do?" She tried to keep the hopelessness from her voice.

He looked down and shook his head. "I have no idea," he said. "You might hide down there but they are bound to find you. Maybe it is better that you come up now? Where are the ladders?"

"I have them here." She pointed to where they lay.

"Then you may as well: I will do all I can to intercede, and see that you are treated properly."

Elizabeth reached for the first ladder and, helped by two others, raised it to the mouth of the hatchway. She climbed and hugged at George, but he roughly brushed her aside, as a group of strangers appeared, clambering down the steps to the lower deck.

"The French," he said in explanation, and then the privateer captain approached with his mate and other seamen close by.

"These are all the female passengers?" Passon asked. Two ladies had followed Elizabeth and were now brushing down and rearranging their dresses.

"They are prisoners," Nichols replied harshly. "I demand that they are treated with respect."

"Sir, you insult me." The captain's tone was low, although his voice remained as strong. "It is not our habit to wage war on females." The second ladder appeared, and soon there were several women on the lower deck.

"*Mesdames*, kindly accompany my officer. You will be transferred to our ship and not harmed in any way although if you display any sign of *désobéissance,* I will not hesitate to have you dealt with in the harshest of manners."

Subdued now, the women formed up and trailed behind Elizabeth as she made her way along the deck. Men from the

French ship watched them as they went, some with curiosity and respect, while others held looks filled with lust and longing. And there were others they recognised—not only seamen from the *Pevensey Castle*, but male passengers who stood in groups under armed guard. Several women saw their husbands or brothers, and there were waves and calls. Elizabeth knew it to be a dangerous situation. Should any of the females be threatened, or give cause for the French to contain them, the British would be bound to rise up. Unarmed as they were, it would be a massacre.

They reached the upper deck, and assembled under the ship's boats. It was now quite dark, although a number of lanterns had been lit and were held by the French. Elizabeth felt a wave of relief when she saw Kate standing next to her husband and the surgeon.

"Is it right that we are going to the French ship?" she asked, as they came together and briefly embraced.

"It is—all senior officers and passengers, and some of the crew as well. We will be kept in separate confinement, though thankfully I seem to have been counted as one of the latter," Kate replied. "Mr King and the juniors are remaining in charge of those left in *Pevensey Castle*."

"Could he not just sail her away in the night?" Elizabeth was looking anxiously about her. Kate smiled.

"No, there will be a prize crew aboard, and I expect the ships to be travelling in close company." She turned as a Frenchman on the gangboard began giving orders in a broad accent. "We shall probably be in France within a few days," she added hurriedly.

Elizabeth could now see Rogers, along with Willis, the first mate. They were walking out along the starboard gangboard and, on reaching the entry port, began to clamber ignominiously off the ship. Mr Paterson followed, then Mr Langlois, almost elegant in his tailored watchcoat, and there was George, last in line. He looked down at her, paused and raised his hand briefly, before being prodded in the back with a pistol held by a French seaman. One last look then he was gone. A cold sensation ran down her and she had the strange intuition that she would never see him again.

* * *

The damage to *Pevensey Castle*'s rudder was not critical, although it would take most of the night to repair. The carpenter had been called to attend and fingered the damage thoughtfully, while one of his mates, along with King and two armed Frenchmen, looked on.

"I'd say a round shot," the elderly man murmured quietly, examining the edges of the damage. "Must have struck at an angle, so I'm surprised it even penetrated."

"Larboard tiller sheave is done for." His assistant collected the smashed block from where it lay, wrapped in a tangle of line. "'Ave to rebuild the fixin' an' mount a fresh block."

"Sweep okay?" the carpenter asked.

The mate turned to the long, curved wooden beam that supported the tiller. "Aye, an' the rest's healthy enough. It's just the mountin'."

"Four hours," the carpenter said, turning to King. He held up the fingers of one hand and loudly repeated, "four" to the guards. They nodded and began to converse in French; the carpenter turned back.

"They might try rigging a relieving tackle," he muttered to King. "Chains to the rudder 'orn, then mount a couple of blocks up to the poop; that'll work her right enough for a time, an' it would be the faster option."

"If it came to it they could probably steer by the tiller," King agreed, his voice low and guarded. "It wouldn't take much to rig a separate internal tackle."

The carpenter looked at him doubtfully. "You gonna suggest it?"

"Oh no," King rolled his eyes "I am in no rush to see France. Let us see if they can work it out for themselves."

* * *

By dawn, the repairs were complete and *Pevensey Castle* was underway once more, beating back against the easterly breeze, with the privateer to windward, less than a cable off and ready to bear down upon her should she show the least sign of wavering. King was in the captain's cabin, which he now shared with Marcel, the French first mate. Both had little more than a smattering of the other's language, although the common currency of seamanship had been adequate to carry them through most problems.

The prize crew consisted of eighteen men, a relatively small number to contain the remaining British seamen, although the French were heavily armed and alert. On arriving in France, *Pevensey Castle* would bring the privateers a handsome profit, a fortune even, and they were determined not to let her slip from their grasp.

Their captives remained in two watches, with each spell of duty now running for six hours to reduce the number of times a watch was changed. The off duty men were confined below, supervised by the French equipped with loaded East India Company blunderbusses. The guards were also working watch and watch about, and had been split, with five stationed on deck and four in steerage. It was a tight system, and at any sign of insurrection, the privateers had made it clear that they would not hesitate to open fire.

Crowley entered with a tray of food; Luck, the captain's steward, having followed his master to the privateer. Marcel indicated Rogers's handsome desk and beckoned King to join him. There were some rather superior biscuits, far nicer that those normally issued, several types of cheese, what looked like a potted meat *pâté,* along with some rather sorry-looking pieces of fruit. Clearly, Crowley had been inspecting the captain's stores. On seeing the spread, King was reminded how hungry he was. He cared little where the food came from, in fact knowing it had been provided by Rogers actually gave it extra flavour. The pot of coffee added an aroma to enforce the point, and soon he was laying into his breakfast like a lad. Marcel, eating well but with slightly less enthusiasm, chuckled quietly as he poured a measure of red wine and water for them both.

"You eat, then you rest," Marcel informed him, indicating the captain's sleeping cabin. "All officers together; I shall be here." He pointed to the large couch in the main room. It would be hard to exit the sleeping cabin other than by passing the Frenchman. The off-duty deck guards from the prize crew were also berthed in the dining room cuddy, so communication with *Pevensey Castle*'s people was all but impossible, except when they were on watch.

King nodded and bit into some more of the cheese. It seemed a reasonable enough arrangement; at least they weren't to be bound and gagged. The Frenchmen must fear the take over of their ship, but then he supposed they were also relying on the fact that passengers and officers were interned in the privateer; each ship was effectively carrying hostages for the other.

Crowley appeared again and spoke to Marcel in rapid French. King strained to translate, and then the steward addressed him directly.

"Your man here reckons it will be a good five days or so afore we reach port."

King nodded. It was what he had been told, but why was Crowley mentioning it, and in such a direct manner?

"So I understand, Michael," he said, eyeing the steward cautiously.

"Well, I think you'll be finding the men will be ready before then," he continued.

King stared at him, uncomprehending.

"I said, they will be ready, sir." Crowley's statement was slightly more emphatic. Clearly he was trying to convey something to King, although the young man's tired brain could not decipher it.

"Ready?" Marcel spoke from the other side of the cabin. "For what is it that they are ready?" His voice was harsh and suspicious.

"For the next watch; they are settled in their quarters," Crowley replied innocently, repeating the answer in French.

Marcel snorted and went back to making up his bed. It was only then that King began to truly understand. Crowley was saying the British crew were prepared to act, to retake this ship or anything that he, as senior officer, might have in mind. They were primed to support him if he chose to make a move, although quite what that move would be remained a mystery. For a split second the very thought appalled him, but then he supposed he had a certain duty, a commitment almost. They had done their bit by showing their willingness to be led. Now it was up to him to do the leading.

"Very good, Crowley," he said, adding a sly wink, although there was nothing in the Irishman's face or manner that showed any sign of collusion or shared understanding. "I will not need you further this watch, you may get some sleep."

Crowley left silently through the dining room cuddy while King made for the small shutoff area that was the captain's sleeping cabin. He had also been looking forward to some rest, but now it seemed there were other matters to consider.

* * *

The British hands had lost their comfortable quarters in the forecastle to the steerage guard of the prize crew and were now berthing with the Lascars. The latter shunned the use of hammocks, however, preferring to sleep on the hard deck and with the French strictly imposing the six hours on, six hours off, system, there was room enough for all. The new watch had just been set, and Ward, Johnston and Khan were tired after working for much of the night. There had been plenty to do in their department. In addition to the main yard, which was now fished adequately enough, several mizzen shrouds had parted during the battle and a fresh main topsail needed to be set. All the repair work was carried out by *Pevensey Castle*'s crew, while the French guards looked on. But then, with just nine men on watch to guard many times that number, their captors could hardly be blamed for giving all their attention to supervision. After a gruelling and overlong trick, the men were not impressed and grumbled openly as they ate the cold burgoo provided for their meal.

"This is nothing less than horse feed!" Ward grouched, while he annoyed the mixture of oats and water with his spoon.

"Galley fire's dead," Johnston informed him stoically. "Don't seem likely they're going to relight it, neither."

Clegg, a topman from Lancashire at the next table, exhaled loudly and swung round on his bench to face them. "Aye, they probably think we're gonna grab hold of burning coals, an' lob them about when they're not looking."

"They'd got the spirit stove in the cuddy pantry alight an' were roasting chickens, last I heard." Ward added bitterly.

The French were certainly taking few chances. All small arms had been rounded up and locked in the spirit room which was one of the most secure stores in the ship. Even the topmen's knives, essential tools for their job, were taken from them.

"Tastes very fine to me," Khan said, a slight smile on his face. "All that butter and sugar is very bad for a man's heart; this will do more good."

Ward, whose proportions were certainly generous, peered at Khan's slight frame. "If you're so bleedin' healthy," he asked. "Why ain't there more o' you?"

"Do you see me tired?" Khan replied. They considered him; certainly, the Indian seemed as fresh as when they started the watch. He looked about brightly. "Maybe if I carried so much fat it might be the case, but as it is I am ready for my sleep, and work the next day."

"So you're not missing your prayers then?" Clegg asked. Khan might be a friend and shipmate, but there was something in the Indian's superior attitude that occasionally nettled, making the northerner long to prick his composed bubble.

"It is regrettable," Khan shrugged. The regular meeting times when men of his faith could pray was one of the first things the French abolished. "But Allah understands and will make allowances." He glanced at them sideways. "Besides, maybe a way will be found for us to continue, before so very long."

* * *

Elizabeth's suspicions proved correct. The women passengers were segregated from the men, and placed in a small dark room that stank of mouldy cloth. It was deep inside the French ship, with no ports or scuttles of any description, and soon the smell of confined bodies made the atmosphere even more oppressive. A door set into the bulkhead at the far end was their only form of ventilation, and that was fully boarded. There were nineteen of them altogether, counting Kate, who the French assumed could never have been an officer, and the very basics for survival had been provided.

The food mainly consisted of ship's biscuit. This was different to the type they were familiar with, but not unpleasant. There was also some soft cheese that she guessed might be goat, although it was so far gone as to be almost inedible. Both were doled out as soon as they settled, and all now had disappeared. Water was provided in two large skeels, one of which had been clumsily knocked over and the other emptied almost as quickly. Since then, they had been left for what must have been six or seven hours, and they were certainly thirsty. The room was only just large enough for them all to squash in, and lit by a single lamp that gave its meagre light at the cost of a dirty wick, which added an unpleasant cast to the strong smell of captivity. There was no furniture, other than the bolts of canvas they were sitting on. For other, more personal requirements, there was a bucket.

Elizabeth wriggled uncomfortably in her seat and whispered a quick apology to the woman on her right, who appeared to have been woken by the movement. Kate was on her left, eyes closed, and probably dozing. Elizabeth tried to join her, but could not relax in such circumstances and for the second time in twenty-four hours, she felt almost frightened to close her eyes. Instead she stared about the room and wondered vaguely about George. There had been no sign of the men by the time they finally boarded the privateer. All was dark, the ship strange, and the French who herded them down to this room were wary in the extreme. Most regarded the women with suspicion, but some seemed to have a different interest, and at least one, a chubby officer with a stupid, thick moustache, did not attempt to hide his look of open desire. She supposed that George and the others were held elsewhere. In a ship this small they could not be far away, but to find them would probably take forever, even if they were free to do so.

"I should welcome some food." Kate's whisper made Elizabeth start slightly. "And a chance to stretch our legs would be nice."

"How long have we been here?" Elizabeth asked.

Kate shook her head and then peered forward in the half-light of the crowded room. "Does anyone have a timepiece?"

Mrs Drayton stood and presented her dog to the women immediately next to her. Leaning closer to the lantern, she consulted an ornate fob watch that was set on the lapel of her jacket. "Half past ten o'clock," she said firmly, then added, "Mind it is like to lose the odd half hour most mornings, so better make that eleven."

Kate glanced at Elizabeth. "I'd say it was time they started to take notice, wouldn't you?"

Without waiting for a reply she lifted her head and shouted "Hello!" The other women looked at her aghast, and when she repeated the bellow, some shuffled uncomfortably.

"It might be better if you did not annoy them." Mrs Crabtree's voice came from the far end. "We are their captives, after all."

"And you know what the French are like," another slightly closer added enigmatically.

"I know they have kept us here long enough," Kate retorted. "And if we don't start to make ourselves known, we might well be forgotten." She went to shout again, but before she did so the sound of keys rattling outside made them all turn towards the door. It opened, admitting a pool of lantern light from the corridor outside and the same moustachioed officer who had leered at them earlier.

He leaned in through the opening and surveyed them for a moment. "Ladies, there is too much noise; continue and you will force me to be harsh." Even in the poor light, it was clear that he would require little persuasion.

"We should like food and some fresh air," Kate said coldly. She was directly opposite and fixed him with her stare. "Also, this bucket is undignified; would you expect your own women to use such a thing?"

The man returned her gaze, his moist eyes standing out in the flickering light. "My women learn to do what they are told," he said, a smug expression sitting easily on his fat face. "As you will also, if you cause me trouble."

"Does the captain permit you to threaten women prisoners?" There was a mutual intake of breath from the others, but Kate's eyes remained set on his.

"The captain has given me the full control, as I speak your *sauvage* language." His look mollified for a moment. "But maybe... maybe if you were kind, I might be able to give you what you want." He reached down and touched the cheek of the nearest prisoner. It was Emma, one of Mrs Drayton's maids, and the girl froze while his hand greedily explored her hair and face.

"Maybe the captain should know you are offering to make deals." Kate's reply caused the man to visibly start, his fingers frozen over Emma's lips. "Maybe if we were all to scream at once he might hear," she continued. "Maybe then he would ask what caused us to react so, and then discover that you are open to inducements."

The officer pushed himself further into the room and stood as near upright as the low deckhead allowed.

"You would not be so stupid." he said.

Kate drew a deep breath and let out a credible scream. The sound echoed about the small room. She inhaled and shrieked again. This time the noise was louder, as Elizabeth and another added their voices. The three women went to repeat the procedure, and it was clear that others intended joining them. The man's eyes grew wide, and he swung round, gesturing violently for them all to stop.

"There is no need to involve the captain," he said, panting slightly.

"Then we can expect some breakfast and an opportunity to exercise?" Kate's voice, though slightly hoarse, lost none of its menace. "Otherwise he will hear of your attitude."

He turned back to her. "There shall be food shortly," he said. "But you would be wise not to annoy me." The frightened look was fading now, and complacency slowly returned. "You will all be in my care for as long as we are at sea; and if any prove to be a problem I shall report them to the captain myself. Once I have done so I am sure he will be happy for me to deal with the situation in any way I choose. We have a number of punishments that are eminently suitable for ladies; some you may know, others might come as the surprise, but all are undignified and I doubt there are any you will wish to experience."

* * *

King had been back on duty for three hours, and darkness was just starting to fall when he decided to make his move. It was a subtle one and must remain undetected afterwards, so choosing the right time was very important. He had long since decided that, should this attempt fail—if he, or his plan, were discovered—there could be no other. Either the French would take far harsher measures in detaining them, or he would be dead.

So far, the day had gone well. *Pevensey Castle* had tacked three times and was still heading in a broadly northeasterly direction, towards the coast of Spain. Even beating against the wind, they must have covered a fair few miles, although by now he had little real idea of their exact position. Two hours of pumping by the previous watch had seen the well almost dry, and they had prevailed upon their captors to relight the galley fire, so there was hot food for all. His plan must remain undetected for several hours, so any relaxation on the part of the French was to be encouraged. Now it only needed him to act.

Marcel was studying the traverse board by the binnacle. King sauntered across. The two were getting on reasonably enough; in fact, he had come to genuinely like the Frenchman, despite their differences in nationality and language.

"I need to use the heads," he said, patting his stomach. On the first occasion, he was accompanied by a junior officer, but since then King seemed to have earned a little trust. Choosing the place was not up to him, so provisions had been made for any eventuality.

"Below," Marcel replied, pointing downwards to the great cabin.

The quarter galleries. He was in luck. King nodded and strode quickly for the companionway. It mattered little if he rushed and might even explain matters should his absence be slightly longer than normal.

On the deck below, the dining lobby in the great cabin was empty. He went in and closed the door behind him, as well as the open sliding door to the larboard quarter gallery. That might buy time if anyone came to investigate. The hatch to the bread room was rarely used and lay under the thick canvas sheeting. It was a far less obvious means of entry than the locked outer door on the deck below, but how could he get the flooring up without a good deal of fuss? He glanced about the room and then noticed a corner, next to the quarter gallery entrance, which was free of furniture. He lifted the canvas up. The heavy cloth came back almost as far as the hatch, and he only needed to move a table and two chairs to clear the opening completely.

The trap door moved easily and made no undue sound. Gently, he laid the wooden cover back on the rolled-up canvas, collected a lantern from an overhead beam and slipped quietly down into the bread room. The lantern lit the dark billowing sacks of hard tack that lay in neat piles. He was banking on the biscuit being stacked clear of the next hatch. If he needed to move any sizeable amount, it might take a second visit, and that could not be until the following watch. He fell to his knees, feeling along the deck for another opening. The bread room was less than fifteen feet long; the lower trap that led to the bilges might easily be the other side of the door. That could be broken down of course, except that to do so might advertise his presence, and probably jeopardise the entire plan.

Luck was with him. The hatch was in the room and just where he hoped it to be, although only instinct and a fair amount of guesswork had actually guided him. This one was far lighter, but the hinges were badly rusted and squeaked as he brought the lid up. He pulled a face to himself, but did not stop. Time was so very important, and this was the most dangerous part of his plan.

Jumping down into the bilges, he felt his feet splash slightly on the wet gravel. *Pevensey Castle* had clearly taken in some water since the recent pumping, a fact that could only give his idea credibility. The lantern light flickered about the dank chamber, and several rats ran scurrying for the darkness. He was at the extreme stern end of the hold. About him were two rows of casks and what looked like spare parts for one of the pumps. He swung the light around, desperately searching, and then noticed the hefty bronze faucet rising up from the ballast shingle.

This was the sweetening cock, a valve set through the hull of the ship which allowed seawater into the bilges. Once a suitable amount had entered, the theory was that the valve would be closed and the water could then be removed by the main pumps, thus diluting and neutralising the ship's odour. *Pevensey Castle* carried three such valves in total. The other two were permanently attached to canvas pipes and used to direct seawater inside the ship. If Marcel had sent him to the forward heads, King would have been forced to tamper with one of those, with a far greater likelihood of him, or his plan, being discovered.

A brass bar was set across the valve. Placing the lantern on the shingle, he took the cold metal in both hands and tried to move it. At first, it seemed stuck fast, then the lever began to ease very slightly. Gritting his teeth he strained until it moved one-quarter turn. He paused, drawing breath, and wiped his hand about the mouth of the pipe. It was quite dry. Back to the valve: a little more effort brought it round a further half turn. The thing was moving easier now, and he stopped when seawater suddenly began to gush from the pipe, splashing over the shingle and thoroughly soaking his boots.

The noise was too great; it might be heard, and could cause the ship to actually sink. The sound of the running water was also playing terrible games with his mind, making him wonder if his fictional trip to the heads might actually prove necessary. Slowly he eased the bar back, until the torrent dwindled to a decent sized flow. The ideal amount was slightly more than the pumps could handle, although he could only guess at what that might be. He settled for a stream that seemed a little greater than that from the scuppers when both pumps were in action. The noise was still noticeable but, being continuous, should soon fade into the background, to be masked by the other regular shipboard sounds.

His lantern was in danger of being soaked. Quickly he collected it and made back for the hatch. The bread room was just as he had left it. He lifted the lower trap carefully, wincing as the hinges moaned closed. Now was the truly dangerous time, if someone had entered the lobby while he was below, they would almost certainly be waiting for him. The opened seacock was bound to be discovered, and all would end badly. He peered up into the room, but there was no movement, just absolute silence. Pushing the lantern ahead of him, he swung himself up and dragged the hatchway closed. The canvas flooring rolled back well enough, and he hurriedly replaced the table and chairs. Now he was short of time. The lantern was rehung and he paused only to open the quarter gallery door, before striding across the room, out to the deck and straight into the bulk of Marcel.

"Ah, you are *malade*?" The Frenchman grinned conspiratorially.

King tried to hide his surprise. "Yes, my stomach." He held his belly and pulled a face. The Frenchman laughed heartily and slapped him on the shoulder, before heading back to the quarterdeck. King followed, his hands, which he plunged deep into his pockets, were cold, wet and shaking, and as he walked along the dry wooden deck, his feet squelched in his damp boots.

CHAPTER TWELVE

For his plan to work, King was counting on a number of things, the most important being the ingress of water remaining undiscovered until the seacock was fully submerged. Then the cause might be put down to damage below the waterline, most likely from the recent action. The valve could still be suspected, of course, in which case it would take little investigation and hardly any effort to stop the leak, while an inner feeling told him that identifying the culprit would be no more taxing.

The other major concern was that the leak would go unnoticed, even to the extent that *Pevensey Castle* might actually sink. But that should take a considerable time, and the fact that there was rising water in the well must surely be spotted before long. With the pumps in action for up to twenty-four hours a day, he hoped she could be maintained afloat, even if the valve remained open. Her waterlogged hull would not sail well, however, dramatically slowing the progress of both ships, and buying precious time before they finally made French waters. At the very least, their recapture by a British vessel would be more likely, although King was hoping for rather more.

In fact, the flooded bilges were not discovered until later that evening, when the routine sounding of the well showed several feet of seawater where only a few inches were to be expected. It was two hours before King was due to go on duty, and he was playing a game of *vingt-et-un* with Marcel in the captain's quarters, when the cabin door burst open and the boy officer erupted into the room.

Marcel stood as the lad began to blurt and babble in French. King could understand little of what was said, although clearly Marcel was immediately concerned. He turned to King, his face creased in surprise and mild panic, and shouted in French.

King shook his head and spread his hands wide, even though some words, like *l'eau* and *le naufrage,* came through clearly enough. The emergency had robbed Marcel of his limited English, and he did not intend to make life any easier for him. Crowley entered, drawn by the commotion. Marcel addressed him in a torrent of French, and King noticed that the Irishman's face betrayed no change as he took in the information.

"Your man here says we are leaking," Crowley told King. "He wants to know how much the well usually draws in a day."

King replied in an equally flat tone. "A few inches, though it can be more in bad weather. How much is there?"

"Just under two of their metres." Crowley's voice was now full of concern for the ship; the answer was what King wanted to hear, but anyone looking at either of them could have thought the opposite.

"More than six feet, that is very serious," he said, turning to Marcel. He found an air of mild panic peculiarly easy to adopt. "We must pump," he said, winding his hands in the air to mimic the pump handles.

" *Rassemblez les hommes!"* Marcel shouted at the boy. *"Et commencez à pomper l'eau!"* The lad nodded and rushed away, calling as he went.

"They're summoning the watch below," Crowley said. "Me'be them at the pumps will make a difference, though six feet'll take a while to clear."

"Especially if the leak is not cured." King was finding it harder to keep the triumph from his face now, and Marcel's eyes were boring down on him.

"What do you know of this?" he asked.

King turned his expression into one of surprised outrage as he shook his head and spluttered, "I can only assume that we are holed."

"What?" Marcel demanded, and swung round on Crowley. The Irishman translated, but the privateer remained unimpressed.

"In the action," King persisted. "You fired on our stern. One man died and several were badly injured. It was a rash act if you had any intention of capturing us." He watched while Crowley translated, hoping that the accusation, together with the inclusion of the casualties, might muddle things sufficiently.

"He says that is not the case," Crowley told him. "The injured were on a higher deck, by the tiller; no shots hit below."

"Tell him he is mistaken," King replied. "We felt damage in the hull."

Marcel shook his head on hearing Crowley's translation, and repeated *"Non!"* several times.

King shrugged. "In that case we are not leaking," he said simply.

The Frenchman clearly understood without Crowley's help and stamped his feet in frustration. It was dawning on King that the danger had been discovered at the ideal time. In the dark of night, communication with the privateer would be that much harder. The prize crew must rely on night signals; both ships might even need to heave to while the emergency was discussed. Of course there was some backbreaking work ahead for the captured British, but the French were no fools. Fewer than fifty men might pump a leaking ship and sail her for a day or maybe two. But to make France could take a week or even longer. Reinforcements would be needed from the privateer, and in the confusion some attempt to retake the *Pevensey Castle* must surely be possible. He felt the excitement rise up in him, and it was difficult to remain calm and still while the ship echoed to the noise of men being roused from their sleep.

Then Marcel suddenly began to babble at Crowley, and before the steward had a chance to translate, rushed from the cabin, and out towards the quarterdeck.

"He says there must be another reason." Crowley raised one eyebrow to emphasise the irony. They were alone, but there was still a chance that others might overhear. "Belike he intends to search the ship."

"With six feet in the well, any leak is likely to be hidden," King replied flatly. He had counted on a minimum of four to conceal the opened seacock, but that did not mean it could not be checked by anyone so determined. "And the lower she sits in the water, the greater will be the pressure. They will have to find it fast, or it will be the worse for them."

Crowley nodded wisely and then caught King with a direct stare. "There will be a fair amount of disorder, sir," he said softly. "Maybe we should offer to assist?"

* * *

Pevensey Castle carried two pumps, both on the lower deck and to either side of the mainmast. Each had a single continuous chain that carried a series of tholes—small leather plugs that fitted tightly into a wooden tube extending deep into the bilges, at the lowest point of the ship. Two large handles on each side of the pump hood turned a wheel that pulled the chain. There was room for two men at each handle, so four men were needed to work each pump; eight for both. They could not be expected to pump for longer than half an hour; more than that and the backbreaking and belly-bursting effort would totally exhaust them. Thus it would take sixteen men an hour to maintain a constant drain on the bilges, and even at the peak of fitness, none could work effectively for more than six hours in any one day.

Johnston, who knew nothing of the cause of the leak, had not actually worked this out while he was being chivvied from his warm hammock. But he realised immediately that the number of men remaining in *Pevensey Castle* would not be sufficient to clear a sizeable body of water. Certainly, if the leak was as bad as the rumours currently circulating, further hands would be needed from the privateer; possibly even passengers as well. Word that they were actually sinking quickly followed, and the estimated time they could stay afloat dwindled with every telling. Johnston was an experienced seaman and used to the lower deck's inclination to exaggerate. But he also guessed that the stories must have some substance and, unless a way could be found to stop the rising water, both pumps would be working until the ship saw land, or the ocean bottom.

He grasped the cold metal pump handle and began to turn the heavy contraption as the last remains of sleep left him. Ward was to his right, sharing the same handle, while Khan and another Lascar worked to the other side of his pump. It took five or six full revolutions before the first of the water appeared in the cistern and began to run down the leaded dales and out through the scuppers. It was a fair flow, and the second pump could be expected to produce as much. But then, they had only just started, and the latest report of eight feet in the well and rising was certainly a good deal of water to move. He looked to his left and grimaced at Khan while the rhythm became established. The Lascars, with their slight frames and lean bodies, were not ideally suited to this kind of work, and Khan's forehead was creased in concentration and effort while he turned his handle. Then he noticed his friend's attention; his expression cleared, and the familiar smile returned.

"Hard work to last for very long," he said, breathing only slightly deeper than usual.

"Aye," Johnston agreed. "Reckon we'll have a fair taste of it, afore the day's out."

"Over ten foot in the well, they tells me," Ward added for good measure from his right. "Say several planks have been stove in below, an' the entire hold's awash."

Khan remained silent, but grew more thoughtful.

"Strange that there were no sign of a leak until now," Johnston added and was about to say more when he noticed the Lascar glaring at him over the curve of the pump hood. The intensity of his stare made Johnston pause, and he considered the situation afresh.

Strange it certainly was. There was no damage below the waterline that he was aware of, and the well had been all but dry only that morning. Johnston's eyes flashed back questioningly to Khan, who winked at him as they continued to turn the heavy pump handles. Johnston winked back while his thoughts ran on. He quickly decided that the leak had been caused by something other than enemy shot. That only left sabotage.

Clearly, there were those in the ship who were working to stop her, and it came as a relief to discover that a chance remained he was not going to end up a prisoner of the French. He continued to turn, but now his back was starting to protest. The pain must inevitably grow until the end of his trick, and by then, he knew from experience, he would be good for nothing. However, the rhythmic movement certainly encouraged thinking, and he let the speculations continue as a distraction to his complaining sinews.

So, the leak could probably be blamed on one of the officers. King, who was on the lower deck and actually walking towards them as they worked, would be the most likely. He had shown himself to be quite a spark in the past. What else was in his mind was a mystery, of course. It wasn't for Johnston to consider such things; his job was simply to follow when led. But he and the other seamen could now rely on the fact that one of their officers had conceived a plan and was in the process of carrying it out. It might prove unsuccessful, of course, although it was unlikely that any officer worth his salt would have failed to properly think things through, so Johnston reckoned that the scheme must have a fair chance of working. Besides, anything—even the wildest of ideas— was better than sitting back and waiting while they sailed themselves into captivity.

The wheel continued to turn, and the water flowed regularly along the dale and out through the scuppers. The only noticeable change in the routine was his back and belly, which were now starting to protest most strongly. If the leak were as bad as they said, it would take more than two pumps to keep *Pevensey Castle* afloat, so further action might be expected sooner than later. He grinned at Khan once more; the Lascar was also showing signs of tiring, although he met his eyes readily enough and nodded in return. Johnston knew instinctively that Khan's mind was running on a similar path, and the serang would be equally keen for the next move to be made. He just wished that a way had been chosen that involved less physical effort.

* * *

Johnston was wrong. When it came to knowing what to do next, King did not have a clue.

There was no overall plan; no finely detailed strategy that covered most major eventualities, leading to the overthrow of their French captors. In fact, there had been a complete lack of foresight. The act of opening the seacock was almost instinctive and based solely on the principle that something which did the French harm must surely be a blessing to the British. Now, though, it appeared to King as the act of a rash young man, one with no idea how to put a leaking *Pevensey Castle* to their advantage.

The enormity of what he had already done, coupled with an expectancy from the other men, instilled feelings of foolishness and inadequacy in him not experienced since he was a lad. He longed to discuss the possibilities that his actions to date had uncovered. But he was still a captive, still liable to constant surveillance from Marcel and the other members of the French prize crew and for the first time he truly knew the loneliness of command.

His thoughts tumbled through his head as he made his way along the lower deck. Ahead of him, the pumps were clanking monotonously, and he could see Marcel standing close to the stern hatch with a group of Frenchmen, their faces strangely distorted in the lantern light. Throughout his journey from the roundhouse, Crowley accompanied him, along with two of the guards who had been sleeping in the dining cuddy. Neither spoke any English, but still he and Crowley remained silent. Even with the relative security of their language, King preferred to say nothing. That way Crowley might not guess that the officer he trusted to lead them out of this mess was completely at a loss.

The hatchway led to the hold and lay open. King pushed past the group, peered down into the gloom below and was surprised to see a floor of black water, far higher than he had anticipated, reflecting the lantern light. As he watched, several small casks floated by, bumping against each other as they went. The hold was almost flooded, even with the pumps working continuously.

He spun round and addressed Marcel. "How much water is there in the well?" he demanded. The Frenchman stared back without understanding, and then switched his attention to Crowley.

"Gained another ten centimetres since the pumps started." The Irishman translated Marcel's reply with just the slightest hint of worry.

"We must get help." King's voice rose with concern, both for the problem and that his part in it might be discovered. He faced the French officer directly. "There are additional portable pumps we can rig, and a bucket chain could be started, but that will take more men."

They had been communicating well until the emergency, but now Marcel's English deserted him, and again he looked to Crowley.

"He says they will have to fire the rocket," Crowley translated.

King's forehead creased. "What rocket?"

"It sounds to me like some sort of danger signal, in case we gets too lively. I reckons there'll be a bunch of armed Frenchmen joining us once it goes up." His eyes flashed at King as he continued. "That'll make a might of confusion, wouldn't you say?"

King nodded. Crowley was right, if they were going to act further and make anything from the opening of the seacock, it must be now.

"We have two fire pumps on the upper deck," he said, turning back to Marcel and pointing at the deckhead. "I'll get them rigged over this hatch and for'ard."

He went to move while Crowley translated, Marcel nodded readily and let him go, while he babbled instructions at the boy officer who had first announced the leak.

The three of them made for the upper deck, with the lad just slightly in the lead. As they went, King caught sight of eight of *Pevensey Castle*'s men, five British and three Lascars, presumably the relief crew for the pumps. He bellowed for them to follow, which they did. Their two guards objected, but the lad shouted them down, and they too joined the group heading upwards, like characters in some absurd fairy tale.

On deck Drummond and the duty watch were grouped about the main and foremasts, watched over by three more Frenchmen armed with blunderbusses. Again, the lad gave an order, indicating towards the poop where two more stood ready. The boy waved his hand, and one peered forward in the dark.

"La fusée! Allumez la fusée!" The guards hesitated, clearly unwilling to carry out such a drastic action on the word of a mere child.

"I'll go!" Crowley shouted, translating quickly for the benefit of the Frenchmen. He bounded along the gangboard and on to the quarterdeck, then mounted the poop ladder. The two men stood back as the Irishman joined them.

"They need you to fire the rocket," he said in English. "Fire the rocket," he repeated. One guard shook his head bewildered, but turned to where a slim brass tube stood ready, its mouth pointing over the side towards the privateer. Crowley grabbed the flint and steel that lay next to it and began to strike; soon a small fire was glowing in the tinder. He looked across to where the French ship's lights could just be made out; she was about three cables off their starboard bow, beating close hauled into the wind. Once they saw the rocket it would take little time to let the wind carry them round, and alongside. The two Frenchmen began to talk rapidly to each other, but Crowley paid them no heed as the flame grew up and was ready. He glanced back at the guards, noticing that the boy officer and two other Frenchmen were making for the poop, with King and his men close behind.

"Fire the rocket," Crowley repeated. At last, one of the guards bent down to the fuse, which could just be seen at the base of the tube. His head lowered as he extended the small length of quick match, exposing it to Crowley's flame. The second guard was leaning over to watch, and it was then that Crowley dropped the flaming tinder and administered a deadly rabbit punch to the back of the man's neck.

* * *

On the quarterdeck, King saw Crowley act and the man fall. The first guard looked up in surprise, and the Irishman neatly despatched him with a sweep from his right fist which sent him spinning to the deck. It was clear from their reaction that the French also noticed. The boy looked back at King, his face a mixture of surprise and confusion, while the other guards shouted and raised their weapons to bear on Crowley. There was no time to think. Without a sound King caught up with the rearmost Frenchman who was in the act of aiming his piece, and shoved him firmly in the small of his back. The weapon flew up and the man crashed forwards, but King had no time to consider him further. A second guard turned to him and levelled his blunderbuss. Without conscious thought, King reached for the barrel and knocked it back towards its owner, just as the trigger was squeezed and the hammer struck the frizzen. A flash came from the pan, but no more—a misfire. King finished the startled man off with a swift punch and saw him fall back and to one side. He turned to take on the rest, but they had already been dealt with by *Pevensey Castle*'s crew, who were standing over them like so many hunters claiming their prey. King's grin owed much to relief as he looked back along the deck. It was now quite dark, but there were no signs of other Frenchmen.

"Tie them up and make sure they're securely gagged," he said. All but the boy were knocked senseless, but there was no telling for how long they might stay that way. King had already taken enough chances and cared little if the gags choked them. There were five blunderbusses lying on the deck, which were quickly gathered up by the men. One also collected the short sword that the officer had carried and handed it to King. Holding the naked blade, he felt more able to plan matters. Crowley was back from the poop and dragging one of the guards with him.

"Good work, Michael." King nodded as the Irishman dumped the senseless body with the rest.

"The other will give us no problem," Crowley replied with strange certainty. "Shall we attend to those Frenchmen below?"

"Yes, two parties," King said with sudden decision. "You four and Crowley take the for'ard ladder; Drummond, you'll be in charge. I'll take the stern with the rest. Clegg, stay at the wheel and try to keep her steady." The midshipman blinked in confusion for a moment while he took in what was said. King realised that this must be his first time in action and slowed down. "Take your men down the hatchway, but no further. Do nothing until you hear us begin, then join in as fast as you can. No one is to use firearms unless they have to. But if it comes to it, don't forget that we have men at the pumps."

The lad nodded, and the men separated. King made for the stern hatch.

"May I suggest, sir?" Crowley was pointing to the fife rail where a row of empty belaying pins sat ready. There were no small arms to hand other than the blunderbusses and the boy's sword, but the short wooden staves would make excellent weapons.

"Yes, take one each if you wish." The unarmed men helped themselves, although King knew that their blood was up and that the seamen would fight well enough with their bare hands if need be. The forward group moved swiftly across the deck.

The only part of the fight which might have been seen from the privateer was that one misfire, but sound could carry great distances at sea, and they had not been silent. The Frenchmen below might also be wondering what was happening, and how long it took to launch a simple rocket. Some may even have come to investigate and seen that the British were in control of the upper deck. Then there was the not inconsiderable point that *Pevensey Castle* was slowly sinking. Even if the British dealt with the prize crew below, they must then attend to that damned seacock, as well as making preparations to receive the Frenchmen from the privateer when they came to retake the ship. Time was certainly of the essence.

He peered down to the deck below; no one was apparently waiting. Ahead he could see Crowley and Drummond in position at the mouth of the forward hatch. He raised his hand to them, then walked slowly down the steps, his sword held hidden against his leg.

Below the French were still grouped about the entrance to the hold, while the monotonous drone of the pumps continued, masking much of the sound of their conversation. Ahead, King could see Drummond cautiously leading his men down the forward ladder. He reached the deck without attracting attention and slipped into the shadows next to the steerage mess. Slowly his men formed up behind him. He paused, looked back and then strode boldly out into the centre of the deck. His boots sounded noisily on the hard deck, but he continued forward, conscious that each step he took brought him closer and made the job easier. He came to within ten feet of the group when one looked round and called out in surprise. Marcel's face was visible for a moment, and he said something that King did not catch. It was time.

With a yell that was very close to a scream, King launched himself forward, swinging the short sword out in front of him. He could hear the thunder of bare feet as those behind followed; and there was Crowley closing in from forward, passing the bemused men at the pumps, while he singled out an opponent. The crowd of Frenchmen broke as they turned to meet them, reaching for their weapons. King noticed Marcel drawing his sword. There was no time for niceties; he made for the man and crashed into him, knocking his body sideways and the weapon to the deck. The crack of fist on bone came from the other group, and one of the British yelled as a cutlass slashed across his chest. King recovered himself, and struck out wildly at one of the guards who was raising a pistol. The blade caught the Frenchman on the forearm, and the weapon tumbled out of his limp hand. Someone fell, knocking King sideways as he went. Then Marcel clambered to his feet, and began to shout in guttural French, before Crowley, striking from behind, silenced him forever with a belaying pin.

The fight ended as suddenly as it had begun. The pumps had ceased to turn with King's attack, the men having abandoned the hated machines in order to join their comrades. For a moment, there was a stunned pause; then all began shouting and slapping each other in victory. King knew it was time to take a hand and called for order. Once more, the injured Frenchmen were secured and roughly moved to a nearby cattle stall.

"Fresh hands to the pumps," King continued, conscious that the men were ready to respond to him, whatever he ordered. He glanced down at the hold; there was no visible change in the water level, but that seacock must be closed without further delay. "Does anyone here swim?" he asked vaguely.

"Yes, sir." It was Johnston and, despite the circumstances, King found himself suppressing a slight smile. He was well aware of the persistent deserter's talents in that department. But Johnston was injured, a cut to his left forearm was bleeding freely, despite his efforts to contain the flow with his right hand.

"See to your wound, Johnston; I will need someone else."

The man was about to complain, but another was there ahead of him.

"I do, sir." King considered Khan, the boatswain, briefly. The man was clearly tired from pumping, but he also carried an air of competence that was obvious to all.

"The stern sweetening cock is half opened," King told him. "Do you know where it is?"

"'Ere, you can't send Abdul, there's nothing of him," Ward complained, and Johnston was looking mildly disgruntled.

"Do you swim, Ward?" King asked. The boatswain's mate shook his head. King glanced at the other men, but none met his eye.

"The valve you mentioned is below the bread room, sir," Khan said softly.

King turned back to him. "Indeed. Can you reach it?" What he actually wanted to know was, did Khan have the strength to close the thing, although to ask such a question of another male was almost impolite.

"I believe so, sir," the man replied.

King looked about. Both pumps were working again, but it would not be long before the water came up to the level of the lower deck. The longer they waited, the harder Khan's task would become, the deeper *Pevensey Castle* settled, and with the increase in pressure, the faster more water flowed in through the valve.

"Very well, Khan. Do your best; but don't take too many risks. If it cannot be closed there will still be a little time, although we might need to defend the ship shortly."

Khan nodded and lowered himself until he was sitting on the hatch coaming, dangling his bare feet above the water. He slipped his cotton top off and handed it to Johnston. The Lascar grinned at him and then gently eased himself over the side. A slight splash, and he swam away into the black depths of the hold and out of their sight.

King reckoned he could remain on the surface for a spell, at least until the deckhead became too low. After that, he would have to continue underwater and in total darkness. The sweetening cock was several feet down; it must be located and heaved shut. King had found it a hard enough job to open: Khan must close it several feet down, before finally returning to the surface. There was a deep ripple as the Lascar's lithe body slipped under the water. Then he was gone.

CHAPTER THIRTEEN

All the men were crowded together in the raider's hold. Counting officers, passengers and the remainder of *Pevensey Castle*'s crew, it amounted to almost fifty. Although the *Espérance* was nearly empty of stores, there was hardly room for half that number. One lantern lit the dismal scene. The seamen had taken to the forward end and made themselves relatively comfortable, even to the extent of rigging makeshift hammocks from the slimy line and scraps of canvas they had found. The gentlemen passengers were next; uncomfortable and in the most part cold, they sat close together and muttered bitterly of the circumstances which had put them in such a position. Several were military men, and nearly all mourned the fact that they had failed to get to grips with the enemy. To have surrendered without a shot being fired, or any form of resistance offered, offended their pride and made the captain's expulsion to the very end of the officers' section inevitable.

He sat there now, alone and for a number of reasons ignored, while Paterson, Nichols and Langlois talked softy in the half-light. Willis slept nearby, and Drayton, who had naturally assumed the status of officer, chewed on the very last of his ration of salt horse. Keats and Manning were not present, having been called for some while ago. They were thought to be treating an injured member of the French crew. The ship gave a slight heave, alerting the sailors present, and then a succession of shouted orders filtered down from above.

"Sounds like a change of course," Paterson said flatly. This was nothing to be surprised about. The privateer was beating into the wind and they were accustomed to tacking regularly. Nichols withdrew his watch and peered at it in the uncertain light.

"A little early," he said. "Belike the wind has shifted slightly." This also was in no way unusual, and the three were content to let the matter drop when Langlois spoke.

"She is not turning," he said, his clear voice edged with certainly. "I'd chance they are backing sails."

There was silence as all considered the implications. The only reason most could think of for the privateer to purposefully slow her progress was trouble aboard *Pevensey Castle*. The merchant might have lost a spar or some other piece of her tophamper, or there could be problems with the British crew. Then the unmistakeable sound of gun carriages being run out came to them.

"I'd say something was up," Paterson chanced. The others nodded and stirred themselves in their cramped seats. Langlois rose, stretching his legs and looking about. The captain was still sitting morosely to the stern, his head down and arms wrapped about his body. They must have been cooped up for almost a day, and yet the only contribution he made was pushing himself forward to be first for the provisions and, inevitably, the necessary bucket. Willis still slept, but Drayton was alert and caught the fifth mate's eye.

"Changes aloft," Langlois said briefly. "Might be nothing, or there could be trouble in the old *Pevensey*."

Now he had the attention of some male passengers, several began to mutter to each other, while two eased themselves up and stretched.

"I don't think there is need for alarm, gentlemen." Paterson's voice rose slightly. "Perhaps it is just a manoeuvre." Panic, in such a confined space, was dangerous. Willis woke and yawned generously, looking about for some reason for the movement, and Drayton clambered to his feet.

"I feel we should make ourselves ready," he said, in a quiet but commanding voice. "We heavily outnumber our captors, and this might be the chance we need to fight back."

His words found a home with many of the men, although

Rogers still sat disconsolately at the end of the line.

"We have no arms." Willis was properly awake now, but showed no inclination to rise. Paterson was up and alert.

"Maybe some could be improvised," he said. "Are all these casks full?"

Men began to shake what barrels remained in the nearest tier. All appeared sound; it would be difficult to broach or break them down to individual staves without crows of iron. Then one of the seamen found a half-opened crate containing jars of preserved cabbage. Using nothing more than his bare hands and determination, he ripped two of the short planks free, before using them to lever apart the others. In no time there were forty short pieces of heavy wood; not ideal hand-to-hand combat weapons, but potentially useful nonetheless. The ship heeled again, and there were further shouts from above. Paterson and Nichols exchanged glances; something was definitely up. They both made their way forward and stood under the hatch cover. It was securely closed, and more than six feet above their heads, so even reaching it was difficult. Paterson looked about.

"Here, let's have a couple of those barrels down," he said, pointing to the water casks nearby. "You two men ease one from the top and let it fall—stand away below or you'll end up under. Then roll it over here."

The men moved cautiously in their cramped confinement, but soon a cask was dislodged and fell heavily on to the shingle. Planting it securely under the hatch, Paterson pulled himself on top and half crouched under the closed cover. He reached up and pressed gently. It gave not an inch. He shook his head.

"Firmly secured," he said. "We shall have to force it."

"Won't that alert the guards?" Willis's voice came from below. Paterson shrugged.

"It is a risk worth taking," he said. A further shout of orders came to them, followed by the sound of bare feet running on deck. Paterson smiled and looked down, "besides, I'd wager they have other matters to consider at present."

* * *

Khan had been gone for several minutes, but that did not mean he had been under the water for that length of time. King fidgeted aimlessly next to the hold. Drummond and Crowley were up on deck, keeping an eye on the privateer. Last heard, she was holding her course, although that was a little while ago. For all he knew, she had turned and was bearing down upon them. Their defences would need to be organised, with men stationed ready when they came. King had already ordered the door to the spirit room to be broken down, and the small arms, cutlasses, pikes and pistols recovered: there was little more that could be done while he remained below. But then, beneath his feet a man was struggling underwater, fighting to close a valve that he himself had opened. Khan was risking his life to save the ship, and the least King could do was wait for him to return.

The sound of someone on the stern ladder made him turn. Drummond was hurling himself down the steps. He stumbled slightly on reaching the deck, but that did not stop him from scampering recklessly towards him.

"Frenchman's spilling her wind," he spluttered when he reached King at the open hatch. "Must 'ave caught the drift of something; Crowley thinks they're going to turn."

"Very good," King replied, momentarily unsure of his next move. He could order *Pevensey Castle* to back sail or even alter course, but the act would confirm trouble aboard the ship, and any such manoeuvre must take time. With the ship waterlogged as she was, chances were strong that the privateer would find them half way through the operation.

He forced himself to think. The leak must have slowed the ship considerably. It was even possible that nothing untoward was suspected, and the enemy was simply allowing *Pevensey Castle* to head reach on them. He peered down at the dim waters that had taken Khan. This would not do. He should be on deck supervising, and must leave the Lascar to his fate. There was little he was actually achieving by standing by the hatch.

"You and Crowley can organise the men. I have to remain a moment longer." Crowley was capable enough to order a defence, and he intended to join them directly. The pumps were still clanking monotonously while King's mind sped on. Even if the French were not coming now, they were bound to soon. Within half an hour matters must be settled either way, and *Pevensey Castle* was not going to sink in that time. He turned to the men at the pumps. "Up on deck with you lads, it sounds as if we're expecting company." The men willingly dropped the handles and followed Drummond.

The chains rumbled to a halt, and as he finally stood alone, King stared once more into the water which now seemed ominously dark and still. It had been too long, much too long, but he could waste no further time waiting. For a moment, he decided to leave and even took a step towards the stern ladder when something made him stop. Stop, throw off his jacket and remove his boots. His feet just touched the water, which felt icy cold, but he was able to ignore that as he slipped off the hatch coaming, and plunged his body into the depths beneath.

* * *

Crowley received the order from Drummond without comment. King was going to be with them as soon as possible; until then they must manage without him. The Irishman went to turn away, when he suddenly became aware that the lad was eyeing him cautiously. Crowley paused for a moment, before remembering that, despite their difference in age, the midshipman was actually the senior.

"I could take charge, if you wish Mr Drummond," he said softly.

"If you would," the lad replied, conscious that the older man outranked him in almost every other sphere.

Crowley nodded. "All right boys, spread out along the starboard rail, and let's see what the French have in mind." The men responded instantly to the voice of natural authority, and Drummond drew a silent sigh of relief.

* * *

In the absolute black of the flooded hold, Khan was starting to lose his sense of direction. He had been in the water for no more than three minutes, and swimming strongly under it for less than one; by his own estimation, that put him in the general vicinity of the sweetening cock. Consequently, the side of a tier of crates that bashed him cruelly on the shoulder came as a shock. He had thought to be keeping to the middle gangway and past such obstacles. Immediately he pushed himself away, and tried to regain the central aisle, only to collide with another hard object to the other side. Despite the breath that was bursting inside his chest, Khan paused for a moment. For him to be amid the main bulk of the stores meant that he could not have progressed very far at all. It was still a fair distance to the sweetening cock. He pushed off once more, knowing that the time left was rapidly depleting. His chest was starting to hurt now, and he released some air to ease the pain. Again, his left shoulder was jarred by a sharp object, and more of the precious air unwittingly escaped as he controlled the instinctive reaction to gasp. But soon he must be clear of the stores, then the search for the valve could begin. His lungs were already fit to burst, and yet he knew that added depth only increased the pressure. Khan stubbornly closed his mind to all thoughts apart from reaching the stern. Once there he would switch to finding the valve. After that the thing must be closed, and then, only then, could he even consider the long journey back.

* * *

The moon was low and to the east as Crowley strode down the length of the quarterdeck and gazed forward at the ghostly spectre of the privateer. She had backed her main and was wallowing in the swell, while *Pevensey Castle* crept up on her. They might reduce sail, but the Indiaman was barely making steerage way as it was, and such an act would only arouse suspicion. Crowley was content to fight the ship on his own if it came to it, and the men were certainly game enough, but still he wondered what on earth could be keeping King.

A light appeared on the privateer, to be covered almost immediately. Then it reappeared and was left to burn brightly for several seconds, before being extinguished entirely. Crowley grunted to himself. It was clearly some sort of signal, and the French would be expecting another in return. He could try to discover what the correct reply was—some of the prisoners were now conscious and might be persuaded. Chances were strong that they would not speak the truth, however. The only signal Crowley knew of was the rocket, and that was clearly meant for distress. They were edging closer, already the hull and most of the privateer's tophamper were quite discernible. The men were formed up and waiting, in the most part sheltering behind the bulwarks. There were a fair number and all well armed and ready to fight, even though many were not experienced in hand-to-hand combat. Activity on the French ship caught his attention. They had brought her back to the wind, and she was starting to gather way.

Crowley watched, transfixed, while the enemy's speed increased, and for a moment hope welled up inside him. Then he saw the yards move and her rudder started to bring her round in a wide, graceful, sweep. They had been rumbled; the French were turning back, and would soon have the wind with them as they swept down. A ship like that was built for speed; it would be no time before she was alongside. Slowly the immensity of what they were attempting became apparent. And where the hell was King?

* * *

The water seemed to grow even colder as it soaked into his shirt and trousers. King supposed he should have stripped completely, but there had been so little time. He swam forward in the dark; a few tentative strokes at first and then reached the first of the heavy frame beams that ran widthways across the ship. The solid oak was nearly a foot deep and almost touched the surface of the water. Ducking under, he emerged on the other side, and immediately banged his head on the deckhead, which was that much lower. The beam sealed off most of the light from the open hatchway, and as he swam forward, the darkness slowly became complete. He continued a little more cautiously, knowing he might reach another obstruction at any moment. It was difficult to judge exactly where he was in the ship; certainly, it would be a good few feet before he came even close to the seacock. The water level must have risen slightly since Khan tried, but not that much, and a feeling of guilt swept over him as he finally understood the difficulty of the task he had allowed the Lascar to attempt. Another frame, again he ducked under, and again the deckhead seemed lower on the other side. He turned and swam on his back, his face scraping against the rough planking while he fought for the very last of the air.

The solid wall of another beam stopped him, and he drew several deeper breaths. It seemed likely that there would be no space between the water and the deckhead on the other side. This was his last chance, before plunging down into the dark and searching for that accursed valve. Taking one final gasp, he ducked down and swam deep into the hold. Almost immediately he hit a cask, one of probably several that contained enough air to lift them from the shingle. He wriggled round it, but the act took much of his breath. Vainly he struck out again, but he knew that his reserves were too low to continue for much longer; certainly not as far as the sweetening cock. What to do, turn back, return to the other side of that last beam, then take in more air and try again? It seemed hopeless. He struck forward and hit another object. This time it was softer, probably a sack or a bundle of material. A firm shove pushed it to one side, but as he did so several things registered; the thing was warm, moving and strangely familiar. It was a man's body.

Any thoughts King might have for the seacock disappeared instantly. Reaching out, he found an arm, which reacted to his touch. He pulled at it, tugging the thing towards him, then slowly started to make his way back towards the hatch. There was some movement, but none that helped in any way. King's lungs were near to bursting now, but still he swam on, moving past the floating cask with effort. The deckhead was still keeping him under, but must surely begin to rise before long.

Painfully he scraped against the pine strakes. The all-enveloping dark was slowly robbing him of his sense of direction until he could only hope he was heading for the hatchway. Fantasies of light and blessed air threatened to take him over while he struck out again and again. The body followed him readily enough, but the movements were diminishing, and it was becoming disturbingly like a dead weight. Still the deckhead was too low, still it kept them under, and yet they could not be that far from reaching that final beam. For a moment, he considered releasing the body and making for air. He could draw breath and return for Khan later, although even while he thought, he rejected the idea. The Lascar might have some semblance of life left in him. Time would be lost, and King may not be able to find the body again. He swam on, his right hand desperately scooping water while the left tugged the lifeless mass behind. His chest hurt, and some unknown muscles began to force his mouth open and his lungs to breath. He wanted so much to gasp, to draw in anything that might satisfy the cravings in his chest. Then he was at the frame, the oak struck him on the side; he must have been swimming diagonally across the hold. He clambered under just as another spasm gripped him. It was no good; his mouth actually opened and, finally giving in to what had become inevitable, he inhaled deeply.

A noise, which must have been his own lungs, filled his ears, but it was not the dark water of the hold that flowed down his windpipe, but cold, clean air. He coughed, retched and gasped afresh, before breathing in once more, then pulled at the body until it was level with him. It was still pitch black; there was no more than an inch or two of air between the surface of the water and the deckhead, but he could breathe. He held Khan's face against the gap and pulled the body further forward. They continued, with the Lascar mumbling softly as each subsequent frame was negotiated until finally, unbelievably, they were under the hatchway.

King looked for some means to get the body up and on to the deck. Drummond's face appeared in the gloom above; the lad must have come down to see what was keeping him. King shouted out, holding his arm high.

"Over here, I can't reach you." The young midshipman stretched out, but their hands remained a few inches apart. King heaved the body across. Khan moved suddenly, striking King a firm blow to the side of the face, but now the boy had a hold and was starting to drag the Lascar out of the water. King helped as much as he could, although Drummond was a strong lad, and the serang no more than a lightweight. Reaching for the coaming, King hauled himself up, pausing to gain breath when his face was level with the deck. Drummond was trying to roll the man to one side. For some reason this was not possible; then he realised that the Lascar was actually resisting, and attempting to clamber to his knees. King managed to swing a leg on to the deck. Drummond reached for him, and soon he was slumped on his side, panting like a dog in summer.

He looked across. Khan was alive and breathing deeply. "Did you manage it?" he asked, still breathless.

Khan's eyes were closed and he appeared to be speaking softly to somebody else. Then they opened, and he registered King's presence apparently with surprise. "Yes," he smiled weakly. "It is done."

King nodded. "Good." The air was starting to revive him now, but still he continued to inhale deeply. "I have no wish to go back," he said.

*   *   *

In the privateer, the prisoners were making slow progress. The hatch cover was solid hardwood and Paterson was attempting to force a plank from the smashed crate up under one of the corners. He guessed that the thing was only lightly secured, but there was little movement when he pulled back. His lever creaked alarmingly, and the hatch stayed firmly closed. Withdrawing the plank, he moved away from the corner, and inserted it nearer the middle. This time the cover bowed slightly with the effort.

"Give me another," he shouted, and a second plank was thrust up from below. He took it, pulled back on the lever and thrust the new piece into the gap. Withdrawing the first plank, he took another as it was passed to him and repeated the process. Soon the hatch cover was bowed along its entire length, although the gap was less than three inches high at the widest point.

"I need something larger," he said, looking down at the waiting group. "Something to force into that hole."

There was a brief movement and some muttering before one of the heavier frames from the crate was handed up. Paterson examined it: a much shorter length of wood, although considerably thicker. He pushed the timber into the gap nearest the corner, and pulled back. The hatchway groaned with the effort and there was one sharp crack, but no more. He tried again with the same result. Then, on the third attempt, another louder snap, followed by the sound of tearing wood, and the cover lifted.

The previously wedged planks released and fell on to the men below, but no one complained or even seemed to notice. Paterson pressed his back against the hatch cover and gingerly lifted it free. He glanced round; the lower deck appeared empty, but he could not be sure. The cask that supported him wobbled slightly, and he peered down to see Nichols scrambling up next to him. When he was settled, Paterson lifted the hatch up again, and the fourth mate squeezed through the gap.

Once on deck Nichols climbed to his feet. A foreign voice, raised in alarm, made him turn and he looked straight into the eyes of a stocky man in a striped shirt. Without stopping to think, Nichols lunged forward. The Frenchman stepped back, but could not avoid the fist that caught him on the side of his chin, or the swift left hook that followed almost immediately afterwards. The body slumped to the deck in an untidy heap and Nichols massaged the knuckles of his fist thoughtfully.

"All clear?" Paterson was peering under the wrecked hatch cover.

Nichols nodded. "Apparently."

The hatch creaked as Paterson pressed up from beneath. Nichols moved towards it and took the edge in both hands. With his feet on the solid deck, he was able to wrench the entire cover free, although he was careful to keep the noise of tearing wood down to a minimum. Below him, Paterson was still perched on the barrel, with the other men in the hold crowding beneath. The seamen, most of the officers and a good proportion of the passengers looked ready to act.

"Lower deck's empty at the moment, but that can't last if you make a lot of noise." Nichols spoke in a clear, soft voice that carried easily and there were nods of agreement from most as he continued, "We'll take the officers first, then the seamen. Gentlemen, your assistance would also be welcome."

The message clearly found a home with some of the passengers, and Paterson received a nod from Langlois. He glanced back up at Nichols, who was standing next to the open hatch, looking along the deck. "Come on then," he said, and reached for the coaming.

"Touch of the dropsies?" Paterson asked, as he clambered on to the deck and noticed the crumpled body of the Frenchman. "Didn't have you down for a pugilist, George."

"In truth, neither did I," Nichols replied. "'Tis lucky he went down as he did: there was little else I had to offer."

Paterson looked about; the lower deck of the privateer was far narrower than that of *Pevensey Castle*. Men's hammocks remained hung from the deck beams, grouped in what must be their individual messes; clearly, the French did not choose to sling them nightly. There was also the usual assortment of storerooms and workshops that might be found on any deep-sea ship. Doubtless the women were incarcerated in one, but they would have to remain so for the time being. Should they be released, it could only mean greater danger for all. There was no sign of any other French, he supposed the activity above demanded all hands. Then the ship began to turn.

A stream of orders came down to them, followed by the creak of spars as the braces dragged the yards round, and the ship heeled on to her new course.

"All appear to be up on deck," Paterson commented.

"Must be truly short handed," the fourth mate agreed, while Willis climbed up through the hatch. Most of the officers were out of the hold now, and the first of the seamen were beginning to follow.

"What of the captain?" Paterson asked, suddenly noticing that he was missing.

"Mr Rogers prefers to remain in the hold," Langlois said flatly. "Though I chance we are the better without him."

"The captain is ill," Willis's tone was stiff and defensive.

"Then what I say holds true," Langlois replied, his voice oddly curt.

The officers were silent, although noises from above continued, and the ship began to heel further to larboard.

"Starboard tack and wind on the quarter," Paterson said, quietly. "I'd say they've turned about."

"Chance is another vessel's been sighted." Langlois was looking intently at the deckhead as if he wanted to see through the planks. "Belike a warship?"

"They could hardly attempt taking another merchant," Paterson agreed. "Not with their numbers stretched so."

"Odds are high that it be British." There were several seamen on deck now and the first of the male passengers also joined them, although it was going to take a fair while to clear the hold completely. Some were brandishing their rough wooden staves as if they were terrible weapons.

"Gentlemen, I think we can find better arms." Paterson indicated the nearby bulk of the mainmast, which had a ring of boarding pikes secured about it. Cutlasses were also to hand in two brass racks to either side, and soon the small group was a proper fighting force.

"If they've sighted a British ship, we might be better to wait awhile." Willis sounded anxious, although no one seemed to be taking a great deal of notice of him.

"My guess is there's trouble in *Pevensey Castle*, and they're heading back for her," Nichols said, gripping his cold iron sword in his swollen right hand, conscious of a strange but not unpleasant surge of energy flowing throughout him. "There is nothing to gain by staying here. Clear the hold of all who are willing and let us act, else the advantage of surprise will be lost." The ship groaned as she took up speed, and when he moved off for the stern hatchway he knew instinctively that the other men were following him.

* * *

The privateer was closing on them fast as King regained the quarterdeck. He glanced briefly at Crowley who appeared to take no notice of his soggy clothes, bruised face and lack of jacket, before turning his attention to the oncoming enemy. She was less than two cables off their bow and bearing down, her topsails, stays and jib picked out by the ghostly moon.

"They're intendin' to come alongside," Crowley muttered, his eyes fixed on the enemy ship. "I wagered to starboard, but now ain't so certain."

King nodded. "Aye, it will be larboard for sure; best set the men."

Crowley stepped forward to the fife rails and directed the crew to the larboard side bulwarks.

"Stay covered 'till we meet her, and then wait 'for them to come across." King addressed them in a clear but soft voice. "Take them on our deck, only attempt to board yourself if there be enough, and you are truly confident of support."

There were several former Navy men who knew the dangers of an enemy deck, and King trusted that the Lascars, together with any dyed-in-the-wool merchant seamen, could control themselves sufficiently. The privateer drew closer, and was almost hidden as she crossed their bow. They had been right; she would scrape their larboard wales. A light showed briefly from her foretopmast, to be repeated after a short interval.

"They've done that afore," Crowley spoke from behind. "I was thinking it a signal but knew not what to reply."

King nodded, then inspiration struck. "Tell them we're sinking," he said.

Crowley looked at him sidelong for less than a second before drawing breath and bellowing forth.

"Nous coulons!"

The words echoed about the quiet night as if shouted in an empty cathedral. A momentary pause, then a guttural French voice replied.

"They're asking us to make the signal," Crowley replied.

"Say there is no time, to come alongside and help; tell them the pumps are out of action and we are taking in water fast."

Crowley's reply rang out, and now the French ship could be

seen clearly as she crept towards their larboard bow.

"Keep covered, lads," King growled, when one of the British seamen on the forecastle raised his head above the bulwark. The same French voice replied, and this time it carried a slight note of panic.

"They say if we don't make the signal they will fire on us," Crowley said calmly.

"So be it," King all but whispered. "They are close enough, and we have put them off long enough." He turned and looked at his friend, both faces dimly lit in the moonlight. "What say we go and meet with some Frenchmen?"

CHAPTER FOURTEEN

Ward and Johnston were keeping down low behind the dubious protection of the forecastle bulwark. The thing was made of sound enough timber and in places measured several inches thick, although it still would not be strong enough to keep out round shot at close range. On a warship it would have been higher, thicker and topped with netting that held any number of canvas hammocks, each tightly rolled and crammed in place to make an excellent defence. But they just had plain wooden planking secured to frame timbers; the bulwark itself was only truly intended to repel high seas and stood barely more than a foot above the deck.

Ward lay next to Johnston, who had Khan's shirt tied about his wounded upper arm, with Clegg, the Lancastrian, further forward and currently peering up over the cathead.

"Less than a cable off," the latter reported, ducking down and regaining what shelter he could. "I'd say they'll be alongside in less than a minute."

Ward fingered his cutlass thoughtfully. The blade was heavy and almost dull, although its worth came not from a razor-like edge. It was built to deliver hard, hacking strokes that severed and slashed and could be as deadly as any scimitar. The weapon was worthy of the job ahead; a true professionals tool, but at that moment Ward felt that it was being held by an out-and-out amateur.

His Navy days were more than ten years behind him and had been free from any genuine action. The previous brush with privateers in the Channel had been inconclusive, and even when *Pevensey Castle* was taken, he had not felt himself in any great danger. Now though, with King in command and the stakes raised so high, he knew this was not going to end without a proper resolution, or in the anticlimax of a speedy surrender. He looked at Johnston who crouched, knees drawn up under him, his back barely sheltered by the bulwark. The man seemed taut and ready to pounce as soon as the chance presented itself. Feeling Ward's eyes on him, he glanced sideways and treated the boatswain's mate to a slow, sly wink.

"Ready, lads!"

Ward jumped at the unexpected voice. Mr King had come forward and must be just behind them. Yes, there he was, peering over the bulwark at the oncoming enemy. He stood half way up the forecastle ladder, dressed in what looked like sodden clothing that clung to his body. Heaven alone knew how he had got himself quite so wet; it was certainly none of Ward's concern. The time stretched on inexorably, with every man at his post—rigid with anticipation or, in certain cases, something else.

And Ward was one. In the past he might have wondered how he would behave in action, but it was only now, now that the prospect of a bloody fight was so dangerously close, that he knew for certain. He swallowed dryly and suppressed the urge to urinate. In a couple of seconds he was going to disgrace himself, and yet there was nowhere to go and nothing else he could do, so exposed was his position. He could feel his heart beating rapidly in his chest, and knew his breathing to be brisk and shallow. It could not last much longer, surely?

Then the slightest of shadows passed overhead. There was a loud crack that was replaced instantly by a horrible grinding noise, and *Pevensey Castle* shuddered and heeled. A whistle sounded, and Ward found all mundane thoughts swept away as he rose up to meet the oncoming rush of Frenchmen.

There were fewer than ten perched on the enemy's forecastle, although one fell to Clegg's pistol before he could even attempt to clamber up the Indiaman's sides. Then Johnston raised a boarding pike and stabbed down on another whose hands were reaching up to grab the top rail, and the shot of a blunderbuss, aimed by someone on the gangboard, accounted for two more. Ward glanced down and along the privateer's decks. The ships drew apart momentarily, and the Frenchman crept slowly by. Aboard her another group of twenty or so were waiting for them to close again by her mainmast. King was also looking and turned to Ward's group on the forecastle.

"Knock out all you can on our decks when they come across. Remember the enemy will be that much harder to fight on their own territory. So don't follow any back, or go on your own. Wait until you get the word."

Ward nodded to himself. He saw the sense in that, and was certain not to get carried away—the very idea of carrying on the fight unnecessarily was quite abhorrent to him. A crash and another shudder, then the yardarms locked and both ships became entwined. This time there were more men reaching for *Pevensey Castle*'s forechains. Johnston, backed by several others, was soon at work with his pike. The sound of a blunderbuss, wielded amidships, rang out above the din, and a tongue of flame from a French swivel gun lit the scene momentarily, although the weapon was aimed far too high and did no discernible damage. Clegg now held a cutlass and was slashing away madly at two men mounting the chains, while shouting the foulest of oaths at the top of his voice. Something caught Ward's attention; to his right a Frenchman had actually made it as far as clambering over the top rail. Instinctively he swung his own cutlass, catching the man on his shoulder while he struggled to stand. The privateer screamed and dropped his sword as his right hand went to the wound. Fired by success, Ward advanced and struck again, this time sending the man backwards over the rail, to fall on any others that might be following.

Now his blood was up, and there was neither the time, nor the need, to worry how he might fare as a fighter. He glared about, eager for another enemy, and immediately spotted one attempting to mount their larboard anchor. The man had a small axe slung about his neck while he used both hands to climb, and was an easy target. Ward wielded his cutlass again, and the Frenchman disappeared with barely a scream.

He looked to his left. Johnston was entwined with an evil-looking brute who was wrestling him for his pike. It was a simple matter to take the man from behind, swipe the hilt of the cutlass down on his neck and finish him off with the blade as he fell. Johnston looked his thanks, but there was no time for more. King, with Crowley by his side, was fighting with two Frenchmen who were apparently on the verge of being beaten back, while Clegg moved further forward, hacking at men as they attempted to board over the bowsprit. Johnston's pike was in use once again, but there seemed no immediate enemy for Ward. He glanced round, his mouth open and eyes wide. A moustachioed face appeared for a moment over the larboard anchor, but vanished just as quickly when its owner apparently lost his footing. Ward stepped forward and peered over the side and saw seven or eight Frenchmen grouped on the privateer's deck below. Some had been pressed back by *Pevensey Castle*'s crew and were clearly wounded, others seemed unwilling to even try. He braced himself and grasped his cutlass even more tightly. His head was filled with fighting madness. They had won; the French were beaten off. Now was the time to press forward the advantage.

Stepping up and over the anchor, he paused for a second. *Pevensey Castle*'s tumblehome, the rounded profile caused by a wide lower deck and narrower upper, meant there was a good three feet between her and the Frenchman, although the latter vessel sat much lower. He braced himself for less than a second before leaping forward, just as someone unknown shouted his name. The distance from his ship to the privateer was easily covered, and he landed with a sizeable thump, absorbing the shock with bended knees. His feet smarted from the hardness of the enemy deck, but Ward was more than ready and sprang up, cutlass raised and a cruel look on his face, to meet the Frenchmen. They stared at him, transfixed, for no more than a second, and he had time enough to fully appreciate their number and the folly of his action, before they killed him.

* * *

King, watching from *Pevensey Castle*'s side, swore under his breath. The man was a fool, of course, but that didn't make the fact of his death any the easier to take. His damp clothes were finally becoming a nuisance, and he shivered suddenly in the chill of the night. He might have just seen off two boarders and the forecastle was now free of Frenchmen, but to take the fight to the enemy was another question entirely—as Ward had already discovered. *Pevensey Castle* was considerably higher than the privateer, and any attack they launched must be that much harder to retreat from. They would be committed, and the chance of failure was high. But then they had been committed from the moment Crowley first felled the guard—from the time King opened that seacock, come to that—and to throw away the advantage already earned would be foolish in the extreme.

"They're clear amidships," Crowley shouted. King looked; sure enough the men at the larboard gangboard had also fought the French back, aided by those on the poop and quarterdeck. All were now without an enemy to fight. Seven seamen stood primed on the forecastle, with only one slightly wounded, and there were at least eleven further back who appeared just as ready to join them.

"Then now's the time, Michael," King said, raising his sword high and looking back for the others to notice. They greeted his action with a roar and were immediately clambering across the bulwark. King too mounted the wooden wall, before launching himself over and down on to Frenchman's deck. A man was directly in front of him as he landed and King dodged the slash of a cutlass which would have all but taken off his arm. He knocked into Crowley as he avoided the blow, but the Irishman was ready with his weapon and cut the man down. King recovered and raised his own sword, sending another privateer, who was making for them, spinning to the deck. More appeared. One, wild eyed and yelling, swung a wicked-looking axe in a manner that seemed every bit as dangerous to the French as the English. Crowley neatly despatched him with a blow from the hilt of his cutlass, and the axe fell harmlessly to the deck. Two steps deeper into the enemy's territory and a pistol ball screamed by King's head. He turned, looking for the source, but saw a man heading for him with a pike instead. A quick side step, and another cutlass landed on the Frenchman's shoulder as he passed. Crowley drew back his sword without a word, and they advanced further.

"We must take the quarterdeck." King shouted once he realised that the forecastle and main were theirs. The Irishman nodded. There were roughly twenty more Frenchmen towards the stern, some having retreated from the main, along with one well-dressed officer who looked like the captain. King had twelve fully fit men on the privateer's decks and it was hardly enough; especially when more enemy were liable to be waiting below. For a moment he considered withdrawing, but the Indiaman's sides were high, and the French were bound to take advantage of the first sign of retreat.

"Back with you lads, we're taking the officers!" Crowley clearly had no such thoughts and, raising his cutlass high, led the boarders in a rush. The Frenchmen on the quarterdeck were ready, some armed with pistols, while others held pikes and swords. King, running forward with Crowley, was preparing himself for a bloody fight when the first of the British prisoners appeared from the stern hatchway ahead of them.

It was Nichols, followed by what looked like Langlois and two Lascar seamen. The boarding party slowed slightly as more swarmed up. Some of the released prisoners turned back and even went to attack King's men until realisation dawned on them that they were friends. But most went straight for the quarterdeck and swamped the stunned French in a vicious onslaught.

The sheer volume of men, inflamed by their recent confinement, was more than enough to swing matters. Within minutes of starting, the fight was over, and the enemy, battered and bemused, began to surrender. King ran on to the quarterdeck just as the last of the Frenchmen were cornered. Nichols was there, his face flushed and an evil looking foreign cutlass in his hand.

"Well met, Tom!" he beamed at King.

"Well met, indeed," King agreed as the shouting began to die down around them. "You came just in time."

Langlois was collecting the remaining weapons from the Frenchmen, who sulkily gave them up as they nursed their wounds. King noticed that the captain was standing alone next to the larboard bulwark.

"No sword, sir?" Langlois asked him. *"Vous n'avez pas d'arme?"*

The officer eyed him morosely, and then his left hand withdrew a small pistol from his belt. Langlois reached out for the weapon but rather than give it up the Frenchman clicked back the hammer with his right hand and fired.

The shot rang out in the relative silence, and the fifth mate looked down instinctively. But there was no wound opening in his belly, and no stab of excruciating pain. The ball must have passed him by no more than a whisker.

"Where is your damned honour, sir?" Langlois angrily demanded as he snatched the hot gun from the officer. The Frenchman opened his mouth to speak when a loud moan from behind made them all turn.

"My God!" Nichols was staring down, almost in surprise.

"Are you hit, George?" Langlois asked. Nichols's look of astonishment was quickly replaced by one of agony. His hands grasped his stomach and he sank to his knees before tipping forward slightly and slumping unconscious to the deck.

* * *

Morning found them weary and strangely subdued. The night had been spent making both ships ready to sail again, and with the first light of dawn men started to stumble and grow quarrelsome. The French were secured in the merchant's forecastle, with some removed in rotation every half hour to attend to her pumps. Consequently *Pevensey Castle* now drew less than four feet in her well, and the prisoners, suitably exhausted, were quiet. A permanent armed guard was placed over them and Kate, at her insistence, took over their supervision, losing no time in introducing some to the wonders of the necessary bucket.

Running repairs were needed in both ships. Several shrouds had parted, which Khan, who seemed fully recovered, attended to, while the carpenter returned to the tiller flat, replacing and improving much of the work carried out when the ship was under French command.

In the sickbay Keats and Manning had also been busy. Besides Nichols, a number of men required treatment. Two arms, so shattered as to be useless, were removed, and numerous cuts and gashes treated. There was only one other bullet wound—a French topman who had taken a blunderbuss shot to the shoulder. It was a relatively easy matter to pull the thing out, and both surgeons were hopeful for a good recovery. Nichols's wound was far more complex however; the pistol ball was lodged somewhere deep in his lower abdomen, and he was not expected to survive.

The British lost eight men in the attack, and there were several quite severely wounded, although all were expected to pull through apart from the fourth mate. The fact that he was about to die played upon the feelings of everyone, so there was little jubilation following their victory. Any relief that they were no longer prisoners was more than countered by the knowledge that another—one who was known to them all and with them even now —was also about to pay the ultimate price for their liberty.

The feeling spread even to the passengers, who readily accepted that their cabins could not be restored until the ship was serviceable again and were eager to cooperate in any way they could. Now, with both ships hove to within a cable of the other, and the scent of wood smoke in the air from the galley fires, most were stood down for the first time, and they finally rested.

The cook had been wounded in the fight, so Susan and Emma were helping at the stove. Mrs Drayton had prevailed upon her husband to donate a side of bacon to provide a decent breakfast, and the heavily salted rashers were even now hissing on a large round copper pan atop the range. A bucket of eggs was supplied by another passenger, even though many of the ducks and chickens that had produced them had been slaughtered by the French in their lust for fresh meat.

Susan rolled her eyes as an apron-clad Mrs Drayton directed and instructed from afar, but she scraped the rashers up carefully enough, while Emma produced another pan and added some of the cook's slush for the eggs. The smell of hot food permeated throughout the ship, and slowly a better feeling followed, although it would take more than a good meal and the knowledge that they now had a fair chance of survival to wipe away the memories of the last few days.

* * *

King was in the privateer and strode the quarterdeck with a proprietary air. He knew of Nichols's wound, but was far enough away from its reality to enjoy the fruits of success. Responsibility for the prize had been passed to him from the outset, and now that there was time to examine the vessel properly, he was extremely pleased with her.

Built almost exclusively for her sailing qualities, the hull was slimmer than most with the armament—a main deck of six-pounder long guns plus a handful of swivels—seemingly added later as an afterthought. Her three masts were higher in proportion to those found on similar British-designed craft, and though she might appear fragile and could well be sensitive and delicate to sail, her performance should be that of a thoroughbred compared to the old *Pevensey Castle*. And, like a racehorse, it would surely be worth putting up with a small amount of careful handling to gain that vital edge. She was at rest in the water now, the seas lapping against her sleek hull and the wind whispering past the raked masts and light spars, but it would take only a few orders from him to set her free. Despite a tiring night when he had brushed close with death on more than one occasion, King simply longed for the opportunity.

Crowley appeared on the quarterdeck with Drummond, one of the midshipmen from *Pevensey Castle* also detailed to the privateer.

"There's a boat headin' across," King said conversationally as the two joined him. It was not an unusual occurrence—for the past few hours there had been a great deal of traffic between the two ships.

"Looks like Mr Langlois," Drummond said, peering down at the cutter as it came alongside. Sure enough, the iron grey hair was unmistakable, and even after such a night, the mate looked immaculate in his frock dress coat.

"Lively little craft you have here," he said as he joined King on the quarterdeck. "Give you longings for the Navy, does she?"

King regarded his friend easily enough, although the suspicion that he might have come to relieve him of command lurked at the back of his mind.

"How are things in the *Pevensey*?" he asked. "What news of Nichols?"

"Not good I fear." Langlois's voice was suitably low. "Mr Keats feels it unlikely he will last out the day."

Nothing was said for a moment, then Langlois raised his eyebrows. "But an interesting situation elsewhere." He motioned King away from where Crowley and Drummond stood at the binnacle.

"Shall we go below?" King asked, guessing that some degree of confidentiality was called for.

"A capital idea, Tom. Lead the way."

It was certainly private in the captain's quarters, and a deal more comfortable as well. King sank down into a soft horsehair armchair, while Langlois selected the upholstered bench under the tiny stern windows. He lay back on the deep buttoned leather seat, with one arm gracefully draped along the sill, as if he were relaxing at his club after a particularly satisfactory meal. King felt he only needed a cigar and a glass of brandy to complete the picture.

"Yes, we have enjoyed some rare conversations," he said amicably when they were settled. "Captain Rogers has surprised us again, although as that is so much in his nature, I chance that it is no surprise at all."

"Is he in command?" King asked.

"Ah, no. No, he is not." Langlois gave a half smile. "Mr Drayton has dismissed him, though it took an hour or two to come to that decision and make it stick."

"Can he do that? I mean, Drayton is the ship's husband and I understand has quite a senior position, but Rogers is employed directly by the East India Company, surely?"

The look stayed on his face as Langlois replied. "Whether he can or whether he cannot, he has done so, and, may I add, he has the full support of all, be they officers, passengers or men. Mr Rogers's status is now no more than that of a passenger, though I note he has not given up the captain's quarters. Any legal niceties can be sorted out later, but we are in a perilous position and reliable command is paramount to our survival."

"Does Willis have it?"

Langlois shook his head. "No, it is Paterson. Willis is to remain chief officer, in name at least, though I fear we will all have to keep an eye on him. And young Taylor will be acting up to stand watch with a master's mate."

It was King's turn to raise his eyebrows now. "I'm sure that went down well with the premier," he said.

"It's the way it has to be. Willis is a fool, and potentially almost as much of a liability as Rogers. He thinks himself a better seaman than he actually is, and the people hold no respect for him. Were it not for the lack of senior men, I think he would have joined his late captain." Langlois's words, though quickly spoken, carried a weight of emotion. "We have two ships to man, and a crew barely large enough for one. *Pevensey Castle* requires attention and is still heavy with water. And there is a fair old distance to travel until we can call ourselves safe. This is not the time for salving hurt feelings."

King nodded. What Langlois said made sense, but he was glad to have been in the privateer whilst it was being sorted out. "So what goes now?" he asked.

"A council of war was held," Langlois continued. "Regrettable that you could not be involved, of course, but I think you will agree with the outcome."

King waited expectantly.

"We intend to sail for the nearest naval force, which we reckon to be Lord St Vincent's at the Tagus."

"Do you know him to be at Portugal?"

"Indeed not, he might equally be off Cadiz, Gibraltar or even back in the Mediterranean b'now, but there will be a presence at least, and we should find shelter."

King mused; Lisbon was still several hundred miles away.

"Estimates vary of course, and a lot will depend on what speed the old girl can make," Langlois continued. "Once there we will await escort and probably continue to Gibraltar; I cannot see Jervis sparing any of his ships to take us to Madeira. Still, there is more extensive warehousing at the Rock. *Pevensey Castle* will need to be unloaded, re-provisioned and her cargo examined. I chance that a few amongst her passengers will not wish to continue with her; and, of course, there is the Rogers question to sort out. I expect us to remain a month or more until all can be sorted.

King was thinking through Langlois's words when he noticed the fifth mate's eyes fixed intently upon him.

"Tell me, Thomas; how many men do you have in this ship?"

"Seventeen, not counting myself or Drummond," he answered readily.

"Is it enough?"

"To sail her, yes, though I would not wish to come across any form of bad weather, nor action, if it came to it."

"Which it very well might," Langlois conceded. He nodded, thinking for a moment while King tried to suppress the question that was simply bursting to come out. Finally it could wait no longer.

"Are you to take command?" he asked.

"Of this ship?" Langlois regarded him with mild surprise. "No, Tom, I fear that is down to you, and by unanimous decision I might add."

King drew a silent sigh of relief as the mate continued. "You have handled a prize on more than one occasion, I understand. None of the other officers have experience of command or even Navy training, save Rogers and myself. No one would consider him worthy, and the idea has little appeal to me."

"I had not guessed you to be Navy," King said.

"Oh yes. I was written in the books of several ships for all of eight years before I finally stepped aboard one. My uncle was the premier of the old *Glorious*, and ended up following Dixon until he was yellowed."

King nodded encouragingly. This was a fresh side to the fifth mate, one he had yet to hear about. "And then?" he asked.

Langlois sat back, drawing his knee up in his clasped hands while he thought. "Well, I served as captain's servant in two seventy-fours and was finally appointed midshipman in the *Panther,*" he smiled. "Passed my board in 'eighty-seven, but only ever acted as lieutenant, and that for the briefest of periods."

King shook his head. "Then you switched to the Indiamen?"

"Aye, and remained with them ever since," he grinned, noticing King's enquiring look. "And rose no higher than a fifth mate, if that is what you are thinking."

King looked away, mildly embarrassed as Langlois continued. "Reasons there be, Tom, but this is not the time to talk of them. Perhaps one day we will speak again?" In a profession where both space and privacy were at a premium, Langlois was not alone in wanting to conceal his past.

"Of course," King said automatically.

"But I will say this now—the two lives are very different," Langlois mused, his eyes searching the deckhead of the tiny cabin. "It takes one type of man to be an officer in an Indiaman and another completely separate to serve in a man of war."

King tried to remember when he had heard a similar statement.

"And you are one of the latter," Langlois continued, his gaze dropping until he looked at King directly. "Not that you have failed in any way; the very reverse in fact. But it is obvious to all that your heart does not lie with the Honourable East India Company."

"In truth, it was not my first choice," King admitted. "I would have preferred an appointment elsewhere."

"I thought as much, and should hate for you to take *Pevensey Castle* for a typical example; indeed, there are many better, and few worse. But you will not find the Royal Navy in John Company. It is a different world, with different tasks. The Bombay Marine comes close, I suppose, but the openings are as restricted there as in His Majesty's ships."

King moved uncomfortably, conscious that Langlois's perception was remarkably accurate. "I am sorry. I have not offered any refreshment," he said hurriedly.

The older man stood and shook his head. "Neither did I expect any. Besides, they gave us a fine breakfast; and I will be back in time for a late bever." He patted his flat stomach appreciatively.

King pulled a face. "Ah, such luxury!"

"Aye, well, I have much to do; an examination of stores awaits me." He paused and grew suddenly serious. "Some cully was foolish enough to open a seacock; ruined our dry goods and made no end of a mess of the rest. Might cost thousands to set right, so they are saying."

King considered him uncertainly while the man hastened out of the small room. He turned as he was about to duck through the low doorway and grinned once more.

"Ask me, Tom, I'd say this little tub is the best place. I'd stay where I was, were I you."

* * *

Elizabeth sat in the darkened sickbay. She held Nichols's hand in hers, and it was all she could do not to grip it so tight as to cause him further pain. His face was quite white; even his lips were without colour, although the eyes that she loved so much still glowed back at her with a deep warmth.

"Won't you have some more to drink?" she asked, her voice soft. He shook his head slightly and winced from the effort. For the past hour or so he had hardly spoken a word, and yet when she first came to him they had chatted like children. A shadow fell over her, and Mr Keats knelt down beside them. Elizabeth released Nichols's hand to the surgeon, who began to measure the pulse against his watch. She looked at him eagerly, but Keats shook his head and said nothing.

"Is there naught you can do?" she asked.

The surgeon's glance went straight to the patient, then he turned back to the girl. "Perhaps we should speak?" he said.

She nodded and gently released the hand she had reclaimed, standing slowly from the bunk as if unwilling to leave. Keats led her towards his dispensary, where he indicated the small chair usually used by patients.

"The wound is very deep," he explained, as soon as they were settled. "To treat Mr Nichols properly must entail a major operation. I cannot be sure what damage has been done; even finding out would mean a great deal of pain and I don't think him to be strong enough."

"So that is it?" she asked, after a moment. "You are to let him die?"

"I have no choice. Any action I might take can only cause further distress and bring death that much the sooner. I think him better left and would chance that, on reflection, you will agree." He paused and regarded her with gentle eyes. "I am so sorry," he said.

* * *

The wind still blew from the northeast, although the course they steered, when both ships finally set sail, meant that it now came across their larboard quarter. King had long ago decided that this would probably be the privateer's best point of sailing, and so ordered just staysails, topsails and topgallants to match *Pevensey Castle*'s full suit that included courses. Sure enough, the little ship sprang forth like a deer, forcing him to back the mizzen and allow the Indiaman to forereach, then take in the topgallants before he finally matched her stately pace. He had allowed himself one short nap, and now that dinner was served, stood on the quarterdeck with just an able seaman at the helm and the rest sheltering in the lee of the bulwarks. He was happy for those on deck to rest whenever possible. The ship was running a two-watch system, although those below would be needed if any changes to their course or sail pattern were called for. King was taking alternate tricks with Drummond and Crowley even though all three might be needed at once. It was not an arrangement that could last forever, but he felt it might stand for the time needed to see them to safety.

Their noon sights placed them at roughly forty-three degrees north. Longitude was less easy to calculate as all the available chronometers differed, but it was generally reckoned that there was upwards of a hundred and fifty nautical miles to cover before raising the coast, and a further two hundred to sight the Tagus. It was a journey they could easily complete within the week, although with the rate *Pevensey Castle* was making, it might be twice that long, and even minor meteorological problems could stretch the time still further. Standing on his tiny quarterdeck, King was already becoming familiar with the motion of his ship through the soles of his boots. She was a lively thing to be sure; he felt he could have taken her to Gibraltar and back in no time at all, were he permitted.

To leeward the *Pevensey Castle* was battering through the swell with all the grace of a clumsy bear. She was riding higher now and must soon be dry, even though a trickle of water from the midship scuppers showed that her pumps were still in action.

Langlois's words, and being aboard the privateer, even for so short a time, were awakening strange feelings in him. There was nothing exactly unseaworthy or crank about the Indiaman. Indeed, she was solidly built and would probably survive three, or even four, more passages to India. He doubted if his present craft could see two without a major refit. But the privateer remained a proper ship, whereas *Pevensey Castle* was simply a barge—one built to bring riches from the East and wealth to her owners. There was no soul in her; she was just a means to an end.

Though larger, his previous ship, *Pandora,* a light and lithe frigate, was surprisingly like the little privateer. A versatile craft, not built for a single destination, and one designed with her sailing abilities very much in mind. The same could be said about most Navy vessels. Even the mighty warhorses, the seventy-fours and above that sat low and were so laden with guns as to be floating fortresses, even they could show a couple of knots to the old *Pevensey.* Watching her now as she dragged herself through the rolling seas, he finally decided that the merchant service was not for him.

He walked back and forth across the tiny deck while his thoughts ran on. Langlois had been right; the two services were very different. Plodding along in a hull weighed down by so much dead weight might suit some, but he yearned for the freedom of a warship, even one confined to a dreary blockade duty. And he missed the company of Navy officers. Paterson, Nichols and the rest had done well enough when retaking the *Espérance,* but with a handful of true fighting men beside him, he was certain the Indiaman would not have been captured in the first place. Thinking about it again he was still amazed at the apathy the others had displayed. In his mind there could be no excuse for allowing such a valuable ship to fall into enemy hands without some form of resistance, yet giving in without a fight seemed to have been universally accepted.

And in a warship there were no passengers, no audience present, to discuss the smallest of orders. It was strange how even a few weeks at sea produced nautical experts from the most unlikely material. He was equally sick of snugging the ship down at night, shortening sail early to ensure that none of these newborn sons of the sea were awakened by something as mundane as taking a reef in the topsails.

He would see this trip out, even though calling at Gibraltar was going to be difficult in the extreme. The Mediterranean fleet were regular visitors; he may well see ships known in earlier times, and meet with former colleagues in the Navy. Then, when he finally quit the merchant service, he could apply again for a proper posting. The time wasted in *Pevensey Castle* might see some important changes in the war; there could be a berth for him then. He knew the chances were slight, but at that moment even to be on half pay in a Navy uniform seemed a better option than service at sea with the Honourable East India Company.

* * *

"That sounds perfectly dreadful," Kate said as she handed Elizabeth a cup of hot tea in the steerage mess. "Though in my experience the Navy does not shrink from important tasks, if at least some degree of success is perceived."

"I know, yet they refuse to act, and it would seem such a relatively simple procedure."

"I fear that any attempt to open a belly could never be considered simple," Kate said, as tactfully as she could.

"Maybe not, but if it be the only chance, surely it is worth the taking?" Elizabeth sipped the hot drink and winced slightly. Kate had sweetened it almost to a syrup, even though she knew Elizabeth did not take sugar. "Mr Keats just has to remove the ball, and repair any damage it might have caused."

Kate nodded sympathetically; she could remember all too well how she felt when her own father was in a similar situation. "I am sure if it could be done it would," she replied. But her words sounded trite, and she could tell that nothing, short of having Keats ordered to operate, could be acceptable to the girl.

"Forgive me, but what exactly is the problem?" Langlois was dining alone at the small table that he had adopted in the corner of the room. Kate acknowledged him for the first time, also noticing how he was taking a glass of white wine with his meal; it seemed a sophisticated accompaniment to a very basic lobscouse.

"George Nichols is in need of an operation," she said briefly. "Mr Keats fears him not strong enough for the pain."

"Cannot laudanum or rum be used?" the mate began to chew meditatively.

"It is a belly wound: the surgeon will not countenance drugs."

"Has he none that need not be ingested?" he asked, himself swallowing a mouthful and taking a small sip of wine.

"I presume not, though you should properly speak with the surgeon."

"It is rare even for an experienced man to contemplate such a procedure," he mused, replacing the glass on the table. "Though I grant that medical matters may have moved on a pace of late."

"If there is something of which you know, I am sure Mr Keats should welcome the telling." As she spoke Langlois became uncomfortably aware that he was holding both women's rapt attention.

"It is probably nothing," he said, then apparently changed his mind. "Let me be straight, it is the pain that remains the problem?"

"Indeed." Kate agreed readily.

Langlois stopped eating now and for a minute sat holding his knife and fork in the air, before placing them both down on the table. "Forgive me ladies, I would not have your hopes raised, but do wonder if there might be something that could be tried."

Both women were looking at him now, and hope was very evident in their eyes.

"Pray, do not take what I say to heart until I have cleared it with the surgeon." He smiled awkwardly as he stood and went to leave the room. "I might be considering something that is quite impossible; but still, I think it worthy of pursuit. You will excuse me, I am sure?"

CHAPTER FIFTEEN

The air in the sickbay was already thick with its smell, and yet only a small fraction of the green lump was actually burning.

"It is important that you breathe in the smoke," Langlois told Nichols, before turning to where Keats and Manning were waiting by the patient's feet. "And equally so, gentlemen, that you do not."

"Have no fear of that, Mr Langlois," Keats said seriously. "I have every intention of keeping my breath clear, and trust that you will also."

Langlois nodded. He was well aware of the responsibility he had undertaken, and secretly felt less than certain he could maintain the patient in a suitably semi-conscious state. But this was not the time for doubt, without surgery Nichols was going to die, and the man had been ready enough to take the chance when offered. He lowered a small brass funnel over the glowing drug and held the dish in front of the fourth mate, who now lay, prone and naked, on the operating table. Nichols's nose twitched slightly, and he seemed to cough. Then his eyes grew darker, and his head fell to one side. Langlois looked back towards the surgeons.

"I think you may begin."

It took less than twenty minutes, and despite the fifth mate's administrations, hardly appeared pain free, although Nichols remained relatively still throughout. Langlois gave his entire attention to the patient, altering the position of the brass dish as minute facial reactions revealed his state of consciousness. He purposefully did not look when Keats wielded the probe and finally caught the small ball in the bullet retriever. It dropped with an important clatter into a pewter dish. The shot was lodged in the man's lower abdomen, and the surgeon had been able to press it against the pelvis to allow the tool to do its work. There was also a small amount of fibre, presumably from Nichols's clothing, which Keats removed. Damage to the gut was mercifully light. Not more than eight horsehair stitches being needed to close the fascia and abdominal muscle, with another twelve of light gut to the skin, administered by Manning who was becoming quite adept with a needle. Keats wiped the ragged scar dry and applied a small lint dressing that he held in place as Manning bandaged. Then Nichols drew his first clear breath as Langlois removed the funnel and extinguished the glowing fire.

"A success, Mr Keats?" he asked, closing the lid and slipping the warm dish into his jacket pocket.

The surgeon shook his head. "Far too early to speak of such things, Mr Langlois. I have only performed one similar procedure in the past and that, I regret, was not a success. Still it is done." His expression lightened for the first time. "And it might not be, but for your help. I thank you."

Nichols's eyes were closed, and it was obvious that he would sleep for some hours although, of all present, only Langlois could guess at the dreams that might accompany him.

"We will discover more in a day or two," the surgeon continued. "But I fear it will be far longer before we know if *sphacelus* infection has been avoided."

"I will inform the ladies," Manning said. By common consent it was agreed that neither woman should be present, even though it had become routine for Kate to assist during surgery. She was carrying out an equally valuable role in comforting Elizabeth, and Manning was eager to tell them both of the progress.

"I must caution you again, you know little of what you do," Keats said, when Manning had left the room. The surgeon regarded Langlois seriously as he wiped his hands on some cotton waste. "Opium is a powerful drug. I concede that without its attributes, and your knowledge, Mr Nichols must surely have perished. But no good will come of such indulgence for pure pleasure; anyone foolish enough to think otherwise can only expect damaged countenance, poor constitution and an early death."

"It is something I have heard before, doctor."

"Then I am telling you again," Keats continued. "It is a dangerous game that you play; one that will likely do you the ultimate harm."

"Death is something that worries me little," Langlois replied, equally sincere. He tapped his pocket, which was growing agreeably warm, and met the surgeon's gaze with equanimity. "Life offers few pleasures, and I am sadly denied one of the greatest; so you will pardon me if I take others where I may."

* * *

"I wish to talk with your master," Drayton told Luck, Rogers's servant.

"I believe he is resting sir," the man replied, with only the slightest hesitation.

"Perhaps you will ask?" It was in Drayton's mind to barge past and force his way into the room, but this interview was intended to settle matters, and that might not have been the ideal start.

Luck returned almost immediately, and Drayton noticed the look of relief on his face. "Very good, sir. Please to enter."

The roundhouse cabin appeared very much as before, except for a small print of King George which was missing from the larboard bulkhead. Rogers was sitting at his desk, although he did not seem settled in any way; it was almost as if he had just placed himself there.

"Sir, we need to speak."

Rogers regarded the man with moderate interest. "There seems little to say, but if you wish it so, then pray be seated."

Drayton sat opposite, his body angled slightly in a manner that was intended to be non-confrontational. "Matters regarding this ship have yet to be consolidated," he said. "There are still a number of points we must consider, and I hope to have these settled before we sight land."

Rogers affected a look of unconcern. "I am no longer captain, sir, so am at a loss how they might affect me."

Drayton nodded. "Very well. I asked to speak with you in private, but if you wish it, then I must communicate with the court of directors."

There was no perceivable reaction from Rogers. Drayton continued. "A situation such as this does no one credit. I am certain the Company's wish will be to keep details as private as possible, and assume that you are of a similar mind."

"Difficult to deprive a captain of his command and say naught about it," Rogers mused, while examining his fingernails. "I'd chance that plenty of folk will be interested in the whys and wherefores." The sudden smile was one of defiance, and Drayton felt his body tense slightly. But he was prepared for some degree of obstinacy, and careful to show no change in his expression.

"That is your prerogative, sir, if you so wish. Sure the newspapers will be only too pleased to make a cheap story; but you will not be seen well, that I can promise you." Of course Drayton cared little how Rogers might be perceived; in the scale of things he was a complete nonentity. But the good name of the East India Company, the *Honourable* East India Company—that was of far greater concern.

The Company prospered, and men like him grew rich because of its reputation for sound business sense. A bad apple like Rogers could do incalculable harm to both the organisation and foreign trade in general. Public confidence would fall, and even those in government might take a slightly different view in future dealings. With Britain at war, a great deal of leniency was being extended to what was basically a private concern. Expansion in both India and China had been left very much to them and their armies. Closer inspection by civil servants could only cramp future developments and might even endanger the valuable monopoly that was the centre of the Company's wealth and its very *raison d'être*. And Drayton would be damned if Rogers endangered either.

The two men considered each other as poker players might when the stakes were rising uncomfortably high.

"I had considered my father to be husband of this ship," Rogers said, taking an unexpected turn.

"Indeed, we agreed that you should be so told."

"And why? Why was I deceived? Why must I find I cannot trust my own parent?"

Drayton could tell that Rogers was about to embark on a personal tirade of injustice and self-righteousness and quickly replied.

"Because he, in turn, felt that his son was not to be relied upon."

There was another silence while this was considered, and Drayton felt that Rogers's face had blanched slightly. "This might be better said by him," he continued, straightening himself in his chair until he faced the man directly. "But since you have chosen to put me in such a position, I shall tell you myself. Suffice it to say that your father has reached the end of his tether as far as you and your care are concerned."

There was no reaction, and Drayton continued.

"Though not exactly the closest of friends, we have been business associates for many years, and I have been very aware of the efforts he has made on your behalf." Rogers's stare remained constant. It was as if he were slightly disturbed by what was being said, yet too intrigued in the outcome to interrupt. Drayton was strangely reminded of his own reaction when his granddaughter began to tell outlandish stories about her younger brother.

"We will not list them now, but you have taken advantage of all his endeavours, yet repaid nothing. He confided in me that this ship, and the arrangements he made for your command, were to be the last."

"I had it that *Pevensey Castle* was purchased on my behalf."

"That was not the complete truth. Your father certainly invested in her, but there are other shareholders, apart from myself. I was unanimously voted her husband, and it was a condition of my associates's involvement that I should accompany you on your first trip. It happened that I was due a visit to several factories, and..."

"So you are telling me that he lied?" Rogers interrupted. His face was alight with indignation, and he brushed Drayton's comments aside like an annoying fly.

"If you wish to take it that way," Drayton replied simply. "Although I might guess that it is probably the only lie you have ever heard from him. Though not, I fear, the other way about."

Drayton had long ago decided that Rogers was not the fastest of thinkers, but upwards of a minute went by before any reaction could be detected, apart from a blank stare that seemed to focus somewhere in the middle distance. Then the face cleared slightly, and a more genial look appeared.

"The ship is not taken," Rogers said, as if registering the fact for the first time. "She is whole and intact, apart from a little dampness in the hold—the fault, I might add, of someone other than myself. We should make Gibraltar safely and ought to be restocked, re-victualled and ready to meet with the next southbound convoy within the month."

A smile was forming, which Drayton purposefully did not meet as Rogers continued. "And we have acquired a valuable prize into the bargain!" The look now developed further, and his stare was fixed hard on Drayton in an endeavour to make it infectious. "In no time we could be turning turtles off Ascension." His expression reached its zenith and Rogers was positively beaming. "Frankly, sir, I fail to comprehend the enormity of my crime."

Drayton resisted both the look and the temptation to close his own eyes. There was little point in continuing; the man was clearly mad or disillusioned. In a moment he would be blaming someone else for surrendering, and doubtless bringing charges against those rash enough to spill their blood on his decks.

"Mr King saved your ship," he said, with an air of finality. "The likelihood of the cargo remaining sound is small. We have yet to reach Gibraltar; if we do, it will be the task of the courts to decide the ownership of the *Espérance*. Should that occur, I hardly think your part in the recapture will make a very good impression." He opened his mouth to say more, then closed it again, suddenly sick of an undertaking that he had feared would end in frustration. The silence hung between them once more, before Drayton spoke again, although the words were almost to himself. "It is indeed a pity," he said, not bothering to meet Rogers's eyes. "I was to suggest an amicable solution, one in which both parties might be satisfied."

Another pause, then Rogers showed a flicker of interest. "How so, sir?" he asked.

It was Drayton's turn to examine his nails. This was a distasteful business, but he was determined to recover what was salvageable, even though any arrangement with this bumptious fool went against the grain of common decency.

"Mr Paterson is currently acting as captain. After we call at Gibraltar his position will be made permanent for the remainder of *Pevensey Castle*'s voyage. I have already spoken with Mr Willis, who agrees that he is not yet ready for command and has expressed a wish for service in another vessel. I have given my assurance that his position within the Company will not be affected by this decision. Mr Nichols, should he be spared, and Mr Langlois will serve as chief and second mates, with Mr King eventually acting as third. Further officers can be recruited at Gibraltar."

"Little appears to have missed your attention." Rogers who had been watching in mute astonishment, stirred slightly. "I assume you have made similar provisions for myself; may I ask what they might be?"

"We continue with you, disabled from command due to injury. On arrival at Gibraltar you will resign as a captain in the East India Company's service on grounds of ill health. The injury to your eye should prove reason enough; it was acquired while on duty. There will be no public investigations or contact with the press on either side. You will relinquish any claim on income from the prize which, if granted by the court, shall become the ownership of the consortium that funded this venture."

Rogers continued to stare at him, and for a moment Drayton wondered if he understood a word of what had been said. Then the cunning look returned, to be replaced almost immediately by a damp smile.

"Go on, sir," he urged, sitting forward in his chair.

"There is little more to say." Drayton met the expectant look with one left intentionally blank. "Obviously there are fine details to be addressed, but I think you have it in essence."

Rogers's eyebrows lowered. "But what benefit do I gain with such an arrangement?"

Drayton knew that the effort in keeping his countenance neutral would soon prove too much. The man was expecting an actual advantage from what he must surely understand to be the only available alternative to personal disaster.

"You retain your integrity, sir," he said bluntly. "Or at least, that is how it will appear to most. What agreement you reach with your father is of your own concern, but the general public will view the matter simply as the recapture of a prize combined with the heroic taking of a privateer. It will be greatly regretted that the captain, sadly disabled by injury, was shortly afterwards forced to relinquish his command, but no more need be said. The honour, prestige and standing of all parties shall remain unsullied."

Rogers continued to consider the proposition, his eyes unfocused and mouth slightly ajar. Then Drayton found himself the subject of his stare once more.

"Nothing more?" he asked. "I am to gain in no way?"

"You are being dealt with leniently, sir." Drayton replied. "A gentleman should be pleased to escape so lightly."

Strangely, Rogers appeared to find some sort of compliment in the remark. The confused expression relaxed, to be replaced by the same sickly smile. "Then it is an offer I am pleased to accept," he said with a hint of victory, while his right hand rose gingerly to his face. "Indeed, I think it to be the better solution; in truth, my eye has been troubling me greatly of late."

* * *

They made poor progress. By the morning of the second day the coast of Portugal still lay some distance beyond the horizon and was likely to remain so for a good while. *Pevensey Castle* was barely making steerage way as she beat against the weather. The wind turned contrary almost from the start, forcing them to tack and tack again to claim any degree of easterly progress. It was an exhausting business, and men made weary by recent events grew tetchy and quarrelsome. A respite, one small piece of good news, or even the promise of better to come was sorely needed, and it was later that same morning when providence provided and Nichols began to rally.

He had been sleeping fitfully since the surgery, attended by either Kate or Elizabeth, using their own private watch on watch arrangement. Kate was present when he started to wake, although Elizabeth, who had only retired a few minutes before, was back in time to see the first true signs of consciousness. She entered the sickbay, eyes already fixed on the body that lay at the far end in the darkened bunk.

"His eyelids were beginning to flicker," Kate told her. "Not like when he was dreaming, it was more as if he were trying to open them properly, and for a moment I thought he might talk."

Elizabeth nodded eagerly while she examined Nichols's pale face. Then she drew back as his breathing deepened and both arms began to move beneath the sheets. The head fell back, and one hand appeared from under the covers and actually touched his mouth.

"It is a common action when awaking from a coma." Manning's voice came from behind. He had also been called and was watching with as much attention as either woman. "He might not be back fully, but I'd say most of the drug has worn off."

"George, can you hear me?" Elizabeth spoke quietly, but the

reaction was obvious to all. His head turned in her direction slightly, and the closed eyelids twitched.

"Try not to tire him." Manning's warning was purely automatic. He was following the progress just as intently, and almost felt inclined to give the patient a firm nudge.

"George?"

The eyes, finally revealed, appeared dilated and bloodshot in the poor light.

"You're going to get better, dear." She said the words as a statement of fact; one that, once made, could not be revoked. His face twitched and a faint smile appeared, to be quickly replaced by a tensioning that might be from pain.

"Leave him a while." Manning placed his hand on Elizabeth's shoulder, although he remained as hypnotised by the waking form as any of them.

"Elizabeth?" Nichols's voice was little more than a whisper, but his eyes opened once more, and now the entire face was starting to look more human.

"Yes, dear." she rested her hand on his bare arm, and slowly both limbs relaxed. "You need to sleep," she said, the words betraying her wishes. "Sleep, and you will be better."

He nodded slightly, closed his eyes and, for a moment, there was silence. Then he drew a deep breath and sleep reclaimed him.

* * *

Since the French had been confined to their beloved forecastle, the senior hands were now messing in forward steerage. This was not as crowded as it might have been, as several of *Pevensey Castle*'s crew were in the privateer, while a few more remained under the surgeon's care in sickbay. And others, of course, were dead.

Johnston was trying not to think of the latter as he slung his hammock. It was the end of another eventful day, one of so many in a voyage that was proving more tiring than most, and he felt ready for sleep. He had been assisting Khan with replacing the lifts on the fore and main topmasts. It was the sort of job previously carried out with Ward in the team, and yet strangely he was hardly missed at all. Now they were off duty, however, Johnston felt his loss far more acutely.

Khan, who along with most of his countrymen, shunned the use of hammocks, was wrapping his near-naked body in a thin blanket and settling down to sleep in a manner that, to Johnston at least, appeared unnecessarily uncomfortable.

"You want to draw another blanket from the pusser, Abdul," he said. "Each man's 'titled to two; if you don't claim yours, the rook will only sell it."

"And he is very welcome." Khan was smiling as he lay down in the folds of the blanket and composed himself.

Johnston noticed the look and grunted to himself. He had long ago abandoned any thought that he might change the Indian's habits, but the loss of Ward emphasised the fact that his lifelong collection of friends was incredibly small. "Well, you'll catch your death if you sleep like that."

He snuggled himself into the warmth of his hammock, well protected by his own two blankets and the shirt and trousers he had been wearing all day long. It was about now that Ward used to think of something to talk about; usually inconsequential and, more often than not, annoying. But some form of comment would be called for from Johnston, ensuring that a conversation was struck up, and neither got any sleep for at least another half an hour. He had cursed the boatswain's mate for it often enough, but now found himself hating the silence every bit as much.

"You are missing Mr Ward?" Khan asked from his bed on the deck beneath.

"Not especially," Johnston lied. "You?"

"I was grateful to have him as a friend," Khan replied after a brief pause. "And hope to meet with him again some time."

"You believe in that sort of thing, do you?" Johnston was fully awake again and listened, strangely eager, for the response.

"I believe in many things, and some are not so different from your Christian faith," Khan said.

"Is that straight?"

"Oh yes, there are more similarities than you might think."

"Well, I never did."

"But most of all I believe that if we start to talk about such matters now, we will be awake for most of the night. It might be a fitting tribute to Mr Ward, although I think that we should also rest."

Johnston grinned, but found his mind strangely cleared of the memories. "Bloody Lascars," he said softly, and settled himself to sleep.

* * *

They continued to beat against the contrary weather for seven more days until finally the dim grey outline of land appeared off their larboard bow and a fresh course could be plotted. The easterly wind stayed constant and was now in their favour, so much so that *Pevensey Castle* began to heel slightly and a credible bow wave could be seen as her stem drove through the dark Atlantic. There still remained a fair way to run, and with the Portuguese coastline occasionally visible off their larboard beam, all settled down to the final leg that should see them raise the Tagus and safety.

The weather moderated two days later. The wind dropped considerably, and a wintry watery sun appeared that gathered in strength, drying the decks and making it almost pleasant to stand watch. Beckoned by its call, some of the passengers came up cautiously from the dark underworld of the ship. Though in the main still shocked by recent events, signs of recovery could be detected. The whist school had already reformed, and there was even talk of a celebratory meal when they finally reached safety. Personal relations also became easier: small arguments and petty squabbles common under Rogers's command all but vanished. This was not due entirely to Paterson's captaincy, or the improvement in conditions; rather now, there was a physical focus for ill feelings. The passengers were united by the one thing guaranteed to create bonds of fellowship—they had a common enemy.

The French prisoners were treated with universal contempt. It was considered that Captain Passon's ungentlemanly action had brought disgrace to all and he, along with the other officers, was herded into the same cramped quarters as the men. Their rare and well supervised opportunities for exercise were often accompanied by hoots of derision and blatant insults from the older male passengers, while some of the ordinary seamen were not averse to a well-timed trip that sent one or other of the prisoners sprawling, to the delight and laughter of the ladies.

But there was one who was even less popular than the French, and that was Rogers. He continued to haunt his quarters in the roundhouse, where meals were eaten and wine drunk in splendid isolation. Occasionally, he emerged and his dark and sullen countenance would stalk the quarterdeck, to be firmly ignored by all, even if the officer of the watch took particular care to avoid the stinging sarcasm that any inattention on his part would elicit. The passengers also gave him a wide berth, although one aged military gentleman was heard to comment that, by rights, he should be confined in the forecastle with the Frenchmen. The observation was quickly taken up and circulated throughout the ship, to the amusement and approval of all.

Paterson, who was feeling surprisingly comfortable in his new position, was secretly shocked by this behaviour. But there was little he could do in such a situation, and he quickly turned his attention to the more complex problems associated with the command of an Indiaman. It was at his insistence that the regular afternoon dinners in the dining cuddy were re-established, and what unspoilt provisions remained were distributed freely without regard to cost or station. The very act of eating well helped restore confidence and generally raised morale, to the extent that for the first time in her current commission, *Pevensey Castle* was showing signs of becoming a truly happy ship.

Despite his recent appointment, and the responsibilities it contained, the shortage of officers forced Paterson to stand a regular watch. It was something he accepted, if only because it brought him back to the more familiar duties he had carried out for most of his time at sea, the only difference being that there was now no ultimate authority to summon should anything prove beyond his capabilities. But this had yet to happen, and Paterson, like the ship, was becoming brighter as the voyage continued and his confidence grew.

It was exactly nine days since he took command, and Paterson had just relieved Langlois and was starting to enjoy the warm sunshine, when Nichols made his first appearance on the quarterdeck.

"Jove, sir." Paterson grinned when he saw him. The man, who lay prone on a bier that was carried by two seamen, closed his eyes to the bright glare of morning and smiled weakly in return. His body was covered in a dark blanket from which his feet, wrapped in white woollen socks, poked out almost comically. "I thought you were to stay abed for the next month."

"And so he should," Kate informed him sternly from one side

of the stretcher. "Though he were impossible to keep still in the sickbay, and, in truth, a little fresh air might help him sleep the better."

"I have used up all the sleep I need to see me until Christmas," Nichols grumbled. "And dreams enough to last well beyond." Elizabeth was walking next to him, and they each held the other's hand tightly, as if afraid of losing contact.

"Just aft of the main will be the steadiest," Paterson said, and the seamen lowered the bed down, resting it on two empty hen coops so that Nichols was suspended just above the deck.

"Think you can make it to a hammock chair, sir?" one of the seamen asked.

"He'll be fine where he is," Kate informed them.

"No, I can do it, thank you." He held his arm out to one of the waiting men, who heaved him up as if he were nothing heavier than a sack of hard tack.

"Steady, Clegg!" Elizabeth held his other hand and together they walked him across to where one of the canvas chairs set out for passengers awaited them.

Paterson nodded as the mate was settled and the women began fussing about him, generous with blankets and cautions. "First sign of ill weather and I'll strike you below." His words were harsh, although he was smiling broadly. "How is it with you, George?"

"Well enough, thank'e." The man showed no inclination to release his grip of Elizabeth's hand, and she knelt awkwardly on the deck next to him. "Belly hurts like Hades, but they tells me I'm better, so I best believe 'em."

"We had thought you lost," Paterson told him, with his characteristic lack of tact. "Glad to see it to be otherwise."

Nichols's face relaxed as he closed his eyes to the sunshine and let out a deep and measured sigh.

"Not as glad as I, John," he said, and squeezed Elizabeth's hand once more.

* * *

The bell struck twice, and the helmsman and lookouts were about to be relieved when a shout came from one of the latter.

"Sail ho, sail on the starboard bow!"

Paterson looked up and then across to where the privateer was sailing to windward on their larboard beam.

"Make the same to Mr King," he said, automatically. The smaller ship had lower masts and would not notice the sighting for some while. Taylor, the young curly haired midshipman, had learned much and was prepared for just such an eventuality. The flags ran up the halyard and broke out as the lookout was adding to his report.

"Two ships on the opposite tack, sailing abreast an' to the north. I'd say it were the 'ead of a squadron."

That could only mean Jervis, or part of his fleet. Paterson took a turn up and down the quarterdeck and naturally caught the eye of Nichols, still seated in his hammock chair, but now apparently wide awake.

"How far are we off the Tagus?" he asked.

Paterson paused. "Expect to sight at any time, belike we have found the Mediterranean squadron first."

"Mr King acknowledges, sir." The signal midshipman touched his hat as the lookout broke in once more.

"Commissioning pennant on one ship at least," he bellowed. "An' I think I can see another's masts beyond."

"Land ho, land on the larboard bow!" It was different voice. The lookouts were changed with every even bell, and clearly the previous man was remaining aloft at the end of his trick. One of them must have had the sense to continue scanning the horizon, even though an important sighting was being reported elsewhere. Paterson made a mental note to find out who and commend him for it later.

"That must be the Rock of Lisbon, or *Cape da Rocca*, as the chart has it; the headland to the north of the entrance to the Tagus," he explained to Nichols. "We stood out to sea last night in case it came across us earlier than intended. The Portuguese are supposed to maintain a light, but there seemed little to be gained in taking chances. We put back at four bells in the forenoon watch in the hope of sighting it."

"Then we're home and dry," Nichols said, a thin smile on his face.

Paterson snorted. "That might be pressing things a touch," he said. Nichols had been out of action since *Pevensey Castle's* recapture, and could know little of her condition, although even he must be aware of the damp and mouldy hold that was already starting to smell abysmally. Elizabeth moved slightly, and Nichols's attention swiftly moved back to her. Paterson looked away, not wishing to intrude upon them.

"But at least we've found Lisbon," he said, watching the horizon for the first sign of the ships. "And the British fleet come to that, so I'd chance that we are one stage closer."

CHAPTER SIXTEEN

"Gentlemen, that is indeed quite a tale." Admiral Sir John Jervis, Lord St Vincent and commander-in-chief of the Mediterranean fleet, sat back in his chair and considered matters for a moment. King used the brief pause to look about; he had been in so few first rates, and *Victory*'s great cabin was certainly one to remember. Stout beams, yet tastefully furnished, she carried an air of understated power and, despite her advancing years, was still considered one to be of the best sailers in the fleet.

"Your prize, Mr King, she is sound?" A senior captain whose name King had missed was addressing him, and he switched back to the real world with a jolt. "Yes sir. I'd say she would show a fair turn of speed." The man spoke in hushed tones to Jervis, who nodded readily.

The summons had come from the admiral barely a quarter of an hour after *Pevensey Castle* dropped anchor. Patterson was unusually subdued, as well he might be, his first official duty as a ship's captain being a meeting with a commander-in-chief. But Drayton seemed unusually familiar with Lord St Vincent, giving his report in a casual, almost conversational, manner that was quite at odds with anything expected in the Royal Navy. King wondered if they had met before, although Jervis had made no mention. But then he was not known as a man who greeted acquaintances particularly warmly.

"Well, I congratulate you on your capture," the admiral

continued. "I have no doubt that the prize court in Gibraltar will move swiftly, and I hope to see her flying His Majesty's flag before so very long. I am sure Mrs Drayton will find the revenue welcome."

"Indeed so, my Lord." Drayton nodded politely, and King's suspicions were confirmed.

"Heaven knows, the smaller ships are at a premium on this station," Jervis continued. "Admiralty thinks that, just because we are not on the other side of the world, all matters must be referred to them for consideration. I'd spend all my time sending messages back an' forth if they had their way, and the public must be aware of what is about before I am."

"The mood in England is hopeful, my Lord." Of the three men seated before the admiral, Drayton was by far the most relaxed. "After Camperdown, and your own victory, the Navy is held in high esteem."

Jervis considered him carefully. "No ill feelings following Tenerife?"

"Not that I am aware; more concern for Admiral Nelson and his wound."

"Ha, that young pup will be up again afore so very long. I could use him now if the truth be known. We cannot be called the Mediterranean fleet and be denied its use, what?"

Drayton nodded. "I should say not, my Lord."

"In fact, the information I have just obtained makes the matter of communication even more important." The admiral regarded the three men contemplatively. "I was about to make myself unpopular by requisitioning that Company packet that docked today," Jervis smiled briefly. "But instead might be presuming upon your prize, in anticipation of the court's decision, of course."

King stiffened slightly in his chair. His command of the privateer had lasted a little less than two weeks, and yet he was already aware of strange proprietary feelings towards her. The senior captain also appeared uncomfortable. "This might not be the best time to talk further, my Lord."

Jervis grunted. "I see no point in hiding matters. The French have been open enough, and it'll be common knowledge with the mob in a week or so." He relaxed further in his chair and set his powdered wig straight. "There is movement at Toulon. Massive armament, and more ships assembling by the day. The country's being swept clear for supplies; even the northern Italian ports are affected. It's clear they have invasion in mind; maybe Naples, Portugal, some even say Africa."

"Africa?" Drayton asked, surprised.

"Egypt, to be precise." Jervis considered him thoughtfully. "Fastest way to take your empire in the East, don't you think?"

"It would be utterly devastating, my Lord," Drayton replied, genuinely shocked.

"Well, we will know little while we stay this side of Spain," Jervis continued. "Gibson, in *Fox*, is currently at Gibraltar. We should look in at Toulon without delay, 'though it might be polite to advise the admiralty if I intend to re-enter the Med. Not that their lack of knowledge will alter any plans, of course, but I will have complied with my orders by informing them. Your capture is larger than the usual, but will suit well enough, and her use will not weaken the British force in any way."

King felt his body tense further as his heart began to pound inside his chest. He had yet to see the privateer under full sail, and already she was to be taken from him. Taken and probably handed over to some dolt of a lieutenant who was bound to treat her roughly and know nothing of her ways.

"I could take her back to England, my Lord."

It was hardly customary for junior officers in the merchant marine to offer suggestions to a commander-in-chief, but, if Jervis was surprised by King's suggestion, he failed to show it.

"I thank you for your offer, sir, but regret this is a government matter, and as such the command must go to a Navy man." He switched his attention to Paterson. "I will see your ship taken safely to Gibraltar; there should be an escort available within a day or two." The old man's eyes twinkled. "But rest assured, we will relieve you of your prisoners before then."

"Thank you, my Lord." They were almost the first words that Paterson had spoken; it was quite unusual for him to remain so quiet. King took a sideways glance at his friend. His face was slightly flushed, and he appeared apprehensive. It was even possible that the occasion overawed him, although that was hardly in his nature. But King was feeling in no way intimidated. The pain of losing the privateer was stirring him into action, and he found himself wriggling in his seat in an effort to break back into the conversation.

"I trust that you gentlemen will find any provisions you need ashore, but if not you may apply to the fleet. I shall not see you go short after such exploits." Jervis was attempting a smile now, and it was clear the interview was coming to a close. King felt the disappointment growing, even though he fully understood that there was nothing intrinsically wrong with what was being planned.

Finally he could contain himself no longer. "Sir...my Lord, I should be happy to captain the prize. I hold a commission as lieutenant in the Navy, and know the ship well."

This time Jervis's look held a measure of annoyance. "You hold the King's commission, sir?" he said, the incredulity obvious in his voice.

"I do, my Lord." King hesitated as all eyes in the room considered him. "And I have served under you." He drew breath. "I was at Cape St Vincent."

"Were you indeed?" Jervis was growing dangerously intense. "What ship?"

"*Pandora*, my Lord."

The expression lightened slightly. "Ah, Sir Richard's little frigate; much missed on this station, but she fared well under Adam Duncan, I hear."

"I was with her until she paid off, my Lord."

"So you were at Camperdown?" the senior captain asked.

"Yes, my Lord...sir."

"But you wear the uniform of a Company man, and a midshipman at that!" Jervis considered him closely, and King could only blush.

"There were not the opportunities, my Lord. And I wanted so much to be at sea."

"Yet now you wish for your rank returned? That speaks little for whoever it was who saw you made in the first place, and nothing for your new employer." Jervis was positivity glaring now, his eyes ranging about the room as if in search of a target. "When a man is promoted to lieutenant, the least his country can expect is a few years' duty. What numbskull approved your commission?"

King swallowed. "You did, my Lord."

A short bark that might have been a laugh made everyone jump slightly, and Jervis leaned forward in his seat. "I made you?"

he asked, aghast. "I granted your commission? When, sir? When did I do such a thing?"

"Just last year; the January of 'ninety-seven, my Lord. I returned as prize master of a French frigate and our first lieutenant had died..." His voice trailed off as he realised that it might not be diplomatic to remind St Vincent of Pigot's death.

"It comes back to me," Jervis said a little more gently. "Sir Richard spoke well of you then, and he is a hard man to please. But that was nought but a few months past!" Jervis was more confused than angry now, and the other men shuffled uncomfortably. He shook his head as if in wonder. "Do you care so little for your rank, and the service in general, as to come and go like a common tradesman?"

Drayton broke in. "Mr King has performed well in the Company's employ, my Lord. Indeed, his will be a great loss, but it was clear from the beginning that he is a Navy man, and will never truly settle to the life of a trader."

"Then it is his bad luck to have made that choice," Jervis replied sullenly.

"It is due to Mr King's actions that we were able to retake *Pevensey Castle*, my Lord," Drayton persisted.

"Indeed, so I understand; but there are many capable officers ready to give their right arms for such a command. They have not left the service for self-betterment, and are entitled to their chance as much as any." Jervis brooded for a moment. "As much as any, and more than some."

"Except that the chance was created by Mr King." Paterson's sudden contribution took them all by surprise. Even he wore a look of mild astonishment.

"Beg pardon, sir?" Jervis queried, his eyes again wide and dangerous.

"I said that he created the chance, my Lord; and yet it appears he is not to benefit by it." Paterson's words were spoken quite clearly, and he more than equalled the admiral's stare. "It might not speak well of him to have left the service, but it could also be said that it was the fault of the Navy that a man so qualified and experienced could not be found employment."

There was a slight intake of breath from the senior captain, but Paterson was well into his stride by now, and continued quite unabashed.

"I have served with Mr King for some while. He is an exceptional officer: I find it strange, and not a little worrying, that one such as he should be allowed to rot on the beach for want of a berth."

"This is not the time to discuss the merits of the Navy, sir!" The senior captain spoke with an edge to his voice; at any moment the conversation might turn into a full-scale argument.

"I should think there never will be, sir," Paterson replied. His complexion was returning to normal now, in fact he appeared completely relaxed. "There are many defects in both our promotional systems, but I submit that the merchant service has no pretence."

"Pretence?" Jervis was eyeing Paterson sharply.

"Positions in the East India Company may be purchased; it is a well-known fact, and one the Navy likes to taunt us with at every opportunity. Yet your own system is just as corrupt, if not so open."

"Mr Paterson, I fail to see quite..."

"Mr King is a capable officer who has proven himself in action, yet he was forced to leave the Navy and serve elsewhere in order to put bread upon his table. There are young lieutenants aplenty in his position. Good men, but brushed aside to allow the sons of admirals, peers and politicians to take up valuable seagoing positions in their place. If it is a system that you approve of my Lord, then I am surprised."

For several seconds no one said a word. Then Jervis sat back in his chair and regarded the mate.

"It is an honest opinion, Mr Paterson, I grant you that. And I thank you for sharing it with me, 'though I chance that you might not have been quite so bold were you directly under my command." His face hardened slightly. "But still I have responsibilities, and it would go badly were I to show favouritism outside of the service." He nodded again, and seemed to consider the matter again, before leaning forward and rising from his seat.

"Gentlemen, I will not detain you longer, I am certain you have much to attend to, as indeed do we all. I congratulate you once more on your prize and will arrange for her transfer without delay. We can provide a crew. There are sufficient men who can be trusted to return to the fleet, as well as those whose injuries mean they are of no further use to His Majesty." He paused and seemed to watch Paterson particularly carefully while the three men stood to leave. "Of course, this will in no way influence any conclusions that the court might arrive at. Your prize will be treated as a hired ship until a proper decision can be made, and you will be reimbursed in full for her use."

The admiral's eyes were still set on Paterson. "Were you in the King's service, sir?" he asked quietly.

Paterson stopped in the act of turning to leave. "Me, my Lord? No, I regret not."

Jervis smiled and nodded. "No, I thought as much. Gentlemen, I wish you all a good day."

* * *

Manning had sorted through the surgeon's instruments and taken those that belonged to him. Now there were only his personal possessions to collect. He walked through to the steerage mess and found Langlois sitting in his customary position at the small table. The man was sketching once more, although there seemed precious little in the room worth recording.

"Patient on deck?" he asked, glancing up from his work.

Manning nodded, "I believe so."

Langlois returned to the pad, his pencil loosely held and apparently moving of its own accord. His eyes were half closed and he seemed so relaxed that, for a moment, Manning wondered if he had been indulging in his own particular style of recreation.

"Are you leaving us?" The words came from somewhere far away, but when the surgeon's mate turned, Langlois came readily from his trance and looked into his eyes.

Manning cleared his throat. "Yes, Kate...my wife and I are heading back to England." His tone was flat in an effort to dissuade further conversation.

"I am sorry to hear it," Langlois returned briefly to his work, but it was clear that the moment was lost, and soon he thrust the pad aside.

"There is news," Manning continued, despite himself.

"Indeed? But not from England, I fancy?"

"As a matter of fact, yes. A packet arrived only yesterday," Manning explained. "The wind that kept us from gaining the coast was fair for them; they made a quick passage. I believe there be post for all." His ditty bag was full now, there were just the two aprons to collect from the store, and the purser to see. He really did not have time to waste on idle conversation.

"Not bad, I trust?" Langlois persisted.

Manning picked up his belongings and was about to leave the room. "Bad enough; my wife's father is not well. She has expressed a desire to be with him once more." He paused, then continued in a slightly lower tone. "It was fortunate that *Pevensey Castle* was recognised at anchor, otherwise we might not have heard until Madeira."

"That is sad indeed; she is a splendid woman."

The anger built up suddenly. Manning did not want for an argument, but there was something about Langlois, and his smooth manner, that always riled him. And this was probably his last opportunity to tell him so.

"She is indeed a splendid woman, that is why I married her." The words, though innocent enough, were delivered in such a way that they might as easily have been a dreadful accusation, and Langlois reacted instantly.

"I do not doubt it," he said, an expression of mild confusion on his face. "And you are to be congratulated—a lucky man indeed."

Manning paused. He knew he was being unreasonable. He had listened to all of Kate's assurances and was well aware of his own defects—inordinate jealousy had haunted him his entire life. He could not possess, create or achieve anything without the accompanying fear that it would be taken from him. And it was a sad fact that, the more valuable or dear the attribute, the greater his terror of its loss.

"Marriage is a precious thing," he said, hating himself a little as he did. "You might do well to remember that in the future."

There was a moment's silence as Langlois considered this, then his face reddened slightly.

"I can assure you, Robert, I have never held any designs upon your wife," he said. "She is a good friend, and I value her as such, no more."

"But the drawings; those sketches..." Manning waved his hands foolishly in the air. "You capture her so well, I..."

"You cannot believe that somehow we are not in love, or at the least, that I am not attracted to her?"

Manning half closed his eyes and nodded.

"Then I am indeed sorry—sorry in so many ways." The silence continued as if time itself was suspended. Then Langlois indicated the chair opposite, and Manning slumped down.

"I will never marry," Langlois began. "Not that I do not heartily respect women, and indeed enjoy their company greatly, but my preferences fall in other ways."

Manning went to speak, but was cut short by the fifth mate's raised palm. "Worry not, I do not confess to any illegality, either moral, spiritual or legal. But it is a fact that, when young, I was dismissed the Navy due to an unusual affection I held for a fellow officer. Set ashore, I think the term is, although in truth the act was a little more unpleasant than the simple boat ride the rubric might imply. Since then I have vowed to a life of celibacy, and it is a commitment I know I shall keep, through no obligation other than my own sincere wish for it to be so." He smiled, and Manning found himself smiling in return.

"I said you were a lucky man," he continued, "and indeed I maintain that you are, though you have nothing to fear from me, or anyone else, if my judgement is correct. But I urge you to consider your ways. As I have said, I know nothing of marriage, nor will I ever; however I do think I have learnt a little of human nature."

There was silence for a moment, then Langlois continued.

"You spoke of your wife as if she be a possession; indeed, it is the way of the world, and I freely admit to being quite at odds with it to disagree. But I would say that, in your particular instance, it is wrong. Wrong, and inherently dangerous. Far better, surely, to regard her as a fellow human being, one you can share pleasure with, and allow her, in turn, to spend her affections where she may. If you insist on inflicting your ownership upon her, you only make her an attribute, and as I think you may be aware, attributes can so easily be lost."

* * *

"Well, that was hardly expected," King said when they were settled, and the cutter was pulling away from *Victory*. "Don't suppose old Jarvie has been spoken to like that in many a moon."

"Me'be I stepped too close to the mark," Paterson said, although there was little regret in his tone. "My tongue carried me away as usual. But those stuffed up Navy types do get under my skin. So full of righteousness and morals, yet their promotions are as crooked as a dog's hind leg."

"I think you might be a little unfair, Mr Paterson," Drayton murmured. "The interest system is ripe for change to be sure, but I gather that it is rarely applied in the more important cases. And it is not completely unknown for talent and fortitude to be rewarded."

"As you will, sir, but that is not my experience," Paterson maintained. "And I am surprised that someone as straight as Lord St Vincent claims to be, stands for it. Promotion and position should be based entirely on merit, it is the only fair way; anything else is plain dishonest—forgive me if I speak plainly."

"It is your habit, John," King grinned.

"And you certainly made your feelings pretty plain with St Vincent." Drayton's tone was neutral, even though he also had a twinkle in his eye. "I doubt that there are many who could have misunderstood."

They were nearing the privateer now, and King looked up at her quiet, graceful lines with more than a hint of regret.

"There is a deal to be done before the Navy has her," he said reflectively. "I wish to see she is left in as good a condition as possible."

"That is completely understandable," Drayton agreed. "Besides, we shall gain a better penny for her were she well set up."

"Shall I send the carpenter and his mates?" Paterson asked.

"If they can be spared. The work will last a day, no more."

"I expect it will take as long for the Navy to gather a crew."

King nodded. "We will meet again on the morrow in *Pevensey Castle*," he said. "I'd be obliged if you'd send the barge for the people."

"Signal when they are ready," Paterson nodded, "'though I expect you will wish to meet with her new commander."

King looked at him dolefully. "It is a pleasure I can easily forgo," he said.

* * *

"It really is beautiful," Elizabeth told Nichols as she looked across the anchorage towards Lisbon. He was recovering exceptionally well, and now sat comfortably in his hammock chair drawing in the last of the afternoon sunshine.

"All foreign harbours look the same," Nichols said. "Seen one, you've seen them all."

"Well, I want to see them all." She was smiling at him as she turned back, and the sun shone through her blonde hair, making it glow about her face like a golden halo. "Or as many as possible—the most anyone can fit into a life." Her expression suddenly became serious when she realised she was forgetting herself. "Just as soon as you are better, of course."

Nichols pursed his lips. "Well, we'd better make sure that both can be arranged," he said seriously.

"Prize crew'll be coming back from the privateer at any time," Langlois told them as he walked across to where Nichols sat. "If you wish, you can take the barge back, or the cutter's in the water come to that. You'll be sharing with Mr Manning and his wife, I chance?"

"Robert and Kate are returning to England with us?" Nichols asked, surprised.

"Apparently." Elizabeth began to rearrange the blanket that was slipping from his shoulders. "Mr Drayton agrees; it seems that word has been received from home that has forced them to change their plans."

"I'm sorry to hear of it," Nichols said, "but will be glad of their company."

"By all accounts, *Pevensey Castle* is due to stay at Gibraltar a fair while," Langlois told him. "There should be plenty of time to appoint a replacement surgeon's mate and make up for the other missing officers."

"It will mean Robert can attend your wound," Elizabeth informed him. "And I shall have another woman to talk to."

"And someone else to order me about," Nichols agreed.

The couple began to bicker playfully, each so totally absorbed with the other that nothing else mattered. But Langlois was not listening, his eyes were now fixed on the far distance. "Still, it is a pity," he said softly, and almost to himself. "She will be missed."

* * *

King was equally surprised. He noticed *Pevensey Castle*'s cutter approaching as he came up on the quarterdeck and quickly identified Manning and Kate in the stern, along with Nichols, who was laid out on a stretcher, with Elizabeth close by. The replacement crew were expected at any time, and he had been assembling all the ship's papers he could find, while the rest of the men were preparing to rejoin *Pevensey Castle*. The cutter soon skipped across the short stretch of water, passed under the stern and bumped against their starboard side. King strode down the deck as a rather tousled Kate hauled herself up and through the entry port.

"'Tis a pleasure to see you, though I were just about to leave myself," King said, as Manning followed his wife aboard the ship. "What brings you both here?"

"A passage back to England," the surgeon's mate replied dolefully. "I have spoken with Drayton, and he was good enough to let us go."

"England?" King looked aghast. "But what of India, the Far East? What of your plans to travel together?"

"Naught has changed, Tom," Kate said. She seemed to have acquired a smudge from the boat, and was brushing her dress down as she spoke. "We simply felt that *Pevensey Castle* has not been a good ship for us. Robert was for finding another berth at Gibraltar, but I have received news of my father. He has not been well, as you know, but it seems things have deteriorated greatly since our departure." She looked away suddenly. "I would see him once more, if it be possible."

King regarded her cautiously. Kate was a strong woman and unlikely to be swayed from what she wanted to do, even by the impending death of someone so close. He wondered for a moment if there was another reason for her wish to be home.

"I shall also be able to attend Mr Nichols," Manning added. "To that end I'd be grateful for a couple of hands and the use of a whip to see him aboard."

"Do you think he will need so much persuasion?" King grinned, then turned to Crowley after everyone had pointedly ignored his joke. "Send a party to the mizzen whip, if you please; Mr Nichols's stretcher will need to be swayed in."

They watched while a line was sent down to the boat.

"I am sorry to hear of your news," King continued, "and will miss you both."

"Be certain you shall be missed also. Let us hope we might sail again together some time," Manning said. "Now will you show us the ship, while you still have command?"

"I'd deem it a pleasure; there is ample officer accommodation below 'though I should stake a claim before the Navy comes aboard. Otherwise you might be beaten to the best berth by the captain of the heads. I say," he stopped, as a thought apparently occurred. "would it be terribly wrong if the both of you shared the same quarters?"

* * *

Within the hour two barges could be seen making for them from the east quay.

"I sees the Andrew is on time," Nichols commented. He was seated in a freshly rigged hammock chair, looking bright and alert. His face appeared pale from the afternoon's exertions, however, and Elizabeth was hoping to persuade him below before long.

"Aye, so I'll be leaving you shortly." King passed a letter to Kate. "Could you post this for me in England?"

"Juliana?" she asked.

"Indeed, though it will take a tortuous journey to find her."

"Will you pass on regards to all in *Pevensey Castle*?" Nichols said. "It wasn't possible to speak with everyone, even if there are some I would rather not meet with again."

King grinned and collected his watchcoat as the first barge was hailed. "So we'll meet in England," he said, shaking hands with Manning. "That's if you haven't found another berth by then." Nichols reached up and shook his hand, and Elizabeth kissed him shyly on the cheek.

"I wish you a good recovery and hope you will both be happy." The couple blushed in matching shades, then he was embracing Kate, before collecting the last of his luggage.

A young Royal Navy midshipman had climbed aboard and was now standing tentatively by the entry port.

"Douglas Barrow; midshipman," he said, uncertainly as he regarded King's uniform.

"Are you to command, Mr Barrow?" King asked.

"No, though I am due to sit my board on return to England."

"Then I wish you luck. Your lieutenant is still to join, then?"

Barrow shook his head. "I was advised I should find him aboard," he said, his frank blue-grey eyes searching King's own. "A Lieutenant Thomas King; I have a note for him from the admiral."

King expelled a breath and smiled ruefully. "Then you had better hand it over," he said.

CHAPTER SEVENTEEN

The transfer of men took less time than he needed. There was a deal to do, and yet King still found himself pausing to gaze stupidly about with the look of a simpleton upon his face.

"There's a seaman that says he is staying with the ship, sir." Barrow eyed him doubtfully. King broke from his trance to see Crowley standing defiantly on the quarterdeck as the last of *Pevensey Castle*'s men were filing into the barge.

"Yes, it has been arranged; he is to accompany us," King lied.

Barrow turned to bellow at the new men who were forming up. King examined them briefly. Most were older, some well into their forties, and several walked with an exaggerated gait, clearly suffering from some form of rupture. A few were missing arms, and in one case a lower leg, but all looked like seamen. Judging by the number, he would have sufficient to man the *Espérance*. King considered taking the opportunity to address them, but he was still holding Jervis's despatches in a tight grip and knew that there was no time to be lost.

"We have the wind and the tide, Mr Barrow," he told the midshipman, "as well as the attention of most of the Mediterranean fleet. What say we get it over with, and up anchor?"

Barrow grinned readily and touched his hat. An elderly boatswain's mate who King was yet to formally meet was also alert and brought his pipe to his lips. The scream cut through the air, and men began to detach themselves, some to attend the single bower, while others made for the lifts, braces and topsail halyards. The Jacob's ladder was removed, while a group of topmen began to scramble up the shrouds. All was done in an efficient and seaman-like manner, and if some of the evolutions were just a little slower than usual, King was not in the mood to criticise. He glanced about the anchorage. They had a clear run to the open sea, with only *Pevensey Castle*, moored three cables off, to negotiate.

"Make sail," he said, giving the time-honoured order of every commander since the time of Drake, and in the same spirit the men responded.

The anchor was to be raised by hand, using a tackle and two blocks clapped to the cable. King had a momentary doubt whether his crew of invalids were up to the task, but they seemed to possess a positive spirit and the thing was done without complaint. Topsails were set just as efficiently, and soon *Espérance* was making stately progress through the water.

"Leaving already?" Manning said, as he clambered up the companionway and on to the deck.

"Carrying despatches," King replied, the satisfaction obvious in his voice.

"Dip ensign!" Barrow at least remembered the courtesy of leaving harbour, and King looked back a little guiltily to where *Victory* was solemnly returning the compliment.

"I have to conn the ship, Robert," King said, and Manning stole away obediently.

Pevensey Castle was passing to starboard now. Looking at her, King felt a pang of regret. There were so many aboard he might never meet again, and some he would certainly miss. Paterson was one. He could see him now as he stood on the quarterdeck watching their departure. King waved, and was pleased to see him lift his hat in reply. But there was no sign of Langlois, or Drayton, or Keats, or even Johnston and Khan. It was a shame he had not been able to say goodbye properly. They were men he would never forget.

"Coming up on the larboard buoy, sir." Once more Barrow was reminding him of his duty. He must concentrate on the job before him.

"Prepare to tack." Turning past the mark would set him on course, but they were still very obvious to the rest of the Mediterranean fleet. There was nothing else for it. He tucked the canvas-covered package into his jacket and collected the brass speaking trumpet from the binnacle. He had been given this command and a chance to re-establish himself in the Navy; now was the time to prove his worth.

* * *

"There are precisely twelve fully fit men amongst them," Manning said. He had joined King in his tiny cabin and was now perched on the upholstered bench below the stern windows. "The rest, well, I'd say we have the basis of a pretty comprehensive medical dictionary."

"As bad as that?" King asked.

"Actually, it sounds far worse than it is. Most are fit enough, if you ignore the loss of a limb here and there. And others, those with the bursten belly or chronic rheumatism seem to manage well enough, as long as their particular ailment is not affected."

"I see. And the rest?"

"Mainly venereal," Manning answered cheerfully. "A few have been dosed up with goodness knows what and are pretty much burnt out, but the majority were caught early and present well. Oddly enough, most are topmen; it leads one to wonder if there be a connection."

"But it could be worse?" King asked.

"It could be indeed. There are a few with tumours, though not too advanced. Three are deaf and two have been blinded, but even they are serving well enough, picking oakum and preparing vegetables. Some have ulcers, and three are quite clearly mad—including one who has a predilection for eating candles—but overall I'd say you have the makings of a fair crew. One that will get us to England, at least."

King nodded; it was roughly what he had expected. These must be the medical rejects from the Mediterranean fleet for the last six months or so, the minor and not so minor sick and hurt who were unable to continue in the service. Some might have been offered berths as junior warrant officers—it was rare to find a cook without at least one limb missing—but the rest were being sent back to England to face an uncertain future at the mercy of the country they had served.

"And there are two others you should be aware of," Manning

continued. He was smiling slightly and King wondered quite what was in store. "Mr Barrow, if you please?"

At Manning's call the frail door opened, and the midshipman ducked through and into the cabin. Behind him were Johnston and Khan.

King rose up from his chair in surprise. The two men stood close together in the tiny space; Johnston's head was ducked down to avoid the low deckhead, although Khan stood upright and serene.

"What the hell are you two doing here?" King asked, his eyes flashing to Manning.

"They stowed away," the surgeon's mate replied calmly enough. "Or to be totally correct, they have apparently deserted the East India Company in favour of the Navy."

King gave a brief short laugh. "Well, that has to be a first," he said. "Have you anything to say for yourselves?"

There was no response from either man, and King was momentarily at a loss. "Do you intend to serve the King?" he asked.

Johnston grinned. "In a manner of speaking, sir."

"Explain."

"We was hoping to return to England with you. The old *Pevensey Castle* was not a 'appy ship; so me and Abdul here thought we might try our luck in 'ome waters."

King shook his head slowly. "Johnston, you're going to have to stop this running. Eventually someone will recognise you, then you'll be for it." He turned his attention to the Lascar. "Mr Khan, what you have done is not so very bad, but you have a respected position in *Pevensey Castle*. A man might be hanged for such an act in His Majesty's service; are you aware of that?"

Khan nodded. "I am very well aware, thank you, sir. Mr Johnston has explained everything, but much I knew already."

"You would do better to stay with the Indiamen," King persisted. "And I am willing to take you back, if you so wish."

"I am certain that you are right, sir, and your offer is much appreciated. But I have served with them for nine years, and now wish to try for the British Navy."

"That wasn't what we said," Johnston interrupted, looking sideways at his friend. "Head back home, then a spell inland. I was to take you to the farm I told you about."

Khan nodded graciously. "It is generous of you indeed, and I should like to see an English farm, but I am not a worker of the land. I understand the sea and ships, and know that it is the place for me. I also have learned that it is better to serve good men than bad." He paused and looked directly at King. "And I wish to follow this officer."

King was mildly embarrassed, although not unaffected by Khan's speech. The man was certainly talking from the heart, and it was quite a compliment. He looked to Manning, who shrugged in reply. There was little either of them could do. King might take them on and allow passage to England. In a hired vessel running an understandably relaxed regime, they would probably go undetected; and if both chose to leave when they entered home waters, he could even deny all knowledge of their existence. They were excellent swimmers, and Johnston was something of an expert at running away, having left at least three ships undetected to King's certain knowledge. But if King was to rejoin the Navy, it seemed clear that Khan intended to follow, and go wherever he went. He knew in his bones that Johnston was not one to be left behind, and it would be just a question of time before the man was recognised and found out. He must, inevitably be caught and was just as likely to meet the noose. If King accepted them on board, it was tantamount to handing Johnston over himself, and after all that they had been through he wondered if he could carry out such an action.

"You may have issues with the East India Company," King prevaricated. "Johnston, you will have drawn two months pay on signing on; some of that time is still owed."

Both men nodded, even though neither seemed exactly concerned.

"But this is a hired vessel, Tom," Manning interrupted. "It might be argued that Johnston is still officially in their employ. When we finally make England, the time will have been all but used, so, as I see it, he will be a free agent once more, and can do pretty much what he pleases."

King looked at him uncertainly.

"Were you in any doubt," Manning continued. "You could always refer the matter to Mr Crowley."

"Crowley?"

Yes, he has come across from the Company's employ with little trouble, and I am sure will be in full agreement."

245

"Very well," King said, blushing slightly and looking swiftly away. "That will do for now; you may return to the other men."

The two seamen knuckled their foreheads respectfully enough and left the cabin.

"Thank you for that," King said, once they were gone. "My first command, and you have me sheltering runners."

Manning's expression was totally bland. "Not so; you heard me say, they are all still Company men. There is nothing with which you must concern yourself."

"Remind me of that when we see Johnston, or whatever he'll be calling himself by then, making one last passage up to a foremast yardarm."

"Look here, Tom, they are fully grown, and can make their own decisions. I've told you the crew we have; all experienced, but hardly in the first prime of fitness. Two more regular hands are a Godsend, and all seem ready to do what is needed to get this ship back to England. You really should not decline such providence."

Of course, Manning was right, although King still could not ignore a measure of responsibility. "Very well," he said finally. "We shall do what we can to make the best of them. Mr Barrow, you can assist Mr Manning in drawing up a watch list."

Manning looked surprised. "Hold fast there, I know nothing of such things."

"We must all be ready to do what is needed, Robert," King told him brightly. "All I want from you is a medical assessment. Mr Barrow will take care of the rest. Divide the healthy men equally between the watches; you might consult with Mr Crowley as well. I have as much confidence in his instinct for human nature as his seamanship."

"Aye, aye, sir." The midshipman touched his hat.

"And see if any are gun crew amongst them," King added as they were about to go. "I'd like at least half our pieces to be manned, should we have need."

"Do you think that likely, sir?" Barrow's eyes held more than a spark of interest.

King snorted. "Mr Barrow, from my experiences in this ship so far, I would exclude nothing."

* * *

His Majesty's hired ship *Espérance* was cutting along at an exhilarating pace with an easterly on her beam, and King had seldom been happier. Freed from the dead weight of *Pevensey Castle* and with the prospect of reclaiming his commission, the future suddenly looked far more positive. This change of heart was heightened by his little ship's performance; she was proving true to every promise. They had covered nearly four hundred miles since their departure. At that rate England should be raised in less than a week, and he could hand over the all important despatches with added pride from a fast passage.

The wind had remained strong throughout. A storm was clearly raging just over the horizon, but apart from giving them a good and steady speed, they were mercifully unaffected. Johnston, now rated as the second boatswain's mate, had taken it upon himself to exercise the men aloft, devising further evolutions on a daily basis for what he referred to as his 'poxed topmen'. But, social illnesses aside, the men were generally well versed in their craft and took Johnston's commands readily enough. By the third day everyone was working smoothly, and as a team; so much so that King wondered if it was actually responsibility that had been lacking in the man's life. Maybe an earlier promotion would have cured him of his pathological need to desert? There were certainly no signs of restlessness or discontent; in fact, he was exhibiting all the qualities of a fine warrant officer.

Barrow, the midshipman, had also revealed hidden talents, being quickly identified as a gunner at heart and given charge of the ship's main armament. Enough men were raised to man four of the long six pounders, which could now be served in quite a credible manner without the use of topmen, although the final act of heaving the heavy guns up the sloping deck was often a trifle slow, and apparently painful.

King was also harbouring plans to organise a small arms drill: three of the sick and injured were marines, one a sergeant. They seemed more than eager to pass on their skills, even though, at the speed she was travelling, it was likely that *Espérance* would be rounding Ushant and on the last leg before they got the chance.

Below, in a locked drawer, were the despatches entrusted to him. Though clearly of little actual importance to Jervis, their early delivery should gain him extra kudos when applying for a position again. He would start by petitioning the admiralty in person before writing to anyone who might hold sway, and calling on former captains and senior officers. All the avenues his juvenile reticence and lack of confidence had previously closed to him would be forced open and followed to exhaustion, until he found himself back on the deck of a warship. The spell in *Pevensey Castle* might not have been happy, but he had grown considerably because of it and now felt ready to take on the adult world with a more mature attitude.

The sound of a whistle cut through the air, and the men began to secure the guns once more.

"Very good, Mr Barrow," King said. "You have made a sound start. If we draw on topmen we might even be able to offer something approaching a full broadside."

The lad touched his hat, and King noticed that his forehead was running with sweat.

"Thank you, sir. It would be good to have a live practice at some time."

"Sadly we are low on supplies, but these men are experienced enough, despite their injuries. I think we can rely on them to make a credible show."

It was unfortunate that much of the French store of powder was in cartridges that had been allowed to grow damp. Some of these were now opened and their contents laid out to dry, but so far the sun was having little effect, and King was hesitant about supplementing it with heat from the galley stove. There was roughly seventy pounds of dry powder left in one keg, which he intended to have sewn into fresh cartridges, but that would only provide a total of thirty-five rounds for his main armament. It was possibly enough for the briefest of skirmishes, but none could be wasted on practice.

"Pipe up spirits, then send the seven bell men to dinner. The others may follow at the end of the watch."

Barrow touched his hat again and hurried off. As soon as the rum was distributed, King decided he would go below and collect his quadrant. They were coming up to noon: time for the daily sighting. This was normally a hallowed ceremony in larger ships, although King, who was naturally taking all responsibility for navigation, allowed any who professed an interest to join him. Khan had been quick to take up the offer, and Johnston, encouraged by his friend's interest, accompanied him. There was little of the navigator in the British seaman, however. His hands, made clumsy by years of hard labour, found the intricacies of delicate instruments hard to deal with and the mathematical calculations were quite beyond him. But Khan was of a different mettle, and showed innate ability. His mind followed the complex computation of figures and formulae so rapidly as to be almost intuitive. If Johnston was a potential boatswain, then Khan might have an equally rosy future as a sailing master. It was a satisfying thought and one that increased King's feeling of well-being still further. This was certainly turning into a golden cruise.

There was a murmur as Kate appeared on deck, accompanied by one of the blind hands supporting a small cask of spirit easily on one shoulder. She walked sedately towards the scuttlebutt with the man following, his left hand resting lightly on her shoulder. A wail of pipes followed, and the men were just beginning to form up for their noontime grog when a shout from the masthead cut through a dozen conversations.

"Sail ho, sail on the starboard bow!"

King's mind jumped back to reality. That was almost directly to windward, and the likelihood was it would prove to be a larger ship than his.

"What do you see there?" All happy thoughts dissolved as he called up to the lookout. A pause, and he had to resist the temptation to peer at the far horizon.

"Sizeable, sir. Masts are well spaced an' she's going some."

"Colours?"

"No, sir, though the sails are white."

King felt his heart begin to pound. "Heading?"

"To the sou'west, I'd say."

Espérance would have to alter course. He had every confidence in both ship and crew and knew that there were few vessels he could not outrun, but they were no match for an actual opponent. The diversion must take them deeper into the Atlantic and, more importantly, would delay their arrival in England.

"Very good," he muttered softly. "We'll take her to larboard,"

Khan, who was preparing to take the noon sight, responded instantly. "Braces there!" The men reluctantly turned away from the promise of grog, and went to attend to the sails while King consulted his chart. There were British ships a plenty in this part of the Atlantic, although the majority were likely to be following the coast, either to the north or the south. A ship heading southwest was probably a foreigner, possibly neutral, but more likely a privateer in search of convoys. Or she may even be a larger stray warship that had escaped from a blockaded harbour.

He must balance the likelihood that they could out-sail this mystery ship against the risk of falling into enemy hands. Manned as she was, *Espérance* could not face any but the feeblest of warships, but most, he knew, would be hard pressed to catch her in a chase. So, should he turn and run, abandoning the highly credible time made to date? Or only alter course to avoid the enemy and, placing total trust in his ship's exemplary sailing abilities, dash past her very bow, and on towards England.

In any event, there was little chance that the despatches would be taken. The package was weighted well enough for just such an eventuality and could be thrown over the side should the need arise. But the very fact that they were not delivered must count against him, and even influence his future employment. For a moment his mind hung in indecision, then sense took hold and he acted.

"Steer north by nor'west." The solid helmsman had seen it all before and began to turn the wheel without comment or show of emotion. Aloft, the spars creaked. The braces were keeping the sails in the wind, and *Espérance* bucked slightly as the hull angle altered, and she began to cut into the heavy rollers.

For a moment King hesitated. He could still change his mind, still order her completely round. Heading on the same course as the sighting should see her sailed under the horizon in an hour or so. But by venturing deeper into the Atlantic, there was also more chance of heavy weather and further complications. His hands were pressed deep into his pockets, and he set his jaw determinedly as he told himself it was the right choice. The enemy might well close on them, but he felt they were fast enough to pass her by, before returning to their original heading. And the main point was they would still be making some degree of progress northwards.

He took a turn back and forth along the tiny quarterdeck, and the movement gave him strange reassurance. It was something he had seen other commanders do a hundred times, and he wondered for a moment how often the simple action disguised acute anxiety.

The thought stayed with him as he considered his options once more. All on board depended on his actions, but then it was the job of any commander to make such choices. He took another turn along the deck, and gradually the tension eased. Clearly, other members of the crew were aware of his quandary. Khan considered him with interest, while Barrow was anxiously looking at the horizon, beyond which the enemy was now bearing down on them. King's expression relaxed as he eased his hands from his pockets and placed them more elegantly behind his back. It was done, he had made his decision and was staying with it. There was certainly a risk, but a small one and definitely worth the taking. He would be careful to keep them out of range. Within a few hours they should have passed in front of the enemy and be able to set a more direct course for England once more. It should still be a remarkably good time, and he would make a reasonable impression as he delivered St Vincent's despatches. The mixture of concern and relief made him chuckle softly to himself, and Barrow and Khan smiled also. At that point no one knew it was a decision that would haunt him for the rest of his life.

CHAPTER EIGHTEEN

On hearing the masthead's report, Kate immediately abandoned any thought of distributing grog.

"Back to the pantry, if you please, Mr Webster."

The man's sightless eyes filled with disappointment as he reached forward and felt for the cask. The temptation for her to rush below and find Robert was hard to resist, but she waited and guided the steward back to the hatchway, while about them men grumbled and muttered as they prepared to alter course.

"Can you manage the ladder?" she asked artlessly, and the man grunted in reply. He had been blind for less than two months, the result of a small powder explosion, although already he was able to find his way about well enough. She followed him through to the pantry, where he deposited the cask back on the counter.

"Thank you, Webster; we'll leave it here for now, though it will probably be called for soon enough."

The man knuckled his forehead, and Kate followed him out of the small room, locking the door behind her.

In the tiny sickbay Elizabeth was passing a bowl of portable soup to Nichols, who was sitting up in the only fixed berth.

"There's a strange sail in sight to windward," Kate said, as she ducked in through the doorway and looked around the room. "Might Robert be about?"

"He was here not a moment ago," Elizabeth told her. "What kind of ship?"

"It sounds to be foreign," Kate said vaguely as *Espérance*'s heel lessened.

"And we are altering course," Nichols spluttered, almost choking on the soup. "I must go on deck." He brushed the bowl away and went to move.

Elizabeth's eyes widened. "But you haven't eaten," she grumbled, returning the bowl.

"Neither have you, neither has anyone," he all but snapped. "And it won't kill me if I miss the occasional meal." He was pushing himself up from the bunk and clearly about to swing his legs off. "Really, both you ladies have been very kind, though I'm getting a bit tired of being treated like an invalid."

Kate opened her mouth to answer, but Elizabeth was ahead of her.

"George, you must take things slowly," she said reprovingly. "At least let me help."

"You could get me my trousers," he replied. His bare legs were now reaching down for the deck. "Else I'll have to go in just my shirt."

"Here, wear this," Kate passed him a greatcoat, then turned away while he stood to put it on.

"Whoa, she rolls!" Nichols had one arm through the coat when a sudden bout of dizziness caught him. He reached out and gripped Elizabeth's shoulder.

"Take it slowly," she repeated. "You have been in bed a long time."

"I'll be fine," he said. There was a shout from above. It seemed that King was ordering more sail. "And will be even better when I am able to see what is going on. My boots? Where are my boots?"

* * *

Espérance was slicing through the dark waters, her stem cutting a fan of pure white spray that soaked all on deck, while her very timbers trembled as she powered through the rolling waves. The wind was now blowing on their starboard quarter. King had added jib and staysails, it was too strong for topgallants, and he told himself repeatedly that there was power and space aplenty to pass the enemy. He had just returned from a brief trip aloft, studying the sighting from the swaying maintop. Three-masted and carrying a good deal of sail, she was clearly a warship and equally obviously making to cut them off. The height of the fore and main topgallants marked her out as a Frenchman, as did her canvas, which was definitely of a foreign pattern, lacking the squareness of British sails. If he could maintain this speed, there seemed little likelihood of their getting within long range. All the same, several unsteady hours lay ahead before they could call themselves safe. King knew he would be in a state of constant tension for every second. The enemy should be visible from the deck shortly; it was an indication of the speed at which the two ships were closing, but then all would be so much clearer when his opponent was constantly in view.

"Carries a fair pace, don't she?" Standing next to him Crowley's eyes were ablaze. Both men were unusually conscious of the movement, as the ship bucked and dived beneath their feet. King envied him, remembering times when he had enjoyed the pure excitement of speed and pursuit. But previously there had always been the reassuring presence of a competent commander. Now that he found himself thrust into just such a position, the stimulus became somewhat less than pleasurable.

A movement forward caught their attention, and both men were surprised to see Nichols clambering painfully through the stern hatch.

"Good to see you, George," King said, making towards him and extending a hand. "Are you right to be on deck in such weather?"

"If the women had their way, I should never see daylight again," Nichols grumbled, while he let Crowley and King escort him to the lee of the starboard bulwark. "Haven't felt the breeze on my face in months, or so it seems, and with an enemy to windward I will end up touched if I stay below."

"Well, see that you do not tire yourself," King said as his friend reached up to grab hold of a shroud.

"I see her!" Barrow's shout alerted them all. The midshipman was on the forecastle, his body wrapped in a dark, soaked watchcoat. King turned to look over the rail and, sure enough, a small smudge could just be distinguished on the horizon.

Nichols shaded his eyes with his free hand as they all considered the oncoming ship. Crowley ran his tongue over his cracked lips. "It'll be a close one, so it will," the Irishman said.

King nodded. The enemy had gained since he viewed her from the maintop. They would still pass a good two to three miles off her bow, but it was closer than he had planned. He glanced up at the sails and then at the weather vane. The wind was still holding strong and steady, although soft clouds to the east warned of change. He could order them a point or two to larboard and their lead might increase, but the moment they actually passed, and the time the enemy finally sank below the horizon, must also be delayed. And even an extra point to the west took them that much further away from their final objective. Enemy ship or not, King still was worried about making a good time to England.

"We'll keep her as she is," he said, answering a question that no one had asked. He turned from the sight, not wishing to discuss matters further, although the doubts inside him were starting to multiply, and he stalked rather rudely away in case he should change his mind.

* * *

Khan saw him go and knew the reason. He could already guess the young man's indecision and was equally aware that no one could share either the worry or the responsibility—certainly not a petty officer from another world and culture.

But an empathy remained, nonetheless. The Lascar naturally acknowledged that he owed far more to King than a few minutes of instruction in celestial navigation would warrant, and regarded himself effectively in his debt. Arriving in England in good time was clearly vital to him, as was delivering the package, a thing that he seemed to treat with even more importance than most Britishers did their possessions. These were factors far beyond Khan's reckoning. He rarely encountered urgency, and ownership of anything beyond the most essential of items was completely against his personal ethos. But they were important to King, the man who had risked his own life to save his, and so assumed some form of reflected value to the Lascar. In the same way that one might play a game of chance with a friend, not for the game, but the company—so Khan was equally concerned that they made England quickly and that the canvas package was safely passed on.

He was also an experienced seaman and knew very well that King was taking a chance in trying to pass the enemy ship so close to her bow. In his mind he felt there was space enough. *Espérance* should clear the enemy ship with room to spare—certainly well out of the range of her guns—but that was assuming none of the many possible mishaps occurred. They could easily split a sail, a spar might spring, the wind alter or even die completely. The sea was an element built on change. It was the main reason Khan had first been attracted to it and, ironically, its ephemeral temperament did much to help him maintain something far more placid in his own countenance. But now that there was reason for worry, even though it be a reason borrowed, he was experiencing an unusual feeling of disquiet.

For probably the first time in his life Khan was acutely concerned about matters that he could not control. He felt a gnawing in his stomach that was quite foreign to him. It was probably a similar sensation to that when the English claimed hunger, although he knew that a simple meal would not ease the pain in any way.

A cry came from the masthead. The man stationed there had identified the type of ship and clearly the news was not being received well by the other members of the crew. Khan looked about uncertainly; another trait that was becoming all too common with him since the start of this voyage. Johnston was on the forecastle, and both were officially off watch, so there might be some benefit in keeping together. He stole towards him, an uneasy expression on his face, and Johnston seemed to greet him with relief.

"How come, Abdul?"

The Lascar relaxed slightly at the sight of the weather-beaten face.

"We have a race on, as I think you say."

Johnston grinned at him. "Aye, that's a fact. An' one we're gonna win."

Khan returned the look, and the two men stood companionably together while they watched the enemy ship gather detail as it bore down on them. It was certainly better than worrying alone.

* * *

By six bells in the afternoon watch, three o'clock, the enemy was in clear sight. King considered her through the deck glass. She was what he would term a light frigate, although the French doubtless used some other name for the type. She probably carried between twenty and thirty guns, either nine or twelve pounders, over sparred in the typically French manner, but with a sleek hull. And she could sail, there was no denying that. Her captain had her trimmed to perfection, and the ship sliced through the broad Atlantic rollers as if she were a toy yacht set free upon a millpond. As King watched his hesitation mounted. Yes, she was certainly fast, but not as fast as *Espérance,* he told himself.

The wind was staying true, and they would not close for at least another hour, probably more. He watched the enemy craft powering through the water, aiming for a point some way ahead. It was a course which, if she raised the speed, should ultimately cut them off. He was still reasonably certain his little ship could pass out of range, but night was only a few hours off. They should start to lose the light in no time, and he wondered again if it might not be better to wear away now.

"Colours!" The shout came from somewhere forward, and King looked again. Sure enough a large tricolour could now be seen on the Frenchman. By his own command, *Espérance* was flying no flag of any type. Even the coveted 'despatches' pennant had been struck some while ago.

"An' a signal." King was reasonably sure the voice belonged to Barrow, but was more interested in the Frenchman's activities. "Looks like a numeral, and two swallowtails that ain't in our book."

Being the ship to windward, the frigate was making the private signal first. *Espérance* would be expected to respond with the recognised reply. Failing to do so was as clear an indication of her identity as any, and must wipe any doubts that might be remaining from the French captain's mind.

"Hoist a French ensign," he said, without taking his eyes off the enemy ship. There was nothing wrong with the ruse at this stage; indeed, it was almost to be expected. He could then follow it up with the private signal he watched the luggers off the Downs exchange. Doubtless it was well out of date and probably irrelevant for this station, but it might encourage some indecision.

King took a turn along the deck as was now becoming his habit. The signal was made, but no response came from the Frenchman. He looked at her for some time, then took his eye from the glass and peered up at the sails and the weather vane.

Yes, he would take her a point or two to larboard, that would lengthen things slightly, and might even bring the time of passing closer to nightfall. His mouth opened to give the order, and he was actually drawing breath when another call from the masthead stopped him.

"Sail ho, sail fine on the larboard bow!"

Instinctively he turned to look, but the blank horizon stared back at him.

"What do you make there?"

A pause followed. The lookout was Fowler, a former topman who must have been standing masthead lookout for many years. Though now well over thirty, and with a rupture that made the long climb a painful business, he still retained excellent eyesight, and King was glad to have someone so experienced on hand. Clearly Fowler had called a warning when he was reasonably certain it was another vessel. To define exactly what type, or course, would take a little time.

"Belike a brig, or maybe a snow," he replied eventually. "Two masted, an' headin' north, I'd chance."

King glanced down at the chart while Fowler gave the bearing. The second vessel was almost exactly in line with his current course, and they were closing with her at a considerable speed. The heading made it likely that she was a merchant, although why sailing independently, and not part of a convoy, was a mystery.

Nichols appeared again at the stern hatchway. He had gone below about an hour ago, and King was not expecting to see him again that day. Obviously the draw of an enemy actually in sight was too much for his curiosity. He pulled himself over the coaming and stood uncertainly on the weaving deck. Elizabeth followed close behind and King's impression was that, even if they were about to be set upon by an entire fleet, her attention would remain solely on her patient.

"How is it with you?" King asked as they joined him in the lee of the bulwark.

"Well enough, thank you," he said. They both helped him to the side, although he was standing firmer now and seemed in no need of her support.

"We seem to have acquired further company," King said, while Elizabeth buttoned up the greatcoat that Nichols had clearly just thrown on. He pointed forward. "There's a brig sighted, heading north."

"A trader, do you suppose?" Nichols asked.

"So I should say," King replied. "And, if British, they will not thank us for bringing a Frenchman down upon them."

"Deck there, I can see her tops'ls," Fowler reported from the masthead. "An' I get a glimpse of her courses an' hull ever so often."

"What is she?" Nichols shouted, then instantly gripped his belly in pain. Elizabeth grabbed his arm, but he brushed her away as King repeated the question with more force.

"A snow I'd say, an' a warship at that," the masthead replied. "Showing a fair roach to the forecourse, and there be no way she were fully laden, not an' travellin' the speed she is."

"Does that mean another Frenchman?" Elizabeth asked.

"There is no way of telling," King shook his head. If so, their position had deteriorated considerably. He could not make that slight alteration now, in fact the only way to truly avoid capture was to turn to the southeast. It was away from England, and all thoughts of a quick passage must be forgotten. But if not, if some miracle had occurred and she turned out to be a Royal Navy warship, the odds had changed just as dramatically. Together they would be no match for even a light frigate, but if the other were properly handled, they might guarantee the escape of both.

"Strange place to find a brig of war." Nichols shifted uneasily, and reached out to the bulwark for support.

"Aye, but she might make a deal of difference were she British."

"Do you think that likely?"

"Starboard escort of a home-bound convoy," King replied hopefully. "I'd not discount the situation. And we can't be certain she is but a simple trader sailing independently."

Nichols shrugged. "Like as not, we shall tell in due course."

King felt a wave of apprehension stir within him. "You think different?"

"I'd say she were another privateer," he said simply. "And I doubt that she is alone. We must be just off the northwest tip of Spain, is that not so?"

King nodded. "Finisterre bears not a hundred mile' to the east." The doubts inside were beginning to grow.

"It is an area ripe with jackals," Nichols mused. "Deep enough into the Atlantic to grab the larger Indiamen, yet close to their home bases, so it need not be a long run for safety. They often hunt in pairs; I'd say there will be another, maybe two, in sight of her."

"But, if you are right, they will be oblivious to the frigate," King said, clutching at a straw.

"Indeed, both forces will know nothing of the other," Nichols agreed. "Though their presence must affect your actions, I'll be bound."

He was right; the turn to larboard was out of the question now. Of course, he could wear round completely and head south with all sail, but such a move must only encourage a chase. Any well manned privateer would be a tough match for *Espérance*, with her crew of invalids and rejects, and that was discounting the powerful national ship that was also bearing down on them. The frigate could sink his little craft with a single broadside and hardly leave a mark upon her own paintwork.

"Wait, larboard ship's turning," Fowler was speaking again. "Yards are amove. She's starting to tack."

King looked again at the map. Presumably the brig was intending to bear round and head for their stern on the larboard tack; another ship, if there was another ship, could come down on their bow. Neither need know of the frigate's presence, they would be simply rounding up an adversary and guiding her closer to the shore, in the same way that a pair of dogs might gather in a wayward sheep. But it was only a question of time before the frigate's topmasts became visible to them. Then the situation must change considerably.

"Take those damned flags down!" King had forgotten all about his ruse. If anyone in the brig noticed the bunting, they would guess that another ship lay hidden from their view. For a moment he even considered using Duncan's trick. He could send up a signal announcing an enemy in sight, in the hope of fooling both. But the French were not so simple and might even be able to read the British code book. He would have to send a bearing. Which would it be? And why had he delayed so long in announcing the presence of the frigate?

"Shall I strike the Frog ensign as well, sir?" Barrow was hauling down the signal halyard himself as he asked.

"No you may let that stay. It may serve to add confusion." King cleared his throat and was about to take a turn or two along the deck, but with Nichols and Elizabeth standing with him he felt unable to break away. The afternoon watch was ending in no time. Dusk would start to fall not long after supper, but night remained some hours off. He looked across at the French frigate, still pounding off their starboard bow. The ship's masts were especially tall, how long would it be before they noticed the brig, and maybe her consort, that had them neatly trapped?

"She's settled on the larboard tack," the masthead reported. "Close hauled an' heading—wait, I see a signal!"

King felt the pain inside his belly grow.

"There're flags breakin' out, and she's hoisting French colours."

Nichols let out a long sigh. It might be a ruse. A merchant captain could be trying to see off what he took to be a privateer. *Espérance* was still flying the French ensign, after all.

"Do you see anything else off our bow?" King bellowed.

A pause, then Fowler's voice came back to them again, although this time there was the slightest hint of umbrage. "No, sir. Just the two sightings...as reported."

King and Nichols exchanged glances. The brig's signal and change of course might still be the gambit of a particularly game merchant captain, even if the evidence indicated otherwise. The two men considered the problem for a while, then Nichols broke the silence.

"I'd say we was in a fix."

For the first time Elizabeth turned her attention away from her patient.

"Maybe you're right," King said, meeting the looks of concern with an ironic grin. "But we have a few more cards to play yet." He spoke the words automatically, as something a captain should say in such a situation, but the others took them well and almost seemed encouraged. Only he felt the ominous signs of approaching depression.

* * *

"Robert, I wonder if I might have a word."

Manning almost laughed out loud. The ship was travelling at speed, her deck constantly vibrating to the motions of the ocean, and there was a tension in the air that only came when frame and fabric were being pushed to the very limit. It was so typical of Kate to choose the wrong time for a chat.

"Of course, my dear, shall we go to our quarters?" They were standing in the tiny dispensary and the low deckhead made such conditions extremely uncomfortable.

"No," she said, surprising him for the second time. "No, I think we should stay here, if you don't mind."

"As you wish," his look became a little less certain now, and he sensed what she wished to say might have greater import. "But at least let us be seated."

She nodded, strangely serious, and propped herself on the edge of Nichols's empty bunk. Manning collected the small chair without a word and wedged it against the bulkhead where it made a steady enough support, even in the present conditions.

"Very well, my dear," he said, regarding her cautiously. "What do you have to say?"

Her eyes lowered, and for a moment Kate did not speak. Then she muttered a hesitant, "I fear it is of a medical nature..."

* * *

King's world was rapidly collapsing about him. *Espérance* might be called his first true command, but even she was nothing more than a hired ship. He had been hoping for a fast passage, a chance to deliver her and the despatches safely, and then effectively reclaim his precious commission. Now it seemed he was to lose all three. At best they would be taken prisoner, with the canvas-covered bundle at the bottom of the Atlantic. At worst, men, and possibly women, would die. Some were his friends, and he would be responsible.

His black thoughts ran on all too readily, spreading further woe wherever they could. And the despatches might be seized—he had to delay throwing them over the side until the last possible moment, but what if something stopped him in that final act? Handing Jervis's private documents over to the French was not the best resumption of his naval career, and could hardly improve his standing, should he be exchanged.

The stain of depression was now colouring his brain completely, and it would have taken very little to have him heave the ship to and surrender. The realisation forced him to turn away suddenly, and he took three or four good long strides, gasping in the cold fresh air that seemed to have been missing in his lungs for a good while. He had known times like this before, times when he allowed his natural pessimism to take control, conjuring up strange fantasies and dreadful conclusions as it did. In the past the problems might have been small, or at least they appeared so in comparison to those which currently faced him. Now lives depended on his judgement and the decisions he made could not be those of a child, one who allowed the devil to take charge of his mind. He looked back at Nichols and Elizabeth. Their eyes were following him in a subtle but considered way, as if watching a jack-in-the-box toy that might operate at any moment. No, it would not do, he told himself. *Espérance* had plenty of fight in her, and there was still much he could try.

He turned from his pacing, and approached the couple once more. "Yes, it is a fix indeed, George," he said, this time with no forced jollity. "But what say we make the best of it?"

Nichols nodded. "Aye, we figured you had something of the like in mind."

"Deck there!" Fowler's voice cut into their thoughts, and all eyes turned aloft. "Sail in sight, fine off the larboard bow." He paused for a moment to consider, the added, "She's headin' close hauled and as tight to the wind as she'll lie."

It was the ship that Nichols had predicted. King noticed that the man was now gripping the rail until his knuckles were quite white.

"What do you make of her?" he called.

"I'd say it were another snow, sir," Fowler replied after a moment. "Just like the first, an' she's aiming to cut us off for'ard."

Strangely King received the news quite well. Rather than sending him down further into the pit, his spirits actually rose, and he glanced about the deck as if this were all some splendid game, one that might end well enough as soon as their mothers appeared and they were finally called in for tea. Crowley, standing next to the wheel, was clearly worried, as was the helmsman, another experienced seamen, and Nichols was looking as if the world itself were about to end. But the spur was just what King needed to pull him up the final step from his melancholy, and he began to chuckle softly to himself.

"A fix indeed," King was actually laughing now, and all were looking slightly more confident; even Elizabeth's eyes were raised and she was smiling slightly. "Well, if we are to be taken, I intend to sell ourselves dear. Does that cause any concerns?" he asked.

"None that I can see." Crowley was the first to reply, but it was clear from the looks of the other men that they were in complete agreement. Only Nichols appeared at all unsure, but then he was still an invalid, King reminded himself. And a merchant seaman.

"Mr Khan, she'll take more sail, methinks." He turned to the boatswain standing nearby. "Worry not if we shake a spar or two, we will be sailing this to the edge and have nothing to lose. We shall take her to larboard and meet with the first of them on our terms, and maybe sooner than they might wish. Rig preventer stays, then we'll have t'gallants. Oh, and you may prepare the stun'sl. booms while you are about it."

Khan knuckled his forehead, his face unnaturally creased with concern. The wind was still blowing strong, even to add topgallants was risky enough. But the studding sails, additional canvas set on extensions to the yards, were made of a lighter material and would be blown out within minutes.

King caught the look and shook his head. "Do not be concerned, Mr Khan, I have no plans of setting the stuns'ls at present. But the wind may yet die, and we could be glad of them afore long."

The boatswain acknowledged the explanation with a silent nod and set about calling up topmen while King began to pace the deck once more. It was the damnedest piece of fate that dealt him such a hand, but there was nothing to be gained in cursing. He was still reasonably certain his ship was the better in an all-out race, although whether she were quicker in stays was something yet to be discovered. He might have an experienced, disciplined and eager crew, but, if the majority were anywhere near the peak of their efficiency, Jervis would hardly be sending them home to retire. But the momentary period of doubt had served its purpose. Now he was determined to see matters out to the end, play on until the very last card. The next few hours might well be the most taxing of his life, and he had to give his all. There would be plenty of time later for regrets.

* * *

"It's hardly long enough for us to tell for sure," Manning said, wiping his hands on a small piece of tow. "And the tests I should normally run, well, they're just not possible."

Kate nodded. It was much as she expected. There were very few things that could have distracted both their minds from the activities on deck, but she had managed to pinpoint one.

"When did the sickness start?" he asked.

"About a week ago, every morning."

"Only in the morning?"

She nodded. "Except when I drank some coffee with Mr Paterson before we left the *Pevensey Castle*; I thought I was going to throw up, and cannot bear the thought of the stuff ever since."

"Well then, I chance that it is pretty certain." The look of concern was starting to fade and a slight smirk replaced it. "And despite all Rogers's efforts!"

Now she was smiling rather hesitantly herself, and she reached out and held his hand.

"There were suspicions, some while back. Which is why... which is why I wanted to head for home," she added with a rush.

"In truth, I had thought there must be another reason."

"You don't mind?"

"Why should I mind?" It was a proper beam now, and one that she was beginning to share.

"But the travel, we were to see the world..." Once more she felt her words fade away as he looked at her face.

"We can still; this will only delay matters for a year or two," he thought for a moment. "Possibly a little longer if there be more."

"More?"

He was positively chuckling now. "These things do happen," he said. "We might have learned that by now."

They laughed together then, as if by an unspoken signal, stopped and held each other very close.

"You don't think me foolish?" she asked, drawing away suddenly.

"Foolish?" it seemed a strange choice of adjective. "No, why ever should I?"

She shook her head. "For wanting to go back to England. When I suspected, I mean."

"I wouldn't say that was foolish, exactly. You could have given birth aboard ship, though. People do."

She laughed suddenly. "Aye, stick me 'twix the cannon like the rest of 'em."

"Well, I wasn't meaning that exactly..."

"I'm sorry, Robert, I just didn't want it that way." She held him to her once more, her voice muffled slightly by his shoulder. "Maybe I've been living in a ship for too long, but now, now that we are starting to be a family, I need something more."

He drew back. "Kate, I cannot give up the sea, not for a while at least."

"And I wouldn't expect you to."

"Maybe when I get my surgeon's ticket I could try for a shore base?"

"That would be fine, but it isn't necessary. I could be happy knowing you were coming home."

"I would always do that, if I were able."

"And I would be there for you."

His face relaxed. "I think I realise that now." he said.

"Do you want to tell anyone?" she asked, her head to one side as she pressed against his chest once more.

"Not yet. "Not before we know for certain. Maybe then Tom, and Elizabeth, if you wish."

"I think she already suspects," Kate sighed. "She was there once when I was sick."

Manning snorted philosophically. "Then let us hope she has sense enough to keep it to herself, until you are ready, that is."

A shouted order came down to them, and the dark and tiny space was suddenly private no more. "We aught to see what is about," Manning said, releasing her from his embrace.

"Yes." Kate stepped back and smoothed her hair into some sort of order. "Belike we should think of other things for a week or so; at least until we get back to England."

Another call, this time accompanied by the sound of running feet. "Sounds as if there be action above." Manning raised one eyebrow slightly. He took her hand in his, and they started towards the door. "Let us hope it is something that will take our minds from the immediate," he said.

CHAPTER NINETEEN

The wind was changing. It had backed slightly and was starting to show signs of faltering, although *Espérance* still sailed crisp enough for now, with shrouds and stays fiddle-string tight and the whole of her tophamper seemingly as one. The first French brig was closing on them, and the shift in the weather was also hurrying the second to starboard, while the frigate had altered course and was heading in at speed from the northeast. No signals had been exchanged between either force, but that need not mean they were unaware of the other's existence. King took a turn about the deck. Darkness still lay some time off. He must meet with at least one of the enemy ships before then, and had been making plans.

The stun'sil, or studding sail, booms were in position, with canvas furled and ready. The wind was still too strong to consider their use for now, but in an hour or so he might be glad of the extra speed. The ship was cleared for action, and the guns, already loaded, were checked and secured. That much was possible using those detailed as gunners, most of whom were suffering from rupture, tumour or the loss of an arm or hand. To actually run all the pieces out called for fully able bodies. It would have to be the topmen, even for the relatively light weight of a six pounder, and that must mean temporarily sacrificing control of the sails. Ideas began to tumble about his brain as he sought solutions, while the ship powered on through the dark waves, with every minute bringing her closer to the nearest enemy.

"I'd say we shall be within range in half an hour." Nichols was studying the brig through the deck glass.

"Your wound does not bother you?" King asked, taking the brass telescope from him.

"Truth is, I had almost forgotten it," Nichols lied.

"Well, I have not." Elizabeth had been waiting in silence for some while. "And if you really must stay on this wobbly deck, can you not avoid standing?"

"Maybe a seat?" King asked diplomatically. Nichols was duly placed on a hammock chair by the nearest gun, and Elizabeth started to arrange his greatcoat about him.

"You might be more comfortable below, dear," he said when she was finished.

"Below?" Elizabeth asked, surprised.

"Aye, we'll be in action in no time," King confirmed.

"But that does not mean I cannot stay and look after George."

For a moment King nearly laughed out loud. There seemed little a young woman could do to stop French round shot. "Remain if you wish, but there will be nothing called for from you, and it will only be placing yourself in greater danger."

"Go, my dear." Nichols reached up and touched her hand briefly. "Tom is right, you cannot do much, and I am well protected."

The girl considered him doubtfully. "I'd say I were in as much peril here as anywhere, but I shall, if you think it right."

"I believe the Mannings were bursting with something when they came on deck earlier," Nichols continued, his own eyes slightly alight. "She seemed as if they had won the lottery, yet neither would speak any more. What say you try and discover their secret?"

"I noticed that, though chance I might already have guessed the cause." She studied his face for a moment, then leant to embrace him. King turned diplomatically away and returned to studying his adversary.

The brig was well set up and being handled competently enough. And Nichols was right, they should be within range before the next bell, although if both held their current course, there would be minimal gunfire. The Frenchman was close hauled on the larboard tack, sailing as near to the wind as she could lie, while *Espérance* had the wind just past her beam. The two vessels were converging almost bow to bow and at a considerable pace. If the Frenchman had any guns facing forward, the British would know of it soon enough, but it should be a spell longer before their broadside armament came into use. He glanced up to the sails, now considerably softer than when the wind was blowing at its peak. The fore and main courses were set, although their roaches were uncomfortably low for a warship. Whoever had fitted *Espérance* out paid scant attention to the needs of a privateer—her lower canvas was certainly of a merchant cut. Were he to use the guns he really should consider brailing them up for safety, as they could so easily ignite. But if this were to be the hit and run manoeuvre he intended, extra power was needed to turn and move on. There was really so much to think about, and yet so little time. Crowley came towards him and knuckled his forehead.

"Can I be issuing a bite of food to the men?" he asked.

Of course! King felt the first signs of depression returning. He had postponed their noon time meal: most had eaten nothing for several hours. If he couldn't even manage to keep his people fed, what chance did he have of conducting an action?

"Yes, speak to the cook and see what can be done," he said, feeling his face flush slightly. "Let no man leave his station, but arrange that all have enough for now, and promise them a hot meal and double grog when it is over."

Crowley moved off, and King's thoughts went back to the problem of manpower. The guns were ready, but all his topmen, and the injured trained as servers, would be needed to man a single broadside, and yet he must also keep control of the sails. He felt that he could solve every difficulty adequately enough were he only given one at a time, and with sufficient space between.

"She's signalling!" Barrow spoke this time. The young man was studying the French frigate through his own glass. Sure enough a line of bunting had broken out, and the second brig, still thundering towards them to starboard, was making some form of reply. So the enemy were now aware of each other and their own strength, although that hardly altered his current problem. He turned to pace again, and was actually raising one foot to move, when the solution finally came to him.

* * *

"Hold her, steady, steady..." King was leaning over the larboard side, his right hand clutching at the mizzen chains as he watched the enemy draw closer. They were now less than three hundred yards apart, with the French brig only marginally off their larboard bow. Neither vessel had opened fire, both lacking any forward-facing guns, but it would take no more than a simple helm order from either to present their full broadside. Such an action was risky, however. Anyone acting so must stake the chance of an important hit against that of losing both position and wind. The battle of wills continued, with each vessel creeping nearer in the fickle breeze. *Espérance* had her fore and main courses furled tightly to the yards, whereas the forecourse was still set on the Frenchman. But then the enemy's sail bore a deep-cut roach that placed it well out of the way of any burning embers, should she use her guns, whereas King's ship was hampered with low-cut canvas that would be more appropriate on a collier.

"Steady," King repeated. He glanced over to Harris, the helmsman, and felt there was no need to worry. The man knew his job well enough and was absent-mindedly chewing on a quid of tobacco while he guided them in. Never was the difference between helming and steering so clearly exhibited. Most hands with the usual share of sight and reason could be taught to steer, but it took a true seaman, one with years of experience and a fair amount of intuition, to feel the way of a ship, predict the numerous variances in a failing wind and keep her on a steady course, when all about her were trying to do otherwise.

The time for subterfuge had past, and the British ensign flapped laconically in the breeze. They were growing closer now. He must not leave it too late. King opened his mouth to give the order, then hesitated. It was no good allowing the enemy room to manoeuvre and possibly recover, but then he also wanted to avoid closing too much. He glanced up at the sails, no longer stiff and starting to grow indistinct in the lowering light. A lot depended on how the addition of courses increased their speed; there would be little time to add studding sails for what he had in mind.

"Take her two points to larboard," King said finally, his voice breaking the tense silence that enveloped the entire ship. It was the order they were expecting, and the men responded instantly. The yards were heaved round, and the ship began to turn almost imperceptibly. It was not enough to bring the enemy into their arc of fire, but the intention was clear and made doubly so when the hands who had been manning the braces rushed to the waiting starboard battery.

"Run them out, lads," Barrow shouted, his hands waving in excitement. The guns rumbled forward on their carriages and were swiftly secured. Again, it appeared a slick enough operation, even though there were precious few men to actually serve the pieces if King had ordered them to be used.

He continued to watch. There was no sign of movement from the Frenchman, and they were each about to enter the other's arc of fire. Then a murmur ran through the crew as the enemy showed its teeth, in this case an irregular line of black muzzles that nosed out from their starboard ports to snarl at them. King forced himself to count; there were nine—the brig was well armed. He peered up at the mizzen topsail, now decidedly slack. It was going to be a close thing. Much would be down to luck and how that luck was used.

"Now's the time," he said finally, pulling himself inboard as he did. "Bring her round and heave on those sheets!"

The enemy could be expected to open fire at any moment—he had judged it to the very last second. Johnston was there with his pipe to his lips, but there was no need for any instruction—the men knew their tasks well enough. With a sound of successive snaps, the main and foresail sheets were heaved, tearing the spun yard loops that were securing the canvas to the yards. The heavy sails had been soaked in water to prevent them catching fire whilst also retaining every last breath of wind. They flopped down and began to billow in the gentle breeze while the yards were braced round and Harris centred the wheel. Then the men were rushing to the guns, this time to run out the larboard battery. King looked to the brig again as the small vessel began to move across their prow and finally settle off their larboard bow again. *Espérance* was moving faster now, but would she be fast enough to avoid the enemy's reaction?

"Take sight and hold your fire." Barrow was running down the deck as the guns were secured. Each had an experienced captain attending to it, even though two of them were lacking an arm and another a leg, while a fourth was muttering nonsense to himself while he signalled the servers to move the gun to point as far forward as it could. "Take your time," Barrow cautioned. "We don't want no fancy broadsides, fire when you're good and ready, but not until I gives the word."

The men knew their business well enough, as they did their aiming point, which was to be at the brig's tophamper, but all were far too intent on what they were doing to make any form of reply. Barrow watched as the enemy crept closer, then finally looked back at King, who gave him a nod.

"Fire as you will, lads," he said. For a moment nothing happened. The pause continued until King wondered if any had truly heard. Then the first gun spoke, and soon there was a long staccato clatter that cut through the cold, quiet evening air, and turned all on deck ever so slightly deaf.

It took hardly any time for the seven six-pound lumps of iron to cover the short distance, but King willed them on every inch of the way. It was a Frenchman's trick to fire at another ship's masts, especially with the wind as it was, but he was not intending to take the brig, or even harm her significantly. If *Espérance* was carrying any chain or bar shot he might have used that, but a well-placed six-pound ball would do almost as much damage to a fragile rig as something far heavier. One shot striking a vulnerable spar should do the job, disable the vessel enough for them to pass and seek shelter in the dying light. One shot, and they were firing seven. It needed an expert gun layer, a man used to his weapon and the motion of the ship, to hit such a small target from a moving platform, but then that was where the luck came in.

"Buckets there!" Stationed further forward, Barrow was clearly keeping his head, and had the sense to check the courses. The fore was glowing slightly at the clew and would be ablaze within seconds if not attended to. Two seamen quickly doused it with seawater, and the danger was abated.

King looked back to the enemy brig. The smoke was rolling down towards her, as he found himself joined by Crowley and Khan at the larboard rail. Then the wind gusted, the evening air cleared, and the group let out a mutual sigh, followed by something far more robust from further forward as seamen on the forecastle registered their success.

"That seems to fit the bill," Crowley commented dryly.

"I could not ask for more," King agreed.

Indeed, the damage was beyond his wildest hopes. The brig lay amidst a confusion of spars, canvas and rope, her main topmast leaning forward and clearly about to tumble.

"We must make for safety," he continued, turning away from the sight and looking up at the sails once more. With a larger crew and no other ships in the vicinity, he might even have taken the Frenchman, but as it was he could only depend on flight and the coming darkness to shelter them.

"She's opened fire!" Barrow again. His shrill call came a split second before the sharp crack of five or six guns fired almost in unison.

"We've little to fear from that," Crowley muttered. "It were fast work for them who ain't ready; half failed to fire and those what did could only have been roughly laid."

King stared back into the gloom. Crowley was right, and even if the French had been prepared at the larboard battery, the confusion caused by a falling topmast could hardly have helped their aim. Sure enough, a line of splashes, some way short of *Espérance,* rose up briefly to disappear almost as fast, and only one, laid slightly higher, skipped across the dark ocean in a series of splashes that finished well before their hull. "Belike we caught them unawares," the Irishman continued, gracing a rare smile on anyone who would have it.

"Take her to starboard!" King ordered, turning aside and almost colliding with Nichols who was stumbling across the deck to see.

"A hit, Tom?" he asked, his face the image of anxiety.

"Aye, we've taken out her main topmast," King said, before turning his attention back to the ship. "Braces there, and rig the stuns'ls!"

The wind was certainly weak enough now for the fragile extensions to the yards to be used. The topmen ran from the guns to the shrouds, and in no time the extra sails were being sheeted home, and the ship truly began to gather way.

"She's in irons," Crowley said, his eyes back on the enemy and his voice rich with satisfaction. Clearly, the slight alteration necessary to allow the Frenchman's broadside had been ill timed. The brig was wallowing in the swell, with her remaining sails flapping impotently as the darkness began to claim her. They had gained a head start and, with the wind now on her quarter, King was quite certain that *Espérance* could out sail any vessel with a damaged mainmast. But then there were still other matters to concern him.

"What do you see of the second Frenchman?" King yelled. A moment's pause, then the masthead replied.

"Hull up and headin' for us, though the light's fading fast."

"Distance?"

"Two mile off or more."

King nodded to himself and spared a grin for Nichols. There was the noise of water bubbling from the stem, and the lower courses were growing stiff and hard: the wind appeared to be rising. Luck was certainly on their side, but would it remain so throughout the night and, most importantly, stay with them until morning?

* * *

Midnight and no moon. The ship was totally blacked out, and darkness completely enveloped them. Only the whine of wind through rigging lines and an occasional slap of water as a rogue wave smacked against the hull proved that *Espérance* was anything more solid than a ghost ship. King was back on deck after retiring below when the enemy finally disappeared into the gloom. There he had nibbled at a scratch meal, rested a spell, and even contemplated sleep before a seemingly magnetic attraction brought him up once more. Now he stood next to the binnacle, his tired body flexing easily with the motion of the ship, while his mind considered the many possibilities before him.

When last spotted, the second French brig was making to the southwest on the starboard tack, while the frigate, being slightly to the north, was on a converging course. The wind was still backing and now came from roughly that direction. *Espérance* had turned, taken in her studding sails and was making good speed close hauled, heading west-by-north. The change had been made in complete darkness, and King was reasonably certain would have gone unnoticed, although there was nothing he could do to prevent the French from predicting his actions.

This was where supposition took over. He could have no idea if there was any change. Both vessels might have continued on their previous headings, which placed them slightly to the east of him. Or they could equally have given up the chase completely. But then *Espérance* was a small ship and easy pickings for the Frenchman. He could not think they would let such a plum prize get away without a chase.

If he was worth his salt, the enemy captain should assume that

King wanted to get to his destination without delay, and attempt to return to his previous course, or as near as he could make to it. And he would be right. With the change of wind, a northerly heading was impossible, but King was sailing *Espérance* as close as she could lie. And if he were doing the obvious thing, could he not expect both enemy vessels to have altered their headings accordingly? If so they must have worked out his likely position, and be aiming to intercept him at daybreak.

But at least he felt he could all but discount the first brig. Since their brief action they had travelled a fair distance and repairs to a main topmast could not be made quickly in the dark. It was probable that she was many miles away by now, or at least so far off as to make any further involvement in the action unlikely. The second brig was still a threat. She appeared every bit as powerful and could probably take King's little ship with ease. But he had already dealt with one of her kind and, in his mind at least, felt able to write her off in a similar manner. It was the frigate that really worried him—she was a completely different proposition.

There would be no chance of disabling her in such a cavalier manner. She was bound to be heavily armed, with chase guns to bow and stern, and her broadside could sink a fragile craft like *Espérance* before he even thought of testing his feeble six pounders for range.

He took a turn or two along the deck, easing his tired muscles into activity, and gaining a small amount of warmth from the action. It was possible that he was reading too much into the problem and could be excused for thinking the French had not guessed his change of course. He might just as well brazen it out and continue on his present heading. Then he stopped pacing and sniffed the breeze. In his bones he knew that, if he did nothing, first light might reveal a powerful enemy vessel in sight, and almost certainly to windward. It was not an attractive thought.

So, what were his options? A few hours ago, avoiding capture had been enough. But now, now that he had gained both a reprieve and the all-important sea room his desire for a quick passage home returned. The recent diversions had placed him behind. To make anything like a credible time he must pass the French and, ironically, it was probably the one manoeuvre they would not be expecting. But only the hours of darkness could make such a bold move possible, and they were rapidly diminishing.

The wind was gradually growing steadier, the earlier gusting having all but levelled off. It also seemed to be settling in the north. Tacking now, he could probably hold a course eastwards; possibly east-by-north. The northward progress would be almost negligible, but he would be in a better position should it back further. Then he could continue with a series of broad reaches until the wind changed again. It would be a bold and calculating move; one that meant turning towards the French, and attempting to slip past. And rather than just a simple exercise, one that would be over in a couple of minutes, this had to last out the rest of the night. For several hours he must hold his nerve, while any second could reveal a dangerous enemy close by. King could not help but wonder if he was truly ready for such a task.

But what was the alternative? They could continue as they were, wasting time and exposing themselves to greater danger while being chased even further from home. With an invisible force at their heels, King could guess how soon the hunters would assume greater powers in the men's minds. He had an experienced crew and to run for an hour or so was acceptable, but a prolonged pursuit must start to tear at their morale. Even if daylight revealed an empty horizon, all would know the French were still out there somewhere. They might continue, surviving the day and the following night, but each mile must take them further from their objective, with the added chance of sailing straight into further enemy shipping growing with every league.

Turning to the south might be a better proposition. They could gain speed, and the manoeuvre might well confuse the chasing French. But the enemy would remain to windward; a danger to be negotiated when he finally found the courage, he could think of no other term, to turn for home.

He flexed his knees and yawned, stuffing his hands deeper into his pockets, confident that the absolute darkness would hide such a deliciously slovenly act. The night was certainly welcome, and he was further blessed by the complete absence of moon, but it only granted a brief postponement. Morning must come, and the first hour of light would show his true position.

"Two bells, sir." Johnston called out softly.

King had ordered that the bell should not be struck once the gloom descended. Two bells. Sunrise was at eight, but dawn started long before that. There were less than five hours of complete darkness before first light. A lot could happen in that time. A lot, or nothing at all—the choice was his. By this time tomorrow he might be heading once more for England, a prisoner of the French, or well beyond the range of all such worldly matters.

And, whatever his eventual position, the only certainty was it would be entirely due to the decision he was about to make.

* * *

After an especially tiring day, Nichols was feeling remarkably good. The wound was healing nicely; apart from a tendency to itch, it caused him little problem. And the pain inside that had been pretty well constant since the surgery was growing less. It was almost as if the recent exercise had actually been beneficial. Sometimes he received a not-so-gentle reminder, and on a couple of occasions he thought he might have pushed things too far; but in general, he felt well.

And he was not dead; that was certainly a point in his favour. During his seafaring career he had heard of many cases where men injured in the chest or belly required medical intervention. Such procedures were carried out only when there was absolutely no alternative, and were rarely, if ever, successful. No, he was certainly a lucky man; that fact was readily acknowledged, and he also felt incredibly glad to be alive. The ship might be speeding into dangerous waters, and they may have several powerful enemy ships on their tail, but that was all but countered by the overwhelming feeling of wellbeing that he now experienced. It was a sensation aided not a little by a most beautiful dining companion, one who currently sat in front of him, and smiled so readily whenever he looked in her direction.

In fact, they had long since ceased to eat, and the remains of their supper was now quite cold, although still they sat facing one another as if frightened that movement by either party might break the spell. Their conversation was conventional enough for two nubile people, even if they gave it a mildly unorthodox slant.

"Or we could ditch the whole idea," Nichols said, his eyes flashing wickedly.

She gave him a warning look. "What exactly do you have in mind?"

"A secret wedding," he beamed innocently. "One with two witnesses that we drag in from the street and a tired old parson who only wants to go back to his pipe and armchair."

"Really, George. You make it sound so attractive."

"It might save a lot of fuss."

"Fuss is what a woman looks forward to most in a marriage," she said primly. "For the ceremony at least."

"Well, I should be happy."

"Doubtless, though my aunt might object."

"I don't want to marry your aunt," he paused. "At least I don't think I do. Is she as pretty as her niece?"

Elizabeth dropped the hand she had been gently caressing and leaned back in her chair. "In a moment you'll be asking Mr King to perform the ceremony at this very moment."

"It's a consideration."

"Can he do that?" she asked, suddenly interested. "I mean just marry people, as a captain?"

"Tom? Oh yes, he can marry whomsoever he likes, 'though I fear he might be already spoken for." He looked at her with ill-concealed glee. "Otherwise you might try introducing him to your aunt."

* * *

Kate and Robert were in bed, their bodies close together, neatly entwined like adjacent spoons in a tray of cutlery. The ship was making her customary rhythmic groans, the flexing of timbers and easing of joints that was usually enough to send them into a deep and trouble-free slumber. Both were fiendishly tired, yet they lay awake, drawing comfort and reassurance from the other's proximity. They moved little and spoke hardly at all, but there was communication enough in the simple sharing of warmth and intention. The new life that was starting between them had yet to assume any form of identity although it was already affecting their relationship. They were no longer Mr and Mrs Manning, man and wife, bride and groom; lovers setting out to make the best of a partnership. Now they had become one single entity, a family, albeit their issue was of doubtful age and completely lacking in individuality. Earlier there had been talk, long and deep, in the darkness of the empty sickbay, even though there was little to discuss, the two being of a common mind and understanding. The future might hold much, and nearly all was well beyond their comprehension or control, but everything that came would be met together, shared in full with the absolute support of the other. It was the first time either had truly known what it was to be as one.

The cause might be both joyful and fearsome in equal measures, but the feeling it evoked was every bit as wondrous.

* * *

"Summon the watch below." King's voice was soft, but the order it carried proved enough to turn the entire ship into turmoil. Johnston touched his hat and raised his pipe, before remembering the need for silence. He turned to a member of the afterguard resting nearby.

"Alert the lower deck," he said, in a gruff whisper. "Turn out the larboard watch, an' anyone else who 'appens to be about." The man ran off readily enough, while Johnston moved forward, peering through the gloom, to raise the watch on deck.

"Who's at the wheel?" King asked as the rumble of bare feet died down.

"'Arris, sir."

He nodded. It was the elderly quartermaster from the previous night. King was glad to have someone so skilled to hand.

"We're going to tack and head back past the French." He was speaking in a normal voice, although the sound carried easily and the men were primed to listen. "With luck we will be past them by daybreak, otherwise there might be a spot of bother, but I don't think you will mind that so very much."

A ripple of laughter came back to him, as he knew it would. The poor fools were in high spirits, clearly happy to risk all and expose the ship and their lives to the enemy.

"I cannot be certain of their exact position, and there is a chance we'll meet with them before dawn. For that reason I want this ship to remain darkened, and repeat my order for silence. Any man who makes an unnecessary sound, or shows a light," he paused, wondering what punishment was suitably harsh for something that might mean the death of everyone on board, "will make me very unhappy," he finally added.

Another series of chuckles, the mood was certainly buoyant, but no bad thing for that. Each of them knew the position they were in and would do their utmost to see that the ship was not revealed without any additional threats from him. He caught sight of the elderly helmsman, his face faintly aglow from the single binnacle lamp that King allowed. Clearly the thought of action when he was expecting to retire had not daunted him in any way, and he was grinning widely. Even faced with an enemy that included a light frigate, and in a ship as small as the *Espérance,* he was confident, if not of victory, then at least that his life was not to be sold too cheaply.

"Very well, prepare to tack."

"Ready about, stations for stays."

King stepped back as members of the afterguard went about their work. Then the sound of Elizabeth's voice came up from below. For a moment he went cold, he had forgotten all about the women, and it came as a surprise to realise that there was more at stake than the lives of a few worn-out seamen.

"Ready, ease down the helm."

He could still change his mind, of course. He was the one in command and nothing was irrevocable. But he waited while the ship moved steadily into the wind and gradually settled on to the opposite tack. The sails were sheeted home, and she gathered way smartly enough. The deck moved under his feet, and soon he felt she was even travelling faster on the larboard tack, although that might be purely an illusion, one evoked by the thought that an enemy was likely to be bearing down towards them. Harris was keeping the ship on a steady course, despite the fact that he could barely see the luff of the topsail a few feet above him.

"Three bells, sir," Johnston muttered softly.

King nodded in the darkness. Three bells, half past one in the morning. If the frigate was on the course he estimated, *Espérance* would be passing her at any time from three o'clock onwards. They might not see her at all, she could slide by several miles off their beam, or so close that action and defeat were inevitable. Or they could survive the hours of darkness, only to be caught at first light, with the entire day for the enemy to close on them. He pressed his hands deep into his pockets, bent forward slightly and slouched his shoulders. It was going to be a long time until dawn.

CHAPTER TWENTY

For a well-found ship, one that was fully crewed, well armed and with a predator's eye, the hour before first light was always filled with excitement and expectation. Dawn could rise faster than any fleeing prey, revealing a tasty prize that might have wandered unwittingly close. Or for the hunted, daybreak might also signal the end of a nervous night; the cold darkness that had sheltered them disappearing to the warmth of the sun, leaving a horizon void of all danger.

And so it was to be for them, King told himself. The night was still black, although he knew it could only stay that way a short time longer; even now there was a lightening in the east, and the slight, low-lying mist was fast disappearing. When the day finally came, the enemy frigate would be several miles to leeward of them, of that he was growing increasingly certain. Probably beyond sight, but certainly out of range. Then they could enjoy a pleasant breakfast, safe in the knowledge that they had given a dangerous enemy the slip and were now well placed to continue for England, home and safety. Throughout the long hours he repeated the calculations in his head, each time reassuring himself of their accuracy and quality, while trying to drive out the *iota* of doubt that stubbornly remained to taunt, tease and tantalise.

Crowley appeared carrying a steaming china mug. King took it gratefully and bent down to sip. It was coffee; he had hardly tasted the stuff in weeks, and was not even aware there was any on board.

The slight dizzy feeling it evoked was both stimulating and welcome. There had been no food since the biscuit and cheese he downed the previous evening, but he felt no hunger, and his watchcoat was keeping him tolerably warm.

He sipped again from the mug and looked about. Yes, there was definitely a hint of dawn in the sky. He took a turn or two along the deck. The new day would come in time, and nothing he might do could bring it forward, but the movement seemed to pacify him, and he continued to walk.

Nichols's head appeared above the hatch coaming; proof of the growing light that enabled King to identify him so readily. He hauled himself on to the deck, with Elizabeth, dressed in a long dark coat that he had often seen Kate wear, following close behind.

"What cheer, Tom?" he asked.

King shook his head. "Nothing so far, though we shall doubtless know more afore long." He studied the man in the gloom. "How is it with you, George?"

"Never better," Nichols responded instantly, his voice painfully loud to those who had stood the quiet night on deck.

"I am glad." His friend certainly sounded bright, and there seemed something extra added. King did not know the reason, but guessed that the young woman who stood near was somehow connected. "Glad, indeed," he said again, with just a hint of envy.

A small sound came from above, one that was instantly cut short. Fowler was at the masthead, along with Barrow who had been sent to join him. The atmosphere became tense once more as King and Nichols exchanged glances. One of them, probably the boy, transferred himself to a backstay and was soon heading for the deck by the second fastest method. Both men looked about uncertainly; there seemed nothing untoward in the growing light, but those at the masthead would have a far better view, and clearly something had alerted them.

The lad hit the deck, having released his hold slightly too early, and stumbled clumsily. King and Nichols made towards him as he turned and recovered himself.

"Sail in sight," he spluttered, pointing wildly. "Off the larboard bow, less than mile away, and headin' to the west."

* * *

King felt the last sip of coffee catch in his throat. It was shockingly close. A wave of anger rose up inside him. By his estimations they should have been past and at least ten miles behind. The enemy had no right to be there.

"It were the frigate from last night," Barrow continued, spewing his words between gasps of breath. "She's under topsails an I'd say were about to set t'gallants."

King cursed silently; that was one thing not counted upon in his plans. The French must have shortened sail during the night, a rare act for a man-of-war. That, or given up the chase completely. He felt his face flush. If he had only kept *Espérance* on her original course, they should have been sailed well below the horizon by now.

But this was not the time for recriminations. The light was coming faster by the minute. King glanced round. Men stood ready at their posts and, for the most part, were watching him, some even stupid enough to think he had anticipated such a meeting. Less than a mile off. The fact continued to reverberate about his head like the echo of a loud and painful noise. It was no distance at all. They were in range of her broadside guns, and the enemy was still to windward.

"There she is!" It was Crowley's voice; the Irishman was on the far side of the deck. King peered out as the gloom slowly lifted. Yes, the dark patch was certainly a ship's hull, and the masts and yards were becoming clearer by the second. It was ridiculously near, and they were even closing as he watched.

"Take her about," he shouted as the blood started to drain from his body. How could he have been so stupid? Why on earth had he not stuck to the safest course, rather than risk all in a foolhardy attempt to pass in the dark? "Stations for wearing ship!"

Espérance shuddered as she was roughly turned and all but wrenched on to the starboard tack. The light was in the east, and a modicum of mist remained. There was the slightest chance that they were still hidden from the Frenchman, although King could hardly dare hope that was the case.

"She's adding royals." Fowler's voice came from the masthead to haunt him. Clearly the lookout had abandoned all pretence at staying concealed. "An' shaving a point or so to have us in pursuit."

There was nothing else for it. He must have left the turn too late, not accounted sufficiently for their lead, or allowed for the enemy shortening sail. But all was not lost. They could make a chase of it, and the interesting part was still to come.

The enemy could yaw and give them the benefit of their broadside, gambling the loss of speed and position against that of scoring an important hit. Or she might trail them, putting all her efforts into closing, whilst taking pot shots with her forward-mounted cannon—powerful guns that could easily rake such a small craft as *Espérance*. Even if they were not damaged, it was going to take some while to sail the Frenchman out of range, and probably the rest of the day to lose her completely. He glanced round the deck and noticed Nichols. The man was watching him closely, clearly concerned.

"Seems that our friends are not so easy to shake," he said, with remnants of his previous good humour still evident.

"Aye, and they're looking for a sailing contest," King forced himself to speak lightly, then turned to meet the eyes of those about him. "What say we show him a thing or two about seamanship?"

The men agreed and laughed readily, as was their right. All knew their craft well enough, and none had made such a colossal gaff as their captain.

"What news of the others?" he shouted up suddenly as a thought occurred. "Do you see either of the brigs?"

A pause, then Fowler continued slowly. "There's a smudge, but I can't rightly be sure, and couldn't mark it as a sighting," he said.

King turned to Barrow. "Back to the masthead," he snapped. "Take the deck glass and tell me what you make of it."

The youngster was at the chains in seconds and soon flying up the shrouds at an impressive rate, the brass telescope swinging from the strap about his shoulders. King focused his attention on *Espérance*, which was settling on the new course.

"Mr Khan, we'll have the stuns'ls on her again, if you please," the boatswain touched his hat and began to shout for his topmen. King must now forget all about a record passage home. The only way he could hope to escape capture was to run, and as fast as his little ship could carry him. "Quartermaster, steer sou'west."

The extra points put the wind on her quarter, their best point of sailing, even if it was also directly away from England. The ship bucked slightly as the breeze caught the fresh canvas, and soon *Espérance* began to fly. Light was gaining steadily; already the frigate was plainly visible from the deck. King studied her intently; she was a well-found ship, beautiful in design and clearly heavily armed. When it came to fighting, *Espérance* could not withstand even one full broadside from those deadly guns. Despite the coffee, his mouth felt inordinately dry—they could expect her to open fire at any moment.

* * *

Khan looked back from his masts, where the freshly trimmed canvas was filling nicely. At least the wind still blew strong and benefited a light hull like theirs more than that of even a frigate.

"Keep your head down, Abdul," Johnston grinned, as he joined him next to the mainmast. "Frenchie's gonna open up at any moment."

The Lascar pursed his lips, even though his face showed little sign of immediate concern. If the enemy chose to fire on him, that was their business and completely beyond his power to control. But still he worried about Mr King. The young officer was standing on the quarterdeck barely feet from him. His body was tense and brittle, with head pressed unnaturally down upon his chest and ridged arms held tight against his sides. He was the very image of distress, and clearly blaming himself for the bad luck he had been allocated.

A commotion from behind drew their attention, and shortly afterwards the solid ring of a single gun reached them.

"They have us nicely," Johnston said, and Khan turned forward to see the last of a substantial cascade of water collapse off and beyond their starboard bow. "That will be a ranging shot," he continued. "From their bow chaser; checkin' we're within their grasp."

"Will they continue to fire?" the Lascar asked, despite himself.

"Like as not," Johnston replied; it was his turn to be nonchalant now. "They'll aim for our rig; Frenchies always do, and they seems to have the elevation. It's a bigger target than the 'ull, though still no sitting duck, even at this range."

"We should make preparations, perhaps?" Khan asked, concern now switching to his precious masts and spars.

"We done all we can until they hits us," Johnston reassured him. "But it's no sure fire bet; yon Mr King ain't so beetle headed as he makes out. He's got them nicely hidden on the quarter at the moment, that's the space between the reach of their bow chasers and broadside guns. The enemy will correct, you can be sure of that, but he'll alter course as soon as they do, and there ain't gonna be no fancy shootin', not while he keeps her so."

Khan nodded, glad that another person was sensitive to King's predicament and that the man himself was still making rational decisions.

Another crack of gunfire, but this time the shot landed unseen.

"Must have been well off," Johnston said. "But we'll be turnin' in no time; before the French gets their eye in. An' he'll keep dodging until they can't reach us no more."

"How long will we remain in range?"

Johnston shook his head. "Can't rightly say, but it won't be forever," he grinned again. "Even though it might feel like it."

* * *

"Take her two points to larboard." The time was certainly not dragging for King. There was too much to think about, too much to do. They must have gained a good half cable on the pursuing frigate and, although the constant changes of heading had slowed them slightly, none of the enemy's shot were landing close. Of course, there was something of an illusion in the last point. The French were aiming high, as was their fashion, so any that missed caused a splash some considerable way off. But some had been wide, extremely wide, and King drew comfort from the fact that he was not facing crack gunners.

Dawn was up now, and a mild sun just started to make itself known. Earlier on Fowler and Barrow had reported one of the French brigs in sight, fine off the larboard bow. She was coming up close hauled on the starboard tack, but still lay a good way off, and King felt he could ignore that particular threat for the time being.

Elizabeth was on deck. She was standing close to Nichols, after bringing him a cup of something from below. King considered ordering her down once more, but finally decided against it. If she were prepared to risk her life, then it was really not of his concern. Everyone made mistakes, after all.

"Should be clear of them afore long," Nichols called across the deck after the second shot in succession had fallen a good way off.

The evidence certainly indicated so, even though King felt they were still a way from being out of danger. But he knew that every change in direction threw the French gunners, and noticed that the first or second shots following a minor alteration were often poorly elevated. It was the sign of a bad marksman, and it might be supposed that the very best was being used at the bow chasers. Sure enough, the third was in line and actually passed through the small ship's maze of rigging lines. Fortunately, nothing was hit, and he hurriedly adjusted their heading. It was not an experience he wished to see repeated.

They were making a fair speed, however, and much of his earlier despondency was gone. The enemy was a good mile off by now and they would be properly out of range within the hour. Then he could abandon this zigzag trail and settle down to the long haul; one that he guessed must last the day and probably most of the night to come. By the time they were properly free and could turn back with confidence, several hundred miles will have been covered. It was quite a distance to make up, and doing so would certainly mean a poor passage time back to England. He was on the very verge of thinking about his commission once more, when the French fired their next shot. The sound that echoed across the empty water was no different to those that had gone before, except this time it was accompanied by a loud crack, and the snapping of lines from aloft.

King stared up, then jumped to one side as a heavy object fell to the deck, barely feet from where he was standing.

"Mizzen t'gallant!" Crowley shouted, tripping as he dodged out of the path of another falling block. King reached out and pulled him from the deck, while a series of loud crashes told where several more pieces of tophamper were raining down.

"Topmen!" King shouted, but Khan was already heading for the weather shrouds, with Johnston and Smith, the second boatswain's mate, following close behind.

"Watch the spar!" The call came from Harris at the wheel. He was staring up at the sky and pointing wildly. King followed his gaze. The yard and upper mast were free now and starting to fall, with much of the topgallant sail still attached.

"Stand away there!" King bellowed to no avail, but then it was hard to know which way to run, as the dark wooden beam speared down towards them. It landed squarely on one of the men, bending the soft body to the deck much as a badly wielded hammer might a particularly stubborn nail.

"Abdul!" Johnston's shout was nothing less than a scream. He rushed forward as the spar fell to one side, its work complete.

"Leave it, boy," Harris at the wheel commanded. Indeed, there was little Johnston could do for his friend, but much remained wanting elsewhere.

"Axes, axes there!" A considerable amount of cordage and the topgallant staysail, were trailing over the side, slowing their progress. Two men made for the bulwarks and began to hack down on the tight lines. King looked about in momentary confusion; then he saw Elizabeth and Nichols.

She was lying in his arms as he bent down and attended to her in an odd reversal of roles. Blood was streaming from her head, and her eyes were open, but clearly seeing nothing. King consciously blocked the sight from him mind; he could spare them no time while the ship was in such imminent danger.

"Topmen!" He repeated his cry of thirty-seconds ago. Johnston was still attending to Khan's body, but Smith responded readily enough, and along with other hands, began to clamber up the weather shrouds.

"How does she feel?" King snapped at Harris. The old man turned the wheel either way.

"It's a difference I can handle," he said guardedly. "The bow is up slightly, an' I'd appreciate the stays'l replaced."

"Very well, we'll see what can be done." Of all of the tophamper, the mizzen topgallant was probably the least important, but that hardly eased the fact that they were hit. Any progress they made now was bound to be that much slower, and, probably just as important to the eventual outcome, the French would be encouraged. King felt the motion of the ship through his feet as he stood on the quarterdeck and glanced back at the oncoming enemy. Certainly, *Espérance* was maintaining her lead and might be even gaining slightly.

Another crack from the bow chaser. They were currently in the arc of the larboard gun, which was still firing every four minutes. Was it really that long since they were hit, or had their success hastened the French gunners? This time the shot fell to starboard and even a little short, so the damage might easily have been caused by fate—a freak combination of power and timing which had thrown what could even have been an irregular ball further and higher than normal.

Smith and the topmen were at the mizzen topmast now and appeared to be attempting to make some order from the mess.

"Can you rig a jury?" King asked.

Smith shook his head. "Not a replacement mast, sir. But I might be able to set a fresh stays'l if we has one."

"We got a main t'gallant stay that'll serve." Johnston's voice— he had finally left Khan's body and was looking up. "Rig a fall whilst I rouse it out."

King nodded, then noticed Nichols and Elizabeth once more.

He had laid her on the deck and was foolishly trying to wipe the blood from her forehead, although the wound was clearly deep and continued to bleed.

"It was a fiddle block," he said, almost conversationally as King joined him. "Fell from above and knocked her cold."

"Is she breathing?" King asked.

"Aye, and there's a pulse." King could see that Nichols's hands were shaking horribly and wondered how he could tell.

"We should get her below." He looked about, but all appeared to be fully occupied.

"I'll take her," Nichols said, and he began to scoop the light body into his arms.

"Wait, you'll do your wound damage. I'll get Manning to come up."

But Nichols was already gathering Elizabeth in his arms. He began to lift, then let out an involuntary cry as he slumped forward over her. He sobbed once, and went to try again. Then Kate joined them.

"Come, George, we can take her together," she said, and King was momentarily struck by her white pallor. She pressed her arms under the girl, and with Nichols half lifting, half trailing, brought her up from the deck and started for the hatchway.

"Can I help?" King asked, feeling vaguely useless.

"You can attend to the ship, Tom," Kate replied, not looking back.

Another shot came from the Frenchman, but that also fell short, and another after that. Then there was blessed silence, a silence that continued far longer than anyone could have hoped. Slowly, it dawned on them that *Espérance* was finally out of range.

The remains of the topgallant mast had been ditched over the side, and Johnston with two other men were manhandling a replacement staysail to the lower mizzenmast. Khan's body was still lying broken on the deck. Two older men made for it, but Johnston cried out angrily, and they let him be.

"Bloody Lascars," Johnston swore softly to himself while he turned his attention to attaching the staysail to the line that Smith had sent down. "Always the first to die."

* * *

King breakfasted a little later, and by the time he regained the quarterdeck, much had changed. The French frigate was still in clear sight, although the lead was now more than four miles. But coming up to larboard, seemingly with a firm breeze, the French brig was gaining fast.

"Take her two points to starboard," King ordered, as he collected the traverse board from the binnacle. They were now heading almost due west and must be more than fifteen points off their original course. The brig was a nuisance, no more. Even with their damaged mizzen, he was confident of eventually out-sailing both vessels. And once that was achieved, there would be little point in repeating last night's disaster. Making England and delivering the despatches late was far better than not arriving at all.

He had left Nichols and Elizabeth in the sick berth. Manning had extended the small room to take in a good section of the lower deck, and already there were several takers. They were minor injuries mainly, men cut or bruised by falling debris, a splinter wound and one who had lost two fingers to another's axe. Elizabeth lay in the sick berth proper, out cold and seemingly many miles away. Nichols was attending to her and, quite understandably, had been rather short when King enquired as to her condition. Manning reassured him that there appeared to be no major damage, although little could be told for certain until she showed signs of consciousness. He, too, had been a little curt, but then this was his first time in overall charge of a sickbay, and King was well aware how heavily new responsibilities could weigh. The still small body of Khan was wrapped in a sheet awaiting the attention of Johnston, who claimed the Lascar as his tie mate and would later deal with him in the time-honoured fashion.

At the dining table King ate cold boiled pork with some pickled cabbage and took a draught of more strong black coffee. It was his first proper meal for twenty-four hours and sustained him insofar as he felt few ill-effects from his sleepless night. Manning joined him briefly, although Kate was strangely absent.

On returning, King sent Barrow and Crowley also to eat and began to pace the empty area, almost enjoying the lack of company until he remembered the reason.

"Sail ho, sail fine on the larboard bow!" The voice of the lookout took him by surprise. It was Cuminsky, a wild-eyed Irishman with a broken nose.

"What do you see there?" he shouted. The likelihood that it was yet another enemy ship was small, but one that still made his heart beat noticeably.

"Two sail, sir." The reply came back after a slight pause. "Large ships, I'd say they was men-of-war, or of a similar size. They're close hauled, headin' west-nor-west, an' just come on to that tack, by the looks of it."

King felt his body go limp. Oh the relief—the glorious feeling of rescue at the final hour. A pair of warships beating against a contrary wind. That certainly didn't sound like Frenchmen, although, even in his elation he recognised it as strange that no smaller vessels were in attendance. He felt the tension flow from him while he looked back at the pursuing French. Both must still be in ignorance of the sighting and were bound to remain so for some while. If he could only lure them into range, they would be snapped up in no time. The ideas began to develop; maybe if he slowed slightly, and waited until nightfall, or perhaps he might signal the ships and bring them down upon the enemy.

"Men-of-war for certain, sir," Cuminsky called again. "I'd say they were heavy frigates, or me'be even larger."

"Are they showing colours?" King asked, as Crowley appeared once more on deck.

"Not that I can make, sir. But they don't look like Frenchmen."

"Any other in sight?" King persisted, nodding briefly at Crowley.

"No, sir, but they're not good sailers." Cuminsky's words held just the hint of doubt. "We're gaining on them fast enough."

Large, slow ships, yet well into the Atlantic. And rather than being on the end of a broad reach, they might just as easily have altered course when they spotted the *Espérance*. After all, she was still, apparently, a privateer. Feelings of disquiet multiplied as his mind ran over the likely options, then the cold truth dawned, to him and Cuminsky, almost simultaneously.

"I'd say they was Indiamen, sir..."

* * *

Now the cat was really amongst the pigeons. He had encountered a wayward pair of East Indiamen. British, if he were to believe the ensigns that were now becoming clear, and they were sailing unescorted. There were reasons enough for such a meeting. They might have been separated from a larger convoy by the recent ill weather, or simply be chancing a run for home without escort, but neither improved his position in any way. Rather the opposite, in fact.

Sailing as they were, almost in line with his present course, meant that he was now leading the French to a far greater prize than his one small ship. Two fat Indiamen must be worth hundreds of thousands of pounds, to say nothing of the cost and inconvenience to his own country. Their presence was still hidden from the French, but it could only be a question of time before they spotted the topmasts and came to the same conclusion.

"More John Company ships," Crowley growled as their significance dawned on him.

King nodded. "Aye, and I could do without their presence." He looked about. With the brig coming up on their larboard counter, and the frigate still sitting on his stern, he was running low on options.

"I shall have to avoid them as if they were Frenchmen," he continued bitterly. "Otherwise we will simply be making a gift to the enemy."

Crowley had totally grasped the problem now. "If only they were being escorted," he said.

"Well, maybe they thought better of it," King agreed bitterly. "Didn't want to wait for the Navy to help them out."

Crowley was watching him warily. He knew the fix King was in.

They must alter course, and as soon as possible, but with the wind still in the north the choices were limited.

"Take her to larboard, head due south." The worry and relief of the last twenty-four hours were encased in that simple phrase, and King all but spat the words out. But the men reacted readily enough, and soon *Espérance* was making a credible speed running before the wind, her stunsails once more straining in the growing breeze.

"We'll keep her like this a spell," King continued. "Then take her to the southwest, when our friend here gets too close."

He was watching the French brig, now growing steadily closer. She had also altered course to maintain her bearing, but still lay three miles or more off their larboard bow. A mile south should sail the Indiamen well under their own horizon and totally mask them from the French.

Nichols appeared on deck once more, but did not approach King. Instead, he looked across to the nearest Frenchman.

"What news of Elizabeth, George?" King shouted, taking a step in his direction.

Nichols nodded, but did not smile. "She is right enough, though still out cold from the blow. Her wound has been stitched, and it's thought she will mend in time."

"Robert has a fair hand with the needle," King said, searching for something constructive to say as he joined his friend.

"What of the enemy?" Nichols asked.

"We have sighted Indiamen to the north-west, so we've turned south."

"You are still running?" he asked, amazed.

"Of course; it is my duty," King replied.

Nichols considered him for a moment. "Yes, I suppose so." His voice now carried a note of dull wonder. "Though I could never carry such diligence quite so far myself."

"It would have done little good to have surrendered earlier," King murmured, then inwardly kicked himself. To Nichols it would have made all the difference in the world.

"I am inclined to disagree," he said quietly.

There was an awkward pause, before King tried once more. "I fear it will be a while afore we are back on course for England." The situation left little constructive for him to say.

Nichols shook his head. "That is not a great concern for me at present."

Sailing before the wind, the lack of sideways pressure on the sails also made the ship's roll more apparent. Nichols staggered slightly as the ship heaved, but quickly recovered himself.

"You should get below," King told him. "There is no good to be served here."

"Aye, I shall attend to Elizabeth, I am sure you can handle things from now on." His words carried a ring of finality that worried King. As the mate made to go, he called after him.

"We will try and evade the brig at all costs; be sure of that."

Nichols turned briefly before continuing for the hatch. King could read no reassurance in his face. The man might have other worries, but there was clearly no further interest in the fight.

"I'll have you home within ten days," King persisted, desperately trying to find something to reassure him.

Nichols gave a half smile in reply. "To be truthful, Tom, I should care little if I never saw England again."

* * *

The words, and Nichols's attitude, stayed with King as he finally brought *Espérance* on to a southwesterly course. The brig was much closer now and heading west-southwest to intercept them. A painful ten minutes work saw both of *Espérance's* broadsides loaded and run out, and now the men were resting, watching the chase continue and waiting for the inevitable outcome. Crowley and Barrow were on the quarterdeck with King, and none had forgotten the frigate, also making to the southwest. Their lead was increasing steadily, but her presence effectively blocked any fancy tricks King might care to play in that direction.

Despite the situation and the knowledge that they were to be in action, and probably taken, within the hour, King found his thoughts returning to his friend. Nichols was clearly thinking of Elizabeth, and who could blame him? Once she regained consciousness and started to show signs of improvement, he would be as keen as any to reach England again, King was certain of that. He might not have a vested interest in the despatches, and there was no commission for him to reclaim, but only a fool could want for a spell in French captivity.

Of course, it should only be a spell. Most, if not all the crew, would be put forward for exchange straight away; the French could have little interest in holding disabled prisoners. The women were also likely to be repatriated without delay. He and the other officers might be held for slightly longer, but even they should be home by the end of summer. It might not be so bad, he supposed.

The Company would lose their valuable prize, however, and when he did return, King would be just another unemployed lieutenant, and one with a less than impressive history. No matter what the odds or circumstances, time spent in enemy hands did not look well on any record. He could apply to serve again, he supposed, and might even find a seagoing position again eventually. But he would be delayed in sending for Juliana, and she could be excused for deciding him a prize not worth the waiting.

"Watch her head!" King growled. Harris must have finally given up his precious wheel to a man who clearly lacked his skill. The mood of the others about him was also altering subtly. Even Manning, at breakfast, had appeared distant and reserved. As King considered this, there came a mild eruption forward. Johnston was haranguing a seaman in unusually harsh tones. King took another turn across the deck, and thrust his hands deep into his pockets. It was possible that the chase had gone on long enough.

* * *

The fickle breeze began to drop shortly afterwards, and by four bells in the afternoon watch they were barely making steerage way. King was now all but stamping about the quarterdeck, his frustration steadily mounting. If the weather deteriorated into a storm, it might be used to some benefit. Even with his damaged rig, a decent squall might enable him to shake off the brig that still crept determinedly closer. And there was four full hours before the dark came to rescue them; long before then all would be settled. Watching from the taffrail he reckoned they might be in range in twenty minutes. The brig was well armed, almost identical to the one they dealt with the previous evening, and he knew that his ship could not sustain any prolonged action with her. Besides, they were low on powder, and the men were showing further signs of growing tired and dispirited. A listless crew did not fight well, and he began to accept that this really was the end. Crowley took some food at lunchtime, although King refused to follow his example. He did leave the deck for two short minutes, but that was only to collect Jervis's despatches from the desk drawer. They were with him now, the weighty canvas bundle sticking uncomfortably into his waistband, a constant reminder of the job he had failed to carry out. It was almost as if by punishing himself he might woo the gods into taking pity, but then he could see little evidence of mercy in the events of that day.

Nichols came on deck once more. King saw him as he clambered through the hatchway and noticed how much easier he moved. His expression was still filled with concern, however, and he ignored King for several minutes, preferring to stare out towards the nearest Frenchman, until King approached.

"What news?" King asked, as he drew closer.

Nichols turned and looked at him as if for the first time. "She is well, thank you, Tom." He gave a faint smile. "She has woken, and is sensible, though her head pains her greatly. Robert has said it's better if I leave her be for a spell."

King nodded. "I am glad," he said.

"And what of this?" Nichols said, looking towards the enemy, now considerably closer. "You are still determined to see all through to the end?"

King regarded him carefully. The man was clearly upset and had reason to be.

"I have to make every effort to avoid capture." He felt as if he were explaining the situation to a simpleton, but then Nichols was not a King's officer, that must be considered.

"And to what end?" Nichols asked, looking at him directly. "What good will come of it? One good man has already been killed, many more wounded, and Elizabeth..." His words faltered.

"George, I have my duty..."

"Pah, 'tis a strange duty that is so reckless with human life," he said. "Were you to have struck at first sight, no one would have thought the worse of you. We are no great prize to the enemy, all might have been back in England before the month was out. What do you think you have here, a squadron of battleships?" He gave a single, sharp laugh. "You have temporary charge of a hired ship, with a crew of invalids to man her, yet behave as if you were Lord Howe himself."

"George, you are a merchant seaman. You cannot understand."

"Oh yes, I am nothing more than a lowly mate on an Indiaman. My service hardly compares with your own valiant Navy."

King felt his anger rise. "There are differences, to be sure. I doubt that a Navy crew would have surrendered *Pevensey* to privateers without a shot being fired."

"Maybe not, Tom, Maybe not. But no one died."

King's look was totally without humour. "So you think I should do the same now, just shrug my shoulders and strike?"

"You could have done so hours ago; it would not have been such a terrible thing."

"George, you are concerned about Elizabeth, and with cause. But you must see that our duties are so very different. If there be an enemy, I must fight him. If I cannot win, I must run. That's the way I've been taught."

"And you are to continue now, when the odds are so very much against you?"

"If we take damage I shall surrender, but I intend to see it through..." he paused, realising what he was about to say, then added, "at least a little further."

Nichols nodded and turned to go. "So be it, then I wish you joy, and trust that not too many men will fall while you follow your duty."

"Deck there, sail on the larboard beam!" Both men's attention was so distracted that it took a moment or two for the information to sink in. King looked up to the masthead, but his mind was still set on Nichols's words, and he saw no reason for excitement.

"Heading west-nor-west," the lookout continued, somewhat disappointed that his announcement seemed to have caused so little reaction.

"What do you make of her?" Crowley asked eventually.

"Difficult to say for sure, looks to be a sizeable vessel—three masts. She's carrying royals and going a fair pace, considering the weather."

King and Crowley exchanged glances for a moment. Knowing the luck they had enjoyed, it might only be another Frenchman coming to join in the fun.

"Do you mind if I take a look, sir?" Crowley asked.

King shrugged. "If you wish, Michael, though I am happy to send Barrow."

"I have a sense about this one," the Irishman explained, as he collected the glass from the binnacle and headed purposefully for the main shrouds.

Nichols smiled a little sadly as they watched him make the climb. "We come from very different worlds, Tom."

"It's something I have been told often enough before," King said, noticing a softening in his friend. "But I confess, did not truly believe it until now."

"Each has advantages," Nichols agreed. King nodded, then his eyes flashed wickedly.

"Though I note the Navy has won a fair few actions of late."

Nichols was grinning now and laid a hand gently on King's shoulder. "Aye, and all we have done is to colonise a nation."

The brig must also have spotted the strange sail. Indeed she probably had made her first, and was now busily turning. Soon she would soon be bustling away, close hauled and under as much canvas as she could carry. She might still pass close enough to *Espérance* for a broadside, but the change allowed King to gain a point or two to the south. His heart began to pound again and, as the order was given he glanced up to Crowley, who had just settled himself at the masthead. The man was studying the sighting and, in King's opinion, was spending far too long on such a simple task.

"She's a British frigate," he said finally, turning from his glass and looking down towards the deck. "*Shearwater*, her what escorted us down south."

The world began to swim slightly, and King reached for the solidity of the binnacle for support. It was all he could do not to break out into hysterical laughter. *Shearwater* —the escort would have released their original convoy further south and probably picked up the next home-bound. It was highly likely that she was looking for the two ships they had sighted earlier on. But the absolute fact remained that there was a powerful friendly warship in sight. In sight, and shortly to be in range, and the French were already running.

"*Shearwater*'s a thirty-six—big enough to swallow that Frog frigate whole," Crowley was positively bellowing in elation. "And still have room for the brig as a chaser!"

The men on deck began to cheer, and Nichols, his hand still resting on King's shoulder, was laughing softly.

"Very good," King said, almost to himself. Then, a little louder, "Take her to the southeast if you please, Mr Barrow; let us make their job a little easier."

EPILOGUE

They had taken rooms at the Keppel's Head, a popular and friendly inn, known as 'The Nut' to most junior officers. But when King walked slowly down the Hard, he was in no rush to return. The spring sunshine was pleasant; certainly preferable to the heavy rain endured throughout their passage up the Channel, and Portsmouth seemed well scrubbed, and even presentable in the bright morning light.

His reception at the port admiral's office had gone well enough, he supposed. A commander, who must have been sixty if he was a day, had taken charge of the despatches and listened with apparent interest while King related his story of the passage home. Jackie Robson, captain of the *Shearwater*, had been ushered through to meet with more important folk, but then Robson was a senior captain, one currently with a ship, and further more he was responsible for capturing an enemy frigate. King could see the prize now as she was being made safe at the entrance to the docks, her sleek lines and graceful form hardly marred by the jury fore topmast that altered the simple symmetry of her rig.

The brig had escaped. At first King wondered if he might have done more to prevent her loss, but there had been no recriminations. In fact all his actions since leaving Portugal seemed to meet with universal approval. It had been a tiring voyage, however, and now his mind was starting to feel quite numb. Even the finer details were becoming indistinct, and he was just so glad to be back. His hands were reaching deep into his watchcoat pockets as he rested against a low brick wall. It was still early; there should be plenty of time for a decent breakfast when he returned to the inn. *Espérance* had come in yesterday, and he finally gave her up late last night. Nichols and Manning then insisted on a celebratory supper, and none of them had reached their beds until the early hours of the morning. King doubted if anyone else would be up for a while, although at that moment he felt no need for human contact. It was enough that they had made it home, delivered those damned despatches, and now all could begin again.

Elizabeth was recovering well, the wound already being barely noticeable under her hair. And the headaches that bothered her at first were now fading to the extent that she and Nichols were actually starting to make plans for the future. King supposed they were to be envied. He had no set ambitions, apart from ditching the East India Company uniform he seemed to have been wearing for an age and beginning the long, slow search for a fresh position in the Royal Navy.

He had made a start at the port admiral's office, and the commander had been reasonably polite. But little had changed since he was last in England. Seagoing positions remained at a premium and, without a word being said, it was clear that most were snapped up by those with connections. King had few influential friends, and suspected it was going to be a long hunt.

From somewhere far off a bell began to strike the hour. It was nine, time enough to be heading back and see if the others were up. King turned and found himself facing a Navy lieutenant treading purposefully along the pavement towards him. He drew back to give the man passage, but there was something in the officer's stance and gait that caught his attention, and he was smiling broadly before he had even properly registered the face.

"Michael, Michael Caulfield!"

The man almost staggered as he turned in the act of passing, and it was only then that King realised the expression had been strangely occupied, as if his thoughts were complex and many miles away.

"Beg pardon, sir?" The face cleared. Then the eyes grew less distant, and were brought to focus on King, standing by the wall in his tattered watchcoat.

"By Jove, its Tom!" The lieutenant grinned and extended his

hand. The months ashore had taken much of Caulfield's tan, and his belly might have been a touch more noticeable, but the man himself seemed fit and lively enough. "Why, I'd expected you to be off the coast of Africa b'now!"

They shook hands warmly, even if Caulfield seemed strangely eager to move on, shuffling from foot to foot as they spoke. "So what brings you back from the clutches of John Company?"

"A long story. Would you have me tell it?"

Caulfield shook his head, "Sadly there is not the time. I have an appointment and cannot be late; but walk with me."

King quickly fell into his step, which was a fast one, and the sun seemed to shine even more warmly as they bounded along the Hard together.

"So what of Robert and Kate, did you leave them well?" Caulfield asked.

"I did." Despite being physically fit, King was not used to walking quite so quickly without a break. "And not more than an hour or so since," he puffed. "We're staying at The Nut."

Caulfield stopped suddenly and turned, causing King to all but jump to one side in avoiding him.

"So Robert is back in England also?"

"Indeed."

"And are you both still on the Company's books?"

"We left *Pevensey Castle* at Lisbon. I have no desire to return, and believe he feels likewise."

Caulfield tapped King smartly on the chest with the back of his hand. "Then you'll both be wanting a posting, I'd wager!"

King gaped. They had only been back on British soil a matter of hours. "I—I cannot speak for Robert; Kate is with child, and her father not long departed."

"But how are you set?"

He felt the need to think, although there really was little to consider. Nothing on land held him back in any way. His only commitment was to find a posting, and here was one apparently on offer. "I am at liberty," he said.

"Would you consider the Navy, that is after the luxury of John Company travel?"

"The Navy?" King brightened further. "I surely would."

Caulfield's expression returned to the well remembered smile. "Sir Richard has been given a ship, a seventy-four, she is fitting out even as we speak."

"But how so? What of his plans for parliament? I thought he had intended to stand?"

The older man shrugged, "Who can anticipate the actions of the blessed? I received a letter a week or so back, and am going to meet with him now. You must come with me."

But King's inherent pessimism was not to be denied. "He may have favourites and not require any further."

Caulfield eyed him with amusement. "I am sure a place would be found, Tom, were you to be interested. And Robert too, I have no doubt. Though we shall be needing a surgeon for him to assist; sadly, Doust could not be tempted back. But Adam Fraiser is to join as sailing master, and there may be others for all I know. Doubtless we will learn more in due course."

King felt his heart skip, all the key officers from *Pandora*, and in a ship powerful enough to sail in the line-of-battle.

"You are certain that the Navy is the place for you, though?" Caulfield asked again, and King noticed that he was examining him quite carefully. "You know of course that we may be stuck in harbour a year or more? Or twice that long on some Godforsaken blockade? There is no chance that you may prefer the life of a merchant seaman?"

King almost laughed out loud. "No chance whatsoever!" he said.

SELECTED GLOSSARY

Able Seaman	One who can hand, reef and steer; well acquainted with the duties of a seaman.
Andrew	*Sl.* The Royal Navy. Supposedly from Andrew Miller, a much feared press gang officer.
Antiphlogistic	Reducing inflammation or fever; anti-inflammatory.
Azimuth compass	Originally designed to measure the position of celestial bodies, a sighting arrangement was provided, often used for taking land bearings.
Back	Wind change, anticlockwise.
Backed sail	One set in the direction for the opposite tack to slow a ship down.
Backstays	Similar to shrouds in function, except that they run from the hounds of the topmast, or topgallant, all the way to the deck. Serve to support the mast against any forces forward, for example, when the ship is tacking. (Also a useful/ spectacular way to return to deck for topmen.)

Backstays, running	A less permanent backstay, rigged with a tackle to allow it to be slacked to clear a gaff or boom.
Barkey	*Sl.* Seaman's affectionate name for their ship.
Beetle headed	*Sl.* Dull, stupid.
Belaying pins	Large wooden pins set into racks or rails. Lines secured to these can be instantly released by removing the pin.
Bever	*Sl.* A light meal, usually taken in the afternoon.
Binnacle	Cabinet on the quarterdeck that houses compasses, the log, traverse board, lead lines, telescope and speaking trumpet
Biscuit	Small hammock mattress, resembling ship's rations. Also Hard Tack.
Bitts	Stout horizontal pieces of timber, supported by strong verticals, that extend deep into the ship. These hold the anchor cable when the ship is at anchor.
Blackwall	London yard where HEIC ships were built and refitted.
Blane	Gilbert Blane, (1749—1834) Scottish physician who instituted health reform in the Royal Navy.

Block	Article of rigging that allows pressure to be diverted or, when used with others, increased. Consists of a pulley wheel, made of *lignum vitae*, encased in a wooden shell. Blocks can be single, double (fiddle block), triple or quadruple. Main suppliers: Taylors, of Southampton.
Blower	*Sl.* A mistress or whore.
Boatswain	(pronounced *bosun*) The officer who superintends the sails, rigging, canvas, colours, anchors, cables and cordage, committed to his charge.
Bombay Marine	Fighting navy of the East India Company.
Boom	Lower spar to which the bottom of a gaff sail is attached.
Bower	Type of anchor mounted in the bow.
Braces	Lines used to adjust the angle between the yards and the fore and aft line of the ship. Mizzen braces, and braces of a brig, lead forward.
Brig	Two-masted vessel, square-rigged on both masts.
Broach	When running down wind, to round up into the wind, out of control usually due to carrying too much canvas.

Bulkhead	A wall or partition within the hull of a ship.
Bulwark	The planking or wood-work about a vessel above her deck.
Bunting	Material from which signal flags are made.
Bursten belly	*Sl*. Hernia.
Canister	Type of shot, also known as case. Small iron balls packed into a cylindrical case.
Cat's paws	Light disturbance in calm water indicating a wind.
Caulk	*Sl*. To sleep. Also caulking, a process to seal the seams between strakes.
Chapbook	A small booklet, cheaply produced.
Company Bahadur	*Sl*. Indian name for the East India Company.
Close hauled	Sailing as near as possible into the wind.
Coaming	A ridged frame about hatches to prevent water on deck from getting below.
Companionway	A staircase or passageway.
Counter	The lower part of a ship's stern.
Course	A large square lower sail, hung from a yard, with sheets controlling, and securing it.

Crank	*Sl*. Description of a ship that lacks stability, having too much sail or not enough ballast. Opposite of stiff.
Crown and Anchor	A popular shipboard dice game.
Crows of iron	"Crow bars" used to move a gun or heavy object.
Cuddy	Area in a merchant ship forward of the roundhouse, on the same level as the quarterdeck.
Cutter	Fast small, single masted vessel with a sloop rig. Also a seaworthy ship's boat.
Deckhead	The underside of the deck above. Also Overhead.
Ditty bag	*Sl*. A seaman's bag. Derives its name from the dittis or 'Manchester stuff' of which it was once made.
Dogwatch	Short two hour watch that break the four hour cycle, giving each watch keeper a variation in watches.
Dolly	Wooden implement for stirring clothes in a wash tub.
Drab	*Sl*. A particularly nasty slut or whore.
Driver	Large sail set on the mizzen in light winds. The foot is extended by means of a boom.

Dunnage	Officially the packaging around cargo. Also *Sl.* Seaman's baggage or possessions.
Factor	Owner or governor of a factory or trading post; a master merchant.
Fall	The loose end of a lifting tackle on which the men haul.
Fife rail	Holed rail to accept belaying pins.
First Luff	*Sl.* First lieutenant.
Flick	*Sl.* To cut.
Forereach	To gain upon, or pass by another ship when sailing in a similar direction.
Forestay	Stay supporting the masts running forward, serving the opposite function of the backstay. Runs from each mast at an angle of about 45 degrees to meet another mast, the deck or the bowsprit.
Foretack	Line leading forward from the bowsprit, allowing the clew of the forecourse to be held forward when the ship is sailing close to the wind.
Founder	Verb, to sink without touching land of any sort, usually during bad weather.

Frapping/Frapped	When not in service the gun, carriage and breaching tackle are lashed together, or Frapped.
Frizzen	Striking plate of a flintlock mechanisum.
Futtock shrouds	Rigging that projects away from the mast leading to, and steadying, a top or crosstrees. True sailors climb up them, rather than use the lubber's hole, even though it means hanging backwards.
Gaff	Spar attached to the top of the gaff sail.
Gaff sail	Fore and aft quadrilateral shaped sail, usually set at the mizzen.
Gangway / Gangboard	The light deck or platform on either side of the waist leading from the quarterdeck to the forecastle, often called a gang-board in merchant ships. Also, narrow passages left in the hold, when a ship is laden.
Gasket	Line or canvas strip used to tie the sail when furling.
Glass	Telescope. Also, hourglass; an instrument used for measuring time. Also barometer.

Gore	The lower edge of a sail, usually scalloped, in the case of a main or forecourse. In warships the gore is deeper (more round). Also Roach.
Gratings	An open wood-work of cross battens and ledges forming cover for the hatchways, serving to give light and air to the lower decks. In nautical phrase, he "who can't see a hole through a grating" is excessively drunk.
Grape	Cannon shot, larger than case.
Grog	Rum mixed with water (to ensure it is drunk immediately, and not accumulated). Served twice a day at ratios differing from three to five to one.
Gunpowder	A mixture of charcoal, potassium nitrate and sulphur.
HEIC	Honourable East India Company.
Halyards	Lines which raise: yards, sails, signals *etc.*
Handspike	Long lever.
Hanger	A fighting sword, similar to a cutlass.
Head	Toilet, or seat of ease. Those for the common sailor were sited at the bow to allow for a clear drop and the wind to carry any unpleasant odours away.

Headway	The amount a vessel is moved forward, (rather than leeway: the amount a vessel is moved sideways), when the wind is not directly behind.
Heave to	Keeping a ship relatively stationary by backing certain sails in a seaway.
Holystone	*Sl.* Block of sandstone roughly the size and shape of a family bible. Used to clean and smooth decks. Originally salvaged from the ruins of a church on the Isle of Wight.
Hounds	Projections at the mast-head.
Idler	One who does not keep a watch, cook, carpenter, *etc.*
Interest	Backing from a superior officer or one in authority, useful when looking for promotion to, or within, commissioned rank.
Jack Dusty	*Sl.* Purser's steward, also Jack of the dust.
Jacob's ladder	Rope ladder (often used for boarding a ship from a boat).
Jib-boom	Boom run out from the extremity of the bowsprit, braced by means of a Martingale stay, which passes through the dolphin striker,
John Company	*Sl.* The Honourable East India Company (H.E.I.C.).

Jury mast/rig	Temporary measure used to restore a vessels sailing ability.
Kinchins	*Sl*. Children.
Lading	The act of loading.
Landsman	The rating of one who has no experience at sea.
Lanyard	Short piece of line to be used as a handle. Also decorative tassel to a uniform.
Larboard	Left side of the ship when facing forward. (Later known as Port.)
Lascar	A sailor or militiaman from the Indian subcontinent or other countries east of the Cape of Good Hope. Employed on European ships from the 16th century.
Leaguer	Water cask, holding 159 imperial gallons.
Leeward	The downwind side of a ship.
Leeway	The amount a vessel is pushed sideways by the wind, (as opposed to headway, the forward movement, when the wind is directly behind).
Letter of marque	A commission, formerly granted by a country or power, allowing privateers to make prizes of enemy shipping. Also *lettre de course*.

Lifts	Lines that keep the yards horizontal, each lift leads from the mast, through a block at the yard arm, and back through another block at the head of the mast, and down to the deck, where it is secured.
Lighter	A large, open, flat-bottomed boat, with heavy bearings, employed to carry goods to or from ships.
Lily white	*Sl.* A chimney sweep.
Lind	James Lind, (1716– 1794). Scottish physician and pioneer of naval hygiene in the Royal Navy.
Liner	*Sl.* Ship of the line—Ship of the line of battle (later battleship).
Listed on the books	The sons, or protégés of senior officers were frequently entered on ships books while still too young to serve. This gave them additional sea time necessary for rapid promotion.
Lobscouse	A mixture of salted meat, biscuit, potatoes, onions and spices, minced small and stewed together.
Loblolly men/boys	Surgeon's assistants.
Lubberly/Lubber	*Sl.* Unseamanlike behaviour; as a landsman.

Luff	Intentionally sail closer to the wind, perhaps to allow work aloft. Also the flapping of sails when brought too close to the wind. The side of a fore and aft sail laced to the mast.
Man Rope	A side rope to aid boarding.
Master-at-Arms	Senior hand, responsible for discipline aboard ship.
Midshipman	Junior, and aspiring, officer.
Mot	*Sl*. Girl, or wench.
Nigit	*Sl*. an idiot, a fool.
Ordinary	Term used to describe a ship laid up; left in storage, with principle shipkeepers aboard, but unfit for immediate use.
Ordinary seaman	One who can make himself useful on board, although not an expert, or skilful sailor.
Orlop	Deck directly above the hold, and below the lower gun deck. A lighter deck than the gun deck (no cannon to support) and usually level or below the waterline. Holds warrant officers mess, and midshipmen's berth, also carpenters and sail makers stores. Used as an emergency operating area in action.
Overhead	The underside of the deck above, also deckhead

Parbuckle	The rig, consisting of two looped lines, used to drag barrels etc. on board without using a davit.
Parbuckle rails	Rails, often near the entry port, that aid items entering the ship, see above.
Peach	*Sl.* To betray or reveal; from impeach.
Pompey	*Sl.* Portsmouth.
Poop	Aft most, and highest, deck of a larger ship.
Portable Soup	A dehydrated (and fat free) meat soup.
Pox	*Sl.* Venereal Disease, Common on board ship; until 1795 a man suffering had to pay a 15/- fine to the surgeon, in consequence, many cases went unreported. Treatment was often mercurial, and ineffective.
Pugilist	One who fights with fists; usually a professional.
Pumpdale	Gully that crosses a deck, carrying water cleared by a pump.
Purser	Officer responsible for provisions and clothing.
Pusser	*Sl.* Purser.
Quarterdeck	Deck forward of the poop, but at a lower level. The preserve of officers.

Queue	A pigtail. Often tied by a man's best friend (his tie mate).
Quid	The quantity of tobacco chewed at one time.
Quoin	Wedge for adjusting elevation of a gun barrel.
Rapper	*Sl.* A particularly large lie.
Ratlines	Lighter lines, untarred, and tied horizontally across the shrouds at regular intervals, to act as rungs and allow men to climb aloft.
Reef	A portion of sail that can be taken in to reduce the size of the whole.
Rib	*Sl.* Wife.
Rigging	Tophamper; made up of standing (static) and running (moveable) rigging, blocks *etc.* *Sl.* Clothes.
Rook	*Sl.* Thief.
Round house	On a merchant this is the better class of accommodation, set where the senior officers cabins would be in a man of war. Also (and confusingly!) the enclosed (private) heads at the stem of a warship. Larboard side for midshipmen, warrant officers and mates, starboard for patients in the sick bay.

Rudder horn	An iron shackle bolted to the back of the rudder, for attaching auxiliary chains should the tiller fail.
Running	Sailing before the wind.
Saw-bones	*Sl.* surgeon, or any medic.
Scarph / Scarphing	The process of joining wood to build keels, masts and other major items.
Sconce	Candle holder, often made of tin, usually large and flat for stability.
Scupper	Waterway that allows deck drainage.
Scuttle-butt	Bucket with holes for line or leather handles used for water for immediate consumption. *Sl.* gossip (the modern equivalent is chatting by the water cooler).
Seven bell men	That part of a watch who are sent to dine early, to cover the others while they eat.
Sheet	A line that controls the foot of a sail.
Shrouds	Lines supporting the masts athwart ship (from side to side) which run from the hounds (just below the top) to the channels on the side of the hull. Upper run from the top deadeyes to the crosstrees.

Skeel	A cylindrical wooden bucket. A large water-kid.
Skylarking	*Sl.* Unofficial exercise aloft, often in the form of follow my leader, or other games.
Slatches	Large cat's-paws on the water, an indication of strong wind.
Slush	*Sl.* Fat from boiled meat, sold by the cook to the men to spread on their biscuit. The money made was known as the slush fund.
Snow	Type of brig, with an extra trysail mast stepped behind the main.
Spick	*Sl.* Spick and span. New, or at least, clean and tidy.
State / State Lottery	The English State Lottery ran from 1694 until 1826.
Stay sail	A quadrilateral or triangular sail with parallel lines, usually hung from under a stay.
Stern sheets	Part of a ship's boat between the stern and the first rowing thwart, used for passengers.
Stood/Stand	The movement of a ship towards or from an object.
Strake	A plank.

Studding sail	Light sail that extend to either side of main and top sails to increase speed in low winds. Made of the thinnest canvas (No 8).
Swab	Cloth, or (*Sl.*) an officer's epaulette.
Tack	To turn a ship, moving her bow through the wind. Also a leg of a journey. Also relates to the direction of the wind—if from starboard, a ship is on the starboard tack. Also the part of a fore and aft loose footed sail where the sheet is attached or a line leading forward on a square course to hold the lower part of the sail forward.
Taffrail	Rail around the stern of a vessel.
Thwart	(Properly athwarts). The seats or benches athwart a boat whereon the rowers sit to manage their oars.
Tie Mate	A seaman's best friend, one who ties his queue, and attends to his body should he die.
Tophamper	Literally any unnecessary weight either on a ship's decks or about her tops and rigging, but often used loosely to refer to spars and rigging.
Touched	*Sl.* Mad.

Tow	*Sl.* Cotton waste.
Traverse board	A temporary log used for recording speed and headings during a watch.
Trick	*Sl.* Period of work time; an hour, when served by a helmsman.
Trotter	Thomas Trotter, (1760-1832) surgeon to the fleet.
Veer	Wind change, clockwise.
Waist	Area of main deck between the quarterdeck and forecastle.
Warm	*Sl.* When describing a person, rich.
Watch	Period of four (or in case of a dog watch, two) hour duty. Also describes the two or three divisions of a crew.
Watch list	List of men and stations, usually carried by lieutenants and divisional officers.
Wearing	To change the direction of a ship across the wind by putting the stern of the ship through the eye of the wind.
Well	A deep enclosure in the middle of the ship where bilge water can gather, and be cleared by the pumps.

Wherry	A sharp, light, and shallow boat used in rivers and harbours for passengers. Also, a decked vessel used in fishing in different parts of Great Britain and Ireland: numbers of them were notorious smugglers.
Whip	A line rove through a single block to hoist in light articles.
Windward	The side of a ship exposed to the wind.
Yellowed	A newly appointed admiral who will not be given a command is said to fly the yellow flag.

ABOUT THE AUTHOR

ALARIC BOND

Alaric Bond was born in Surrey, England, but now lives in Herstmonceux, East Sussex, in a 14th century Wealden Hall House. He is married with two sons.

His father was a well-known writer, mainly of novels and biographies, although he also wrote several screenplays. He was also a regular contributor to BBC Radio drama (including *Mrs Dale's Diary!*), and a founding writer for the Eagle comic.

During much of his early life Alaric was hampered by Dyslexia, although he now considers the lateral view this condition gave him to be an advantage. He has been writing professionally for over twenty years with work covering broadcast comedy (commissioned to BBC Light Entertainment for 3 years), periodicals, children's stories, television, and the stage. He is also a regular contributor to several nautical magazines and newsletters.

His interests include the British Navy 1793-1815 and the RNVR during WWII. He regularly gives talks to groups and organizations and is a member of various historical societies including The Historical Maritime Society and the Society for Nautical Research. He also enjoys Jazz, swing and big band music from 1930-1950 (indeed, he has played trombone for over 40 years), sailing, and driving old SAAB convertibles.

DON'T MISS ALL OF THE EXCITING BOOKS IN THE FIGHTING SAIL SERIES BY

ALARIC BOND

His Majesty's Ship

A powerful ship, a questionable crew, and a mission that must succeed.

In the spring of 1795 HMS Vigilant, a 64 gun ship-of-the-line, is about to leave Spithead as senior escort to a small, seemingly innocent, convoy. The crew is a jumble of trained seamen, volunteers, and the sweepings of the press; yet, somehow, the officers have to mold them into an effective fighting unit before the French discover the convoy's true significance.

Jackass Frigate

How do you maintain discipline on a ship when someone murders your first lieutenant—and a part of you agrees with their action?

For Captain Banks the harsh winter weather of 1796 and threat of a French invasion are not his only problems. He has an untried ship, a tyrant for a First Lieutenant, a crew that contains at least one murderer, and he is about to sail into one of the biggest naval battles in British history—the Battle of Cape St. Vincent.

True Colours

While Great Britain's major home fleets are immobilised by a vicious mutiny, Adam Duncan, commander of the North Sea Squadron, has to maintain a constant watch over the Dutch coast, where a powerful invasion force is ready to take advantage of Britannia's weakest moment.

With ship-to-ship duels and fleet engagements, shipwrecks, storms and groundings, True Colours maintains a relentless pace that culminates in one of the most devastating sea battles of the French Revolutionary War—the Battle of Camperdown.

All Fireship Press books are available directly through our website, amazon.com, via leading bookstores from coast-to-coast, and from all major distributors in the U.S., Canada, the UK, Europe and Australia.

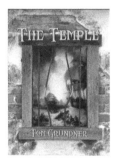

9 781611 791693